Vita Sackville West

PUBLIC FACES

PUBLIC FACES

HAROLD NICOLSON

Private faces in public places
Are wiser and nicer
Than public faces in private places.
W. H. AUDEN

LONDON
CONSTABLE & CO LTD
1932

First Published 1932

This edition reprinted by Cedric Chivers Ltd., Portway, Bath. 1968
at the request of the London & Home Counties Branch of the Library Association
by arrangement with the copyright holder.
Printed offset lithography by
Redwood Press Limited of Trowbridge, Wiltshire.

To
SIBYL COLEFAX
without permission

Introduction to 1968 *edition*
by Nigel Nicolson

HAROLD NICOLSON wrote *Public Faces* in three months, between April and July 1932. At the end of 1929 he had resigned from the Foreign Service, ending his twenty-year diplomatic career as Counsellor in the British Embassy in Berlin. Then followed two years when he worked unhappily as a journalist and recklessly as a politician, first as Lord Beaverbrook's employee and then as an adherent of Sir Oswald Mosley's New Party, for which he edited the Party's weekly journal *Action*. When the Party turned Fascist, he broke amicably but irrevocably with Mosley. He was left without a job, without money, without prospects, and with a sense that he had made a fool of himself. He decided to write a novel as a financial stop-gap, and to restore his reputation and his spirits. It was his only novel apart from *Sweet Waters*, published in 1921.

Those were the circumstances in which *Public Faces* was written. But the roots of the book went deeper. Now that he was unhampered by the need for official discretion, he could write more freely about diplomatic life than he had done in *Some People*, or than a career-diplomatist would dare to risk. He could put down, in the form of a novel, the fruits of his experience. It was not to be a serious analysis. It was written to entertain.. But it did convey, to those who would realize it, his deeply held opinions about politics and international negotiation. In the subtlest and most amusing way he was preaching the lesson that political honesty always pays off in the end; that to do the right thing is usually the right thing to do; and that the most admirable and useful qualities in a diplomatist are truthfulness and precision. That is the moral of the novel.

But it has another theme. Throughout his life Harold Nicolson was fascinated by the element of chance, the fall of a little pebble that precipitates a landslide in great events, the effect of upbringing, prejudices, taste, habit, friendships and even personal appearance upon the characters of men who hold responsibility, ultimate or intermediate, in public affairs. He was well aware how important these things were in the Foreign Office and at the higher levels of politics, for he had watched the leaven at work. He was the first novelist to lift the lid off Whitehall, to show how the system actually operated, to trace the relationships between senior Ministers and junior, and between Ministers and their civil servants, always in terms not of constitutional rights and obligations, but in terms of human character, with its pride, little vanities, loyalties and sheer pigheadedness. *Public Faces* is really about communication, or the lack of it, between people who think that they speak the same language.

It is a satirical novel, but it is kindly. The percipient reader will notice that no characters are introduced, however briefly, without attaching to them qualities which are likeable, or at least amiable. There are no villains. There are no cyphers. Nobody is wholly ludicrous. There is, throughout, very acute observation. A footman, tucking a rug round the Foreign Secretary's knees, a departmental official or a Guards officer glimpsed casually across a crowded room or parade-ground, are all identifiable personalities, rounded out by hints, conveyed often by a single word, of the private sorrows or shortcomings which lie behind their outward conformity and calm. Similarly with dress, tones of voice, the small movements of hand or face, and the contents of people's rooms: all are used as indications of character. Harold Nicolson missed nothing, forgot little, and wasted no experience, whether his own or related to him by others. Once my brother, at Henley Royal Regatta, stretched out his hand to congratulate the mother of a member of the winning crew, and she, misunderstanding his gesture, gave him her binoculars. You will find this tiny incident reproduced at the top of page 29. Perhaps twice in his life Harold Nicolson had read in a French newspaper an article on women's fashions: in one of the funniest and most dramatic scenes in the book he echoes the tone of such articles exactly. Only those who knew him well will understand how closely the weft of his experience was woven with the woof of his imagination. The love-affair of Jane Campbell and John Shorland, which runs through the book like a strand of silver twisted through the hemp, is one example of this. The two characters were based on real people, both bachelors—Hilda Matheson, the first Director of the Talks Department at the B.B.C., and an Oxford don who is still alive—but their wooing, conducted in two separate monologues, each in turn forbidding the other to interrupt, is Harold Nicolson's version of how two such people would have talked and behaved if they had been the sort of people who wooed. The two Cabinet meetings, surely among the great comic scenes in English fiction, are nevertheless plausible. Politicians could behave like that: they have behaved like that. Like all good novels, *Public Faces* is a combination of truth and fantasy. It is scintillating, witty, original and convincing.

The novel was an immediate success in England and America. But thirteen years after it was first published, it acquired a new fame unforeseen by its author. He was hailed as the prophet of the atomic age. The plot of the book turns on the discovery of a new material, found only on an island in the Persian Gulf over which Britain held concessionary rights. This material " might produce in large quantities an element so unstable that beside it radium would be as dull as lead ". A single bomb made of this substance " could by the discharge of its electrons destroy New York ". Harold Nicolson was much amused in 1945 when journalists telephoned to ask him how he could have foreseen, by name and function, the atomic bomb. He had no scientific knowledge even of the most rudimentary kind. But he needed a trigger for the crisis round which his plot revolves, and it had long been a commonplace of popular science journalism that the splitting of the atom might have incalculable results. The name ' atomic bomb ', and sufficient jargon to make the idea sound plausible, he owed to his friend Gerald Heard, but the idea was his own. He saw atomic energy as a possible propellant for rockets, for which it has not yet been used, and he did not foresee its wide civilian uses as a fuel. But he forecast with considerable accuracy the destructive power of the bomb, and the tensions which the discovery would produce between governments and peoples. It was a remarkable forecast, but it was due to luck, not insight.

The action of the novel covers four days, 2nd-5th June 1939, seven years ahead of the date when he was writing. When these actual days came round, he made no reference to the fact in his Diary, being then engaged on other work and his mind occupied by a real-life crisis which soon led to war. The device of setting his plot in 1939 enabled him to link the established past with the imagined future. He was able to erect his spire on an existing tower, to refer to incidents which had actually occurred, and to develop from them a series of events which were improbable but not impossible. His fiction was not much stranger than truth. It also enabled him to tease his friends as well as his readers. We find real people—Churchill, Robert Boothby, Philip Noel-Baker and many others—translated to important political posts, and his diplomatic friends, English and foreign, promoted to Embassies which some in fact came to occupy. His guesses were usually wrong. No matter. They gave authenticity to a plot which was otherwise far-fetched. If it had been set fifty years ahead, *Public Faces* might have been regarded as science fiction. Seven years was long enough to make the improbable seem possible, but not too long to alter the scenery and types of character with whom he was dealing. He made little play with changes in English habits or institutions during the intervening years. It is recognisably England of the 1930's and some might say of the 1960's too.

To publish a new edition thirty-six years after the first therefore needs no excuse. *Public Faces* is not a literary curiosity, nor is it yet a classic. It is a novel which still sounds a contemporary note. Its people still inhabit our world, since it is a novel about human nature under stress. The context has not changed, particularly in so erudite a profession as diplomacy. Nor has the reader's appreciation of a fast-developing plot, of a set of characters drawn partly from knowledge and partly from a rich, observant and inventive mind, and of the facility to point a moral and adorn a tale without either affectation or offence.

CHAPTER I

(1)

ARTHUR PEABODY, that evening, was feeling displeased. Beyond the circle of his immediate awareness lurked an experience which, when recollected would, he knew, arouse not pleasure : but pain.

He lay in his bath conscious of this small irritant, as a man is conscious of a blackberry seed embedded in some distant tooth. He did not probe or peer for the source of his disquiet. He merely lay there, feeling displeased.

The rubber sponge, as he circled it across his chest, foamed lavender soap-suds : the water around him steamed with the scent of verbena. A sedative atmosphere ; and, as such, calculated to reassure. Arthur Peabody, placing the larger of the two sponges as a cushion for his head, indulged in self-assurance : his indulgence was not unqualified : for he knew that something, that afternoon, had pricked him with a poisoned thorn.

Yet, after all, there was much in the external life of Arthur Peabody to cause complacency. For seven years now he had been Principal Private Secretary to His Majesty's Principal Secretaries of State for Foreign Affairs. He would, on occasions, repeat this formula to himself, deriving pleasure from its rich alliterations, enjoying the after-taste of scarlet and gold. Yes, he had been Private Secretary to Sir John Simon in 1932, to Sir Samuel Hoare in 1934 and again in 1935: and when in the autumn of that year Mr. Neville Chamberlain had composed his Ministry of All the Talents, Arthur Peabody had retained his post, servient to the new Foreign Secretary, Mr. Noel Baker. The wedge driven into the Third National Coalition by the Anglo-Egyptian crisis of December 1935, the subsequent " Union Jack " election and the return to power of the Churchill—Mosley combination in March of 1936 still found Peabody ministering from the Private Secretary's room. He served the new Foreign Secretary, Mr. Brendan Bracken, with unabated efficiency: he was invariably available: sleek and civil, he was always there.

There were occasions, it is true, when the flaming zeal of Mr. Bracken, the push and rush of the whole Churchill system, caused inconvenience to Arthur Peabody, and even disquiet. Mr. Bracken treated British foreign policy as a malleable element, as something which could be both handled and shaped. This curious theory upset Mr. Peabody; he had always (and perhaps rightly) visualised foreign policy as a slow but majestic river, flowing sedately in a uniform direction, requiring merely, at moments of crisis, a glib but scrupulous rectification of the banks. Yet, even then, only in places; and, even then, not for very long. Mr. Bracken had a nineteenth-century, an almost Palmerstonian, conception of his task. He took risks which, in Peabody's conception, were awful risks. He settled the Egyptian crisis by occupying the Alexandria customs : he settled the Maltese crisis by threatening (publicly) to blockade Genoa and Trieste : his intervention in the affair of the Chinese Northern Railway caused Mr. Peabody an actually sleepless night : and thus when the Anglo-French Agreement of October 1937 (erroneously called "The Clive–Tardieu Protocol") led to the fall of the Churchill Government, Arthur Peabody had smoothed his thinning hair and sighed relief.

All would have been well with the Clive–Tardieu protocol had it remained a secret. An indiscretion in the Quai d'Orsay led, however, to its publication (in facsimile) by the *Vossische Zeitung*. The centre and the left, headed by Walter Bullinger and Mr. Noel Baker, had made much capital out of this disclosure. The protocol provided in effect that in return for our support of the French scheme for Danzig and the Polish corridor the French Government "would not for their part oppose" the fortification by Great Britain of the Gebel Musa on the Moorish coast of the Straits of Gibraltar. In vain did Mr. Bracken contend that Gibraltar was no longer tenable, that he had secured British control of the Straits without sacrificing a single British interest. The conscience of the House of Commons, as happens in times of security, was sensitive and even alert : no gratitude was felt, or even expressed, to the Churchill–Mosley Cabinet for the economic revival which their industrial and currency reforms had already induced : the House of Commons voted ; and Mr. Churchill resigned.

At the general election of December 1937 the

Central Block, which Mr. Spencer Furnivall had formed so slyly in April of the previous year, were everywhere triumphant. The British public had much enjoyed their excursion under Mr. Churchill : they were feeling proud, acquisitive, patriotic ; but a little unstrung. They welcomed the sweeter, simpler assurances of Furnivall and Bullinger They desired, under the ægis of Geneva, to consolidate their gains. They thus returned the Central candidates,—those former liberals, those left-wing Tories, those remnants of the Labour Party of pre-coalition days,—with a substantial patriotic majority. The King, as was fitting, sent for Mr. Furnivall in the first days of January 1938 : and Mr. Furnivall, as was also fitting, although a trifle languidly, sent for Walter Bullinger. From that moment Bullinger ruled in Mr. Bracken's place.

In the room adjoining that of Mr. Bullinger, Arthur Peabody remained : and still, with a rapid gesture of his shapely hands would he unlock the despatch boxes of Mr. Bullinger as he had unlocked the despatch boxes for Sir John Simon, Sir Samuel Hoare, Mr. Noel Baker and Mr. Brendan Bracken.

The Cabinet key dangled alone upon a gold chain attached to the trouser button on Mr. Peabody's right side. To the trouser button on his left side was attached a silver chain, from which hung a " B " key ; the latchkey of the side door on the Horse Guards Parade ; the latchkey of No. 11 Tite Street ; and (in a podgy truss of their own) the key of his William and Mary writing-table ; the key of his dressing-case ; a key which fitted each of his four suit-cases ; another key which was a source of

distress to Mr. Peabody as being of unknown **origin**
and application ; and finally the key of that **drawer**
in the dining-room in which, labelled with parch-
ment tags, lay all the other keys which locked **or**
unlocked the several casements of his ordered life.

The gesture of Arthur Peabody when handling
the gold chain differed from the gesture with which
he extracted the silver chain from his left pocket :
the Cabinet key would be flicked out deftly in a
flash of gold and tinkling steel : the left-hand keys
would emerge more corporately : when he used his
latchkeys, Mr. Peabody would twist his left thigh
sideways : becoming, for him, ungainly.

(2)

On that evening, however, of Thursday, June 2,
1939, we find Arthur Peabody without his keys, and
as such diminished. We find him aware of some
irritant in his unimmediate memory, and as such
displeased. We find him gazing at his own two
knees, slimly conjoint above the opaque water, and
as such meditative.

Not that Arthur Peabody frequently indulged in
meditation. He was a tidy man, and one moreover
who proceeded in grooves of habit. He called
them " my experience." They were excellent
habits. He was honest, industrious, clean, truthful
and efficient. He spoke French with a French
accent, German with a German accent, and Italian
with an accent which was slightly Polish. His
memory was frequently infallible : his instinct,
quite often, sure : his judgment, on more than one

occasion, had proved demonstrably sound. He had received a C.B.E. in 1932, and a C.M.G. in 1935. There was every prospect that in the impending Birthday Honours . . .

Arthur Peabody moved his sponge hastily: he did not wish, even when thoroughly alone, to anticipate the Birthday Honours.

No—at the age of thirty-eight there was little really wrong with the material life of Arthur Peabody. This very evening, for instance. He would (in fact he *must*) leave his bath. He would dry himself upon that large white towel which Porson had hung over the chair: he would put on those blue celanese combinations, those black silk socks, those slippers from Gane's at Eton, that violet dressing-gown from Sulka. He would pass into his bedroom, exchanging the thin softness of cork linoleum for the fat softness of moleskin pile. He would put on his evening trousers, those slightly old-world trousers with the braid along the seam: he would lace his lacquered shoes: his shirt thereafter, with its small pearl stud: his O.E. braces, and then the two key chains,—that gold one on the right, and on the left that cumbered chain of silver. The stud at the back of his neck would pop slightly as it pierced the collar: the stud at the front of his neck would slip more silently into place. He would comb his black hair forwards over his brow; an effect, for the moment, of a dishevelled Arthur Peabody,—a most unwonted effect. He would shake his bottle of Delhez No. 10, allowing a few drops to drip stealthily upon his head. He would then comb his hair backwards, straight and neat away from his receding forehead : the comb, cold and dentated, upon the nape of his neck : that final touch with the silver brushes where the hair above his ears bunched greyly. Then, lovingly, would he take the C.M.G. from its place above his folded handkerchief : lovingly would he raise shirt-sleeves behind his neck and clip the hidden hook and eye upon that blue and scarlet ribbon. A tug to see that the enamel cross hung the correct 2½ inches below his collar stud. And then the tie ; and then the waistcoat ; and then the coat with its velvet collar. A dab of lavender upon the handkerchief : my cigarette case : the notes for £2 10s., those two dollars and one shilling in the right trouser pocket; a final stare at the mirror : Arthur Peabody is dressed.

Yet, on that particular June evening, this process did not fill him with the habitual exhilaration, with that usual sense of achievement, that sense of something nimbly, neatly done. He gazed at the mirror more fixedly than was his wont, a faint frown raising his eyebrows in a stare of pained enquiry. There was a glint of white scalp between the symmetrical comb-marks in his hair. There was a crease (there were two or even three creases) around the eyelids: not very good-humoured creases, rather fussy they were, almost petulant. And when he dropped his chin into the fold of his collar there was a slight pouch or pucker of the skin. Yet Peabody was, by nature, a thin, and as such expectant, man.

He stepped back from the illumination of the dressing-table into the softer shadows of the room. A tall slim figure faced him from the larger looking-glass : he grasped the lapel of his coat and let the other hand rest lightly in his trouser pocket. " Distinguished "—that's what he looked. And young for his age. . . ..

The word " old," after all, was frequently employed as a term of comradeship ; even of affection. It may have been in that sense that John Shorland had used it. . . .

At this, Recollection, no longer repressible, rose up and stabbed intensively with its poisoned thorn. Yes, *this* was the unpleasantness which had for long lingered in his mind. He winced.

It had all happened at 4.50 p.m. that very afternoon. There had been that fuss going on about the telegrams from Persia. The Secretary of State and the Permanent Under-Secretary had both spent most of the afternoon at the India Office. Peabody had left the room and then returned suddenly. John Shorland, from his table in the corner, was telephoning to someone at the Air Ministry. He had not noticed the return of Arthur Peabody. " O.K.," he had said, " I'll remind old Peabottle. But you know he hasn't quite caught on to the whole business. He regards the Abu Saad concession as something commercial. As something for the Directorate of Overseas Trade. But I'll see to it all right. If the worst comes to the worst I'll tell the Secretary of State myself. We can't let the D.O.T. handle this business."

Was that a pleasant thing to overhear ? It was not a pleasant thing. It was unpleasant for three reasons. The expression " O.K." was not one which should be used in the Foreign Office, and least

8

of all by an Assistant Private Secretary. The word
" Peabottle " was certainly derisive. And the term
" old " . . .

Arthur Peabody passed into the sitting-room.
He looked at the Cromwellian clock : it would take
him fifteen minutes to get to Carlton House Terrace :
he had five minutes to spare. He mixed himself
a glass of Vermouth.

" Old . . . Old Peabottle . . ."

No, there were four, not three, unpleasant things
about John Shorland's remark. For what had he
meant about " not having caught on " ? A young
man of only two years' experience in the service.
Conceited, he was, disloyal, and pert. That's what
came of encouraging those All Souls' people to
enter the Foreign Office. They got above themselves. And Shorland in particular was a disagreeable young man : able, of course, and even efficient :
but he had no tact : he was rigid, and, yes, rude.
Definitely rude.

Sighing at the inveterate tactlessness of his
subordinate, Arthur Peabody mixed himself a
second glass of Vermouth. He sank into a chair.
He opened the last number of the *Connoisseur* and
read, with but scant concentration, an article about
seventeenth-century Pump Room tickets at Tunbridge Wells.

" Interesting . . ." he murmured, and replaced
the paper on its walnut stand.

Porson, blinking white but respectful eyelashes,
was waiting in the hall with his master's hat and coat.

" Good-night, Porson," said Peabody.

" Good-night, Sir," said Porson.

9

An excellent man. A truly excellent man.

Yet what had Shorland meant by " commercial " ? The Abu Saad question was a perfectly straight-cut, if not very savoury, issue. The Persian Government claimed the island as Persian territory : they also wished to expropriate a certain Major Morris. Well, why not ? And why all this fuss ? True it was that the Air Ministry had purchased a controlling interest in the Morris concessions. But such things, with a little experience, could be arranged. Such things always, if one displayed patience, if one possessed experience, settled themselves. And after all, damn it all, it *was* a matter for the D.O.T.

"Tut," said Arthur Peabody, as he entered his cab.

(3)

The taxi which, on that June 2, 1939, bore Arthur Peabody to Carlton House Terrace sped rapidly through Eaton Square. Peabody sat there erect, holding his top hat neatly upon his knees. At the corner of Grosvenor Gardens stood the home of Walter Bullinger. Peabody leant forward and observed the lit blind in his chief's dressing-room : a scarlet blind it was, and it shone like a dispensary poised above the Mews. " The Secretary of State," thought Peabody, " is also dressing for dinner. A singularly successful man."

Yet Walter Bullinger, struggling at that moment into a velvet dinner-jacket, was not feeling successful in the least. He was feeling more than unsuccessful, he was feeling uneasy. He was feeling more than uneasy, he was feeling alarmed. For (unlike

Peabody) he knew the true proportions of the Abu
Saad question : he knew that the British Empire,
nay the World, nay the Cabinet of which he was
himself a member, were, on that June evening,
faced with a crisis of unexampled perplexity and
danger. And what made it all so terrible,—" so very
terrible," he muttered to himself, panting slightly,—
was that upon his own shoulders, upon those intimate
shoulders which at that moment had struggled into
a velvet dinner-jacket, would rest the responsibility
of defining, of controlling, in fact of explaining, of
justifying, the infinite complexity, the appalling
force of impending events. "*I do so hate violence,*"
he muttered, as with fingers, trembling fingers, he
tied his tie. And yet violence,—encircling, com-
pressive, ineluctable,—appeared to hem him in on
every side. The gentle heart of Walter Bullinger
fluttered in panic, seeking for escape.

It was not the fault of Walter Bullinger that his
centre was not exactly in the middle. There had
been his father in the first place : a solicitor of
Cheltenham : conservative : Church of England :
jubilantly precise. There had been his mother in
the second place : winding wool : fluttering with
nervous brown hands among the sweet-pea stalks :
murmuring " Walter darling, I tremble to think
what your father would say,—if he knew." A tacit
understanding existed between Walter and his
mother, that, except in case of enormity, old Mr.
Bullinger should never know.

This had been bad for Walter. It had created
a divergence, almost a conflict, between the practical
efficiency which he inherited from his father, and

those subtler, more critical, less complacent instincts which came to him from his mother. He was not, consciously at least, an insincere man : he was not lacking even in intelligence and courage. Yet there existed an error of adjustment, a lack of frank communication, between his objective and his subjective faculties ; and from his childhood he had acquired the habit of stilling his inner promptings by evasiveness, optimism, and on occasions by actual self-deception.

His father had been so brisk, so authoritative, so certain : his mother had been so vague, so elusive, so questioning. He had found, when at Harrow, that the cheery anglican certitude of his father's pragmatism had proved more remunerative than the negligent wistfulness of his mother's elasticity. This truth had been confirmed for him at Magdalen, —it was always possible, he found, when assailed by self-distrust, to take refuge in the code of an English gentleman ; to fall back upon the public-school spirit : the doctrines of good form ; the doctrines, even, of the church.

Inevitably, and to his mother's secret distress, he began to adopt his father's voice and gestures. He would enter the dining-room shining, panting almost, from his cold bath. " Splendid ! " he would say, rubbing blue hands above the breakfast dishes, " excellent ! excellent ! " As if he were a Wykehamist and not a Harrovian : as if he were at New College and not at Magdalen. And, on observing this, his mother would smile with distant distress.

In this fashion, brisk and god-fearing, he had spent eight months at Angers learning French : he had been called to the bar: he had unsuccessfully contested by-elections at Langport and at Stroud: and had finally, at the age of twenty-nine, entered the House of Commons: a left-wing Tory: a useful, and indeed a coming, young man.

As Under-Secretary to the Board of Control he had, in Mr. Baldwin's second Government, won his spurs. In the National Government of 1934 he had, owing to his knowledge of the French language, been appointed Under-Secretary at the Foreign Office. His name had not been included in the Ministry of All the Talents formed by Mr. Chamberlain in 1935. He thereafter . associated himself with the left-wing tories and the right-wing liberals; had spoken with force and acumen upon the Anglo-Egyptian Crisis; had been a firm supporter of the League of Nations Union; and had taken a prominent part, on the formation of the Churchill–Mosley Cabinet, in attacking the machtpolitik of Mr. Brendan Bracken. From the earliest days of its inception, in April 1936, he had adhered to the Central Block created by Spencer Furnivall, and it was thus inevitable that, with the fall of the Churchill Ministry and the return of Mr. Spencer Furnivall's Centrals, he should have been chosen by that languid if adroit politician as Minister for Foreign Affairs.

Yet, in spite of this success, Walter Bullinger was not a man at peace with himself. There was his outside self,—confident, convivial, voluble: there was his inside self,—dispirited, self-critical, tongue-tied. He was painfully aware of this divergence. It was as though he possessed two separate charts of his own individuality: he visualised them vaguely as two targets painted in concentric circles of red and black. The Bullinger target was contrived of stiff white cardboard : it was highly ostensible : the central bull's-eye was plumb and emphatic : the surrounding circles were unwavering and firm : they represented his " position," they represented his " belief," they represented his " long Parliamentary experience " : his " career." The Walter target was of a different quality : now that he came to think of it, it wasn't a target at all. It was like a Japanese flag printed on tissue paper : it was a splotch, a protest, a disavowal. It was a most flimsy, inconvenient, and indeed disconcerting object. Life would be so infinitely simpler, so far straighter, for Mr. Bullinger were it not for Walter and his Japanese flag. Since scarcely ever had he achieved that unity within himself which enabled his inside to regard his outside with complete conviction.

On that evening of June 2 the inner self, dormant for so long, had suddenly renewed its negations. For the last eighteen months these moods of self-dispraise had been infrequent, doped by the glamour of his own success. Since that January morning of last year when Walter Bullinger—pink, matutinal, redolent of camphor and high intentions—had strode with his jubilant colleagues along the white-and-scarlet corridors of Buckingham Palace, the inner questionings had been almost stilled. When examined tentatively on the subject, when probed by a thin wire of research (as if an exposed nerve), the inner self had evolved a theory by which the outer self had for long been flattered and assuaged. " There is," thus had the inner comforted the outer man, " there is, there must be, a quality in you and me which, for purposes of convenience, we may call ' the quality of success.' The fact that this quality is difficult to isolate or to define, does not mean that it lacks what you, Bullinger, would call ' a spiritual value.' It is a valuable quality: we possess it: I congratulate us: I bow to this unknown, this, I admit, surprising force within us."

Happy in those days, although rare, were these colloquies between the inner and the outer man: a new solidarity, based upon this strange phenomenon of success, established itself in Walter Bullinger. For some eighteen months a single personality was almost achieved: the centre of Bullinger, during those happy active months of 1938 and 1939, became almost stationary in his middle. He was, for the first time, at ease with himself: for the first time he ceased to regard the outer façade as an imposition and a fraud.

Yet on that evening of June 2, 1939:—on the afternoon, to be more precise of that historic day;—this unity, this happy new-found unity, had again been dislocated. Mr. Bullinger, behind his scarlet blind, was wrestling not merely with the intricacies of a velvet dinner-jacket; not only with the impending intricacies of a world disaster: but with the jarring inner intricacies of his own temperament.

" Hell ! " said Walter Bullinger as he brushed his abundant hair.

(4)

It had all arisen out of that beastly Abu Saad concession. It had all arisen from the Livingstone

15

alloy. It was all the fault of that disastrous Churchill Government.

Mr. James Livingstone, an irrepressible geologist from Nottingham, had, in the summer of 1935, discovered a unique deposit of ore on the Island of Abu Saad in the Persian Gulf. He had experimented with this deposit and claimed to have composed from it an aluminium alloy,—harder, lighter and less corrosive than any of the steel alloys. In May of 1936 he had communicated this unfortunate discovery to the Committee on Aeronautical Research, presided over at that time by Lord Lympne. He had suggested to them that his alloy could supply an explosion chamber capable of resisting unlimited charges of any of the fulminites. He had insisted that with this explosion chamber the problem of the rocket aeroplane was finally solved.

With that reckless impulsiveness which had from the outset characterised the actions of the whole Churchill group, Lord Lympne had, without consulting the House of Commons or even the Treasury, immediately acquired the concession then held by a certain Major Morris for the mining of all natural deposits upon Abu Saad. Major Morris himself had been aiming only at extracting beryllium : but the terms of the concession which he held from the Sultan of Muscat would also cover the mining of this new ore which young Livingstone had christened " Deposit A."

Further experiments on the part of the Research Committee had proved not merely the justification of Mr. Livingstone's contention, as also of Lord Lympne's intemperate action, but had led to the surmise that this new alloy which transformed aluminium into what was to all intents a new metal, might itself be refined and made to yield an element which could have revolutionary possibilities. If that proved true, here was a find of incalculable importance. It was averred that Deposit A might produce in large quantities an element so unstable that beside it radium would be as dull as lead; an element, some physicists began to speculate, that as soon as it was reduced to its pure state must transmute itself, as radium transmutes itself into lead, but with infinitely more violence; in fact with an explosion that would destroy all matter within a considerable range and send out waves that would exterminate all life over an indefinite area.

Mr. Bullinger was not very clear in his own mind as to the nature or potentiality of this second line of research. He knew only that the experts had begun to whisper the words "atomic bomb" and that Professor Narteagle in April of the previous year had explained to the Cabinet (looking mildly at them above rimless pince-nez) that a single Livingstone bomb, no longer than this inkstand (and at that he had indicated the wholly pacifist inkstand of Walter Bullinger), could by the discharge of its electrons destroy New York.

The Cabinet of Spencer Furnivall, that liberal and high-minded Ministry, had been acutely embarrassed by this information. Only three months before they had ousted the Churchill Government on a charge of adventurism. And here, in the April of their life, was a weapon of adventure such as no British Government had ever possessed before. What made it all so awkward was that Mr. Churchill, to say nothing of the impetuous, the flaming, Mr. Brendan Bracken, must know, or at least surmise, that this weapon of world dominion lay within their grasp.

A silence, on that April morning of 1938, had descended upon the Cabinet. Professor Narteagle peered over his pince-nez to the right side and to the left. He did not know whether this really ominous silence meant that it was fitting for him to withdraw. And, if he ought to withdraw, ought he to do so briskly as he might leave a lecture-hall at Glasgow, or ought he to say something valedictory and nice? He glanced at the Prime Minister. Mr. Furnivall was leaning back in his chair, his elbows on the baize cloth, his fingers joined, his eyes fixed vacantly upon the two Ionic columns which framed the door. He glanced at Walter Bullinger. Bullinger was staring down and in front of him at two hands joined in a gesture which was almost a gesture of static supplication. He glanced at Mr. Hore Belisha, the Home Secretary, who was drawing cubes on his blotting-paper, his lips architecturally pursed. He looked at Mr. Philip Noel Baker, the Secretary of State for India, who was thinking. It was quite obvious that Mr. Noel Baker was thinking, since he had started to run his fingers through his hair and they had remained there, poised in the centre of the skull. He glanced at Sir Charles Pantry, the Air Minister : the purple face of Sir Charles Pantry was raised expectantly, expecting some remark. He glanced at Mr. R. S. Hudson, the First Lord of the Admiralty, but Mr. Hudson was also drawing cubes upon **his** blotting-paper. He glanced at Mr. Aneurin Bevan, the Minister of Labour, and observed upon the lips of Mr. Bevan a suppressed but still sardonic smile. He glanced at Mr. Robert Boothby, the Secretary of State for War, but Mr. Boothby was reading a letter with a German postmark. The Professor then glanced at the clock. The clock was ticking out the little lives of men.

Three minutes passed. The Prime Minister separated his finger-tips, which, during the last sixty seconds, had ceased to prop against each other motionlessly and had begun to tap against each other in an expectant rhythm. Mr. Furnivall leant forward.

"Tell me," he said, "my dear Professor, how many people know of this?"

Mr. Boothby, at that, replaced his letter in his pocket and thrust firm arms upon the table. The other Ministers also inclined expectantly towards the Professor. The Cabinet table ceased to resemble a splayed and full-blown rose: it resembled a rose emerging from the bud: it no longer spread and lolled: it concentrated.

"Well," began the Professor, "there is Livingstone in the first place. And then the Aeronautical Research Committee. . . ."

"I can answer for them," said Sir Charles Pantry.

"Of whom I am one," added the Professor—glancing upwards at the Air Minister, not wishing to be taken so much for granted.

"Of course, my dear Professor," murmured Mr. Furnivall.

"And three," continued the Professor, "or four of Livingstone's assistants."

" Reliable ? " asked the Prime Minister.

" I hope so," said the Professor. " And of course," he added, " the three Air Marshals."

" Of course ! " there was a general murmur of agreement.

Another pause followed. An awkward pause. The thin white fingers of the Prime Minister had resumed their almost impatient tapping.

" And Mr. Churchill," he asked at last, " and Lord Lympne ? "

" Well," replied the Professor, " they knew about the alloy, of course, and they knew about the explosion chamber for the rocket. The second, the later theory, the theory of the atomic bomb, had, *I think*, been mentioned to them. But only as a surmise. I am practically certain that they knew of it only in the form of a possible development."

" Practically certain, Professor ? " It was Mr. Boothby who spoke : and with his usual incisiveness.

" Well, I couldn't be sure. They were so interested, you know—so, if I may use the expression, acute."

It was evident that the expression was not liked. Yet the Professor had used it. Mr. Hore Belisha started to shade his cubes, with quick impatient strokes of his pencil.

" And this rocket," the Prime Minister had continued. " You think, Professor, that it would be of any *commercial* value ? "

" None at all," the Professor answered, " except for mails, of course. After all the thing does six hundred miles an hour : it could fly to America and back in a June daylight."

" Really ! " said the Prime Minister. And a hum of relieved animation passed across the room.

" Thank you," added Mr. Furnivall. " My dear Professor," he continued, " we are much obliged."

The Professor gathered his papers together. He bowed. He awkwardly left. The door closed behind him, enclosing a silence of the sort which is known as " embarrassed."

" Well, Pantry ? " said the Prime Minister in his most languid voice.

The Secretary of State for Air was by nature neither voluble nor discreet. " Well, it's really like this," he began, and having thus begun he paused to consider what, after all, it was really like.

" I think," he began again, " if I may say so," he added, " that this Deposit A is of the most essential importance. Most essential. The fact that by possessing the Abu Saad concession we hold a monopoly of this essential element may prove, and in fact is," Sir Charles paused, squinting with his swivel eye at the reluctant face of the Prime Minister, " essential," he concluded—being representative of the youngest of the fighting services.

" Commercially ? " enquired Mr. Furnivall, bland.

" Not exactly," hesitated Sir Charles, reddening, " you know what I mean. The stratospheres have proved a failure for military purposes. If we were provoked, if we were attacked, this deposit would give us an advantage, an almost overwhelming advantage, against any aggressor."

Again a silence descended upon the room. They knew what he meant. The knowledge was hateful to their whole tradition. And yet, in the depths of their consciousness, stirred demons of domination waving Union Jacks.

Walter Bullinger, still gazing at his interlocked hands, realised that those hands had become clammy. Yet conscience, and a sincere humanity, urged him forward. The thought of toppling skyscrapers, of vendors of ice-cream crushed beneath the Manhattan building, was extremely painful to Walter Bullinger. He believed sincerely that public affairs should be guided upon a basis of private morality. He was moved.

" I think," he said, " that we should face the situation. We may be in possession of an engine of destruction more powerful, more lethal, than any known in the whole history of man. Such a weapon could be used, should be used, only in the last extremity of national danger. We are entitled, in the interests of commerce and human progress, to exploit to the full the potentialities of the Livingstone explosion chamber. We are entitled, that is, to perfect our experiments upon the rocket aeroplane. But it would be unwise, nay it would be impious, for us to dabble in the satanic potentialities of the atomic bomb. That is a matter for the Air Ministry alone, in consultation with their expert advisers. As a Cabinet we should, in my opinion, proceed no further with the atomic bomb."

" But," said the Prime Minister, smiling with ferocious gentleness, " but, my dear Walter, what if Churchill *knows* ? "

" Well," replied Bullinger, " he can't *say* much anyhow. After all, the thing's no good once it ceases to be a secret."

And as he said so (for he was a moral man) he blushed.

It was in this manner that the Cabinet, on Bullinger's suggestion, shelved the question of the atomic bomb. That had happened in April 1938. And on that June evening of 1939, when the complications had gathered like a swarm of raging bees around that act of hesitation, the details of that Cabinet meeting, the very smell of the baize cloth, returned to Walter Bullinger in a wave of self-reproach.

(5)

His inner conscience allowed him no escape from the sharp realities of his own responsibility. The Cabinet, fourteen months ago, had been informed by the greatest British physicist that the Livingstone alloy rendered probable, or at least possible, the construction of an atomic bomb. The possession of the Abu Saad concession gave us a monopoly of this alloy : it thereby, as Bullinger had pointed out, placed us in sole possession of the greatest engine of destruction ever known to man.

The Cabinet, when faced with this proffered omnipotence, had recoiled in fear. True it was that their acute distaste for the bomb (the way they had all winced—even Boothby had winced—when Professor Narteagle had so gently murmured " New York ") did credit to their humanity, to their state of civilisation. Yet this was no ostensible excuse. The Cabinet, undeniably, had shirked the issue. And it was on Bullinger's own motion that they had deftly side-tracked the problem; shunting it off to the Air Council.

Obviously, on that April day of 1938, they should have taken one of two courses. Either they should at once have resigned and allowed a new National Government to cope with this devastating invention. Or else, as a pacifist Cabinet, they should have summoned the Assembly of the League of Nations, and laid before it the potentialities and the details of the whole discovery.

They had done neither of these things. They had temporised: they had clung to office: they had disclaimed all moral responsibility for the bomb, while leaving it to the Air Ministry to continue their experiments: they had, with timid optimism, allowed fourteen happy months to pass. And now, on this June evening, they were reaping what they had sown.

The Air Council, the Committee of Aeronautical Research, had not during those fourteen months been idle. Profiting by the blank cheque equivocally, nay ambiguously, given to them by the Cabinet, they had continued their experiments. The alloy had been manufactured: the rocket aeroplane had been constructed: and only a fortnight before the Livingstone Rocket I.A. had sped in five hours from Croydon to New York. This achievement, as was to be expected, had aroused intense disquiet among the other Powers. They were aware of the purchase of the Morris concession by the Air Ministry. Immediately they had exercised joint pressure at Tehran. And, as the first heavy thunder drops before the storm, the telegrams that afternoon had been pouring in from three Continents.

It was clear that the Powers knew about the Abu Saad deposits: it was obvious also that they connected these deposits with the Livingstone alloy and the Livingstone Rocket I.A. Did they also know about the bomb? Did Mr. Churchill know about the bomb? And what, after all, had the Air Council been doing, all these months, about the bomb? Pantry, in the Cabinet, had been his usual squinting muffled self. The Prime Minister, affable and aloof, had avoided the subject. Boothby, it is true, on one occasion had raised the question. "And what," he had said, "about that bomb?" Pantry had squinted outwards towards the window. "It requires," he mumbled, "very careful experiment." "It must indeed," said Boothby. And the matter dropped.

And now they were faced, over this Abu Saad concession, with what was obviously concerted action on the part of the Powers.

To give way would entail humiliation, national danger, and perhaps even the fall of the Furnivall Cabinet.

To resist might entail . . .

Yes, it might entail the atomic bomb.

Mr. Bullinger, crushed by this Manhattan of responsibility, collapsed into the dryad chair beside his dressing-table. One thing at least was certain: it was certain that he could not, that evening, face a solitary dinner with his wife. He loved Edith: he loved her tenderly: yet he loved her less tenderly when he was feeling overcome. "What's wrong," she would be bound to say, " with pater to-night ? Tell old Edith."

He loathed being called pater. The term, in fact, was employed by Mrs. Bullinger as compensation for Jennifer, as an attempt to invest that chilblained, that hay-fevered, that wholly unsatisfactory, that snivelling, that only daughter, with the glamour of cricket bats and play-boxes, with the atmosphere of that desired school-boy (he would now be in his second year at Harrow) whom she had never borne. And Mr. Bullinger (although obscurely) realised that the term was one, if not of reproach, then at least of disappointment.

No, to-night, at least, he would not tell old Edith. He would ring the bell. He would order a cab. He would dash into the drawing-room, busied but not over-tired, and explain to Edith that he had been summoned hurriedly to No. 10. He might have a little supper later at the Travellers. No, nothing to worry about. . . . Merely something about to-morrow's Cabinet.

And it was in this way that, at the very moment when Arthur Peabody, in Carlton House Terrace, dangled his first asparagus above a bird-like mouth, Walter Bullinger, at the Garrick Club, propped the *New Yorker* in front of him and began to eat his soup.

Yes, he might play bridge afterwards. Yes, he *would* play bridge afterwards. No good dwelling on worries at this hour of the night. It would all seem simpler, less ineluctable, to-morrow : he could think the whole thing out during his morning's ride. For Bullinger, being very English, believed in unconscious cerebration.

CHAPTER II

(1)

JOHN SHORLAND had, at that very moment (it was 8.40 p.m. on Thursday, June 2, 1939), realised that he was in love. He was not only in love, he was desperately in love. He was in love with the Parliamentary Under-Secretary of State.

The realisation of this fact came as so sudden a shock to him that his hand, in the act of reaching out for the Armagnac, retracted suddenly, and poised, in the shape of three central fingers, upon the table-cloth.

It was not merely the realisation that he was in love which had provoked this spurt of astonishment, this physical retraction. Frequently had he been in love before, and with all manner of people. Yet this, his sudden awareness, was something different. His first feeling was therefore one of difference. His second feeling was one of enlightenment, of recognition. " Of course," he exclaimed, " *that's* what it was,"—and his three fingers (as if to propel across green baize the knave of diamonds) descended upon the cloth. Yet in fact he was pulling the card towards him, he was not pushing it away.

His third feeling was one of alleviation, a sudden

27

purging of perplexity, such as one experiences at night-time, when the brain shakes off its bemusement and establishes the fact that it is one's own hot-water bottle which, tepid and disgraceful, has sullenly (and for some hours) leaked.

" Well," exclaimed John Shorland, leaning back against the maroon velvet, " this is very odd indeed."

These were his first impressions : a magnesium flash of recognition : a sudden loosening of perplexity. They left him blinking, there was a constriction at his throat. And thereafter came the clamorous little waves of reaction.

It was grotesque, of course : it was ungainly : it was almost perverse. There was the difference of age, in the first place, a difference of nine years. John Shorland, that very evening, was celebrating his twenty-fourth birthday : the Under-Secretary had left Oxford in 1927, and must therefore be thirty-three or thirty-four years of age.

Then the whole business was so unmanageable : so difficult to adjust. There he was, an Assistant Private Secretary : Assistant to Arthur Peabody : he could intrude upon the Secretary of State only when Peabody was absent and the buzzer buzzed. His relations with the Parliamentary Under-Secretary, however comradely, must have as their background the conscious, constant, gulf which exists between a Civil Servant and a tenant of the Government Bench. The actual manipulation of the business offered possibilities of shamefulness : of gawkiness : of those estranging moments when physical gestures are falsely interpreted.

A hand, stretched forward to reach for papers, is

warmly pressed : a hand, desiring to press warmly, is given a pair of opera-glasses.

John Shorland was perhaps unduly sensitive to all forms of physical or mental bungling : as he sat there, leaning back against the restaurant settee, his mind became as an ant-heap, flurrying innumerable with whole corridors of busy awkwardness. Even the angles were so difficult : the angles of approach : the actual moment of initiation : the excruciating angle of continuance. One might begin to begin : one might even begin : but how, with all those red boxes about, with all those incessant telephone calls, would it be ever possible to continue ? There was something about office life so crushingly quotidian. Those pegs behind the door displaying hats and bowlers : the typists, at 4.45, fussing like hospital nurses above the gas-ring : those cups with a pattern of violets across the yellow : that cup with a chip in it which one would have oneself on Friday and observe, on the following Tuesday, being used by someone else : that fuggy feeling about 6.50, when one's hands felt dirty, and one's shirt felt old.

Yet not this only,—not the fact merely that their official connection offered the maximum of severance combined with the maximum of propinquity, offered the greatest possible disadvantages of both. The whole setting, with its incessant small preoccupations, was inimical to a delicate, a complicated, a most unusual affair of the heart. The words " Office romance " twirled in his consciousness in a spiral of disgust. No—this startling experience, this strong new preoccupation in his heart, must be protected against the quotidian, must be preserved against the every day.

A second, more immediate, wave assailed him. What, actually, was he to do? To-night? To-morrow? His passion, if avowed, might startle and confuse. Yet, if unavowed, in what manner could it possibly be furthered and conveyed? One might be reduced to facial expression. Shorland, at that, grinned grimly. He saw himself casting glances of adoration at the Under-Secretary behind the office-keeper's back.

" Good God ! " he exclaimed at this, and aloud.

A woman at the table opposite raised startled eyes across the narrow restaurant. Her glance, resting upon John Shorland, meeting his defiance, ceased to be surprised and became appraising. " That woman," thought Shorland, " imagines that I am sensational and drunk." He was wrong. She had merely noticed his hands. " Dear me ! " she was thinking, " that young man opposite . . ." and she dropped her eyes.

This interruption created a pause, a diversion. The little troubled waves ceased suddenly to clop and flurry : there was a momentary silence in his mind : and a great tide—dark, noiseless, overpowering—swelled up within him. He felt embarrassed by the actual organic quality of this sensation : he blushed : his hands dropped to his thighs, holding them with tautened fingers : his brain struggled to resume again its wonted dominance. " This," said John Shorland to himself, " is what they call a gust of emotion." The sound of his mental voice, the renewal of his own mental habit, reassured him.

He released his thighs from that twin grip and completed, with an easy gesture, the movement which three minutes before, three centuries before, had been so strangely interrupted. John Shorland reached his right hand towards the Armagnac: he filled his glass: he drank.

" Life," he decided, exuberant, " begins to-morrow ! "

It did indeed.

(2)

Jane Campbell, Parliamentary Under-Secretary of State for Foreign Affairs, was a woman of tact, gaiety, and determination. She was, in addition, a tidy woman—liking india-rubber bands, desk trays, and cardboard envelopes marked " answered," " unanswered " and " suspense." Her office table, unlike the office tables of other Ministers, was un-encumbered. A mahogany waggon on her left side received the boxes which had not yet been opened: a mahogany waggon on her right side received the boxes which she had dealt with and which were passed on for further circulation. A nest of little pigeon-holes upon the desk itself con-tained the buff, the green, the pink labels which she inserted into these incessant boxes.

She was pleased by her own deftness.

She would turn to the left, open the topmost box, extract a file of papers, transfer the box, still open, to her right side, slip off the white ribbon which held the file together, smooth the top paper flatly with her palm, read the minutes, read the despatch, stretch forward for her fountain pen, flick a neat little tick against the letters P.U.S.S., initial the neat tick " J.M.C. 2/6/39," blot the initial with a silver pad, stretch forward again for a clean label, insert the label over the two brass teeth which would grip it when the box was closed, slam the lid sharply, turn the key, reach towards the bell-push, say " African Department, please " to the resultant office-keeper, glance for a second to assure herself that the correct box had been taken : and then relax.

" Well," she would say, relaxing, " and what can I do for you ? "

Jane Campbell was a confident woman. She regarded it as quite natural that a person of her attainments, both academic and parliamentary, should, at the surprising age of thirty-three, have reached so garish a position. She had no patience with those of her women colleagues who conducted themselves self-consciously as if still in 1930. She herself liked being female : she displayed this liking in every curve of her trim body. The tables under the two gaunt windows of her office room contained large Venetian flower-vases stuffed with roses : and in January she would have hyacinths in pots, which she watered daily from the water-bottle supplied by the Stationery Office. She also liked, and exceedingly, being Under-Secretary of State. Here again she made no concealment of her pleasure. " Heavens ! " she would say, " what fun this all is ! Now sit down there—no, *there*, you fool—and tell me all about it. These supplementaries, for instance. I know you think I went too far, but that ass MacClintock. . . ."

Even the most permanent official was delighted when the telephone invited him to a consultation with the Parliamentary Under-Secretary. " She is so alert," they would say, " so intelligent, so humorous." " She is more than that," remarked the head of the Consular Department, who had a weakness for the right word ; " there is no dust upon her : she shines."

Arthur Peabody, alone among the senior members of the office, did not care for Jane Campbell. He called her " the mongoose." It was true that Jane Campbell had a curious nose, which, at moments of intense self-expression, appeared to twitch at the tip. Yet it was not an ugly nose, exactly :—a trifle snouty, perhaps, a shade inquisitive even, but all the same pertinacious and amused. It was a nose, moreover, which burrowed openly : there was no furtive peering on the part of Jane Campbell's nose : it burrowed openly, accompanied by chucklings and little squeaks of delight. It was a sporting nose, a terrier nose,—and, after all, why not the nose of a mongoose ?

" Yes," Peabody would say, " I see your point " —he was always seeing people's points and informing them slowly of this act of vision—" I see your point. But she routs things out : she takes them away. She kept the Danzig file in her room for three whole days. And when I protested— you know that hoydenish way she has—she said, ' But I was reading it, I really was.' Now in the old days the Parliamentary Under-Secretary was never, under any circumstances, allowed to read current papers. It delays things so."

D　　　33

No,—Peabody disliked Jane Campbell. He showed his antipathy by treating her with elaborate politeness, opening doors for her, rising when she entered the room, saying " Allow me . . ." when she reached for a box. He believed that this his marked chivalry annoyed her. In this belief he was mistaken. She was not in the least sensitive to male courtesy : it amused her, and moreover it was frequently convenient, and at times actually pleasant. If she thought of Peabody at all, she thought of him as a poop. " A what ? " John Shorland had asked. " A poop, John. I'm sorry, I know I oughtn't to abuse your superior officer. But he is a poop, John, he is, isn't he ? " " No," said John, " I don't think so. He's limited and conventional. You hate that, I know. But Peabody's perfectly real as far as he goes. And we require a brake sometimes : he's an excellent pneumatic brake."

Jane, at this, had raised her nose to an angle which in someone else would have presaged a snort of contempt : it twitched at the tip, which showed that it was being used as a banner. One could be certain, when that twitch began, that Jane's nose was being used either as a trowel of investigation or as a banner of freedom. She waved it towards the ceiling, triumphing over all those who had been born with nineteenth-century minds.

(3)

The Parliamentary Under-Secretary, on that night of June 2, 1939, dined alone. She was glad of this respite, since she had had an exciting afternoon : she was still feeling puzzled and a trifle sorry. She was feeling sorry for Bullinger. She was feeling puzzled by the intricacy of a situation which the Secretary of State that evening had, a little shamefacedly, disclosed—looking away from her as he did so, looking out over the lake towards the sunset gathering green and gold behind the Palace.

Jane was fond of Bullinger : in a way she respected him. She was quick to realise that under his bouncing evangelical manner lurked an uneasy diffidence : that those confident clerical gestures, that assured episcopal laugh, were but the frontage to a house of many shy chambers : that his complacency concealed a puzzled realisation of his own intellectual and spiritual incompleteness. Somewhere within this affable and unhappy man high qualities of brain and heart floated inconstant and submerged. Were this inconstancy and this submersion the fault of heredity or upbringing, of defective will-power, or of just ordinary indolence of mind ? Jane was inclined to ascribe the unreality of Bullinger to sheer cerebral cowardice. He resembled some soft-wooded creeper which, if supplied with trellis or with wire, would ramp vociferously : yet which, deprived of external support, would wilt, limp and mud-stained, upon the soil. When confronted with the expected or the measurable, Bullinger would be lucid, authoritative, alert : yet in face of the unexpected or the immeasurable he crumpled supinely, seeking querulously for some familiar, even if wholly irrelevant, support.

It was that crumpled effect which she had observed in him this evening. Her heart went out to him in sympathy. He had seemed so conscience-stricken, so bewildered, so alone. He had stood there by the window explaining his dilemma : telling her the facts : yet even then he had blinked away from the essential disclosure. He had not explained to her (although she had guessed it) that the Cabinet on that April morning of 1938 had tried to hedge.

The crisis, when it came, had come suddenly and in a wholly unexpected form. Jane Campbell, as the rest of the Foreign Office, had been aware, of course, that the achievement of the Livingstone Rocket I.A. had caused uneasiness abroad. They had known also that the Air Ministry held a controlling interest in the Abu Saad concession of Major Morris. Their attention, moreover, had been called by the Berlin Embassy to an article written by Hauptmann A./D. Hans Ritter in *Die Luftwacht*, in which the Livingstone alloy had been described as introducing a revolution in aeronautical construction, and in which it had been indicated that if Great Britain had really secured for herself a monopoly of this material she would, inevitably and for many years, enjoy the mastery of the air. The article had caused some trepidation in France and the United States. It had been reproduced textually in *L'Aeronautique* and in *Aviation*. The Air Attachés of the several Embassies had buzzed like hornets around the circular corridors with which Sir Edwin Lutyens had so lavishly provided the new Air Ministry in Whitehall Gardens. There had been a murmur even, and from Washington, of concerted foreign action. Yet it was not till 3.20 p.m. on that June 2 that the dull undertone of an ordinary office afternoon rose to the high, insistent buzz of a first-class crisis.

Jane Campbell, sitting in her room on the first floor, had become aware of this unwonted animation. She had crossed to the Private Secretaries' room hoping to find John Shorland. A hum of perplexed irritation seemed to rise from those tessellated corridors, and the door communicating with the India Office stood open at the end of its long passage. Two harried officials of the latter department pushed by her, muttering distress. They ran down the staircase on their way to the Permanent Under-Secretary. Jane paused in the passage : her nose began to twitch. The I.O. officials returned bringing with them Sir Reginald himself. Gaunt and imperturbable, the Permanent head of the Foreign Office accompanied them on their return journey. They yapped around him like excited terriers. "Quite," he was saying as they passed Jane in the passage. "Quite, quite." Sir Reginald always used the word "quite" when he meant "I see." It was a neutral, dilatory expression. Sir Reginald was a non-committal man, and not one whom it would be possible to fluster or to rush. They passed through the doorway into the dim recesses of the India Office. And Jane for her part entered the Private Secretaries' room.

"Come in," said Peabody, rising virile, "please come in, Miss Campbell."

"Where's John ?" Jane asked him.

" He's gone to the India Office, I think. The Secretary of State is over there in conference. They have just sent for Sir Reginald."

" What's up ? " said Jane.

" It's about this Persian telegram. You must have seen it. The Persians claim that Abu Saad is Persian territory. They have asked us to evacuate the coaling station."

" But I thought," said Jane, " that it belonged to Muscat. Surely it was from the Sultan of Muscat that Major Morris obtained his concession ? "

" I think so—yes, I think so. An unsavoury business. But not one, I think, which justifies all this excitement. I have never seen Mr. Bullinger so unlike himself : he was irritable, Miss Campbell, it's so seldom that he becomes irritable. And all about some shady concession."

The door opened and John entered. " Halloa, Jane," he said, smiling carelessly. Peabody felt an inward twitch of irritation. He loathed these slap-dash manners. John walked to his table and picked up the receiver. He smiled again at Jane, holding the receiver in his hand, looking upwards and across at her. He said " Library, please," to the exchange, and then he smiled at Jane again. " Is that Library ? " he went on. " Private Secretaries here. Can you look up the Muscat Treaty of 1857 and anything we have regarding the Sultan's lease of Abu Saad ? Yes, very urgent : the Secretary of State's in conference at the I.O. I'll come down in three minutes and help in the search."

Still holding the receiver, still smiling across at Jane, he joggled the rest. " Exchange," he said,

" I want the Cabinet Office at once—get it on the Treasury circuit." He put back the receiver and walked towards Jane, who was still standing in the middle of the room. " Well, my dear," he said, " here's a nice sort of mess—what about Geneva now ? " The bell rang before she could answer him. He strode back to his own table. " Cabinet Office ? " he said. " Private Secretary F.O. speaking. Mr. Bullinger wants a Cabinet to-morrow at eleven. He's in conference over at the I.O. at present. It's about this Abu Saad business. Can you get on to the P.M. and let us know ? "

" I must dash," he said, turning to Jane. She followed him out into the passage.

" What's it all about ? " she said.

" Abu Saad," he laughed, hurrying to the staircase. He strode down the wide steps three at a time. His head, against the darkness of the lower corridor, shone like gold.

Jane returned to her room and sent for the Persian telegrams.

(4)

The British Empire, in that summer of 1939, was anything but a popular member of the community of nations. In fact, never, since the distant days of the South African War, had we been so universally hated and despised.

The origins of that wave of anglophobia which attacked three continents during the later months of 1938 and the spring of 1939 can be ascribed to causes over which neither Spencer Furnivall nor Mr. Bullinger had any control, and for which even the Churchill Government were not entirely responsible.

There was in the first place very widespread disappointment at the fact that the British Empire still continued to exist. The French, feeling our survival to be illogical, ascribed it partly to hypocrisy and partly to an unworthy desire on our part to score off M. André Siegfried, whose book, " Carthago Deleta," had been published so long ago as 1936. The Germans, having been positively assured for ten years in succession that civil war and separatism were impending throughout India, blamed, not Mahatma Gandhi, but Lord Lothian, who, they felt, had let them down. The Russians, who, in the unemployment crisis of 1933, had climbed to dizzy peaks of expectancy, had since conceived for the bourgeois of the so-called British proletariat a contemptuous loathing which thirsted for revenge. And in the United States they had been assured that the great slump of 1934, the Mexican weevil even which had providentially ruined the harvest of 1935, were both directly attributable to the British default of November 1933, and still more to our unscrupulously sudden resumption of payments in the spring that followed.

To these, so to speak, subjective causes of resentment, were added other factors of a more practical nature. The French, already alienated by the tariff war of 1933, already wounded by the, to their minds, pro-German attitude adopted by Sir Samuel Hoare at the fourth and fifth Preparatory Disarmament Conferences, had been incensed beyond measure at the Egyptian conflict and at the high-

handed, and successful, action of Mr. Brendan
Bracken. The repudiation by the Central Cabinet
of Mr. Spencer Furnivall of the Clive–Tardieu
protocol had been taken by each individual Frenchman as a personal affront. Marooned upon a
mountain of gold, the Banque de France regarded
with loathing and apprehension the " insane bi-
metallism " of Lord Waley, dreading lest at any
moment Rumania, Czechoslovakia, nay Poland
even, might join that disastrous sterling club :
becoming daily more disquieted by the currency
position in Cochin China, by the flood of George
dollars which had already spread like a blight across
Northern Africa.

The Germans, having, on the advice of their
Consul-General in Calcutta, decided that Britain,
preoccupied as she would be with civil war in India,
would of necessity steer her policy in the wake of
the Wilhelmstrasse, regarded the Clive–Tardieu
protocol as an act of gross betrayal. It was thus
England, and not France, who bore the odium of
the League decision regarding Danzig and the
Polish corridor. And moreover, that very May,
Great Britain had won not only the Christie trophy
but also the Davis cup.

In Moscow, the leaders of the Union of Agrarian
Republics, while recognising that they themselves
owed much to the intervention of Mr. Brendan
Bracken in the affair of the Chinese Eastern Railway (for had it not been the discomfiture of that
defeat which had proved the first premonition of
the fall of Stalin and their own accession to power ?)
were none the less conscious that their happy rural

collectivism possessed little of the fevered vehemence, the tense energy, of the old bolshevik religion. The red blood had ceased to pulsate with its old pressure : the Central Asian Republics were becoming cold, atrophied, almost independent. The moment had arrived when Russia must again make herself felt at Khiva and Tashkend, at Samarcand and Bokhara. Yet across the path of their infiltration, blinking a trifle mangily, lay that same old lion who, they had been told so frequently, was already dead.

And Mr. Hans P. Scholle, President of the United States, was much under the influence of his young and charming wife. He was thinking already of a second term of office.

It was not surprising therefore that the chancelleries of Europe and America, on realising the implications of the Livingstone rocket ; on learning that the manufacture of this extremely rapid vehicle depended upon the Livingstone alloy ; on ascertaining finally that this alloy could be manufactured only from the Abu Saad deposits ; should have taken counsel together with a view to preventing so unfair an advantage falling into the coarse and brutal hands of Great Britain.

The cables, during those warmed nights of May, had hummed continuously between Paris and Washington, between Paris and Berlin, between Paris, even, and Moscow. Seldom had concerted action been so rapidly achieved. It was Mr. Alexei Rubinstein, Russian Commissar of Foreign Relations, who first evolved the idea of a local rather than a general action. The State Department, for

their part, had at first suggested a collective note
in London insisting, with disguised menace, on
the principle of the open door. Mr. Rubinstein
had suggested that it is always safer to close a door
than to open it. He had addressed to his Ambassadors at Paris, Berlin and Washington a circular
instruction, proposing that the four Representatives
at Tehran might suggest to the Shah of Persia that
Abu Saad was in fact a Persian island, that the
Sultan of Muscat had no right whatsoever to claim
sovereignty over any such territory, and that the
Morris Concession was therefore null and void.
It would at the same time be put to the Shah that
in view of the international importance of these Abu
Saad deposits a new concession should be accorded
by the Persian Government, and approved by the
Majlis, under which exclusive mining rights in Abu
Saad should be granted to a consortium of French,
Russian, German and American interests.

The Governments of France, Germany, and the
United States warmly welcomed the proposal. On
May 29 the four Ministers had presented a joint
note to the Persian Prime Minister at the Gulistan
Palace. On May 30 they had been granted a
joint audience by the Shah at Dilkusha. They had
assured His Majesty that his juridical rights to
Abu Saad were open to no question. They had
assured him also that, should Great Britain contest
this opinion, the four Governments would insist
at London on the dispute being referred to the
League : and that Persia could rest assured of overwhelming support on the part of the League Council.

The Shah had received these assurances while

sitting on a pink velvet chair among the salvias of his private garden. He had expressed his gratitude for the interest displayed by the Great Powers in the integrity and independence of Persia. He had promised to instruct his Cabinet to address an immediate note to the British Minister in the sense desired. And he had also promised that the matter of the consortium would in the same manner receive his immediate attention.

They left him, bowing gleefully like turtle-doves, walking backwards along the gravel path, between the salvias. In the outer courtyard of the villa they had found their four motors, one behind the other, crackling under the Persian sun. They had shaken hands with each other, doffing top hats, sweating in their thick black clothes. Hooting dustily, the four motors swayed back to Shimran.

The Shah, on their departure, cleared his enormous throat and spat with fervour among the salvias. He sat there hunched in his pink armchair, turning his beads slowly in his heavy hands. Suddenly he had an idea. It was clearly a gay and bright idea, since he began to chuckle heavily, hunched with great shoulders in that pink armchair. He clapped his hands for an attendant. Chuckling heavily, he summoned his Minister of the Court.

(5)

It was not till after six on the evening of that Thursday, June 2, that Jane Campbell had obtained access to the Secretary of State. She hesitated in the doorway, seeing his empty chair pushed side-

44

ways from the desk. Walter Bullinger was standing by one of the western windows gazing intently at the pelicans beside the lake below. He appeared bowed and uncertain : he seemed even, a little, crushed.

" May I come in ? . . ." she said.

At the sound of her voice he straightened his shoulders, becoming dapper again, becoming anglican : and having done so, he turned, chest protruding, to meet her eyes.

She thought : " How pathetic, how lonely, he looked against that western window ! He drooped. He was drooping lonelily when I came into the room. How like him to straighten upwards when he heard my voice ! "

He thought : " How girlish she looks there in the shaft of sunset, her hand like that upon that heavy doorway ! A gracious presence. How tight, how trim, her skirt around those little thighs ! "

" My dear," he said, advancing towards her with his springing curate's gait, opening wide anglican arms, " my dear Jane, pray sit down. This Persia business—it will cause us trouble in the House."

She thought : " How like a bishop he is ! That pink, that bouncing look. I suppose that very religious people when overworked always get to look a little like bishops."

He thought : " She feels I am behaving confidently. I always find myself behaving confidently when I get tired. She doesn't understand. She thinks I'm all of a piece. But I'm two different bits : they chafe and hurt."

She said : " For God's sake, Walter, give me a cigarette."

45

He said : " Which cigarette ? "

" My dear man," she said, " you really *are* overworked."

" No," said Bullinger, " I'm not overworked, Jane. Just inadequate. We're in a mess."

" I know," she said, striking a match slowly, giving him time.

Walter Bullinger leant back upon the leather sofa. " You see," he began, " you do not know the whole story. We kept it dark. Old Narteagle—you know about him—told us in March—no, in April—of last year. It was shortly after we came into office. He made it all quite plain—or rather, plain enough."

Jane, her nose twitching, decided not to interrupt.

" You see," he began again, " it's not only the rocket. We don't mind about that. We don't mind much about Abu Saad or the concession. All that could be arranged. But it's the bomb that bothers me."

" The bomb ? " said Jane.

" Yes," he sighed ; " you see, we think the Churchill crowd suspect."

" Suspect what ? " said Jane, nosing.

" Suspect about the bomb," said Bullinger, nodding at the fireplace like King Lear.

" But *what* bomb ? " said Jane again.

" Atomic," answered Bullinger, nodding sombrely. And then he adjusted himself to explanation. He leant forward, stroking his chin. Each point, as he made it, was marked by a raised index, a raised middle finger, a raised third finger, a splayed little finger. Walter Bullinger did not raise his thumb, having been taught at Harrow that the thumb is the most plebeian of all the fingers. Yet he made his points. Jane listened, sympathetic and aghast.

" I see," she said, when he had concluded. " The Government have fallen between two stools. That comes of hedging."

" I don't quite follow . . ." he protested, a faint swirl of self-importance, of Cabinet dignity, rising in his cumbered brain.

" But yes," said Jane, her nose neither a banner nor a trowel, but a pointer indicating points.

" But yes," she said, " it's quite obvious. Concentrating on the rocket aeroplane, you have aroused, in very intricate circumstances, the Great Powers against you. You must either surrender to their dictation, or resist. They do not know about the bomb. You do. So, perhaps, do the opposition. Yet even you are not yet certain about the bomb, and even if you were you would loathe to use it. The opposition aren't certain about the bomb, but were they in your place they would certainly use it, if only as a threat. And in any case they would not, if possessed of the information which you possessed in April of last year, have done nothing about it. They will press you hard : above all if we are threatened publicly with concerted menaces on the part of the Powers. They will ask you what you have been doing about the bomb all these fourteen months. . . ."

" They can't," interrupted Bullinger, " ask such a question across the floor of the house."

" Walter ! " said Jane.

" Yes, I know," he answered, " but you were talking about the opposition."

"No," she continued, "it's far more than all that. The House—and you know it, Walter—doesn't matter in the least in these sort of questions. It's the facts that matter. And the facts are horrible. They boil down to this. You are faced by a ramp on the part of the Powers. You possess a secret which would enable you to defy them all. Your opponents have at least an inkling that you possess that secret. You hesitate to use the weapon which Fate has placed within your hands. It is very noble of you. But if the opposition were in power they would give to this country the unquestioned domination of the world."

Bullinger squirmed upon his leather sofa. His tongue passed across dry lips.

"My dear Jane," he said, "do you realise? That bomb, a bomb no bigger than that inkstand, could destroy New York. It can't be done."

"No," said Jane, prodding towards the fireplace with her nose, "it quite certainly cannot be done."

"So we must give way?" said Bullinger, turning pink cheeks towards Jane, pink wobbly cheeks.

"No," she said, "not that. We must gain time." She cupped her little hand upon her knees. "Yes," she said, "time is everything. Time and confidence."

Walter Bullinger sighed. A puppyish sigh.

The baize door into the Private Secretaries' room opened discreetly. Peabody appeared, with papers in his hand. Jane and Walter relaxed their tension. They became relaxed.

"An urgent telegram, sir," said Peabody, "from Tehran."

Bullinger stretched a wearied and receptive hand.

48

He read the telegram.   He handed it sadly to Jane Campbell.

" Decypher," she read :—

" *Decypher : Sir A. Yencken : Tehran*

$$d.\ 8.30\ p.m.\brace r.\ 6.30\ p.m.\ \Bigg\}\ June\ 2.$$

No. 328

My immediately preceding telegram.

I learn from reliable source that French, German, American Legations and Russian Embassy have offered Shah consortium with unspecified capital for exploitation of Abu Saad deposits.

They have also assured H.M. that their Governments will in event of British action refer matter to Geneva and have in that event promised support.

Shah is personally (? deeply) involved.

I venture to submit (two groups undecypherable) secured by immediate ultimatum backed by measures likely to convince Shah that we mean business.

Such measures would be : (1) Blockade of Gulf.   (2) Landing at Bushire and sequestration of southern customs.   (3) Mobilisation at Quetta and possibly in Iraq.

I gather that legal adviser to Persian Foreign Office has examined Muscat dossier and is confident that juridically Persia has a good case.   My informant adds that Shah is, if we resist, determined to appeal to League.

Repeated to Govt. of India, Baghdad, Bushire and Angora."

E   49

" He wants instructions ? " said the Secretary of State, petulantly.

" No—I don't think so, sir," Peabody answered.

" I expect he does," said Jane.

" Well," said Walter Bullinger, " it's all too clearly a Cabinet matter—all too clearly."

" All too clearly," repeated Peabody. " The meeting is arranged, sir, for to-morrow morning."

" At eleven ? " sighed Bullinger.

" At eleven," Peabody answered.

The baize door opened again. John Shorland appeared, holding a second telegram.

" And," Jane continued, regardless of this interruption, " you will have to tell them what to do."

" Yes," said Bullinger, gazing sadly in front of him. " I shall have to tell them what to do."

Shorland interrupted. " Another telegram," he said, " from Tehran. A very odd telegram."

Again Bullinger held out wearied and receptive fingers.

" Decypher," he read aloud :—

> " *Decypher : Sir A. Yencken : Tehran*
> $\left.\begin{array}{l} d. \;\; 10.5 \; p.m. \\ a. \;\;\; 7.0 \; p.m. \end{array}\right\}$ *June* 2.
>
> *No.* 329.
>
> Clear the line. Very urgent.
>
> My immediately preceding telegram (Of June 2. Abu Saad.)
>
> I hear from reliable source that Cabinet, on personal instructions from Shah, have drafted Bill for immediate submission to Majlis providing for effective confiscation of all conces-

sions held by foreign nationals in Persian territory.

Bill will provide that foreign concession-naires are awarded compensation for value of their concessions in the shape of interest-bearing bonds guaranteed by Banque d'Iran. Actual market value of concessions to be determined by commission appointed by Shah himself.

My United States colleague, whom I questioned this evening, assures me that such a measure would be in conflict with assurances given by Shah to himself and his three colleagues. Such assurances were probably in connection with consortium mentioned in my immediately preceding telegram.

It looks as if Shah has double crossed, and hopes to secure Abu Saad deposits for himself.

Repeated to Govt. of India, Baghdad, Bushire and Angora.

Presume you will repeat to Paris, Washington, etc."

" Hooray ! " said Shorland.

Peabody looked at his colleague with ill-concealed disgust.

" You mean ? " said Walter Bullinger, a little helplessly.

" Well," said Shorland, " you see there are the Caspian fisheries which are a Russian concession, and the tramways which the French acquired from the Belgians, and the Northern Railway which was financed by the Deutsche Bank, and the Southern Railway, plus the oil which the Yanks got in 1936. It will hit them hard."

Jane laughed. Bullinger sighed. Peabody looked respectful.

" Well, said Bullinger, " it's all very obscure. Besides, it's getting late. I shall think it all over before the Cabinet to-morrow."

" Anyhow," said John Shorland, " we have dislocated the block."

" Block ? " said Peabody reprovingly.

" Obviously," answered Shorland, with a touch of impatience, " the Powers, after this, will not be united at Tehran."

Walter Bullinger by this time was already at the door.

" Good-night," he said, " good-night all "— assuming his pulpit tone.

" Good-night," they answered.

" I think," said Jane Campbell to John Shorland as they walked out together into Downing Street, " I think you were a little bumptious to-night. That's all."

" But Jane . . ." he protested. She was already beckoning to a cab.

Half an hour later Arthur Peabody, as we have seen, was in his bath.

Half an hour later, Walter Bullinger, as we have seen, was struggling into a smoking-jacket.

An hour later John Shorland was drinking, perhaps too repeatedly, the Armagnac of Monsieur Boulestin.

And Jane Campbell, at St. Leonard's Terrace, was settling down to read the Persian file.

CHAPTER III

(1)

THE morning of Friday June 3 dawned still and cloudless. The plane trees in St. James's Park, their upper branches radiant in the rising sun, their lower branches shrouded in the shadow of the lake, greeted the day with motionless expectancy. The pelican, on whom the evening before Walter Bullinger had gazed with such sad fixity, was only half awake upon his plot of lawn : he hunched there, round-shouldered and depressed, comforted by the firm feel of his beak against his crouching spine, opening one pink ophthalmic eye upon the enshrouding mist, upon the growing radiance in the upper air, upon the bronze and violet forms of irises emerging, all about him, into light.

It was 5.0 a.m. Already, over there in Paris, the men were watering the lawns, the begonias, the gravel, and the wide asphalt of the Avenue Foch. The Arc de Triomphe rose above them flushed like a cliff which faces to the east. They jerked their jointed hoses this way and that way across the asphalt; the little balls on which the hoses were set scurried busily; the tap in the wide gutter spurted clean blue water, making a rivulet which sparkled down the Avenue Foch : a gay morning

torrent rushing downwards towards those gratings
by the Porte Dauphine.

A car, hooting ill-temperedly, swung round the
Place de l'Etoile and headed down the avenue
towards the bois. The hoses were jerked sideways
to let it pass: the wet asphalt hissed and crackled
at its passage: it was a powerful car and it was
driven fast. It contained M. Jules Boursicaut,
special courier to the Quai d'Orsay, bound for the
Buc aerodrome on his way to London.

M. Boursicaut disliked aviation in any form.
He had been displeased, the previous evening, on
being told that he must fly at dawn to London.
M. François Poncet, the Foreign Minister, had
addressed an urgent despatch to M. René Martin,
his Ambassador at Albert Gate. M. Boursicaut
was to deliver it by hand: an aeroplane would, at
5.30 a.m., be waiting for him at Buc.

M. Boursicaut, sitting in the ministerial car, felt
discontented. His hand, gloved in dogskin, rested
upon his knee: it clasped the leather portfolio
which contained the despatch. He leant back in
the car, stretching out his buttoned boots, con-
veying the impression that he was at his ease. He
pulled down the upholstered arm which, in the
luxurious car of the Foreign Ministry, separated
the right seat from the left. Boursicaut lolled
sulkily upon the cushions, bouncing at moments as
the car swayed and flashed along: letting himself
bounce a shade more than was necessary, indicating
thereby his assurance, his ill-temper, his resentment
at the Quai d'Orsay: hoping that he might break
a spring. (The smell of disinfectant in the Rue

Taitbout, the smell, in the Rue de Rivoli, of plaster and benzine, the smell, when he woke the porter at the Quai d'Orsay, of last year's anthracite and bees-wax.) Undoubtedly M. Boursicaut had a grievance. His wife had said so : for once Thérèse was right. (The smell of newly watered dust in the Avenue Foch, the vanilla smell of laburnum as they entered the bois.) For what, as she had said, was the point of all those clerks and cyphers ? What, after all, the point of all those telephones,— if a message of urgency and importance entailed upon Boursicaut (upon Thérèse also) the need of rising early ; entailed that possible sickness over Beaulieu, that certain sickness by the time they reached Amiens ; entailed, since that had already happened, a disagreement with his wife ? (The smell of the Seine as they crossed the bridge at St. Cloud, that smell of pond mud, of soft water and decaying piles.) Always, as Thérèse had said, it was Boursicaut who was chosen. " Good old Boursicaut ! " the Assistant Secretary had said last night, smiling foolishly. M. Boursicaut did not care for M. Massigli : he disliked the glib manner of the Ecole Normale : finding it patronising : and inconsiderate. Boursicaut bounced viciously as they crossed the octroi cobbles at Versailles.

The pilot at the Buc aerodrome tittered slightly when M. Boursicaut gave him his name. That was another of his misfortunes : to have a name which, inevitably, made young or ill-mannered people smile. Grasping his portfolio sulkily, yet not without a sense of importance, Jules Boursicaut clambered to his seat.

The machine rose heavily in the fresh and

windless air, droning north-westwards to where, after thirty minutes, the sea shimmered like a silver curtain in the sky. M. Boursicaut munched his buttered roll. It was very calm. Already they had passed over Beaulieu, already the twin towers of Amiens circled below them on their right. M. Boursicaut, for once, was scarcely feeling ill at all: he descended at Croydon yellow but intact: he entered the Embassy car and sped to Albert Gate.

And thus it happened that when, at eight o'clock precisely, M. Boursicaut, clasping his portfolio, walked up the steps of the French Embassy, Mr. Walter Bullinger, clasping a crop, was mounting his horse within a hundred yards of M. Boursicaut, and unconscious, fortunately, of what that slim portfolio contained.

At that very moment, from his office in the Kremlin, Alexei Rubinstein, Commissar of Foreign Relations, was telephoning, with but scant audibility, to Baku.

At that very moment, in Tehran, under the white blaze of noon, the Shah of Persia was eating a large nectarine, turning it over in his red and clumsy hands, biting it fiercely till the juice glistened on his fingers. And wondering whether, in spite of everything, he had not gone too far.

And at that very moment, Mr. Hans P. Scholle, President of the United States, slept at Bar Harbour, his windows open to warmed western stars.

(2)

Walter Bullinger, from his early childhood, had been taught that constant physical exercise was the

56

most potent among those many processes which rendered the English gentleman superior to the gentlemen of France, Italy, Germany, and other places abroad. This doctrine had been strongly emphasised at Harrow: had been repeated even at Magdalen: and had, in middle age, become one of the less movable articles of furniture in Walter Bullinger's mind.

Mr. Spencer Furnivall, it is true, who much disliked exercise, had on one occasion, and with that seeming graciousness which masked a really disagreeable nature, rallied his Foreign Secretary upon his absurd prejudices regarding the necessity of exercise and open air.

Walter Bullinger had been hurt by the Prime Minister's ridicule: he had always contended that Spencer Furnivall, in spite of his great gifts as a Parliamentarian, was a trifle un-English. Yet so fluid were the convictions, even the deepest convictions, of Walter Bullinger, that the Prime Minister's sneers had left their mark. Bullinger, at moments, would admit that this need of exercise was a somewhat unnecessary physical habit; a habit which, had he been better educated, he might never have acquired. He felt uneasy, even, when he considered how many hours, how many George dollars, he had expended on his belief in, his conviction of, and after all his constant urge for, physical exercise. He admitted also that, as a habit, it was exacting. At Angley Manor it was all so easy: he could dig: he liked digging: he found it purposeful, creative, hesiodic, and very welcome to the popular Press. In London the whole business was so far more complicated. It was ungainly for a Cabinet Minister, however plump and pink he might be, to play squash with any frequency at the R.A.C. There remained the Park: there remained that horse, waiting at 8.0 a.m., in sight of the twin stags of Albert Gate.

Not that Bullinger really cared for horses. It seemed wrong to him that something potentially so powerful should have become so ambulatory, so domesticated. He had a strong sense of nature, and it was apt to take original forms. It seemed wrong to him, on the other hand, that something so domesticated, so suave, should possess this wholly unregulated capacity for causing alarm.

The horse, a symbol of this habituation, a target for these infrequent criticisms, waited that June morning at Albert Gate. Being an unobservant animal, it had failed to notice M. Jules Boursicaut climbing the steps of the French Embassy, clasping a portfolio pregnant with anglophobia. Yet it did observe the simultaneous arrival of Walter Bullinger, since that entailed two lumps of sugar (tendered amateurishly on a wash-leather, rather cringing, glove)—and thereafter thirteen stone seven.

Walter Bullinger, on reaching the saddle, looked downwards at his right stirrup, and downwards at his left stirrup. A practised glance. He had noticed in the old days (when staying rapturously at Belvoir) that Lord Lonsdale, on mounting, had indulged in that expert, and to him almost automatic, preliminary. It impressed the groom. There were moments when Walter Bullinger was not quite certain whether it really did impress the groom.

That morning of June 3 was one of those on which, regarding this point, he was not quite certain. He was considering the point, a little dimly as usual, as he trotted off.

It was a dull ride. It was more than dull. For even as the French Ambassador (eating sausages up there in his sitting-room, dressed in grey flannel trousers and a jumper, faced by M. Boursicaut, also eating sausages, although with a tentative gesture, not being used to Ambassadors who asked him to breakfast, not feeling very well inside, and still wearing the black button boots, the stiff shirt, the black suiting, even the dogskin gloves, in which —how long ago it seemed!—he had flown from Paris)—yes, even as M. René Martin, Walter Bullinger, that morning, was thinking hard, was trying to think hard, about the crisis.

M. René Martin, for his part, did not feel in the least drawn to Jules Boursicaut, nor yet to the Persian question. He propped the despatch open with a fork. He read it carefully. It struck him as a foolish, slightly hysterical, despatch. He waited till his mouth was quite full before again addressing M. Boursicaut. "Plâit-il, Excellence?" said the latter, in a tone almost, although deferentially, of reproof. Clearly M. René Martin was of the newer school of diplomacy. M. Boursicaut reflected that these young Ambassadors tended to become un-French. He let his eyes, his thoughts, wander regretfully over the faded Aubusson of M. de St. Aulaire.

(3)

Walter Bullinger, by then, had reached the bridge over the Serpentine. He was " arranging his thoughts." He would be obliged, within less than three hours, to put the whole situation before the assembled Cabinet. His statement must be long but lucid. He would divide it into three main sections, namely, (1) analysis, (2) synthesis, (3) conclusions. " Let me commence this morning . . ." thus would Bullinger open his statement, tidy and matutinal, straightening the blotter on the baize cloth, placing his right hand (no, his left hand) upon the pile of telegrams at his side. " Let me commence this morning by telling you the facts of the situation as they emerge from the happenings, the interviews and the correspondence of the last twenty-four hours. I shall then give you some insight. . . ." No, ' insight ' wouldn't do at all, it sounded patronising, it sounded as if in the past he and his office had been secretive. " I shall then," he corrected himself, " try to give you a picture of the facts *behind* the facts." His right palm (no, his left palm) might descend slowly upon the pile of papers underlying the word ' behind.'

Bullinger was pleased with this his second phrase : it was calm, it was authoritative, it was modest : and yet it was determined : it was unpretentious, solid, British. He decided to trot.

He had been told by his doctor that it was a good thing, when trotting before breakfast in the Park, to avoid rising in the stirrup and to let himself jog loosely upon the saddle. Bullinger was by nature an obedient man and his subservience to doctors was extreme. Not that he liked this jogging business. He hated it. It made his cheeks wobble: it generally gave him a stitch: and he was aware that it conveyed to the casual passer-by the impression that he was not wholly at his ease upon a horse. In the hope of diminishing this impression, Bullinger had developed two alternative techniques: he would interchange the forward with the backward seat: when he leaned backwards he went *jug, jug, jug*; when he leaned forwards he went *jig, jig, jig*. There was, in fact, small difference between the two movements: yet the fact that he could, at will, exchange one movement for the other reassured Walter Bullinger, giving him a sense of selection, an added sense of control.

On reaching the Marble Arch, Walter Bullinger tightening reins in a wash-leather glove, slowed down to a walk. That would suffice this morning, in so far as trotting was concerned: he could canter down the Bayswater stretch upon his second round: meanwhile he would allow his horse to walk—a hand grasping slack reins and resting upon the pommel; a head bent forward slightly, " arranging thoughts." Thus would he ride along the frontages of the Park Lane hotels—a British Foreign Secretary grappling with a policy, even as Palmerston, even as the Duke of Wellington had grappled, similarly riding in Hyde Park. At the mention of the Duke of Wellington, the shoulders of Mr. Bullinger, already bowed under imperial responsibility, bowed an inch further. Should he meet a friend upon the way—Lady Athelhampton it might be, or Lord Fairlawne—he would wave a crop in greeting, amicable but dismissive, indicating pre-occupation with affairs of State: waving them away.

"You are not," murmured his inner conscience, "getting on very well with your statement."

Walter Bullinger pulled himself together. "First," he said to himself firmly, "*analysis*." He had reached Apsley House, and as he turned into Rotten Row his horse began to jig slightly, feeling it effeminate with such a stretch of tan before one, on such a radiant morning, to merely walk.

"Woa!" said Mr. Bullinger, "woa! boy," adopting thereby an agricultural turn of phrase rather than a current term of equitation. His horse grunted and resumed its statesman stride. A docile animal. "First," Mr. Bullinger repeated to himself, "*analysis*. Point 1 . . ."

It was indeed a lovely morning. The lawns to the left and right of him sparkled with fresh dew. The great trees above him towered symmetrical and immense. Passive, unquivering and operatic, they drank the morning sun. A slight steam rose from the broad tan avenue. From beyond the rhodo-dendrons came a warm puff of new-cut grass. The heart of Walter Bullinger tautened into longing for Angley Manor. He had promised himself a long week-end on Saturday—and that was, that would have been, to-morrow. He would have left by the 1.18 from Paddington. He would have lunched in the train—those nice oatmeal biscuits, those little radishes, wet and cool. He would have reached Angley by 5.30. The cedars would already be

throwing slit shadows on the upper lawn : the smell
of azaleas would still be lingering in the bog-
garden : those new rhododendrons which Mr.
Perks had sent him from Wales : and, oh damn !
the *Magnolia Parviflora*.

Now, in all probability, he would have to go to
Chequers. How he loathed Chequers ! That unreal
feel, the provisional feel, that exhibition feel, that
" please-do-not-touch " feel, that slippery staircase,
those beastly walks with Furnivall upon the down.

Bullinger admired the Prime Minister : he
admired him immensely : but he did not feel at
ease in his company : in fact, when he came to
think of it, he felt extremely ill at ease. There
was something pejorative about Furnivall : something feline and unfair. Bullinger, in Furnivall's
presence, found himself becoming the sort of
Bullinger which Furnivall so evidently thought he
was. Bullinger's best qualities when faced by the
Prime Minister became frightened somehow and
hid in corners. Whereas his worst qualities, at
Furnivall's ill-disguised solicitation, advanced to
the footlights and showed off, disgustingly.

" You are not," murmured his inner conscience,
" getting on with your statement."

For the second time, Bullinger pulled himself
together. " Point 1," he exclaimed defiantly.
What was Point 1 ? At the mention of Point 1
Bullinger had a momentary glimpse of all the other
painful, galling points mustering behind it like
Army officers at a levée. These things were so
difficult to work out except with pen and paper.
He began again from the beginning. " Let me

commence this morning . . ." No, 'commence' would not do at all: he had read somewhere that in such cases it was less bourgeois, and far more cultured, to use the simpler word 'begin.' "Let me begin this morning by telling you the facts *behind* the facts. . . ." No, he had left out the bit about the "happenings, the interviews, and the correspondence of the last twenty-four hours." That was rather a good bit: almost Curzonian. And in any case it was the skeleton of the thing he wanted to get straight: the actual words would come easily enough when at 9.30 he dictated his statement to Miss Ramsden. What he wanted at this moment was to get the preparatory headings clearly differentiated in his mind. The main divisions were obvious—(*a*) Analysis, (*b*) Synthesis, (*c*) Conclusions. Now under (*a*) came Point 1 . . ."

"Good-morning, Mr. Bullinger," said Lady Athelhampton.

How lovely she looked there in her riding clothes, that big grey horse, that champing curb-chain, those tiny little hands!

"My dear lady," said Walter Bullinger, "this is indeed a pleasure! And on such a morning too!"

Smiling, episcopal again, released from care, Mr. Bullinger turned his grateful steed and cantered back along the Row with Lady Athelhampton.

"I must say," he panted—for Lady Athelhampton cantered fast—"I must say, our parks in June, one can say what one likes, but I must say . . ."

"What?" said Lady Athelhampton.

Bullinger, increasingly breathless, repeated his remark.

An hour later, at No. 34 Grosvenor Gardens, Miss Ramsden waited, pencil poised on pad, for the Secretary of State to finish his breakfast. Her eyes, pained but patient, were fixed upon the clock. Three urgent boxes, showing double labels (that pink label which meant "immediate," that smaller, almost marsupial label which shrieked " I'm very urgent indeed "), had already arrived from the Foreign Office. The Resident Clerk had telephoned twice. And the Cabinet meeting was fixed for eleven.

At 10.10 a.m. Bullinger entered, brisk and busy. " Good-morning, Miss Ramsden. A lovely morning. I have been thinking out the heads of my statement for the Cabinet. Dear me, how late it is ! You had better take it straight on to the machine. Only rough notes, of course—just headings and a few words under each. Head it ' Cabinet Statement. June 3, 1939.' Next main heading. ' A. Analysis.' Underline ' Analysis.' First main sub-heading, ' Point 1.' Now let me see . . ."

Mr. Bullinger paused, swaying upon his patent-leather shoes. " Point 1," he repeated. And then he saw the despatch-boxes. " Oh, excuse me a moment. Urgent . . ." The phrase died on his lips as he fumbled for his keys.

It was in this way that Walter Bullinger arrived at the first of many Cabinet sessions on the Abu Saad crisis, with a mind suffering, but unprepared.

(4)

Jane Campbell, on the other hand, had read the Persian file with great precision. She had even been sent by Shorland, and at 10.20 p.m., a flimsy copy of the Library memorandum on the Muscat leases. Being a tidy person, she had classified the issues in her mind. She had gone further. She had risen early the next morning and, on the back of an old invitation card, she had summarised these issues in tabulated form.

Her little analysis ran as follows :—

BOMB CRISIS: June 3, 1939

A. Statement of problem.

(1) Summer 1935. James Livingstone unearths strange deposit at Abu Saad. He experiments with this deposit and finds that it furnishes an alloy which transforms aluminium into a new metal. He is convinced that this metal will produce an explosion chamber rendering possible a high-power aeroplane rocket.

(2) May 1936. Livingstone submits result of his first experiments to Aeronautical Research Committee. Latter report to Lord Lympne, Churchill's Air Minister, to effect that Livingstone premises seem justified. They add that Abu Saad concession is held by a certain Major Morris, who obtained this concession from Sultan of Muscat in 1922, and who is now in financial difficulties. Lord Lympne thereupon purchases on behalf of Air Ministry 80 per cent. of the shares in Morris' Abu Saad Exploration Company.

(3) Summer 1937. Research Committee report that Livingstone Rocket is a feasible

proposition and request authority to experiment at once. Authority granted.

N.B.—At this interview with Lympne and Churchill it is more than likely that Narteagle and the other experts indicated possibility of the atomic bomb.

(4) December 1937. Fall of Churchill Government. General Election.

(5) January 1938. Furnivall Government.

(6) April 1938. Cabinet meeting on Livingstone alloy. Narteagle tells them definitely that Livingstone alloy has potentiality far wider than a mere rocket aeroplane. The rocket is now a certainty, and will be ready in a few months. The next stage is to experiment with the atomic bomb. Furnivall and Bullinger hedge. While giving official sanction to rocket aeroplane, they refuse officially to consider atomic bomb, while at same time hinting that Air Ministry should follow up this development.

(7) May 19, 1939. Rocket aeroplane, on its first flight, reaches New York in five hours. Excitement abroad. Foreign Governments realise that rocket depends on alloy for which Abu Saad deposit is essential. Fearing monopoly on our part, they urge Shah to claim Abu Saad as Persian territory and then to hand over concession to a joint consortium. Shah does former, but cheats about latter, and endeavours to cancel all foreign concessions and to take Abu Saad deposits for himself.

(8) Thursday, June 2, 1939. News of this

reaches London. Bullinger is alarmed by joint action of Powers and uncertain of Sultan of Muscat's legal rights over Abu Saad, and consequently of validity of Morris concession. He fears that if matter goes to League, Council will decide against us. On the other hand, he recognises that the whole thing is a ramp. He holds trump card in the shape of atomic bomb which could crush all foreign opposition. He does not wish to use this weapon. He fears, however, that Churchill group know enough about the atomic bomb to insist upon a strong attitude towards Geneva and the Powers.

(9) June 3, 1939. Government are thus faced with alternative of having to surrender to pressure of Powers or having to use against them this tremendous new engine of destruction. The Opposition, having an inkling of the atomic bomb, will be able to concentrate on Livingstone rocket and argue that in surrendering Abu Saad concession without a struggle we are sacrificing opportunity of enormous reductions in Air Estimates (meaning thereby easy and durable mastery of air). Churchill group in lobbies will indicate possible developments of Livingstone alloy and render our position untenable. If we fall, a " patriotic " Cabinet will succeed us. Therefore we must not fall.

Having got as far as this, Jane Campbell found that there was no more room, even for her classic calligraphy, upon the invitation card, although the card was embossed and big. She stretched for a sheet of notepaper and continued :—

B. *Our objectives.*

If the Furnivall Cabinet are to remain in power, they must, as an absolute minimum :—

(*a*) Uphold Sultan of Muscat's claim to Abu Saad.

(*b*) And, as corollary to this, establish the validity of the Morris concession.

Now (*b*) depends wholly on (*a*). The immediate issue, is therefore :—

" *Is the Sultan of Muscat legally entitled to claim sovereignty over Abu Saad and to grant concessions in that island ?* "

This question entails examination of :—
The Muscat leases.

(1) Our case is based on :—

(*a*) A perpetual lease of Abu Saad granted by the Sheikh of Elvend to the then Sultan of Muscat in 1836.

(*b*) A rescript addressed in 1862 by Nasr-ed-Din Shah to the then British Minister at Tehran. It runs as follows :—

" This 16th Shawal. My dear friend. As regards Abu Saad, you well know that, if God will, we may be in agreement on this matter."

(*c*) That for more than 1,00 years the Sultan of Muscat's rights over the island have remained unchallenged.

69

(2) To this they answer :—

    (*a*) That the Sheikh of Elvend, although in 1836 enjoying certain rights of provincial autonomy, was in fact a tributary of the Shah of Persia. He had no right to dispose of Persian territory to a third party.

    (*b*) That the rescript of Nasr-ed-Din Shah implied, not that he agreed with the British Minister, but that he hoped the Minister would one day come to agree with him.

    (*c*) That prescription cannot be invoked to justify flagrant violations of sovereignty.

Conclusion. (1) The Hague Court and the League will almost certainly support the Persian contention.

(2) We cannot hope, therefore, to gain our objective by purely juridical arguments before an international tribunal, or under arbitration.

We must therefore concentrate on either (*a*) force or (*b*) diplomacy.

(*a*) Force, if only from the fact that we possess it in a wholly devastating form, is, at least for the Furnivall Cabinet, out of the question.

There remains (*b*) diplomacy.

On reaching the word (*b*) diplomacy, Jane sighed deeply and laid down her pencil, her sheet of notepaper, and the *Architectural Review* which she had been using as a rest. She poured herself out a third cup of coffee, since, after all, she was having breakfast. She pursed her lips Her nose, feeling dispirited, remained wholly stationary. She glanced at the clock: it was only eight-thirty: that was the advantage of getting up early. She would have a good hour in which to think it all out carefully: she could reach the office, if she took a taxi, by 9.45. Bullinger would be certain to look in there about 10.15 before the Cabinet.

Jane Campbell, eating oatmeal and honey, sat there thinking hard.

(5)

Arthur Peabody, round the corner in Tite Street, was also thinking: but he was not thinking very hard. He was thinking that the dinner last night had, after all, been a very agreeable dinner. Mrs. Wickham Schultz certainly knew how to do things. It was clever of her, for instance, to have induced Hans Dammert to play his own Symphony in B Minor. Not that he had played it well: Peabody, who was conscientious about music, felt, indeed, that Dammert had played it very badly: yet it had been a curious and not unpleasant experience to sit there in the tapestry chairs of Mrs. Schultz and to observe a famous composer concentrating irritated and astigmatic eyes upon the complexities of his own score.

Nor was this all. The Prince, even for him, had been excessively charming: no, not excessively charming, just *positively* charming. He had said, before dinner, " Halloa, Peabody ! How's the F.O. ? " And after dinner, as they had all walked up the black marble staircase, H.R.H. had turned round: had smiled at Peabody: and had said (indicating thereby that he recognised Peabody as an initiate of Carlton House Terrace)—had said, " They won't mind, will they, if I take my cigar ? "

Fingering his C.M.G., smiling a smile which appeared impersonal (but which in reality represented the after-glow, the Alpine glow, of that smile with which he had answered " Of course not, Sir," on the subject of the Prince's cigar), Arthur Peabody, in the immediate wake of His Royal Highness, had joined the ladies.

How lovely they all looked !—rising together like that as the Prince, shy but genial, entered the room : a flutter of lemon silks, of apple silks, of silks the colour of cucumber. How effective, in the presence of royalty, was the dip and sway of the new Mexican crinoline ! How lovely those piled tresses upon those tulip necks ! Peabody, although by then engaged in conversation with Dr. Kleinroth, the Counsellor of the German Embassy, was thinking about tulip necks : the carriage of heavy regal heads upon a slender stalk : Darwin tulips.

" Then you agree," said Dr. Kleinroth, " that the Powers were in fact justified in their intervention at Tehran ? "

Arthur Peabody, with an almost imperceptible jerk of his back muscles, changed quickly from the third gear of tapestry chairs and cucumber silks, into the second gear of official awareness. So delicately was he lubricated that the change was scarcely noticeable : a mere internal adjustment of greased and practised cogs : a continuance of his conversation with Dr. Kleinroth, yet with a difference, the difference being that Peabody was no longer thinking of tulip throats, he was thinking of what Kleinroth was saying: a continuance which, while cancelling any affirmatives which in the preceding few minutes he might absent-mindedly have uttered, would none the less convey to Dr. Kleinroth that these affirmatives (had they escaped his lips—and Peabody had a slightly uneasy feeling that they had) were but preliminary passes in an ensuing exercise of finesse.

" I always," said Peabody, answering Dr. Kleinroth's question, " agree with everybody and everything after I have been dining with Mrs. Schultz. That Moselwein, for instance—Lorchheimer Riesling, if I mistake not, and Auslese, and I should imagine 1932. What a year! So baked, so cool: cool as the cherries on the road to Lorchheim. Tell me, my dear Kleinroth, does your Ambassador still retain his vineyards? I always say that the von Schubert wines are the best in all Germany. But they do not travel so well as some of the Rhine wines. Not nearly so well. I remember when I was staying with the Schuberts in 1932—no, it must have been in 1933; no, sorry, it was in 1932—I remember that one evening Herr von Schubert . . ."

" Yes, of course," said Dr. Kleinroth, insistent, " but this Abu Saad question. Surely, Mr. Peabody, you agree with me that it is exceedingly delicate. What think you? "

" My dear Kleinroth," smiled Peabody, a polite Olympian, " I remember my first chief (Lord Graham as he is now) once saying to me when I was a youngster—and perhaps a trifle too keen upon my job—' My dear fellow,' said Sir Ronald, as he then was, ' take my word for it, never fuss. Unimportant questions are unimportant questions.

Important questions settle themselves.' A wise man, was Sir Ronald: a fine diplomatist of the good school: I often feel that we do not breed that type to-day."

" But please," said Dr. Kleinroth, a little fretful, rising on his toes, " but please, Mr. Peabody, what will your Government do if the Persians appeal to the League ? You well know that the Council are prejudiced in favour of Eastern nations ? "

Peabody had not the slightest conception what the British Government would do if Persia appealed to the League of Nations. To tell the truth, being incensed at John Shorland's bad manners of the previous afternoon, Peabody had taken against the Abu Saad question : preferring to regard it as " unsavoury " : as one of those tiresome subjects which Shorland and Miss Campbell were always, as if two spaniels, routing out. Peabody, although he had not as yet registered the fact, even in his own consciousness, had already decided to boycott Abu Saad. He would have nothing to do, either with the concession itself, or with the perfectly foreseeable complications to which it had led. Peabody had a deep conviction that the Government, and above all the Foreign Office, should what he called " keep their fingers clean " by eschewing all commercial questions. He was rather glad that the Abu Saad concession had landed everybody in a mess : he had, as a matter of fact, but slight conception of the nature of that mess. This gap in his knowledge, in his industry, must not, however, be disclosed to Dr. Kleinroth : for the moment Kleinroth must be fenced with ; Kleinroth must be staved off.

" The Cabinet," replied Arthur Peabody, a slight note of the pontifical underlining the commas of his statement, giving to it that communiqué feel—" the Cabinet, I believe, are meeting to-morrow morning to consider this very matter. Obviously, my dear Kleinroth, you cannot expect me to prejudice, to anticipate, in any way, their decision. You will allow me, I know, to say a few words to my hostess."

That was neatly done. Firm and courtly. The memory, next morning, of the expert, the col-leaguely, the almost confederate, the withal authori-tative smile with which he had left the side of Dr. Kleinroth caused him satisfaction. There was a certain way of doing these things : a knack it might be merely, but still a knack which it took many years of experience, of professional experience, to acquire.

Thinking of these things, Arthur Peabody, on that morning of June 3, stirred his China tea, and opened *The Times* newspaper. He was still in bed, since he never breakfasted till 9.30. The hour from 8.30 till 9.30 was perhaps the pleasantest hour in the day. His morning tea in the little lustre set which he had bought that Easter of 1932 (or it might have been 1930—yes, it must have been 1930) at Taunton. The cigarette sending aromatic spirals across the heavy bedroom air. *The Times.*

Peabody loved his morning newspaper. He looked at the picture page first, he then read the leading article, and then the weather forecast, and then the society column. Yes, there was an account of last night's dinner-party. And he then turned to the foreign news. A speech by M. Labourdère at Toulon : a rather aggressive speech. A speech by Dr. Löbe, the President of the German

Reich, to the recruits at Döberitz : not a pleasant speech, not the sort of speech one would have expected from that charming little Löbe. A Government communiqué in the *Izvestia* about the " counter-revolutionary movements in the allied Republics of the Middle East. Movements which were causing serious preoccupation to the Council of Commissars." A statement made to the Foreign Relations Committee by Senator Patrick G. Lowry, of Chicago : rather a confused statement about the American people guarding with their flaming sword the open door of human prosperity and intercourse : but still a statement definitely anti-British, clearly menacing.

Peabody was distressed by the foreign news that morning and turned to read the third leading article, which always soothed and stimulated. It was headed " Other People's Dogs." Peabody experienced a foretaste of pleased amusement : he hated other people's dogs, since they deposited dung upon the neat white doorstep of No. 11 Tite Street ; and he loved the deft, the witty, the scholarly manner in which such matters of common interest were dealt with in the third leader. " The spirit of Charles Lamb," thus had Peabody once defined these articles, " infused with the spirit of A. A. Milne."

His pleasure that morning was, however, interrupted. For as his right eye travelled down the third article his left eye, wandering indiscreet, had caught sight of the contiguous and all-too-legible heading of the middle article. That heading caused Peabody a twinge of displeasure ; nay, of pain. It consisted of two words only : the first word was " Abu," the second word was " Saad."

No, whatever happened he would ignore Abu Saad : he would leave it to Shorland, who enjoyed that sort of thing : he would tell the Secretary of State quite frankly. " No, sir," he would say, " I'm afraid I'm no good on this Persian question. It fills me with distaste. You must rely on Shorland, who has studied it carefully." Mr. Bullinger would understand.

Relieved by this decision, Arthur Peabody returned with renewed zest to the article upon other people's dogs.

And yet the finger of Destiny, moving inexorable across the page of time, paid scant attention to the resolve of Arthur Peabody. He was enabled, it is true, to detach himself from the Abu Saad question even when that incident, hour by hour, swelled into a world crisis. Yet in the end, it was Peabody's vanity which played a not inconsiderable part in the ensuing futilities.

(6)

By 9.15 a.m. Jane Campbell had finished thinking. She rang the bell. " Rose," she said, " call me a taxi. I've no time to lose." " And what," said Rose, " about Rikki, Miss ? " Rikki was Jane's terrier. Hearing his name mentioned, he looked up from the paper basket from which he had just extracted the monthly catalogue of the Army and Navy Stores. He showed the white of his eye self-consciously : not knowing why his name had been dragged into the conversation : not certain that it was a popular, though doubtless an amusing, thing to destroy the catalogue of the Army and Navy Stores. Jane had a theory, not shared by her friends and colleagues, that Rikki was an obedient animal. He was not an obedient animal: upon the very slightest excuse Rikki appealed to the doctrine of self-determination. "I'm sorry, Rose," said the Parliamentary Under-Secretary, "I'm very sorry —you will have to take Rikki for a run yourself."

Rose sniffed: she was not politically minded.

Jane began to write down her conclusions upon a final sheet of notepaper:—

"There remains," she wrote . . .

"There remains (*b*) Diplomacy.

1. *As regards the immediate issue*

(*a*) It would be optimistic to hope . . ."

Rose, at this, reappeared in the doorway, looking pleased. "The taxi's coming, Miss, and that Mr. Shorland is here to see you." Rose liked John Shorland.

"Mr. Shorland?" said Jane. "Oh, ask him to come in."

"John," she said as Shorland entered, "it was good of you to send me that Muscat Memorandum. What made you know I wanted it?"

"Well," said John, "I wanted to send you something. It was my birthday, you see. I guzzled alone at Boulestin. Then I went round to the office and found the memorandum on my desk. I brought you round the flimsy. I didn't come up, as I knew you were busy."

"Well," said Jane, "it was useful. But what an unexpected thing for you to do! Just wait a moment, John, I must jot down a few notes. I've got a taxi coming, I can give you a lift."

78

John Shorland picked up the *Economist* and walked to the window. He did not read the *Economist*, since his eyes were fixed upon the neat hands of Jane Campbell, writing neatly.

" to hope " continued the Parliamentary Under-Secretary in her Oxford script :—

> " to hope that this crisis can be confined within ordinary diplomatic channels. We must face the fact that a definite international block, of great strength, has been organised against us. The problem must be envisaged in terms, on the one hand, of a resounding diplomatic humiliation, and, on the other hand, of war. Only by fixing these two points as the limit of our measure can we hope to see the thing in right proportions.
>
> (*b*) The League of Nations . . ."

Having got as far as this, Jane paused. She frowned and sucked her pencil. A school-girl gesture.

" Jane," said John Shorland, grasping the *Economist* in tense hands, " I love you desperately."

" Of course you do, John "—she was gathering her papers together as if she had finished—" of course you do " (yet she had heard : she heard : something leapt like a strong young fish within her). " Now, look here, I must just powder my funny nose. I'll be with you in a second. And I've got a new hat, John. Such a funny hat : a June hat."

John was silent in the taxi : letting Jane talk about the Abu Saad question : feeling crushed.

And Jane knew that a great excitement had come to her that morning : a thing to be examined only when she was alone.

CHAPTER IV

(1)

WALTER BULLINGER failed, that morning, to call at
the Foreign Office on his way to the Cabinet. The
reasons for this omission were personal, and not very
praiseworthy.

His large blue Humber had, since 9.30 a.m., been
waiting for him at No. 34 Grosvenor Gardens. It
was not till 10.40 a.m. that the footman appeared at
the front door and made to Jakes the chauffeur an
upward movement of the head, signifying " He's
coming "; indicating " You had better throw that
cigarette away." Sulkily Jakes flicked his stump of
Craven A under the mudguard. He opened the
door of the car and took from its recesses the fawn-
coloured wrap which, in the leafy month of June,
covered the knees of the Secretary of State: he
held the door open, looking away from the footman
towards the distant statue of Marshal Foch; not
having been on good terms with Edwin since the
previous Tuesday; being unwilling, across that
stretch of pavement, to catch Edwin's eye.

For in truth Jakes, at that moment, was feeling
angered: he did not care to be kept waiting unnecessarily: he had much disliked the gesture of Edwin
when he had opened the front door—a patronising

gesture, he had found it: a gesture which implied that the indoor servants knew more about the movements of the Secretary of State than did the outdoor servants; that, armed with this inner knowledge, they could give instructions to the outdoor servants by a mere upward movement of the chin.

Walter Bullinger advanced bustling from the shadow of the hall. Edwin followed, the red boxes in his arms gleaming almost purple when inside the house, and springing into scarlet as he stepped with them out into the sun. Jakes arranged the wrap around his master's knees, and, taking the two despatch-boxes (rather jerkily) from Edwin's arms, placed them upon the floor of the car. He then leant forward to receive Mr. Bullinger's orders, holding the door widely open with his right arm across it: he leant a little further into the car than was necessary, wishing to suggest to Edwin that the communications exchanged between him and the Secretary of State, when inside the Humber, were of a nature which the indoor servants were not entitled to overhear.

"Downing Street, if you please, Jakes."

Bullinger, even in moments of distress, never forgot his geniality.

"No. 10, sir," Jakes queried, "or the courtyard of the orfice?"

"No. 10—of course," said Bullinger, with a shade of impatience.

The car slid off, away from a slowly closing front door—a door which, as they receded, did not close absolutely, but remained a high slit, giving a halved glimpse of the blue livery of Edwin, of his silver buttons, of his contempt for Jakes, and of his still possessive eye as he watched the silvering curls of Mr. Bullinger swaying against the back window.

The Secretary of State was thinking that Jakes, although an excellent mechanic, was not, after all, a highly intelligent man. When had they ever in the last eighteen months used the Downing Street entrance to the Foreign Office? Never! Every day had he driven to the little side door on the Horse Guards Parade. It adjoined his private lift. It was stupid of Jakes to suppose that the words "Downing Street" could mean anything but No. 10.

Bullinger, at the thought of such stupidity, felt quite cross.

The car by then was gliding blue and heavy down Birdcage Walk. Bullinger's reflections upon the air-pockets in the mind of Jakes were interrupted by an increasing consciousness that something unusual was happening. A detachment of police crossed the roadway, walking busily with swinging arms. The railings of Wellington Barracks were clustered thickly with the backs of British citizens gazing inside. Above the row of heads could be seen many bear-skins moving this way and that.

Bullinger thought: "I wonder why it is that policemen always look so much younger when in a detachment than when they are detached. Even quite a young policeman looks about forty when walking alone: even middle-aged policemen look boyish when walking in a detachment." Bullinger thought: "How similar are the backs of men— identical as the clustering backs of flies stuck to fly-paper." Bullinger thought: "The bear-skins of guards officers, when seen above a crowd like that, move at the same level and with a continuous, swaying movement. Like cormorants."

Bullinger thought: "Good God! It's the King's birthday!"

He started at this recollection, remembering that only two hours before he had invited Lady Athelhampton to watch the trooping of the Colour from his room at the Foreign Office. She would arrive at 11.50. The ceremony began at 12.0. The Cabinet could certainly not be over much before 12.30. He would stop and warn Peabody that he must look after Lady Athelhampton until he could himself arrive.

On realising this necessity, Bullinger began that struggling movement entailed upon elderly people who, from the depths of their luxurious cars, decide suddenly to address the chauffeur. He tautened his abdominal muscles, preparing to lean forward, to slide the glass panel in the front window, and to say: "Jakes, I think after all I must call in at the Foreign Office. Go to the side door. I can walk round to No. 10 later."

Yet even as he prepared to say this thing, a feeling of aversion rose within him. He relaxed his muscles. He sank deeper into the back cushions. "After all," he said to himself, "I can always get someone to telephone across from No. 10."

The policeman at Storey's Gate saluted Mr. Bullinger as the car entered Great George Street. The Secretary of State, pink and beaming, waved a gay response. "Cheery old bird!" thought the policeman.

Seldom, however, had Walter Bullinger felt less like a bird. It was not going to be a pleasant Cabinet : it was going to be a most exacting Cabinet. And there was something else. There was that shrill voice of the inner conscience. It was saying : " You funked going to the F.O. this morning. You were late deliberately in order to give yourself an excuse. And why ? Because you knew they would insist on your obtaining from the Cabinet some precise definition of policy. You knew that they would come to you with a piece of paper saying, ' These are the points on which we must have a definite decision.' And you also knew that you would be quite unable to induce the Cabinet to be anything but vague."

As the car turned cautiously into Downing Street, Big Ben gathered itself hugely and struck the eleventh hour.

(2)

Walter Bullinger sprang lightly from his motor, but the door of No. 10 was opened by the assiduous Hancock before he could ring the bell. Hancock flung the door wide (since, after all, Bullinger was a Secretary of State), yet with a gesture, at its final extension, of almost hesitance. As if prepared, should Bullinger not apologise for being late, to slam that historic portal in his face. Hancock, standing there sleek and tubby, his thin hair combed greasily around his yellow forehead, seemed a bland reminder that Cabinet Ministers must reach a Cabinet five minutes before the stated time.

" Good morning, Hancock," beamed Bullinger,

panting genially as a result of having sprung so lightly from his car, patting his two breast pockets, as a man pats when assuring himself that he has not forgotten either his handkerchief or his letter-case— " Good morning! I hope we are not the last to arrive. It took me a full twenty minutes to drive here from my house. I was held up at least three times in Birdcage Walk."

Hancock, on receiving this apology, smiled in forgiveness. He manifested by his smile—presbyterian rather than subservient—that in his judgment also, the last should be first.

For nearly thirty years had Hancock been doorkeeper at No. 10. He remembered the old days of Mr. Asquith and the suffragettes : and the moment when Mr. Lloyd George had pushed past him to announce the armistice : and the charm of Mr. Baldwin : and the way Mr. Ramsay MacDonald would sort out his own letters in the post-room : and the way young Mr. Randolph (" such a pleasant young gentleman he was, always a civil word ") behaved, domestically speaking, during the Churchill period : as also (so Hancock remembered) the sweeter, simpler period of Mr. Neville Chamberlain. This store of old-world reminiscences gave to Hancock a permanent, an almost posthumous, attitude of mind. He had seen so many Ministers come : he had seen so many go : he, and his leather beehive chair, remained. And thus, with the passage of years, Hancock had come to adopt towards Cabinet Ministers a manner which, while paying tribute to their office, indicated that their persons (unlike his own) were transitory. Even when addressing

Secretaries of State there was a touch in Hancock's deportment of the obituary. He treated lesser Ministers as welcome intrusions. And to Under-Secretaries his attitude was pitying, paternal and aloof.

" Hancock," panted Mr. Bullinger, " would you be so very kind as to telephone for me to my Private Secretary, Mr. Peabody, at the Foreign Office ? Tell him I have come straight on here as I was late. And tell him that some ladies, my wife and Lady Athelhampton, are coming to view the trooping of the Colour from my room. I may be late in getting through with our present business. Would he see to it that they are accommodated and entertained ? "

Hancock signified acquiescence : yet, even then, only vicarious acquiescence : he made it quite clear by an outward gesture of the hand that it would be someone else, someone more in the background, who would convey that message.

Bullinger passed along the passage slowly. Recovering his breath. He paused to gaze upon a photographic group of the Imperial Conference of 1934. There they all were ; Ramsay MacDonald and J. H. Thomas in the middle : six British statesmen cheek by jowl with fourteen statesmen from overseas : facing the same camera. Bullinger sighed, touched by the mutability of human affairs.

" . . . accommodated and entertained "—that sounded pompous. It was odd how pompously Hancock always made him behave. Just as Furnivall made him talk in terms of cotton wool. Bullinger winced at the remembered sound of his own voice talking in Furnivall's presence : not his natural voice: a high voice, becoming cheeky, becoming joyous, becoming easily sentimental, becoming unctuous. Curse!

Yet he really wasn't pompous: yet he really wasn't insincere; deep down, he wasn't. Disquieted once again by the fluidity of his own temperament (that damned flexibility!), Walter Bullinger placed his fingers upon the handle of the door. Beyond that door waited the assembled Cabinet: beyond that door there lay in wait for him the smile of Spencer Furnivall.

Bullinger braced himself for his own entry. Bracingly he entered.

It was characteristic of Spencer Furnivall that, although punctilious on the subject of the 10.55 rule, he made no allusion to Bullinger being late. Another man might have said, " Halloa, Walter! Here you are! "—and Bullinger could then have repeated that passage about Birdcage Walk. Furnivall, however, gave him no such opening. He was standing talking to Philip Noel Baker, the Secretary of State for India. He went on talking to Mr. Baker, desiring thereby to make Bullinger appear even later than he actually was. For certainly he must have been aware of the latter's jubilant and asthmatic entry.

That was so like Furnivall. Putting one always at a disadvantage: waiting always until one's manner had worn off: catching one always between one manner and the next: getting between the ribs. In a few seconds now he would turn round as if surprised that the whole Cabinet were at last assembled. He would say, " Are we all here now?

Bullinger? Ah yes, there you are! Now we had better begin. Let's see, this morning we have . . ."

At that moment Furnivall broke off his conversation with Noel Baker.

" Ah ! " he said, " I see that we are all here at last ! We had better begin. It's this Port of London question, isn't it, Hankey? Oh no—of course not! How stupid of me! It's Abu Saad! My dear Bullinger, good morning. Perhaps you can now tell us about Abu Saad ? "

The Cabinet took their places, each in front of his own plot of blotting-paper.

" Well, Bullinger," resumed the Prime Minister, now seated in the centre of the table, " and what are we to do about this strangely inconsiderate question?"

(3)

Walter Bullinger laid his palm flat upon the pile of papers at his left side. A gesture at once purposeful and decisive: a prelude to purpose, an overture to decision.

Yet was it " inconsiderate " that the Prime Minister had said ? If so—then just another of his tiresome verbal affectations. Or was " ill-considered " the epithet which he had used ? In that case the Prime Minister was being rude; deliberately rude; rude on purpose. Bullinger, fluttering between these two alternative interpretations, boggled his approach.

" Point 1," he began, " analysis." And at that he cleared his throat.

" I should wish," he continued, " to commence, to begin, this morning by giving you . . ."

Bullinger paused at this, and his palm descended for a second time upon his pile of papers. He glanced across at the Prime Minister. Mr. Furnivall was leaning back in his chair staring at the ceiling. His silky, grey-flecked beard was pointing upwards. His soft silk collar hung loose around a soft silk neck. Bullinger much disliked the beard of Spencer Furnivall: it got on his nerves: it seemed an anachronism; it seemed un-English; it grew unnaturally upon that capon skin: it was a false beard: Bullinger loathed it.

" . . . the facts," Bullinger continued, a shade disconcerted by his own digression, " *behind* the facts."

He paused again, staring with a challenging eye at the gentlest of his encircling colleagues—at Mr. Petticue, President of the Board of Agriculture and Fisheries. The Prime Minister's elbows were resting on the arms of his chair. His eight finger-tips were joined, as were also the tips of his two thumbs. Bullinger knew that if Mr. Furnivall became irritated the thumbs would press together till the nails whitened. Yet if (as was more probable) Mr. Furnivall became merely bored, then the eight fingers would dance a quadrille together—separating and joining, separating and joining. . . .

Bullinger pulled himself together. " You see," he began again, fixing the embarrassed Mr. Petticue with powerful concentration—" you see, this is something far more than a departmental matter. It is more than a Cabinet question ; more even than a Party question. It is a national question. The whole future of the country is at stake. I can, I shall, put before you the main issues in a perfectly objective form. But the decisions to be taken on these issues must be taken by the Government as a whole. And these decisions must be immediate, effective, and above all," (Bullinger's hand descended upon the pile of papers, pressing them down firmly, as the hand of a botanist presses gentians gently between the blotting-paper of a Swiss hotel)— "*precise.*"

The emphasis given by Walter Bullinger to this concluding word was most unwelcome to his colleagues. No Cabinet ever appreciates that sort of language. It is felt to be speculative, rhetorical, emotional, uncolleaguely and tasteless.

Spencer Furnivall, symbolising the general disapprobation, stopped the movement of his fingers and pressed his thumbs together till the nails whitened. Bullinger did not observe this symptom : he was staring (a bull-dog look) at Mr. Petticue.

"And what," said the Prime Minister, still gazing at the ceiling, "and what are the facts which, as you so lucidly informed us, are *behind* the facts ? "

"Well," Bullinger began, allowing his palm to press heavily upon the pile of telegrams, gaining confidence from this wedge of printed matter, as if the whole staff of the Foreign Office had rallied as a pack of cards to his support—" Well . . ."

At that he altered his key. He leant forward towards Mr. Petticue, who for his part was drawing a picture of a windmill, pretending to be unaware that Bullinger had fixed him with a chubby but argumentative finger.

"Well, you see, it's like this. All the four Great Powers have combined together to turn us out of

Abu Saad. The plan was to induce the Shah to claim Abu Saad as Persian territory and then to transfer the Morris concession to a consortium or group of French, German, American and Russian interests. On Wednesday—the day before yesterday—our Minister at Tehran received an official Note from the Persian Government to the effect that the lighthouse and coaling station at Abu Saad, at present administered by the Marine Department of the Government of India, should forthwith be evacuated. The Persian Government were unable, so the Note stated, any longer to tolerate this continued violation of Persian sovereignty. Yes, it was a stiff Note: an impertinent Note. It represented the First stage of the plan.

" The second part of the plan, in so far as we can make out, has gone wrong somehow. For instead of handing over the Morris concession to a group representing the four Powers, the Shah is placing before the Majlis an emergency Bill, providing for the cancellation of all concessions held by foreign nationals in Persia. He will claim, of course, that in presenting this Bill to his parliament he imagined that he was acting in accordance with the wishes expressed by the four representatives at Tehran. He will apologise for the misunderstanding which has arisen. But in fact it's pretty evident that the Shah, realising that such unwonted unanimity among the four Powers meant that Abu Saad was of more importance than any one had as yet supposed, has decided to use it as a lever and an excuse to rid himself in one swoop of all foreign concessions in his country."

" What," asked the Prime Minister languidly—
" what *are* the other concessions ? "

" Well," said Bullinger, pleased at knowing the
answer to this question, " in the first place, there's
our own Anglo-Persian concession, which has still
some twenty years to run. Of course, now that we
have been concentrating for the last ten years upon
the Irak fields, our concession in Perisa is of less
vital importance than it once was. We might even
welcome some equitable arrangement for closing
down. The other Powers will feel differently about
their own concessions. The Russians have the
Caspian Fisheries, the Germans have the Northern
Railway with a kilometric guarantee, the French
have the Tehran and Ispahan electrification schemes,
and the Americans the Southern Railways plus
certain oil rights in Khorasan. Each of these concessions has cost money, and not one as yet has
shown a profit. . . ."

" You mean," interrupted the Prime Minister,
" that, apart from these Abu Saad deposits, which
we can, for the moment, leave on one side, the four
Powers actually stand to lose more heavily by the
Shah's interpretation of the advice they gave him
than we do ourselves ? "

" Undoubtedly, if you except Abu Saad—but
that is a large exception."

" Yet surely," the Prime Minister continued, his
eyes still fixed upon the ceiling, his beard still up-
raised, his fingers tapping—" surely, my dear
Bullinger, it follows from what you say that our
policy should be wholly non-committal ? Surely we
should wait until the somewhat original (although,

I confess, amusing) action on the part of the Shah of Persia has complicated, not to say embittered, his relations with the four Powers ? I see no need for any action whatsoever pending further developments."

"But Abu Saad ?" began Bullinger. "You see, unless we consent to evacuate immediately, the Persians intend to appeal to the League. They have already, I hear, telegraphed to the Secretary-General at Geneva asking him provisionally to insert the Abu Saad question in the agenda for next week's council— for to-day week—that is, for June 11. Now, although in equity and by prescription our claim, or to be more accurate the claim of our tributary the Sultan of Muscat, is strong enough, yet if the matter is dealt with, as I fear it will be dealt with, upon a strictly juridical basis, then there is little prospect of our winning our case either at Geneva or The Hague. It is in this sense that I have described the issue as one of national significance. We are, in fact (and it would be mere optimism not to face this necessity), in presence of two alternatives, each of which entails highly obnoxious consequences. On the one hand . . ."

The beard of the Prime Minister, as Bullinger approached this inconvenient passage, dropped suddenly : his elbows jerked away from the arms of his chair : he ceased to gaze at the ceiling : he leant forward and gazed at Bullinger very hard.

"Yes, yes," he interrupted, "we all know about that. I think perhaps, if I may say so, my dear Bullinger, that you exaggerate the extent of our dilemma. There is always some middle way, if one can find it, between unpleasant extremes. But before we proceed further I should like to hear the views of the Air Minister."

Sir Charles Pantry blushed an even deeper red at finding himself thus suddenly addressed. His swivel eye made a motion as if to turn in the direction of the Prime Minister, but thought better of it and wandered off on its own, gazing glaucous at the cornice.

The Secretary of State for Air was not (clearly he was not) a professional politician. He had, at the age of fifty-two, returned, after an arduous and sensational career, from the outposts to the hub of Empire. He had organised air services in Irak, in India, in the Malay States and in New Guinea. And thus, when Spencer Furnivall desired to fuse the military and civil branches of the Air Ministry under a single expert head, Sir Charles Pantry was returned as Central Candidate for the Combined Universities, and shortly afterwards appointed Secretary of State for Air.

There were moments when Spencer Furnivall regretted this appointment. Cabinet Ministers who possess technical knowledge of their work are inconvenient both to the Cabinet and to the Ministries entrusted to their charge. Moreover, Sir Charles Pantry—as so often happens with strong, shy, silent men—possessed an acute though furtive instinct for publicity. While almost inarticulate in Cabinet, he had none the less managed to impress the proprietors of the F.L.N. (the Federation of London Newspapers) with his prowess, his sturdiness, his patriotism, and the possibility that, if occasion arose, he might supply front-page evidence against the weak-kneed policy of Spencer Furnivall. Pantry (his strength, his shyness, his silence) had thereafter acquired news value. The Prime Minister had a feeling that of all his colleagues Sir Charles Pantry was the one whom he could least afford to lose. He did not like having that sort of feeling.

"Well, Sir Charles . . .?" Furnivall repeated his invitation. The blush upon the face of Pantry became purple, and then almost blue. His eye stood out against it, sideways.

"It isn't easy," began Pantry, apoplectic but tactless, "it's not easy to explain these sort of things to civilians."

"Oh, but please . . ." beamed the Prime Minister, delighted always when people said things calculated to annoy his colleagues.

"Well," continued Pantry, gobbling in his high, tight collar—"well, about Abu Saad. We've *got* to keep it. And when I say 'got to'—I mean simply got to. The public will not easily forgive you if you allow a potty little country like Persia to rob us of a source of power which may well give us, in the shape of the rocket and the bomb, the mastery of the earth. . . ."

A tremor ran through the more liberal members of the Cabinet, a shudder as of poplars before a storm. Even Pantry, not usually very sensitive to external impressions, noticed the quiver which had passed down the table. . . .

". . . the mastery of the earth," he repeated, forcing his errant eye from the cornice and turning it in the direction of the portrait of Lord Oxford and

Asquith, " I for one," he continued, stumbling over the loose cobbles of his own truculence—" I for one, and I don't mind saying so, should not dream of remaining a member of any Government, not for one moment I shouldn't "—and here the voice of Pantry rose to the even louder note of inverted commas, " of any Government," he thundered, " which sacrificed the vital interests of the nation to a weak-kneed toadying of the cranks and internationalists of Geneva."

They knew what he meant. The very phrase he had used was one of the most powerful and frequent of the thunderbolts which had recently been hurled at the head of Furnivall by the *Morning Express*.

" Oh, come ! My dear Pantry, really . . ." The Prime Minister expostulated politely.

" Not but what," said Pantry, " I don't see a way out. I do. And it's this. The four Powers imagine that we have only one of these aeroplanes. That counts for little. As a matter of fact, we have more. What I always say is that one or two isolated machines make little moral effect. You remember the stunt that Farman put up in 1932 at Toussus-le-Noble ? They sent up Lucien Compet with the first stratosphere. He reached the record of 450 miles an hour. For a week or two we were disquieted. And in February of 1933 Junkers produced the Levius stratosphere, which climbed eleven miles and worked out at 900 kilometres an hour. It was invisible, inaudible, supreme. Yet what happened ? It couldn't carry weights, gentlemen. It could observe from a distance, but it could not aim. Now our rockets are a completely different bag of tricks. They can fly lower than any petrol-driven engine. And they can carry enough bombs to blow London to pieces. And safely, since they would be half a mile away before the explosion. And if we get the atomic, then nothing (and they well know it) can stand up against them. With ten such rockets we can reduce any foreigner to silence: with one hundred we could rule the world. And it requires so little. One can assemble at Cardiff a sufficient quantity of that deposit so that the other fellow doesn't matter. See what I mean ? "

The Cabinet did not see what he meant: they showed it.

" You see," he explained, " you only require some 2 per cent. of the deposit with your aluminium to make the alloy. A hundred truck-loads would see us out till 1979."

" 1979 ? " said Petticue, pushing his windmill aside and beginning to take notes.

" Well, say 1980—give you a round number. If we have the guts to act quickly, we shan't need any more after 1960 "—and at that Pantry showed discoloured teeth in what was intended for a smile.

" 1960," wrote Petticue, not quite certain how it had come that he among his silent colleagues was taking so prominent a part in this discussion.

" Of course," continued Pantry, truculent and unappeased—" of course we've begun already."

The rustling of the poplar leaves was at that universal. Even Furnivall shuddered slightly, " Begun *what*, Sir Charles ? " he enquired ingratiatingly.

" Begun getting away the stuff. Why, in March

last, when it was already obvious that this Livingstone rocket was the thing of a century, I arranged with the Government of India . . ."

" India ? " gasped Mr. Noel Baker, running his fingers through his hair.

" With the Government of India, *direct* " (the word was flung at Mr. Baker like a snarl), " as well as with the Anglo-Persian Oil Company, to send some coolie detachments from Bombay and a few tankers. The deposit is easily got at: not much blasting required. I calculate that by November we shall have extracted as much as we can possibly need, and left mighty little for the other fellow. I put our outside requirements at (apart from the reserves needed for the bombs) 400 rocket aeroplanes, and a stock sufficient for 1000 more. That is, of course, in addition to the eleven which we possess already."

The poplars at this rustled formidably, showing the white underside of their leaves. " Excuse me," said Spencer Furnivall, " did you say eleven ? "

" Yes—eleven. There's the original one which went to New York last month. And the ten new ones for experimental purposes. They do their trials to-morrow."

It occurred to Bullinger that it might, at this stage, be opportune to enquire over what area these trials were to be held. With a man like Pantry, with machines so explosive and so rapid, one could never tell. The question rose to his lips : he dismissed it as irrelevant.

It was not irrelevant.

For had Bullinger pressed that question, on that

morning of June 3, it is possible that the Furnivall Cabinet, to say nothing of this story, would have ceased to exist.

" . . . and after that," concluded Sir Charles Pantry, " I shall need 389 more."

There was a pause. A hush of horror. It was broken by the small voice of Mr. Petticue. For Mr. Petticue was still under the, wholly incorrect, impression that for some reason he occupied a frontal position in this discussion.

" And what," he asked, " about the bomb ? "

" My dear Petticue . . ." exclaimed the Prime Minister.

Mr. Petticue wished that he had not asked that question. It was evidently not a popular question. It had escaped inadvertently from his lips. He began to shade the wings of his windmill with rapid downward strokes.

" The final experiments," shouted Sir Charles Pantry, enraged by the hen-like attitude of those around him, " take place on Sunday at dawn."

And, at that, the clock struck noon.

" Dear me ! " said the Prime Minister, " twelve o'clock already—you must excuse me—King's Birth-day—we must continue this discussion, this vitally important discussion, to-morrow—10.55, as they say for 11.0. It creates disquiet to have a Cabinet on Saturday, but it can't be helped. We shall, I feel, welcome a little time to think things over . . ." and as he said this he rose abruptly from his chair— leaving his papers on the table—moving rapidly towards the door which led to his study.

" But, my dear Prime Minister," wailed Bullinger,

struggling to rise also, struggling to intercept Furnivall in time. The Prime Minister had reached the doorway. He waved with a slim hand towards his colleagues. " Till to-morrow then . . . ! " He beamed : he went.

Bullinger was outraged : Bullinger was mortified. This was by no means the first time that Spencer Furnivall had played this sort of trick. He approached Miss Rathbone, the First Commissioner of Works. " My dear Eleanor," he began exuberantly, patting his two breast pockets, " I really must congratulate you on the Park. I assure you that this morning before breakfast, one can say what one likes, but really you know—just like a gentleman's park—a regular *rus in urbs*."

Even at Harrow Walter Bullinger had not been very good at Latin : and at the moment he was feeling disturbed. He passed out with Miss Rathbone towards the door. Chatting joyously.

The Cabinet had held its sitting.

(4)

The Secretary of State's room at the Foreign Office possesses six gaunt windows, of which three look westwards upon St. James's Park, and three look northwards across the Horse Guards Parade.

The embrasures of the northern windows were, on that June morning, occupied by three distinct groups of visitors. In the centre window stood Lady Athelhampton, wearing a huge straw hat on which imitation cherries tockled aridly. She was accompanied by her son, Lord Clonrig, who had that

morning come up from Eton on account of adenoids.
She was also accompanied by Mr. Adrian Hart, a
dark man with gold teeth and large-rimmed spec-
tacles. An amiable, solicitous and snobbish man
was Mr. Hart, employed in some subordinate
position in the National Portrait Gallery. He was
being very amusing, so Lady Athelhampton assumed,
about the military.

In the second window stood Mrs. Bullinger,
feeling dowdy: not liking Lady Athelhampton:
not liking that Walter should have a room like this
all of his own: a grand room in which she was no
more than a guest: feeling that, as the only wife
of the Secretary of State, she should, somehow, and
on such an occasion, occupy a position of more central
prominence. Mrs. Bullinger had brought Jennifer
with her—that unfortunate daughter. They were
being entertained by Arthur Peabody, who was
making himself agreeable.

And in the third window stood Jane Campbell and
John Shorland—leaning outwards, with their elbows
on the sooted sill.

Below them, on the wide gravel of the Parade,
five regiments of foot guards performed evolutions
which, though complicated, and sometimes rippling,
were precise. The officers, slim and tight-trousered,
would at one moment find themselves behind their
men, and then beside their men, and then, with a
scarcely noticeable scurry, in front of their men.
The bands of the different regiments marched up
and down indignantly, facing right about turn when
they reached the garden wall of Downing Street, the
gold and silver of their instruments being exchanged

suddenly for the scarlet of their backs; a blaze of sunshine succeeded abruptly by a dull red cloud. Some of the bands played slow tunes and some of them played quick tunes : the moment one stopped the other began : music continuous and mobile spread upon the summer air.

Immobile amid all this purposeful mobility waited the King, on a white charger : the blue of the Garter ribbon detached itself glaringly from the scarlet of his coat : around him, uniformed and diverse, clustered the Princes, the Generals, and the foreign Attachés. The windows and the stands on either hand were bright with the pink-and-blue parasols of women, and, as an edge to all this resonant and coloured symmetry, clustered the public—a jagged fringe of black and brown against the encircling green.

The pelicans beside the lake were out of it : they huddled together, resenting this clamorous intrusion : being used to having the pond-mud and the admiration to themselves.

" Jane," said John Shorland, " I want you to listen. I want you to listen carefully. I am going to say something important. Tell me before I begin—are you listening seriously ? "

" Yes," Jane answered, speaking very deliberately, pausing at each comma, making at each comma a slight prod of a now serious and sisterly nose— " I'm listening, John. Dear John. I know what you are going to say. You said it this morning. It took me by surprise and I pretended not to notice. It was all so awkward. I should like you to say it again, John—you have no conception how odd you looked—flushed and fierce, crushing the *Economist* in your hand. It must be lying there at this moment all crumpled in the window-seat.

"Yes, John, I should like you to say it again. But not now. It's all so awkward. I haven't been alone with myself since you said it. I am not prepared, John. I just feel grateful about it and excited. I don't want to say things which I should regret. I should like to say straight, clear, intelligent things about it. But my mind flutters.

"No—John—you must say it again some time, but not now. Not with all this noise going on, and all those soldiers, and Mrs. Bullinger here and that awful girl, and Lady Athelhampton here, and the Secretary of State about to emerge at any moment. I want to get away with the idea, all by myself somewhere, like a dog with a bone.

"Oh, don't look at me like that, John. See, we can both stare out at the soldiers. Look, over there to the left a man has fainted. How small his head looks without a bear-skin! Yes, we can lean out like this, pointing like this at things which happen— we can lean out like this, with all this red movement below us as an undertone, and I can say things, stark things, which I might not dare to say were we really alone, John, were it necessary for me at the end of my sentences to meet your eyes.

"No, John, this is a monologue. You mustn't interrupt. Stare out in front of you. Take your hand away from my arm. You can wear any expression that you please. I shall not look at you. I am not going to look. I am looking at that Colonel over there (do you see, John?) trotting across the parade to say something to somebody. Yes, this all gives one an alibi. I can say things which I could not say to you were we alone.

" I love you, John. I know that I must love you, since when you said it this morning it was as if some new young muscle had been born in my heart. Something strong and living twitched in my heart which has never been there before. And then this sense of excitement, all those flags and colours fluttering for me alone, all this silly music according with the triumph in my heart. It's so much more than being pleased, John, or grateful to you. Though at present my most stable feeling is one of gratitude.

" I love you, John. Let us at least be equal in this. Let me tell you without modesty that I love you even as you have told me. Let there be no lies between you and me, and no lies in our own hearts. Let us face this problem with all the intelligence, with all the frankness, at our command.

" It isn't my age that matters. When you are my age I shall be over forty. When you are over forty I shall be past middle age. That doesn't frighten me, John. Love, such as you and I might have, would be independent of that. While passion lasts we shall be young enough to satisfy it; and when passion dies, as it must die, the other thing, which is love, would grow and flourish (oh, my dear John—how strong our love could be l), however much our bodies may decay.

" No, it is not age that frightens me. It is just ourselves. Our personalities. Our independence. You can hardly know, John, how much my single-ness, my combative singleness, my being just Jane

Campbell, has always meant to me. It is stronger than myself. It has nothing to do with virginity or any of that nonsense. It's a sense of personal dignity, of personal aloofness; in a way, I suppose, it's a satanic pride. But it's there, John. The thought of marriage, of being half of someone else, fills me with repulsion. For a year or two I might conquer that feeling. But it would return, John: it is the greatest force within me: it would return, and you and I, John, would be unhappy: I should feel you had robbed me of something all my own.

"I do not suggest that we should live together, John. We care too much for that. Nor, I think, am I in any way affected by the actual awkwardness of marriage, the grotesque details, the complications it would entail for your and my career. It's the singleness that is so insistent upon me: I am a single letter, John: I am 'J': I refuse with my whole being to become a diphthong. Look, John, they are beginning to march past now. How jerkily they walk! It's so undignified to make grown men jerk in that way: I hate soldiers. Oh, John! I dare not see your face. Have I hurt you? John, you mustn't answer me; we must go on looking at the soldiers, and then Bullinger will come in and I shall turn round (without looking at you)—I shall go up to Bullinger, I shall go across with him to that other window and talk to Lady Athelhampton. Oh, John, I know that I have hurt you—yet I am right about it all—you know yourself that I am right. I have said it all so badly, so boldly. But thank goodness you will understand. Oh, John, say something—no, don't say anything—

I should like to get away from you now at this moment, I should like . . ."

The door opened widely and with brisk geniality Bullinger sailed into the room, patting breast pockets.

" My dear ladies," he exclaimed, " I really beg your pardon. I was kept at No. 10. A most exacting meeting we had. Ah! Lady Athelhampton! And Tony too—got away from Eton, I see? And how are you, Mr. Hart? So you got here safely, Edith? I was held up three times myself in Birdcage Walk. And Jane—— Oh, there you are—my dear, how white you look! What on earth's the matter? Edith, doesn't Jane look ill? It's overwork; you've no conception how this little woman overworks. Ah! I see they are marching past at this moment. A fine sight indeed. I always say that . . ."

Jane moved behind them to the centre of the room. She did not look at John Shorland. She hesitated for a moment, and then she opened the heavy door into the passage and slipped away.

John Shorland remained there in the window, his elbows leaning upon the sill, his unseeing eyes fixed upon the circling wedges of scarlet figures, his ears humming with the incessant shrilling of fifes, the intermittent, punctuated, rattle of the kettle-drums.

He thought: " How vulgar life is! How beastly unfastidious! How unreliable! Here is this love, this lust, business which gathers to itself the whole force, the whole power, within us. Yet to expend that force we need the collaboration of a second person. The most individual of all our problems must depend for its solution upon the ghastly self-consciousness of the female species."

He struck the sooted stone with clenched fist. It seemed intolerable to him that Jane Campbell should have intruded herself upon his love for Jane. His hatred of women welled up in him, indignant, rebellious, fierce.

He thought: "It was someone else who spoke to me just now. A woman graduate of Lady Margaret Hall. Trying to dramatise herself: the modern woman, emancipated, sisterly and frank, talking as man to man. She used those ghastly feminine commonplaces: she spoke of 'straight, clear, intelligent thinking'—— Good God! She said that 'some new young muscle had stirred in her heart.' Absolutely shaming it was! I hated her. I hate her. How dare she say she loves me? I belong to myself."

He thought: "Well, that's finished, anyhow!" —and as he thought it the sunshine and the music died from the June air. A gust of loneliness, of depravation, blew chill upon his heart.

Jane Campbell was in her room, alone. Her hands strayed over her flower-vases, loosening a rose here, pushing in an iris which had slipped sideways in the water.

She thought: "It would have been better if I had said nothing. Trying to explain those sort of situations always leads to one becoming dramatic and self-conscious. Besides, this 'man-to-man' business between the sexes is terribly Girton. John must have hated it. At this moment probably he is making pompous phrases about it, being very young, bless him, and very selfish, damn all men. God! How I hate them! Their assumption that they can intrude their beastly love upon our privacy, and that if we respond we are being indelicate and shy-making. How badly everything is arranged! One can't even *talk* sensibly about love without becoming missish and using absurd phrases. And just because of this John will dislike me now—become fastidious. Anyhow, I have myself. I am Jane.

" Yet, I should like to marry John."

CHAPTER V

(1)

AT the moment when the clock struck noon in Downing Street the watch upon the moist and chubby wrist of Leon Judenitch stood at 4.5 p.m. He sighed wearily and pressed the bell. " Rahim," he said to the servant, " I am expecting a visit from the French, German and American Ministers. See that chairs and whisky-soda are placed in the verandah. I shall receive them there."

Again did Leon Judenitch sigh wearily: disliking diplomatic conferences: having something very unpleasant to say to his three colleagues; being even more uncertain of the French language than was Mr. Shearman, the Minister of the United States: and above all feeling that even up at Zerguendeh, even in the Summer Embassy, the heat of a Persian afternoon was all but intolerable.

He rose from his cane chair, his little thighs in their silk trousers making a slight sucking sound as they parted from the hot and sticky seat. He put on his tussore jacket: from the breast pocket he took a comb and, walking to the looking-glass which glimmered at the end of the shuttered study, he passed the comb through the stubble of red hair which grew like young mustard on his bullet head.

The semblance of a perspiring gnome faced him from the mirror. For the third time he sighed wearily. He was constantly being disappointed by his face.

Leon Judenitch, Ambassador to Persia of the Union of Agrarian Republics, or, as he preferred to call himself, Russian Ambassador at Tehran, did not like being a diplomatist, and least of all a diplomatist upon the Persian plateau. What really interested him in life were the diseases of the cotton plant. It was the importance of his researches in this branch of horticulture which had originally induced Stalin to place him in control of Khlopkostroi—the vast cotton-growing and spinning area in Turkestan. His efficiency in administering that concern (certainly the most successful achievement of the whole fifteen years' plan), the influence which he exercised over the planters and the spinners, above all his discovery of an ammonia compound which rendered the plants immune to the Elmer fungus, had given to Judenitch a prominence which he neither desired nor deserved. And thus, with the advent of the Agrarian Party to power, he had found himself promoted and exiled to the Embassy at Tehran.

He was a shy little man, conscious of his own limitations, very much afraid of the Kremlin, distressed by his own circular figure, by his inability, especially when dealing with professional diplomatists, to keep the correct note. Leon Judenitch was acutely aware that in the concert of the Powers he was apt to sing a little out of tune. Dignity was not a quality which came readily to him, and he maintained it only in a series of spasms. When he remembered to be dignified he would frown : when he forgot to be dignified he was merry, querulous, effusive, a trifle unctuous, and coy. When he shook hands with people he looked away from them, avoiding their eyes : partly from shyness : partly because, as a boy, he had observed Prince Dolgorouki greeting the notables of Tamboff with just that allusiveness : and mainly because it gave him a Slav feeling, made him feel Russian, Scythian, aloof.

The sound of a large motor reached him, crackling upon the dry gravel. He replaced the comb in his pocket and walked tubbily to the verandah, rubbing his palms upon the seat of his trousers, since he knew that they were damp. Another car followed, and then a third. The three Ministers, cool and composed in their white duck, holding their sun-helmets in their hands, stepped out from the dark hall on to the verandah. The fresh reed mattings, which hung like blinds over the western arches of the verandah, cast green lights upon the creases in their clothes. The Ambassador waddled coyly towards them, clasping their hands in both his puggy own. " Chères Excellences ! " he crooned to them, leading them to where, beside the blue tiles of the fountain, the chairs had been arranged. He then sat down abruptly and stared intently away from them with a frown upon his face. They followed the direction of his gaze : a gardener, with one trouser leg rolled up above his thigh, was watering the paths by splashing at them from a petroleum tin. They saw no reason why this familiar and indeed refreshing sight should have caused His Excellency such displeasure.

Leon Judenitch jerked his eyes away from the gardener—and towards the syphon. He made in its direction a friendly, adulatory gesture, indicating that they should help themselves : not at all the right sort of gesture to have made : a bazaar gesture, not ambassadorial : aware of this, he seized the cigarette box and with a brisk boyar movement thrust it beneath the nose of the French Minister, who selected a cigarette carefully, examining it through his thick-lensed pince-nez as if it were some new type of locust.

" Excellences . . ." began Judenitch sharply. For after all he, being the only Ambassador among them, was in the chair.

In halting phrases, with movements of his hands at one moment menacing and at another solicitous, he placed the issue before his colleagues. They smoked in silence, gazing at the tips of their cigarettes through half-closed eyes. Not for one moment did they manifest either resentment or surprise. The nervousness of Judenitch was much increased by their reserve.

Although clumsily worded, and most ungrammatical, the statement of the Russian Ambassador was clear enough. It amounted to this. He had himself, that morning, received a telegram from Moscow instructing him (if possible in conjunction with his three colleagues, but otherwise immediately and alone) to address to the Persian Government a Note to the effect that the Union of Agrarian Republics could not, and would not, accept the cancellation of their concession. They would find themselves reluctantly obliged, should the Bill pass the Majlis, to " take all suitable measures to protect Russian interests in the Caspian Fisheries." He, the Ambassador, had thus invited his three colleagues to this discussion in the hope that they would agree, in so far as their own interests were concerned, to make simultaneous representation in this sense.

" And what," said the United States Minister, " do your folk mean by ' suitable measures ' ? Surely, Mr. Ambassador, in the diplomatic lingo those words signify something pretty close to using force ? "

Judenitch shrugged his shoulders, opening his palms wide in a movement at once racial and deprecatory. " I believe," he said, " that instructions have been sent to our gunboats at Baku to hold themselves in readiness."

" Obviously," said the French Minister, removing his pince-nez with a deliberate thumb and forefinger, " our Russian friends dispose of means of pressure more immediate and more efficacious than any of us more distant Powers. I, also, have been instructed to protest against this act of bad faith on the part of the Persian Government. I shall carry out these instructions. Yet I consider that our representations, although concerted, should be neither simultaneous, identic, nor joint."

" Well," said Mr. Shearman, " I reckon I can do much the same. The telegram I received this morning from the State Department gives me a fairly free hand."

" I should wish to suggest," began the German Minister, speaking with all the authority of his experience and years : " I should wish to suggest, if you will permit me, Your Excellency, that it might be more useful if the non-limitrophe Powers were merely to associate themselves, by verbal representations, with the more definite protest which you, M. Judenitch, will make. The Shah, as we all know, is a man of strong impulses. It is possible that, if faced with anything in the nature of a joint ultimatum, he would swing round to the opposite direction and come to some arrangement with Great Britain. He might, in such a case, conceive that it would be more to his advantage to promise the British a confirmation of the Abu Saad concession in return for their recognition of the island as Persian territory. I fear we must face the fact that such inconsistency is not impossible. And the British might, if they attach to the Abu Saad deposits the importance which we suppose, even consent to some arrangement terminating the oil concession. Were such a situation to develop we should find ourselves in an awkward position. Very awkward indeed. Allow me, as an old soldier, to state the issue in military terms. Our four Governments in this matter have committed two blunders, one strategical, the other tactical. It was an error of strategy to select as our field of opera-tion, not the firm ground of London, but the shifting sands of Persia. For that error M. Alexei Rubinstein is to blame. It was an error in tactics to duplicate our objectives, to aim not only at depriving Great Britain of the deposits, but also at securing the deposits for our own consortium. That error is also to be attributed to Russian advice. By this

unfortunate manœuvre we have exposed our flank
and the Shah, observing the falsity of our position,
has launched this offensive against the concessions.
We occupy at this moment a salient which, in my
opinion, is untenable. At any instant the Shah
may effect a junction with the British behind our
backs. If, as M. Rubinstein now seems to desire,
we advance still further, that junction becomes a
certainty. It is for this reason that I advise a
momentary withdrawal to a securer line. It is for
this, moreover, that I would venture to ask Your
Excellency whether it would not be possible for
you to induce the Kremlin somewhat to moderate
the terms of the Note which you are now instructed
to deliver."

The French Minister, with thumb and forefinger, replaced the pince-nez on the bridge of his
nose. The American Minister grunted as he leant
forward to mix himself a drink. Leon Judenitch
moved with sticky uneasiness upon his chair. What
was so maddening about Graf Pyritz was that
he was subtly patronising, gently insulting, and
obviously right. It was Judenitch himself who
had put in that bit about the consortium : perhaps
it was a mistake : he was always making mistakes :
yet it was not for an effete Pomeranian Junker to
point out these mistakes : he'd be damned if he'd
allow himself to be patronised and made to look
foolish by a German Count, a territorial magnate,
a man who spent his leave grinding the faces of his
peasants in the dust.

The fountain tinkled merrily in the dry white
silence of the afternoon.

"I know, I know," said Leon Judenitch, placing his dimpled hands upon knees, which shook with nervous rage. "I had already suggested such a possibility. But my Government have their own internal difficulties. They feel this to be an opportunity to show that they are still a Great Power. You see, the Usbeg Republic has of late . . ."

The Ambassador checked himself, observing from the expression of agony which had appeared behind the pince-nez of the French Minister that, once again, he was being undiplomatic.

"In short," he continued, "the reply to my suggestions was a repetition of their previous instructions. I have an appointment with the Minister of Court this evening at Sultanatabad. The Note which I shall hand to him is already typed and signed."

"And what," said Mr. Shearman, drawling with southern intonation, "will happen if the Russians send gunboats to Pahlevi and if the Persians appeal to the League, not against Great Britain, as we advised them, but against ourselves?"

"My Government do not recognise Geneva," barked Judenitch, frowning.

"Nor do mine," continued Mr. Shearman, "but the show exists all the same. I don't trust the Persians myself not to blurt out the whole story: it would be deuced awkward for us if an account (incorrect, of course, and incomplete) of the many representations which we have all made to them in the last fortnight were handed in at Geneva and circulated to all League members. We should be much attacked in the Senate and in the republican Press."

Leon Judenitch sank back in his chair and tugged a large green handkerchief from the tight recesses of his trouser pocket. He mopped his wet and freckled forehead. He was thinking how far more pleasant than diplomacy were the diseases of the cotton plant: how far less manageable were the functions of an Ambassador than those of Khlopkozav at Ferganeh. He was thinking that the Kremlin were difficult to persuade and quite impossible to disobey. He was thinking how much he disliked Graf Pyritz. He glanced at his watch.

" I realise," he said, " your difficulties, gentlemen. But I have my instructions. And what is worse—I mean what is more—I have an appointment with the Minister of Court in half an hour."

" I cannot," replied Graf Pyritz, " but record my regret. I feel strongly that I myself, and I trust my two colleagues also, must endeavour by subsequent verbal representations to mitigate, if I may use that word, the unwisdom (you will excuse me, my dear Ambassador) of the Russian ultimatum. I shall see the Minister of Court to-morrow morning. And I shall suggest to His Highness that my Government might consider some modification in the terms of our present concession, such as the appointment to the board of directors of one, or even two, highly placed Persian officials."

" Well," said the American Minister, " I am perfectly ready to come in on that. We must play for time."

" And our united front ? " enquired the French Minister. " It is dislocated ? "

" No, no ! " the German Minister assured him,

" not in the least. Our objectives remain the same
—namely, to prevent these deposits falling into the
exclusive possession of Great Britain. We differ
only in our conception of the tactics by which this
common objective can be attained."

Leon Judenitch had not followed the last remark.
He said, " Sure! sure! " thus lavishing upon the
German Minister the whole resources of his store
of English. The French Minister shrugged his
shoulders and acquiesced dimly. The Ambassador
rose effusively. For the second time that afternoon
they were exposed to the joint pressure of his hands.

The motors, as they departed, crackled upon the
dry gravel. And ten minutes later Leon Judenitch,
accompanied by his Oriental Secretary, and grasping
a sealed envelope, drove down to Sultanatabad.

(2)

In London, at that precise moment (namely, at
1.20 p.m. on that Friday, June 3, 1939) the British
Foreign Secretary came to a decision.

" No! " he said to himself, " I shall walk."

In general he drove to his luncheon. It entailed
driving up the Mall, and then through Marl-
borough Gate, and then the whole way back along
Pall Mall to the sedate doorway of the Travellers'
Club. If one walked, one merely cut along the
edge of the Park and thereafter tripped up the
Duke of York's steps. It was quicker; better;
cheaper; to walk. Yet it had three disadvantages.

In the first place, there was Jakes, who, having

been kept waiting since 9.30, would have a sense of
wastage, almost of disintegration if one said to him
at 1.22 : "All right, Jakes, I'm going on foot.
Call for me here at 6.30." Jakes was not the man
to take that sort of thing very well.

In the second place, if one walked along that
path which edged the shrubberies one was apt to
meet other people, and even Civil Servants, flocking
to their food. This also entailed embarrassments.
Walter Bullinger had achieved a wholly adequate
technique for coping with acquaintances when
encountered head-on, when encountered coming
from the opposite direction. He would wave at
them gaily, and, if he happened to remember their
names, would exclaim quite quickly, "How are
you, Sullivan ? " and thus pass on.

It was a different matter, at the luncheon hour,
to manage these encounters when the encounterer
was moving in the same direction as oneself. They
would overtake one—not always deliberately, but
frequently with shamed surprise—being unaware
how, when you overtake a Foreign Secretary inadvertently (being a quick walker oneself and he
only jaunty), you should behave. Such encounters
were all the more poignant when executed with a
member of Bullinger's own staff. The Assistant
in the African Department, stepping out briskly
on his way to Soho, would, only when abreast of
Mr. Bullinger, recognise him as his own Secretary
of State. An awkward shambling might (and had)
result (resulted). That business about falling into
step. That predicament, if one *did* fall into step,
of having to make conversation with a shy young

man the whole way to the Travellers' Club. That predicament, if one did *not* fall into step, of having either to pause dismissive, or to shuffle later into the conjoint and posthumous step of obviously unintended companionship.

In the third place, there was the detective—Mr. Gerald Snelgrove. Bullinger loathed his detective. With much difficulty he had persuaded Scotland Yard to let him off Mr. Snelgrove when he drove in his car. But on the point of walking, The Yard were adamant. "Egyptian students," were the words they used. And thus, if Bullinger walked to his luncheon, Mr. Gerald Snelgrove, clad in a brown reefer suiting, followed airily behind. His presence, his unwanted and coldly ignored presence, produced in Bullinger a tickly feeling between the shoulder-blades. Mr. Snelgrove suffered, all too obviously, from eczema. This unfortunate infliction increased, in Walter Bullinger, that sense of cuticular irritation in the back.

In spite of these three important disadvantages, he decided, that afternoon, to walk. He wanted to think. It was a thoughtful Bullinger who, along the path between the rhododendrons, directed his unhappy feet towards the Travellers' Club.

" I ought," he ruminated, " to claim, to *insist* on claiming, an interview with Furnivall this very afternoon. But at three he will be at the House and I have the Argentine coming, and the German, and then the French Ambassador at four. And after that, the meeting at the India Office, and then the American at six, and I am speaking at the D.O.T. dinner at 7.30. No, I shall have to write

Furnivall a minute. A carefully worded minute. I can think it over at luncheon."

Bullinger was relieved at feeling that circumstances would oblige him to put it all in writing. He tripped up the Duke of York's steps more rapidly than was prudent in a man of his advancing years. A pavement artist under the statue of Franklin had completed his design for the morning. It consisted of the words " Good Luck " outlined widely in white chalk and filled in with little coloured pictures of boats and canaries and freesias. Bullinger read the message and felt grateful. Pausing, he laid a dollar in the artist's cap. It was an almost blithe Bullinger who ran up the steps of the Travellers' Club.

Having washed and brushed, he ascended the staircase slowly, grasping, as befitted an elder statesman, the handrail which had been affixed to the banister for the use of Prince de Talleyrand. In his other hand he held a copy of *Truth* and five square sheets of Club note-paper. He chose an isolated table, standing modestly while the waiter pulled it out. He slipped round it, sank into his chair, ordered some galantine and half a bottle of Brauneberger, and then placed the copy of *Truth*, with the note-paper above it, on the table-cloth.

" June 3/39," he wrote in the top right-hand corner. Then in block letters he wrote the words " Prime Minister." He underlined these two words. And then he launched out neatly upon his minute : conscious as he proceded that he was composing a State Paper of great importance. " I fear," he wrote :—

"I fear that I failed to gather from this morning's Cabinet what exact policy you and my colleagues wish me to pursue :—

A. I was left with the impression that you yourself felt that we could well afford to wait until the four Powers should have quarrelled, both among themselves and with the Persian Government, over this concession question.

B. On the other hand, I derived from what Sir Charles Pantry told us a distinct apprehension that the Air Ministry have gone further, both in regard to the Livingstone Rockets and in regard to the atomic bomb, than the Cabinet, as a Cabinet, have been allowed to suppose."

"Galantine, sir ?" said the waiter.

"Thank you, thank you," Bullinger replied.

He was not irritated by this interruption. It gave him time to appreciate the double reproach implied in his last sentence. Smiling with unwonted asperity, Bullinger began to eat. After four mouthfuls he laid down his knife and fork and resumed his pencil. He underlined the words "as a Cabinet" and he underlined the word "allowed." He read the sentence again. And then he crossed out the underlining under the word "allowed." He smiled a second time, warily, and continued writing. "As regards," he wrote :—

"A. *As regards your own assumption*, I venture to disagree. I admit of course that the Shah's action in cancelling all foreign concessions will have thrown the battalions arrayed against us into some confusion. I feel convinced, however, that this confusion will be only momentary. My reasons for this conviction are the following :—

(1) The main purpose of the four Powers is to prevent our obtaining exclusive possession of the Abu Saad deposits.

(2) To achieve that purpose, they are prepared to exercise strong pressure upon Persia and concurrently to make important sacrifices themselves.

(3) However indignant they may be at the Shah's action, they will not allow their indignation to lead either to a rupture with Persia or to any dislocation of their own united front. They will, in fact, reason as follows :—

(a) Any lack of unanimity on their part will at once be noticed by the Persians and taken as a sign of weakness.

(b) Any violent pressure on their part may tempt the Shah to swing to the opposite direction and do a deal with us on the basis of Abu Saad for Persia and the deposits for us.

(c) They will fear also that the Shah, if he turns nasty, may blackmail them by threatening to publish through the League the whole shoddy story of their recent transactions.

(4) I am therefore convinced that the Powers will not furnish the Shah either with a motive or with the opportunity to make overtures to ourselves.

I am also convinced (though it is only fair to say that some of my experts do not here agree with me) that for us, at this stage, to make overtures to the Shah would be to expose ourselves to a rebuff and to a serious loss of prestige.

For these reasons . . ."

"Brauneberger Juffer 1932," said the wine waiter, inclining himself confidentially over Bullinger's table.

"Thank you, thank you," Bullinger replied.

He poured himself out a glass of that dew-fresh vintage. It tasted like a grass-stalk pulled and nibbled in some May meadow. Bullinger erased the word 'shoddy.'

He had, in the last eighteen months, evolved a system of his own for writing minutes. On the one hand he had adopted with relish the departmental habit of paragraphs and sub-paragraphs. He had a secret hope that one day his sub-paragraphs would become so intricate that they would exhaust the stock of English numerals and letters, and that Greek letters would have to serve as rubrics. Not too many of these, of course, since after passing delta Bullinger was scantily aware of the Greek alphabet. But enough to give diversity, and a touch of the humanities, to his page.

On the other hand, he tried to give to his minutes

and memoranda just that personal note which differentiated the pronouncements of Cabinet Ministers from the suggestions of Civil Servants. A homely turn of phrase here and there: the avoidance, generally, of technical or professional expressions: the introduction even of a few topical catchwords, of a few examples, even, of current slang.

Yet 'shoddy' in a State Paper of this importance would not do. For, after all, the thing might be published: if not in a Blue Book, then at least in his own memoirs. "*How Britain nearly came to War*," by the Right Honourable Walter Bullinger, 10s. 6d. Yes, if this crisis developed, it would make an interesting monograph. Bullinger poured himself out another glass of Brauneberger and resumed his pencil :—

> "*For these reasons* I am of the decided opinion that we shall gain nothing by delay, and may lose much."

That sounded a somewhat lame conclusion. He crossed it out. "I shall," he said to the waiter, "have my coffee here—and a small kümmel." "A double kümmel did you say, sir?" "Yes," answered Bullinger, lying deliberately.

> "*For these reasons* I am of the decided opinion that the honour of this country, and the peace of the world, depend upon our adopting in this question an attitude at once unambiguous and open. And I feel that this attitude should, not later than next Monday, be put before the House and the country from the Government bench."

That was better. Yet, now he came to think of it, what *was* the attitude which in this manner was to be expounded so openly on Monday afternoon? That was a question which Furnivall was bound to ask him. It was an important question. A cloud gathered over the sunshine of Bullinger's enjoyment of his own memorandum. "Well," he thought, "better leave it at that for the moment. I can think out the synthesis later. Best get on with the analysis at this stage."

B. *As regards Sir Charles Pantry's disclosures.*

It is evident from what he told us that the Air Ministry, without specific Cabinet sanction, have :—

(1) Manufactured ten more rocket aeroplanes.

(2) Persisted in their experiments with the atomic bomb.

(3) Prepared a programme of further rocket manufacture on a large scale.

(4) Sent a wholly unauthorised expedition to Abu Saad for the purpose of accumulating stocks of the deposit.

N.B. (*a*) I am aware that Sir Charles Pantry contends that the Cabinet decision of April of last year gave him authority to prosecute these experiments as a purely departmental concern. I have myself frequently regretted that the discussion which took place in April of 1938 was not more extensive and that the resultant decisions were so imprecise.

But the general *feeling* of the Cabinet at the time was one of disapproval, if not of the rocket, then certainly of the bomb. And, if I may say so, I think that Sir Charles should have shown a greater regard for this feeling.

N.B. (*b*) There is a further point which, had not the Cabinet been so abruptly dissolved this morning, I should have wished, under this heading, to emphasise. It is this. Eleven rocket aeroplanes are a very different business from one rocket aeroplane. One rocket can be regarded merely as an experiment, yet even as such we have had good cause to realise the amount of uneasiness which can be aroused by such an experiment abroad. Eleven rockets, on the other hand, constitute a striking force. I much fear that Sir Charles Pantry may already regard them as such. It is for this reason that I should, had I been allowed the opportunity, have insisted in Cabinet that any trial flights conducted by these eleven or ten rockets must be of the most discreet and unprovocative nature. Anything approaching a demonstration is strongly to be deprecated.

C. *Our present position.*

On the *one* hand you have the Cabinet, who are responsible to the House and to the country, relying upon the vague, and to my mind unjustified, hope that our antagonists will fall out among themselves. On the *other* hand, you have the Air Ministry, who seem to be responsible to no one, determined to exploit these Livingstone inventions to a point where they will give us complete supremacy in the air.

It is my duty, as Foreign Secretary, to record the anxious opinion that this mixture of a negative attitude on the part of responsible Ministers and of a very positive attitude on the part of one of the fighting services can only edge us into a position which will render inevitable a cruel and unnecessary war.

As a Cabinet we are pledged to peace. So long as I remain a member of the Cabinet I must insist that these pledges be fulfilled. And again I record the opinion that by our policy of drift we are violating these pledges.

Mr. Bullinger stirred his coffee slowly and read his minute from the beginning. The Prime Minister, with thin white fingers, would stroke his silky beard below that hateful smile. " Yes," he would say languidly, " yes, my dear Bullinger, I agree with every word you say. A very neat exposition of our present difficulties. An exposition which you might well have given us at yesterday's Cabinet. But not, if I may so suggest, a very constructive paper. It is all too easy to contend that the Government should have a clear-cut and open policy. The *Morning Express*, I see, makes that very suggestion in to-day's issue. But the difficult thing is to state what exactly that policy is to be. I should in all probability be ready to adopt any definite scheme which you might propose. But what, my dear Bullinger, *do* you propose? I may be very stupid. But after reading your minute carefully I am still quite in the dark as to the policy which our Foreign Secretary has advanced."

Mr. Bullinger, foreseeing that question, visualising the exact gestures with which it would be accompanied, anticipating the acid wording which Furnivall would use, winced. It was again, and in spite of the kümmel, a desolate Walter Bullinger who descended the staircase of the Travellers' Club. Mr. Snelgrove was waiting for him in the Porter's Lodge. Slowly the two, in Indian file, walked back to the Foreign Office. The pavement artist had wiped out his previous design and was sketching in a battleship upon an angry sea.

"Well," Bullinger decided, as he entered the lift, "in any case I shall send my minute across to the P.M. I shall have it typed at once. It serves at least to disengage my own responsibility, to make my own position clear.

"Clear enough . . ." he sighed as he entered his room.

For Bullinger, as has been indicated, was an essentially honest man.

(3)

Friday was the day of the week selected by the Southern Railway on which to accord to the residents at Tunbridge Wells the privilege of a cheap return ticket to London. Jane Campbell's mother availed herself of this privilege. Not that Friday was for her a convenient day: there being no matinées : and the flower-shows at Vincent Square being held on Tuesdays. Yet Lady Campbell felt that, in justice to the Southern Railway, it was incumbent upon her to come to London on Fridays : and thus, on that particular Friday, clasping a black silk reticule, she came.

Lady Campbell's had been an adventurous and wide-flung life. True it was that she had been born and partly bred at the Rectory at Lamberhurst, and had thus, until the age of fifteen, been lulled by the certainties of a kindly Victorianism. Yet when the Rector died in 1894 she had been taken to live with her uncle, Sir George Wakehurst, at that time High Commissioner in Cyprus. At Nicosia, at Troodos, had Mabel Wakehurst passed the next eleven years of her life : it was there that she acquired that complete mastery of the Romaic language which in after life was a constant source of dissatisfaction to her, as being an accomplishment at once distinctive and incommunicable : it was there that she acquired the flat, the cognisant, the initiate expression which she assumed when other people discussed the British Empire, our Mediterranean possessions, and the Near, the Middle, or even the Far, East. And it was there that she acquired Professor Andrew Campbell, who at that time was excavating Minoan remains at Kerassini.

At the age of twenty-six she married Professor Campbell, although he was twenty years her senior. For the ensuing quarter of a century she followed her Andrew from Knossos (where her Greek had come in useful) to Luxor (where it hadn't) : and from there to Entebbe, the Gobi desert, Patagonia, New Mexico, Iceland and Sierra Leone. In her flowing but very legible script she would make loving although inaccurate copies of the papers contributed by the Professor to the scientific journals of two continents. Yet in spite of this diversity of experience she remained always the daughter of the rector of Lamberhurst, the niece of dear old Uncle George up there among the wild lavender and gum-cistus of Troodos. Her adult experience had left only two impressions on her mind. The first was a deep veneration for the memory of the late Sir Andrew Campbell. The second was a feeling that Jane, so often separated from her in childhood, was always, in spite of her affectionate nature, being taken away.

As so frequently happened on Friday mornings, Lady Campbell was unable to read her novel. The railway carriage, constructed to seat at the very most eight persons, contained twelve. And, being thus tightly wedged between two other ladies, who had also felt it incumbent to profit by the generosity of the Southern Railway, Lady Campbell could with difficulty hold her book. Being a woman who all too readily abandoned her own desires, she renounced her book. It was put back, rather clumsily, into the black silk reticule, which was indeed of an enormous size. Lady Campbell just sat and thought; looking out at the gay gardens of Orpington.

She was sorry about her book. It promised to be a nice book. So few books, nowadays, promised to be nice. Even if they began nicely there was surely something nasty on its way. "What I expect from a novel," thus had she informed Jane only last Friday, "is that it should be comfortable." "You mean 'comforting,'" Jane had suggested. "No," she had answered, a little sharply, "no, dear, not in the least. I didn't mean that at all. You always take the words out of my mouth. All I ask is that authors should write agreeably about agreeable people, that they should avoid writing about horrid things or laughing at nice things." Jane had smiled at that, stretching out her hand and patting affectionately. "Darling Mummy!" she had said. Lady Campbell had jerked her arm away in unconcealed irritation.

She had often tried, in a timid and not very penetrating way, to explain to herself that under-feeling of dissatisfaction, of irritation, of resentment even, which was the cloud upon the sun of her love for Jane. It wasn't Jane's fault: she admitted that: Jane, considering how over-worked she always was, behaved in a manner which was always dutiful, affectionate, gay. Yet Lady Campbell had observed, with some perplexity, that, especially of late, she had parted from Jane with a feeling almost of remorse, with the consciousness of having been unnecessarily snappy and disapproving.

Lady Campbell was at a loss to account for this new and most unwelcome element in her own nature. She was so proud of Jane, so wrapped up in her, so confident in the firm foundations of their mutual love. How came it that she was so frequently cross to Jane when they met? It must be jealousy. Not, certainly, of Jane's success:

that to her was a bonfire in her winter dusk: but jealousy of all the interests which separated her from Jane, of all those public affairs in which her daughter was so intimately involved and in which she, her only mother, could never hope to share.

" Yes," Lady Campbell had confessed to herself, " it's just jealousy. You're jealous of all those politics getting in the way. Well, isn't that just mean of you and small ? "

She was much comforted by this discovery, feeling that jealousy of Jane for Jane's own sake was a not ignoble failing. Yet, had she known it, the causes of her dissatisfaction went far deeper than mere extraneous jealousy. Her maternal instinct, never fully assuaged, had returned to her in the evening of her life: she resented the fact that Jane, once so dependent, should now be so self-sufficing, so detached. This unrealised craving for past motherhood assumed the strange form of a desire to reduce her daughter once again to the status of a little child: and as a symptom of this she was constantly, when they were together, reproving Jane, disagreeing with Jane, diminishing Jane: saying, in effect, " No, darling, I'm afraid you mustn't ": as if they were still back together in 1910.

Yet there was more to it than merely this. Unconsciously Lady Campbell identified Jane with herself, trying in the Jane Campbell of 1939 to revive the Mabel Campbell of 1912. Seeing herself in the terms of Jane's active combative life, she recoiled with timid diffidence from the ordeals which her daughter faced so gaily: it was not that she resented Jane being so much braver than she had ever been herself: it was that, by a muddled form of identification, she became frightened at the fact that Jane should oblige Mabel to live a life to which the latter was so strikingly ill-adapted.

"Well, anyhow," decided Lady Campbell, as the train crossed Hungerford Bridge, "I shall be careful not to nag at Jane this morning. It only gets bad once I start. . . ."

And so thinking she drove to the Army and Navy Stores.

(4)

Lady Campbell loved the Army and Navy Stores. There had been a period, of course, when she had openly regretted the modernisation of that emporium, even as she had openly regretted the introduction of illustrations into *The Times*. That period was now over. Lady Campbell trod with possessive glee upon the rubber flooring of the dear old Army and Navy, even as she would flaunt, with pride of possession, the picture page of the dear old *Times*. Each of these innovations in one of her established institutions had been for her, at first painful, and thereafter glorious. No rubber flooring now seemed to her so sedate, so soothing, as the rubber flooring of the Army and Navy Stores. No illustrations now seemed to her so soothing, so sedate, as the illustrations to *The Times*. "Look at that . . ." she would exclaim, extending triumphantly a photograph of Salisbury Cathedral viewed from a bucolic distance. "I always say . . ." she would affirm, introducing thereby her recurrent eulogy of the Army and Navy Stores.

" Cash ? " the assistant would enquire, when, after processes of much elimination, she had selected just that trowel, just that cake of Windsor soap— " Cash, Madam, or deposit account ? "

" Deposit account," Lady Campbell would answer giving her number with glib efficiency. " R. 47.38."

A sense of privilege, of initiation, of solidarity. A sense of position, of basis, of Nicosia, of having, for over forty years, " belonged." A reassuring feel.

It was thus a reassured, a satisfied, Lady Campbell who, on that stainless June morning, entered an omnibus on her way to the Wilmot Club in Hans Crescent.

The trouble about the Wilmot Club was its atmosphere. It was an atmosphere of trim conviviality, of joyous daintiness. It was a club fated primarily for the widows of Colonial Governors, for the unmarried sisters of still extant Civil Servants. The secretary of the club, Miss Joyce Hetherington, had realised from the very outset that such a club, if left to itself, might become a trifle dim. She did not leave it to itself. She swayed about the premises with a wide marine tread, and when she ceased swaying she would hitch her thumbs within her bead necklace, straining it outwards, as if a male impersonator straining at the armholes of a waistcoat. In spite of this marine, this ostler, exuberance, Miss Hetherington realised that the members of the Wilmot would desire to encounter in Hans Crescent all the refinements of a home. She provided these refinements. There were large daisies in green pottery upon the luncheon tables : the chairs were of the variety known as Windsor :

the napkins were of superfine Japanese paper, and
the mustard pots had been purchased at Dinard,
being of Breton ware. The ash-trays, for their
part, came from Taormina. But the food was
recognisably English. Jane, when she lunched
there on Fridays, loathed the food.

Lady Campbell regarded the Wilmot with mixed
feelings. In the first place, it was a club : in the
second place, it was her own club. She could say
to Mrs. Ledwine, when they met on the platform
at Tunbridge Wells—" As a matter of fact," she
could say, " I generally find it more convenient to
lunch at my club." That was a satisfying remark :
competent, and almost advanced. In so far as
Mrs. Ledwine was concerned, Lady Campbell was
fully content with the Wilmot. Yet Mrs. Ledwine,
after all, was only incidentally concerned.

On the other hand, when she left her bus (" You
do stop at the corner of Knightsbridge, don't
you ? ")—when, as happened on that gay morning
of June 3, she walked slowly with her black reticule
down Sloane Street, a sense of apprehension assailed
her, a not very confident hope that Miss Hetherington, that morning, might have taken a day off.
Lady Campbell found it very difficult to adjust
her own conduct to the manners of Miss Hetherington. She found it irksome to counter the gay
manliness of Miss Hetherington's welcome, feeling
that in the eyes of the club secretary, she, Mabel
Campbell, appeared a most unclubbable woman ;
appeared dowdy, dumpy, damp, feminine and black.

She would endeavour, on entering the Wilmot,
to slink unobserved towards the more remote re-

cesses of the building, emerging therefrom with a timid briskness, hurrying preoccupied towards the lounge. There, in a wicker settee (a product of Madeira), she would hide behind *The Queen*, her little black gloves holding that weekly in front of her, hoping that Miss Hetherington would fail to spot her until Jane were there to help. Since Miss Hetherington was impressed by Jane: although Jane, that morning, was late.

Lady Campbell read with uneasy concentration an article on the impending confirmation of Princess Elizabeth. The voice of Miss Hetherington—that Newmarket, that Newhaven, voice—resounded from the drawing-room. "And so," Miss Hetherington was saying, "I told the old frump exactly what I thought. I told her that there were certain things that were done, and certain other things that were not done. I was right, don't you think? After all, one can't run a club like this without . . ."

Miss Hetherington's unseen victim made conciliatory sounds indicative of the opinion that Miss Hetherington had been right.

"You see," continued the virile voice of the club secretary—"you see, two-thirds of our members are half-boiled, and the other third are frankly lousy. They seem to imagine that the whole place exists for them alone. Now take Lady Freemantle, for instance. You know mother Freemantle—that aggressive woman with the bony hands—well, she had the cheek the other day . . ."

Lady Campbell peeped at the clock over the corner of *The Queen* furthest removed from Miss Hetherington's voice. It stood at 1.35. It was really most inconsiderate of Jane to be so late that morning—most inconsiderate.

" Upon the Japanese table," Miss Hetherington was saying, "just like that. And with an ash-tray six yards from her very nose. Luckily I spotted it just in time. I can tell you, I told her off properly. As it is, the thing has burnt a mark in the lacquer—I'll show you—it's that little corner table in the lounge . . ."

Lady Campbell quailed. Her thoughts veered regretfully to the no less dainty but far less personal A B C in Sloane Street where, in those cloudless, clubless days, she was wont to have her cup of coffee on Fridays and her luncheon scone.

" Hulloa ! " Miss Hetherington had by now entered the lounge, " who have we here ? Oh, it's Lady Campbell ! And how's life ? "

That was just the sort of thing which rendered Miss Hetherington so disconcerting. There she was—strident, welcoming, and above all standing up. Six foot of hearty English womanhood arrayed in brown tweed. And there, below her, cowered Mabel Campbell upon a Madeira settee, a small figure, black and round, a timid uncertain figure, clasping a now unprotective copy of *The Queen*. Ought Mabel Campbell to get up ? No—that would be a most unclubbable motion. It was most unusual, she felt, for people in clubs to rise from their seats when welcomed by the secretary. Yet how, if she did not get up, could she cope with the exuberance of Miss Hetherington, peeping up at her like that, peeping small and black and round ?

" I'm very well, thank you," said Lady Campbell,

fluttering shy lashes, moving *The Queen* nervously upon her knee.

"Good for you," said Miss Hetherington, striding onwards to the Japanese table, intent on showing Miss Garlock exactly where Lady Freemantle had left her cigarette.

Lady Campbell disappeared again behind *The Queen*. How badly she had managed it this morning! Even worse than usual! She had bowed slightly in answering Miss Hetherington: yes, she had made a downward movement of her head. Her smile, her voice, that inclination of the head, had none of them been club movements: they were tea-party movements: vicarage tea-parties: the rector's, even the bishop's wife. Half-boiled, lousy old frump. . . .

"Oh, here you are, Jane!" exclaimed Lady Campbell, almost angrily. "Late as usual."

"Sorry, Mummy, but I was kept at the office."

"*Of course*," said Lady Campbell. She flung into the word a cloud of disapproval, self-pity, satire, and motherly forgivingness.

Jane smiled. They walked together towards the dining-room.

"There's mutton hash," said Lady Campbell, reading the dainty menu card, "and silverside of beef. I know you hate hash, darling."

"Sorry, M'Lady," said the waitress, "the beef is out."

"Oh, I don't mind hash," said Jane, wishing to be daughterly. "I rather like it once in a way."

"Well, hash," said Lady Campbell, glancing at the waitress with unmerited severity.

" And now, dear," she turned to Jane, " tell me all your news."

Jane winced.

Not that she was unprepared for this question : she had already braced herself for it, knowing that, once luncheon had been ordered, the remark would, as always, be her mother's opening move. She had been looking forward, even, while in the taxi on her way to Hans Crescent, to telling her mother all about John. Here—at least, at last—was an experience, a wild excitement, which her mother would understand and share : in this, at least, they would find themselves upon the same human plane. How happy would her mother be on learning this tremendous secret ! What a busy, planning, expectant little heart would be carried back with her that evening to Tunbridge Wells ! Jane, driving down to Hans Crescent, had almost looked forward to that moment when her mother would ask her all her news. To-day it would be all so different : for once the inevitable question would not be a barrier, but an open gate. " Well," she would answer, " well, Mummy, I've got a great piece of news for you. Something hugely exciting. I give you three guesses." She had pictured an ensuing scene sparkling with surprise, animation and love. Yet now, when the moment had arrived, nothing seemed less feasible than to tell her mother about John Shorland.

" News, Mummy ? " she echoed vaguely, gaining time.

" You're looking white, dear. You're not looking well at all."

" There's been a great deal of work these days. Quite a rush. I was up late last night reading files."

Lady Campbell, at that, pursed her lips. She signified by this expression : " It only shows, dear, what I have always said. We women have not the physical strength for public life." She signified, " Well, dear, and who's to blame for that ? " She signified—" I told you so."

Jane would on the whole have preferred if her mother had said, and not merely looked, these things. A feeling of numb discouragement crushed upon her. Life, after all, was a small and squalid thing. The thought of John, the grotesque and ugly thought of her marriage, which had but half an hour ago flamed in June sunshine, crumpled suddenly to the proportions of a sponge-bag forgotten upon the towel-rail of a seaside hotel.

" Naturally," she thought, " I can never marry. Two is an impossible number for any relationship."

" Well, Mummy," she began affectionately, " there's heaps to tell you. We're in for a really first-class crisis . . ."

" Eat your hash, dear," said Lady Campbell, " it will be getting cold."

CHAPTER VI

(1)

M. RENÉ MARTIN, Ambassador of France to the Court of St. James, although an intellectual, was humane. He owed his rapid promotion to the fact that, when in charge at Sofia in 1929, the style of his despatches had attracted the attention of M. Philippe Berthelot. The then Secretary-General of the Quai d'Orsay pronounced that they combined the realism of Malraux with the traditionalism of Jean Schlumberger. Martin's reputation was made.

M. Berthelot, being among the more enlightened of twentieth-century diplomatists, was apt (and rightly apt) to judge the intelligence of his emissaries by the more subtle qualities of their style. He had therefore sent M. Martin to Prague, and thereafter, much to the fury of the Action Française, had appointed him Ambassador in London. M. Berthelot had not himself repented of this action. In spite of his marked francophil tendencies, M. Berthelot was at heart an internationalist. He understood that other countries, notwithstanding their barbarity, did, in fact, exist. He understood that Great Britain was a phenomenon which could properly be comprehended only by extreme eccentrics; and he was therefore glad that he had sent the shy, the outspoken, the untidy, the unmanageable, the occasionally neurotic, René Martin to Albert Gate.

In the year 1938, unfortunately M. Berthelot had resigned, being desirous of completing a monograph in three volumes upon the ceramics of the T'ang dynasty. His successor (who shall be nameless) did not care for M. René Martin. And although M. Massigli—the Assistant Secretary-General: although M. Léger—the Political Director, would quite often refer to the Ambassador in London as "our dear René," yet M. François Poncet, the Foreign Secretary, fell under the influence of his Secretary-General, and was all too apt to become bothered about M. Martin, to regard his despatches as lacking the Latin spirit; as in fact too outspoken to allow of any but the most truncated reproduction in a yellow book.

The instructions which M. Jules Boursicaut had that morning, and at great personal inconvenience, brought to London were not the sort of instructions of which M. René Martin (or for that matter the Quai d'Orsay) was inclined to approve.

They owed their origin to a concatenation of unfortunate circumstances.

M. Labourdère, Minister of the Colonies in the Cocquebert Cabinet, had for long been trying to convince his chief that their position in the Chamber of Deputies was being rapidly undermined by an unholy alliance between the Centre and the Right. What was required was a "diversion," some gesture which would silence the rumour that the policy of the Cocquebert Cabinet was pedestrian, anti-national, ignorant, and inert. The President of the Council was impressed by these exhortations, having of late been himself disquieted by the manifest and increased concord between the Right and Centre deputies. He had thus gladly consented to join with the other three Powers in a spirited endeavour to oust Great Britain from Abu Saad. During the last week he had, by hints and winks, let it be understood in the lobbies that some great diplomatic coup was in contemplation. Already the words Abu Saad had appeared frequently in the French papers, and, through them, had trickled into the British Press.

M. Raoul Thierry, the main coadjutor of M. Paul Sebire in the plan for the formation of a Right–Centre block, was also, and most regrettably, a Director of the Persian Tramways Company. Late on Wednesday night he had received from his Manager at Tehran a telegram reporting that the Shah was about to cancel all foreign concessions. He at once visited M. Cocquebert at his private house, and threatened to interpellate him in the Chamber and thus to expose the damage to French interests which "his inept and vacillating diplomacy" had caused.

Faced by this menace, M. Hippolyte Cocquebert lost his head. He confided to M. Thierry that the issue was far more vital than a mere tramway concession in an oriental capital. He murmured something about "the menaces of the London Cabinet." In a few trenchant phrases he divulged the potentiality, if this monopoly remained in British hands, of the rocket aeroplane. And he concluded with an appeal to M. Thierry not to hamper the Government in their task of safe-guarding "the honour, the dignity, nay the very security, of France."

M. Thierry, reluctant and not wholly convinced, had consented to postpone his interpellation till Saturday. And M. Cocquebert had retired to an uneasy pillow aware that before Saturday something sensational would simply have to occur.

At the Cabinet next morning M. Cocquebert startled his colleagues by informing them that he had received private and absolutely reliable information from London to the effect that the British Government were about to offer to the Shah " important inducements " with a view to reaching a direct agreement with Persia and thus short-circuiting both Geneva and the four Powers. It was thus essential that the British Government should receive an immediate and categorical warning that France and her three coadjutors could not, in any circumstances, disinterest themselves in the Abu Saad question, and summoning the London Cabinet immediately to restore the island to Persia.

M. François Poncet pointed out that any such intimation would provoke grave resentment in London : that if it became known it would render any future adjustment extremely difficult : and that in any case it was a step which could only be taken in agreement with the Governments of Germany, Russia and the United States. M. Cocquebert insisted. The matter was put to the vote. And M. Poncet found himself in a minority. It was with great difficulty that he was induced to withdraw the resignation which he had at once tendered.

The Note was drafted. M. Martin was instructed to seek an immediate interview with Mr. Bullinger and to inform him that the four Powers, confident that the Shah's gesture was for internal consumption only, had in no sense relaxed their determination either to maintain a united front as between themselves or to render all possible assistance to Persia, both at Geneva and elsewhere, in her endeavour to "regain" possession of Abu Saad. He was in fact to leave with Mr. Bullinger a Note Verbale to that effect.

(2)

M. Martin had not liked these instructions when he read them at breakfast. He had liked them even less when, after luncheon, he read them again. And when at 3.20 p.m., preparatory to his appointment with Mr. Bullinger, he read them a third time, he pronounced them to be clumsy, provocative, and ill-timed.

There were, in his opinion, only three means by which a British Cabinet could be driven into positive action. The first was the fear of being made ridiculous. The second was the fear of being thought afraid. The third was the suspicion that foreign Governments were suggesting to them what they ought to do. The instructions which M. Martin had received that morning seemed to combine each of these three propellents.

Fully conscious that in executing his instructions he might be goading the British Cabinet into a policy, M. René Martin, in grey flannels and on his lips a smile of sardonic distaste, drove down to the Foreign Office.

He found Mr. Bullinger affable as always, yet a trifle too exuberant in his welcome—a manner which descended upon the British Foreign Secretary in moments of nervous lassitude. M. Martin delivered his instructions word for word. "I have been instructed," he said, "to make to you the following communication . . ." And then he read the text of the Note Verbale in a tone which indicated that every word was enclosed in inverted commas, that every word was alien, and in fact obnoxious, to himself.

"Well," said Mr. Bullinger when he had concluded, " I call that pretty stiff ! "

The shell-like pink of Mr. Bullinger's complexion had turned to purple. Mr. Bullinger was more than angry : he was perplexed.

" It *is* stiff, isn't it ? " repeated Bullinger, gazing with a hurt and indignant expression at M. René Martin. " And what's more," he added, " it doesn't make sense."

M. Martin indicated, by a wave of his cigarette, that he could not, in loyalty to his own Government, signify how heartily he agreed.

Mr. Bullinger rose from the sofa where he had received the Ambassador and walked to the window. The pelican, for some reason, had retired behind the gunnera. Mr. Bullinger returned to the sofa and sat down. He had recovered his composure. " Well," he said, " what are we to do ? "

" I think," said M. Martin, with that slight cockney accent which he had acquired from his English nurse, " I think that it might be useful were your Government, at this juncture, to define their attitude. . . ."

" That's what I've just said," Bullinger interrupted. " I have only an hour ago told the Prime Minister, or rather written him a minute, in that very sense."

" Yes," said M. Martin, " but time presses. Public opinion in my country, as well as in Germany, is at present as a lake of petrol. It requires a heavy dose of sand. It would be most unfortunate if, before you people here were ready with the sand, someone else were ready with a match. You follow my meaning ? "

Mr. Bullinger had understood this allegory quite clearly. He thought it a good allegory. He would use it, to-morrow morning, in Cabinet.

" There is," he answered, " a meeting of the Cabinet to-morrow morning. I shall probably have to go to Chequers for the Sunday. I hope that we shall be in a position to make a statement in the House no later than Monday afternoon . . ."

" Much too late," said M. Martin, flinging the end of his cigarette into the grate. The brass grate of Mr. Bullinger was at the time decorated with a large paper frill like an expensive ham. The cigarette of the Ambassador threatened to ignite the frill. Mr. Bullinger rose and removed the stump with the fire-tongs. M. Martin watched him without rising : he was thinking how difficult it was to persuade the English statesmen to recognise the urgent or the unusual.

" Much, *much* too late," he repeated when Bullinger was once again seated beside him on the sofa.

" But, my dear sir," protested Mr. Bullinger,

148

" you don't seem to realise.   How could we possibly act any sooner ?   After all, to-day is Friday.   The Cabinet meet to-morrow, Saturday morning—in itself a thing which may cause comment in the country and on the Exchange.   Then after that comes the week-end.   Chequers, I suppose.   No—clearly Monday afternoon is the earliest possible moment."

M. Martin (loving the English) smiled.

" My dear Secretary of State," he answered, " you seem to forget that at moments of crisis there is no week-end in Paris, nor yet in Berlin, nor yet in Moscow or Washington.   You are wasting time.   Your Cabinet, I fear, must meet to-night. A communiqué, if the House of Commons is not sitting, must be issued to-morrow.   If you consider that improper I could arrange for you to give an interview late to-night to the correspondent of the *Temps*.   A man in whom you can place every confidence."

" To-night ? " echoed Bullinger, aghast.   " No —it's impossible.   It would cause a panic in the City.   Besides, I have to make a speech at the D.O.T. dinner, and the Prime Minister always goes to bed at half-past ten.   And, after all, man, why this hurry ?   I really do not follow you."

M. Martin leant forward and tapped the right knee of Mr. Bullinger with two firm fingers.

" Yet you must meet to-night," he said, " unless the very gravest consequences are to result.   My messenger flies back to Paris to-morrow at dawn. I shall do myself the honour of calling on you again, at your private house, at midnight.   You will by then have consulted the Cabinet and will be in a

position to tell me what reply I am to return to this "
—and at that he flicked a contemptuous finger-nail
at the paper in his hand—" this communication. For
the moment I shall trouble you no further." And he
dropped the Note neatly on the little table by his side.

" But, my dear Ambassador," protested Bullinger,
turning round anxiously upon the sofa, " I really
do not understand. What on earth can happen
during the week-end to make it all so desperately
urgent ? "

" By Sunday," replied M. Martin, " every newspaper in France and Germany will know that I
have delivered to you a message which the British
Government cannot accept without humiliation.
It will by then be too late for my Government, or
the German Government, to retreat from the position
they have adopted. Your only hope is to do something definite before the inevitable leakages begin at
the Quai d'Orsay or the Wilhelmstrasse. You have
about sixteen hours in front of you. But that is all."

" Well," said Bullinger, rising numbly, " of
course there's something in that. Yes—there's a
good deal in that. We have had those leakages
before."

For the second time he turned to the window and
stood there gazing down upon the lake.

After a few minutes he joined M. Martin at the
fireplace.

" I take it," he said (since Bullinger, when dealing
with the concrete was not a fool), " that you are
hinting to me, and in a manner which does you
credit, that this communication of yours is a ramp
on the part of your Cabinet to take the wind from

the sails of the Centre and extreme Right in the Chamber. You mean, in fact, that the French Government wish, for internal reasons, to use this Abu Saad question, and the fact that on this you have the support of the other three Powers, in order to gain a diplomatic victory over this country, or in other words to subject this Empire to a resounding diplomatic humiliation. Your Monsieur Cocquebert is, as a politician, astute. I quite see that my friend M. Poncet is not in this at all. I quite see that he and you, my dear Ambassador, wish me to assist you as against your Monsieur Cocquebert. No—you need not reply to that. I know this sort of situation all too well. But it is all more difficult than you think. Your communication is so worded as to mean everything or nothing. M. Cocquebert can represent it as an ultimatum to which we have succumbed. Yet if we ourselves were to represent it as such to the House of Commons they would merely laugh, considering it merely a silly diplomatic gambit like any other. I foresaw this sort of thing. I warned the Cabinet this morning. You confirm my apprehensions. I am grateful to you. I know that you foresee our possible dangers as vividly as I do myself."

M. Martin, perhaps belatedly, became discreet. "I shall now," he said, "take my leave. I ask only, my dear Minister, that you will not delay."

Again effusive, Bullinger conducted the Ambassador to the corridor.

On his return he pressed the bell-push which communicated with the Private Secretaries' Room.

"Ah!" he exclaimed, "my dear Peabody.

Please ring up No. 10 and say that I have this moment received from the French Ambassador a communication of the utmost importance. It requires an immediate answer. Say that I must beg the Prime Minister urgently to summon a special Cabinet for 10.30 to-night. Make it quite clear that I should not make so unusual a request were it not a question of hours."

Peabody showed, but did not express, his disapproval. " To-night, sir ? " he repeated.

" Yes," answered Bullinger sharply, " to-night at half-past ten."

Peabody closed behind him the green baize door which separated the room of the Secretary of State from the office of his private secretaries. He sighed.

" My dear Shorland," he sighed, " remember this. Rush is always dangerous."

And at that he sat down at his desk and telephoned dutifully to the Cabinet Secretariat in Whitehall Gardens.

(3)

Ponderous and uncertain is that relation between pressure and resistance which constitutes the balance of power. The arch of peace is morticed by no iron tenons : the monoliths of which it is composed are joined by no cement. Impressive in their apparent solidity, these granite masses lean against each other, thrust resisting hidden thrust. Yet a swarm of summer bees upon the architrave, a runnel of April water through some hidden crevice, will cause a millimetre of displacement, will set these monoliths stirring against each other, unheard, unseen. One night a handful of dust will patter from the vaulting: the bats will squeak and wheel in sudden panic: nor can the fragile fingers of man then stay the rush and rumble of destruction.

Such was the menace which on that June evening hung above the western hemisphere. A cloud, no larger than a man's hand, had risen in the East, and even now it had swollen to a heavy barrier, creeping onwards across the sunlight—impending, imminent, dark. Walter Bullinger leant against the embrasure of his window, looking down upon the placid pool of June. The ducks were scurrying among the irises, probing each other in the neck: the pelicans, aloof from such farmyard intimacies, slept. Motionless against the already declining sun the plane trees stretched their branches. Yet, even against this placidity, the storm appeared to Bullinger to creep nearer: it was as if, at any moment, the first heavy raindrops would splash to circles upon the happy sunlit lake.

The Ambassador had been right: René Martin was generally right. There was no time, there was scarcely an hour, to be lost. Already the great grey monoliths had shifted: already the situation, with dumb impetus, was sliding away from the scope of calculation to that of force: already a faint shrilling in the air presaged the wind of emotion. In sixteen, in twelve, hours the horrors of open diplomacy would hold Europe in its butcher's grip. There remained but a little hour or so in which the custodians could cope with the danger alone, secretly, intelligently, unharassed by the shrieking of the herd.

Gazing down at the ducks, the pelicans, Walter Bullinger sighed deeply. In a sudden rush the full wave of his perplexity assailed him. He raised his hands to his white locks in tortured dismay. Why had this thing come thus suddenly upon him? How unnecessary, how unjust, that he, Walter Bullinger, should be goaded by so fierce a predicament! The whole thing was ruthless, remote, intangible, distant, compelling. He felt himself distantly surrounded, encroached upon, hemmed in, captured. There was no opening anywhere for postponement, alleviation, or escape.

"Unnecessary" was the word that recurred to him. It was all so unnecessary. Yet withal so urgent, so compelling. A wave of anger flushed his temples. Why could not other people be as considerate, as helpful, as mild even, as he was himself? It was enraging that a man like Cocquebert, a man of no value whatsoever, that a man like the Shah of Persia, a man of primitive mentality, could thus disturb the serene intentions of Bullinger, could thus endanger the peace of half the world. His brain, throbbing through angered temples, reeled with the question, "Yet what am I to do?"

Then it was all so unreal, so distant. Surely with a little patience, a little good-will, a little reason—surely with a closer contact, a little more time, a little less space—surely . . . And what business had that young Livingstone to unearth that beastly deposit? What business had Lympne to involve the Air Ministry in that loathsome Abu Saad concession? Either the deposit was vital or it was not. If not, then it had been a mistake to secure that monopoly. If vital, then surely any ass could have foreseen that the other Powers would combine against us ?

Diplomacy, Bullinger felt, was almost wholly a matter of correct timing. A proposal which, on Monday, would seem a reasonable suggestion would, if deferred till Wednesday, become a humiliating retreat. An answer which, on the Tuesday, would be regarded as helpful and conciliatory, would by Thursday be condemned as " a rejoinder which no Nation, conscious of her dignity as a Great Power, could possibly accept." What had happened in the interval ? The crisis had become public property : the vanity of the thick-headed crowd had become involved : the crisis, imperceptibly, had become a matter of prestige.

Bullinger, being an honest Liberal, loathed prestige. He was aware none the less that Spencer Furnivall, being a politician, thought it " necessary." He was aware also that to Sir Charles Pantry it was the very breath of life. He was aware, beyond anything, that his other colleagues, as between Pantry and Bullinger, would not be very sure.

Yet, if for one moment prestige were allowed to intrude its plebeian snout into this tangle, war would result. Bullinger repeated this phrase to himself quite calmly. " War," he said, " will result." The very shape of those three letters, the very conjunction of *w* with *a* and *r*, caused his gorge to rise. He had seen it in 1916. He saw it always as a man with yellow curls : that man he had passed beside a shell-hole near Armentières : a man clutching his tumbling guts in slim red fingers, a man biting fiercely in the mud. No, anything but that again, anything but that. Bullinger struck the woodwork which framed the window. A cold sweat broke out upon his forehead. " Yes, anything," he murmured through clenched teeth, " *anything* is less terrible than that."

And, after all, was the situation really so very critical ? None of the Powers could intentionally desire war. All that they wanted was a diplomatic triumph. Let them have their victory. It was a victory of the emotions only, it would not be a victory of the mind. Let them have it. And if Furnivall desired a scapegoat, then Bullinger could resign. We could reply to the French Note with dignified acquiescence. We could say that His Majesty's Government would be all too ready to consult with the French Government as to the exact terms in which this Abu Saad question should be referred to the League of Nations. That surely would assuage M. Cocquebert and the Right–Central block. That should abundantly satisfy Moscow, Berlin and Washington, who could each in their own way represent it to their local opponents as a resounding diplomatic victory. And even we ourselves, in the House, could stress the League of Nations, could to some extent save our face.

Yet we should lose Abu Saad. Would Furnivall, would Pantry, consent to such a sacrifice ? And if Bullinger tried to force it upon them by the threat of resignation would they not, relieved and even delighted, let him go ? The thought of his successor, over there seated by his very table, shot through Bullinger with a twitch of angered pain.

Why should he sacrifice himself in such a manner? Why show, and for no reason, so little fight? The combative instinct to which, as an English gentleman, he had been trained since childhood, stiffened within him.

And why, after all, should Great Britain, should the British Empire, surrender without a word to this conspiracy of footpads? We had the right, we had the power, to resist. We could crush the whole combine in the space of a few hours: and if Bullinger hesitated, if Bullinger, at this moment, showed himself unmanly, then some more virile successor would take his place. Nor in fact need the thing be so very destructive. One could employ a progressive series of ultimatums. One atomic bomb on the Landes, a second in Arizona, a third upon the Lüneburger Heide, a fourth upon the Steppes. An area of thirty almost desert miles could in the territory of each of our enemies be ravaged in a single minute. Then would come the first ultimatum: " Unless by midnight on Thursday we receive an unconditional demand for an armistice our air forces will before dawn on Friday destroy Detroit, Tourcoing, Halle, and Magnetogorsk." There would be no need for any second ultimatum.

And yet supposing, supposing that they did not at once give way? Detroit, Tourcoing, Halle, Magnetogorsk. Women in white aprons spattered with infant brains. " No," Bullinger repeated for the second time, and again between clenched teeth, " no, anything, any humiliation, rather than contrive such evil."

Yet even as he said it he knew that along that current, that swift black current, a wisp of straw, called Walter Bullinger, was being swirled.

His left fist was still clenched in pacifist determination as he walked back from the window towards his desk. He pressed the buzzer which summoned Arthur Peabody. "Telephone," he said, "to Downing Street. Ask them to tell the P.M. that I must see him alone this evening before the Cabinet. I shall be there soon after ten."

As Peabody, on leaving, opened the green baize door the sound of chinking tea-cups came from the Private Secretaries' Room.

(3)

Shorland and Jane Campbell dined at the Jardin. They were not embarrassed. The sense, even, of an outer circle of embarrassment created an inner radius of calm—the hushed centre of a typhoon alive with birds.

They talked of Abu Saad.

"Jane," said Shorland, leaning forwards, fingering the tissue-covered toothpicks in their china trough, "Jane, let us speak of realities, let us talk about ourselves."

He shifted the trough nervously between long fingers, staring intently at the nest of paper toothpicks inside.

"Yes," said Jane.

"You see," John began, shifting the trough this way and that upon the table-cloth—" you see . . ."

He flung himself back upon the settee. His hands, twirling a toothpick in its paper sheaf, rested upon the edge of the table.

"You see, Jane, we live in a difficult age. This—" (he turned his head slightly in her direction, and then again his eyes rested upon the toothpick in his hand) —" this is *my* monologue. You mustn't interrupt. You can look across there at Mr. Hugh Walpole, who, I observe, is dining with the Swedish Minister. You must look outwards, Jane, and from time to time you may nod when you agree. For this monologue is mine.

" We live in a difficult age. We are transitional. I sometimes wonder, Jane, whether you realise, whether I even realise, how beastly transitional we are. ' Male,' we are assured, ' and female created He them.' That doesn't apply to-day. You and I, Jane, belong spiritually to the third sex. And the third sex has not, as yet, been officially recognised.

" It is the sex, Jane, to which the movements of the mind—the movements of the heart if you will— are more vital than the movements of the body. Yet the body exists. Physically both you and I are normal animals : some strange normality in our thyroid or our pituitary glands has saved us from being physically inverted. Yet psychologically we are both members of the third sex—and it is this which makes it all so extremely awkward.

" Let me explain. I have been thinking it out. I have been thinking out why something exists between us which both attracts and repels. It all comes from our being transitional. We have all the instincts of the Neanderthal, and all the hesitations of the mid-twentieth century. We are too fastidious, too civilised, not to be dismayed by the crudity, the unfairness, the waste and bungling, of nature.

"The human race is divided between the fecunding and the parturient, between the male and the female. The former, enjoying the wild spasm of a moment, are liberated, militant, questing, acquisitive. The latter, gestating through heavy months towards a culmination point of agony, are defensive, fleeing, cautious, economical.

"No, don't interrupt, Jane. I am not becoming sententious. You always say I am becoming pompous when I try to think things out. Yes— economical. I know that it is a wounding, ugly word. But I am not being unkind, or coarse, or pompous, Jane—truly I'm not. I want to get to the root of all this. You must hear me out.

"From this divergence, this conflict, this vile necessity of pursuit and surrender, has arisen a theory—an instinct, it may be—that man takes and woman gives. To animal or savage natures this glaring inequality has some compensations. The savage, in imposing upon his woman those nine months of haggard endurance, those hours of ferocious agony, repays her by protection, by the sheer bulk of his own biceps. And the uncivilised woman, for her part, enjoys this sense of protection and control, and imagines, even, that in the maternal instinct, in the protracted and diffused sensualism of maternity, she finds her own reward. I think she does. I quite agree that to those timid barbarians of the nineteenth century these compensations were actual, almost physical, realities. Yet, Jane dearest, they can never be realities to you or me. We are too civilised to regard mere physical muscles as an excuse for such monstrous inequality. We are not civilised enough to have evolved a relation between man and woman which can be liberated from all the savage instincts. We belong to an age of transition. The third sex, dominant and self-avowed, has yet to be established.

" Take your own case, Jane. My body wishes, and I may add ardently, to possess you. Yet between that desire and your possible acquiescence there comes this barrier of sex. I admire you, Jane : I respect your character and your intelligence : and it revolts me to subject you to this obscene and savage mechanism of sex. I feel a barrier as instinctive as the barrier of incest. I think of you always as liberated, equal, alone : my very love for you winces. . . ."

She put her hand upon his arm to stay him. She was very white.

" John," she said, " you are being very young and silly. You have got the whole thing wrong. You make me unhappy because you have got it wrong deep down inside yourself. It will be difficult to disentangle. I know you have got it wrong, but as yet I can't see exactly where. I'm afraid I feel a little bit shocked, John. I find it rather shocking to be clever about one's own inside. I am sorry John—it will be better to-morrow. But I think I'll go now, if you don't mind. We can't go to the Phœnix after this."

She rose and smiled sadly at him. Her feet dragged slightly as she walked to the door.

"Waiter!"—John was flushed and angry—"some Armagnac."

At that moment Walter Bullinger, leaving the D.O.T. dinner at the Hotel Victoria, was driving to Downing Street.

(4)

He found the Prime Minister seated in an armchair in front of a wood fire: yet the night, for London, was warm.

"Come in, my dear Bullinger," said Spencer Furnivall, laying aside his detective novel with marked regret. "Really! This climate of ours. It is the only thing which we are allowed these days to describe by that pejorative adjective 'English.' Yes, pull up that chair. We have a clear fifteen minutes in front of us: let us indulge, my dear Bullinger, in what you call 'a chat.' Yes, I have read your minute. I have also read the French Note which you circulated. And apart from these two important documents, I have a letter from Pantry."

The Prime Minister paused, gazing, with silky and uplifted beard, at the ceiling.

"He threatens to resign," he added in the softest of soft voices.

"Resign?" said Bullinger.

"Yes," said the Prime Minister, smiling at his own tapping fingers. "He accuses me—and you, my dear Bullinger—of being what he calls in his aerial fashion 'chicken-livered.' I fear that the French Note, and our reply to it (since I presume you have drafted a reply), will confirm him in his impression of our pullet defects. Unless of course . . ."

" Of course," echoed Bullinger, shrinking sideways from what Furnivall might (or might not) have said.

The clock for eighty seconds ticked against a silence. Bullinger cleared his throat.

" I was thinking," he began, " that we might envisage two simultaneous courses of action. Each of these courses would go far to counter the French Note. In the first place, we might reply to René Martin by saying that we are prepared— are in fact happy—to discuss with the French Government the terms in which the Abu Saad question could be referred to the League of Nations. That, you see, cuts both ways. It might satisfy Cocquebert, and it is really quite defensible in the House. . . ."

" At which," murmured Spencer Furnivall, " Pantry would incontinently resign."

" And simultaneously," continued Bullinger, wagging a plump finger, " we should approach the Shah with a direct and remunerative offer."

" But, my dear Bullinger, if I recall your minute aright, any such overtures at Tehran might expose us to a rebuff. If I am not mistaken, you thereafter introduced that tiresome word prestige."

" Not at all," Bullinger answered. " What I wrote was ' at this stage.' That was written at luncheon. Since then we have had the French Note. That stage is no longer this stage."

" Charming," said the Prime Minister, " positively charming ! " And at that, with pointing beard, he laughed a mirthless laugh up at the ceiling.

" Of course," he continued, " I am as a child in matters of diplomacy. Yet is it customary to assure one Government that you will consult with them preparatory to submitting a dispute to Geneva, and concurrently to negotiate a direct settlement with the interested party ? "

Bullinger flushed. " It's often done," he murmured.

" Often done ! " echoed the Prime Minister, savouring that foolish phrase upon his fastidious palate.

" I thought perhaps," began Bullinger desperately —" I thought perhaps that you yourself might propose some such solution to-night in Cabinet. There might then be some chance of inducing . . ."

" No, no," said Furnivall sharply. " No, no, my dear Bullinger, that won't do at all. You can't get out of it like that, my dear fellow. This is your show, and your show it remains. They wouldn't like it in the least. Ah ! I see it's 10.20. We must join our dear colleagues. We must be getting, as you say, along."

The Prime Minister, at this, rose languidly. Languidly he shuffled off his jaeger slippers, and shuffled on a pair of pumps which lay beside the fireplace. Bullinger, his feathers ruffled, followed him along the passage. The remaining members of the Cabinet were already assembled. They took their seats. The Prime Minister called upon Bullinger to make his statement.

(5)

That was all very well. But what *was* his statement ? It had been filched from him, but four

164

minutes ago, by the sardonic beard of Spencer Furnivall. Bullinger paused, his palm resting as that of a confident statesman upon the pile of papers on his left. He was about to address the Cabinet. Ponderously his palm pressed upon the papers. And what on earth, with Furnivall smirking over there, could he find to say ?

He cleared his throat. " I should wish," he began, " at the outset . . ." he continued. And then he paused again. The door, unexpectedly, had opened. There was Hancock peering deferentially round the door. He held a red box in his hand, and he made towards Bullinger a pointing gesture of his smug face, indicating " This box is urgent, and for you." " Very well," said Bullinger, " what is it ? " Hancock advanced into the room, tip-toeing even as the verger tip-toes at evensong. He handed the box to Bullinger. It bore a special label. " Very urgent," he read, " for the S.O.S. in Cabinet."

" Excuse me a moment," muttered the Secretary of State as he fumbled for his keys. He opened the box. It contained a single telegram. He read the telegram. He read it twice. " Decypher " he read :—

" Decypher : Sir A. Yencken : Tehran
d. 11.30. p.m.⎫
r.   9.50. p.m.⎭ June 4.

Urgent and Confidential.

Minister of Court has just been to see me and has delivered following communication from Shah.

Russian Ambassador this afternoon delivered what amounts to ultimatum on concessions question. Shah is replying insisting on sovereign rights of Persia, etc., and adding that if threatened he will appeal to League. Meanwhile he wishes to 'disembarrass himself' (sic) of Abu Saad dispute. He asks whether we should be prepared to recognise Persian sovereignty over Abu Saad and agree to Morris concession being transferred to company nominally Persian but in fact under British control. Immediate reply essential.

Addressed to Foreign Office. Repeated to India and Baghdad only."

Bullinger blushed. He read the telegram a third time and then he recovered full self-possession. He replaced the telegram in its box ; he turned the lock ; he fumbled the keys back again into his trouser pocket. He then turned to his colleagues with an evangelical and apologetic smile.

" I am so sorry," he began, " an urgent telegram . . ."

And then for the third time he cleared his throat.

" As I was saying," he continued (lying), " you have all had by now a copy of the Note delivered to me this afternoon by the French Ambassador. I am sure you will agree with me that this Note is not only insolent in form, but unacceptable in substance. . . ."

Having said these words, Bullinger circled with a firm and patriotic eye the surrounding features of his colleagues. The Prime Minister, he was delighted to observe, looked a trifle surprised. Sir Charles Pantry, for his part, appeared startled. He gobbled above his high collar, " Wholly unacceptable," he gobbled, purple.

"I should therefore propose," continued Walter Bullinger, serene and dominant, "to send the French Ambassador to-night a reply which, although extremely courteous in tone, would make it abundantly clear that the question of Abu Saad is one which concerns the British and the Persian Governments alone. And I should indicate that we have already come to an agreement in the matter fully satisfactory to both parties. . . ."

"Agreement?" gobbled Pantry, voicing the general query.

The expression upon the face of the Prime Minister was more than perplexed: it was positively startled.

"Yes," continued Bullinger, endeavouring with small success to keep from his voice that note of triumph. "The Shah has offered us, and on his own initiative, an arrangement whereby we recognise Abu Saad as Persian territory, and he, in effect, confirms the Morris concession."

"But surely . . ." interrupted the Prime Minister.

Bullinger laid a solemn palm upon the box which contained the telegram. "Yes," he answered, "I have this moment received confirmation of this excellent news."

The Prime Minister flung himself back in his chair and with uplifted beard laughed soundlessly at the ceiling. And then he leant forward.

"Well," he said, "I think we may congratulate ourselves, and above all you, my dear Bullinger, that this Abu Saad crisis is now terminated."

A pleasant hum of approval spread through the Cabinet, even Sir Charles Pantry gobbled acquiescence. Bullinger, flushed, grateful, triumphant, gathered his papers together. " I must hurry," he beamed, avoiding Furnivall's eye, " I must telegraph at once to Tehran ; and then there is the reply to the French. I promised René Martin that he would have it before midnight." Bustling and evangelical he left.

It was a happy Bullinger who three hours later laid his silvery locks upon the pillow. " Providential," he murmured to himself, and then he remembered that he had forgotten to say his prayers. He knelt by the bedside. And as he did so the inner conscience rose to remind him of two highly unpleasant things :—

(1) " I have this moment received confirmation of this excellent news." That was a lie, Bullinger. It was not confirmation : it was merely the excellent news itself. And what was worse, Furnivall must have known it to be a lie.

(2) You forgot, you were frightened, to ask Pantry over what areas the ten rocket aeroplanes would experiment to-morrow. Pantry had said something about " dawn on Saturday." It is already Saturday : it is 1.0 a.m. : that trial flight will take place within less than four hours.

Bullinger, on regaining his pillow, sighed. A sigh of guilt. A sigh of apprehension.

Yet had he known how abundantly that apprehension was justified he would not have slept.

He slept.

CHAPTER VII

(1)

ARTHUR PEABODY, as we have seen, possessed a mind recipient only of the orderly and the expected. Instinctively would he close the doors of his attention against the confused, the anomalous, or the unusual. For him the current of events did in fact stream continuously between firm embankments: yet all too frequently that current was but a mirage flickering above his own arid conventionality; nor were the embankments those of actual human life: they were the embankments merely of Peabody's habituation.

His experience of public affairs had been too intimate for him to maintain his early belief that great happenings can be shaped by the will of individual men. Yet, being too vain to surrender to determinism, he had evolved for himself this comforting picture of the "current of events," feeling solaced by the compromise it offered between predestination and free will. True, he confessed, that the will of any individual cannot suffice to reverse, to retard or to hasten this current, yet the sum of many wills, a general habit of efficient conduct, can canalise the current, directing it into useful channels, correcting artificially both spate and drought.

Peabody believed in this facile little theory with that obstinate affection displayed by the unadventurous for the compromises which bring them comfort. He visualised himself as a part, as a not unimportant part, of the embankment; and with no little complacency did he welcome this his imagined function.

Had Peabody been braver, or more inquisitive, he might have learnt from the crisis of those four days that if in fact there be any current of events, it can be likened, not to the continuous streaming of a river, but to the more recondite currents of the greater seas. Shifting, discontinuous, submerged, the flux and reflux of these hidden influences veer with wind and tide; nor can the little knowledge of man suffice to foretell the force or destination of such energies.

Peabody was thus by temperament too agreeable to confess that the course of events is determined not so much by the conscious processes of human volition as by the unavowed weaknesses of human character. Had he been less preoccupied with the more pleasant, the more flattering, aspects of man's endeavour, he would have observed those eddies of chance, those swirls of foolishness, those whirlpools of inadvertence, into which his current of events had, in those first few days of June, been twisted and twirled. The central factors were stark and simple enough. Great Britain, in that she possessed a monopoly of the Abu Saad deposits, threatened to achieve a universal mastery of the air. The four Powers, acting through the Persian Government and the League of Nations, wished to deprive her of that monopoly. The issue, had it remained a straight issue, would have been one between surrender on the part of Great Britain, or resistance. Yet, as always in international affairs, the central factors ceased almost from the outset to be determinant. The current of events became deflected by chance obstacles, by tiny landslides where the embankment was weakest, by successive collapses along the line of least resistance. Observant people like René Martin or Jane Campbell saw Peabody's current of events as a stream which was rapidly being deflected from its usual course, which was already gathering an unnatural impetus, and which, if once public excitement streamed through the locks, would burst all embankments and churn into some blind cataract of destruction.

It is easy, of course, at this distance of time, to see the whole business in a correct perspective : to observe those elements of chance and weakness which, on that fourth of June, threatened to enlarge the Abu Saad dispute (in itself a problem of comparative triviality) into a world conflict : and to show how, in its subsequent development, that crisis was determined, neither by the anxious endeavours of the well-meaning, nor yet by the sinister purposes of those who thought in terms of war, but by the interaction of several human frailties, and by the intrusion of the tiny pebbles of chance.

Had Professor Narteagle, at that Cabinet meeting of April 1938, been able to state definitely whether Mr. Churchill and Lord Lympne did or did not know about the atomic bomb, it is possible that some clear-speaking might from the outset have occurred.

It was his uncertainty on this point which had edged the Cabinet into a shifty compromise between pacifism and belligerency: on the one hand they had disclaimed all moral responsibility for the bomb; on the other they had, in effect, urged Sir Charles Pantry to go ahead. The Abu Saad crisis would have arisen in any case: but it was the fact that eighteen months earlier the Cabinet had shirked the problem by adopting the most pitiable of evasions, which led them, when the crisis actually arose, to approach it with all the hesitations and half-truths of a guilty conscience; and this barrier to outspokenness had been created by the circumstance that Professor Narteagle, on that April morning, had not seen the point, and that no member of the Cabinet had possessed the bad taste to press him further.

Had the Shah of Persia, toying with amber beads among the salvias of Dilkusha, been less impressed by the genial and unwonted unanimity of the Representatives of the four Powers, he might not have conceived the fateful idea that the Abu Saad question furnished him with an occasion to obtain possession of all foreign concessions in Persia. And the issue would not have been diverted by this unforeseen complication.

Had that morning of Friday, June 3, been less radiant, had Walter Bullinger been feeling less averse from speculation, had the hand of Lady Athelhampton been less slim upon those double reins, it is possible that the Secretary of State might have evolved the heads of a policy upon his morning's ride, and have reinforced them by previous consultation with his own officials.

Had he not arrived late, flustered and unprepared at the Cabinet on Friday morning, he might have summoned courage, not merely to outline a precise policy of his own, but to cross-examine Pantry upon the immediate intentions of the Air Ministry.

Had he been less mortified by Spencer Furnivall's incivility, had he been less flustered by the Prime Minister's arrogant inhumanity at their evening interview, he would not have jumped with such impetuosity upon the Shah's offer of direct negotiation, nor have allowed himself, relying on that offer, to reply to the French Note in a manner which could only estrange the two Governments still further.

Had M. Leon Judenitch been more at his ease as a negotiator, had he been possessed of more influence with his own Cabinet, had he not been irritated by the patronising tone adopted by the German Minister, he would not have delivered to the Persian Government so crude an ultimatum, or one which was bound to fling them into the arms of Great Britain.

Had M. Hippolyte Cocquebert been less afraid of his Minister of the Colonies, had M. Raoul Thierry not been a director of the Persian Tramways Company, had François Poncet not known that by his resignation he would be abandoning the Quai d'Orsay to the gross incompetence of Mr. Dumesnil, it is probable that the French Note of June 3 would never have been despatched. Had M. Cocquebert been less preoccupied by the imminence of M. Thierry's threatened interpellation, had he troubled to read the urgent note which M. Poncet at 11.40

that next evening sent down to the Chamber, had he possessed a more personal experience of the horrors of open diplomacy, he would not, on that Friday night, have blurted out the whole story to the lobby journalists.

And had Sir Charles Pantry not been constantly humiliated by his own ungainliness in Cabinet, had he taken a less professional view of his own function, had he been a more modest and less stupid man, he would not have lent so flushed an ear to the encouragement of the F.L.N., nor have determined to keep his colleagues in the Government so unaware of his immediate intentions.

These small animosities, these trifling hesitations, these personal fears, had, by the night of June 3, altered the whole nature of the Abu Saad problem. The issue had ceased to be a straight issue : it had become entangled in the countless strands of human personality. Furnivall, Bullinger, Sir Charles Pantry, the Shah, Alexei Rubinstein, M. Cocquebert had each drifted into positions from which they could not now retreat without loss of prestige. Each of them knew that the position in which he was entrenched was a false position : each of them was determined not to admit this falsity : each of them trusted vaguely that something would occur which would render their position either triumphantly strategic, or honourably evacuable : each of them hoped that the other, at this stage, would make some glaring mistake.

Yet in fact, with each hour that passed, retreat became more difficult. The indiscretion of M. Cocquebert (pestered by lobby correspondents as

he left the Chamber) had by midnight on Friday,
June 3, rendered this conflict of private vanities
a conflict of public vanities. The great goose
patriotism had already begun its cackle. And
while Bullinger slept peacefully enough behind his
red blind in Grosvenor Gardens, the linotypes of
the Paris newspapers flicked and tinkled with high
patriotic exhortations.

(2)

" Ooooo ! " screamed M. Jules Boursicaut.
" What was that ? "

His shrill ululation reached the ears of the pilot
above the drone of the engine. The pilot paid no
attention at all. He was straining forward in the
cockpit, his eyes bulging with tense bewilderment.
There was nothing in the blue expanse of the Pas de
Calais either to be seen or heard. The thing, whatever it was—that sudden scarlet screech above them
—had come and gone. The pilot made a gesture of
hopeless amazement. M. Boursicaut looked across
at him with sick and frightened eyes. Then he had
an idea. He tore a sheet of paper from his pocket-
book, and wrote on it, in trembling block letters, the
query " Meteorite ? " He passed this note through
to the pilot. The young man read it and shrugged
with a dismissive grin. It was evident that neither
M. Boursicaut nor his suggestion had been taken
seriously.

" And yet," reflected M. Boursicaut, " it *must*
have been a meteorite. It must have been several
meteorites. They fell within a few yards of us."

At this reflection he leant back in his seat, giddy with dread of this new and supernatural addition to the horrors of aviation. " We are passing," he thought, " through a shoal of meteorites. They always go in shoals."

Jules Boursicaut prayed to God.

It was in this way that, at 8.20 a.m. on Saturday, June 4, 1939, the first of many million Europeans heard, and even saw, the rocket aeroplanes.

M. Jules Boursicaut, on his return flight to Paris, would not thus suddenly have been startled by a scarlet screech above him, had not Sir Charles Pantry believed in what he called " the moral effect." Having spent many years in the Middle and the Far East, Sir Charles had convinced himself that diplomacy is based upon prestige, and that prestige in its turn depends upon the rapidity and certainty with which one is able to inspire alarm. As an expert in aviation, he well knew that the sudden appearance of ten rocket machines would inspire a state of alarm more extensive and more acute than that created by the stratosphere aeroplanes of 1933. As a patriot, he had been incensed by the wording of the French Note on Abu Saad. As a man of action, he had felt that a little independent decisiveness on his part would strengthen what he regarded as the palsied hand of Walter Bullinger. And as a master of indirect self-advertisement, he well knew that the sensationalism of his intended action would blind the British public to its disloyalty and danger.

From the outset, as Bullinger had suspected (although too gentleman-like to voice his suspicion), Pantry had meant these trial flights to be something

of a demonstration. Yet on reading the French
Note he decided that this demonstration must be
more sensationally timed. Dawn was not the
dramatic moment for such exhibitions. And thus,
on leaving Downing Street on Friday night, Sir
Charles had crossed to the Air Ministry and telephoned to the Marden aerodrome, where the ten
rocket machines had been secretly assembled.

"Look here," he bawled down the telephone.
"On second thoughts I feel that these trial flights
would have a greater moral effect if timed to start
soon after eight, rather than at dawn. They would
thus get to Paris at about eight-thirty, to Berlin some
fifty minutes later, and be over Moscow before
eleven, or at one o'clock West Russia time. On
their return they might pass over London during
the luncheon interval. That will do for the five
which are doing the Europe trials. The three for
America should reach Lakehurst at 8.15 or so by New
York time, and be back here by 6 p.m. As regards
the two for Asia, they had better make straight for
Tokyo, but it is essential that they go round via
Cairo, Tehran, Samarcand and Bokhara. They
must be back at latest by five, as I want the complete
story to be ready for the news bulletin and the late
editions of the evening papers. And, look here,
remind the pilots that they have got to fly low, as
low as possible, over all the larger towns. Except
London, of course. Now, have you got all that?"

"O.K., Sir Charles," the voice answered from
Marden.

Pantry replaced the receiver, feeling that he had
done the State, and above all himself, some service.

In this he was mistaken. For alarm, especially
uncertain and dramatic alarm, has no sedative effect
upon Western democracies. Nor was it Jules
Boursicaut alone who, on that bright June morning,
was startled by that scarlet screech across the sky.

The Secretary-General of the French Foreign
Office, for instance, while shaving that morning in
his bathroom, leapt suddenly into the air, making at
the same instant a deep incision in his chin. He
rushed to the window. He flung it wide. The
Avenue Lyautey below him was peopled with con-
cierges and chauffeurs gazing upwards through
their own excited gestures. And even as he
watched, a dray lurched round the corner of the
Rue de la Pompe, swaying behind two panic-
stricken horses. There was no driver to be seen.
The Secretary-General returned to his bathroom and
dabbed some medicated cotton wool upon his wound.
And then he crossed to his sitting-room and telephoned to the Ministry of Aviation. The number
was engaged. It was some time before he was able
to establish contact with the Under-Secretary of
Aviation at his private house. M. Lemoine was
anything but calm. " Yes," he shouted, " of course
I heard it. The whole of Paris has heard it. The
boulevards are blocked by frightened horses, and
there have been serious accidents at the Halles.
Yes, of course it's the English, damn their souls !
It's their beastly rocket aeroplane. There must
have been four at least. And have you seen the
papers this morning ? Very opportune. Really
our friend Cocquebert has a genius for doing the
right thing at the wrong moment. Not seen them

yet? Well, my dear friend, just read the *Figaro*. I can tell you—we are in for a pretty tangle."

The Secretary-General, still pressing medicated wool to his chin, passed on into the dining-room. His coffee was not yet seated upon its little stand. But the papers were there, displayed orderly beside his plate. He seized the *Figaro*. He gasped "Our Government," he read in stream headlines, "puts England in her place."

The Secretary-General returned to the bathroom. His fingers trembled violently as he cut the court plaster to its correct shape.

Fifty minutes later, in Berlin, the German Secretary of State, who was confined to his house with earache, was drinking a belated cup of coffee. He was reading with uneasy astonishment the telegrams which had come in over-night from Paris. M. Cocquebert, it seemed, had, soon after midnight, informed the assembled journalists that he had addressed to the British Government a Note summoning them to restore Abu Saad to the Persian Government. Herr von Dieckhoff had not heard the screech in the air above him, since his ears were still stopped with medicated cotton wool. Yet at 10.15 a.m. a faint droning sound did penetrate these oil-soaked coverings—a sound as of a powerful but distant siren. "Dear me," he thought, "I am in for mastoid again. I knew it was that." And so thinking he sighed deeply and replaced his cup upon its saucer. At that very moment the door which led to the servants' quarters burst open violently, admitting Martha, his housekeeper, and Elena, his Polish cook. They waved wildly at him, and

Martha, being the more resourceful of the two, indicated by her wavings that he should remove the wadding from his ears. He did so. " Your Excellency," she screamed, " a star has fallen upon us." " Jesus," added Elena in the Posen dialect. Hearing this, Herr Dieckhoff, not without a certain dignity, rose from his breakfast table and walked into the Herrenzimmer. From there he could survey the length of the Keith Strasse. And even as he looked, a brewer's dray swung round the corner, and rocked wildly towards the Tiergarten, spilling barrels. Herr Dieckhoff, being of the calmer school of diplomacy, lit a cigarette. " It is nothing," he said to his servants—" it is only the Funkturm trying experiments with a new valve." And at that moment the telephone rang. " Hoesch here," a voice said. " That Dieckhoff? Come round at once to the Reichskanzlerpalais. Doesn't matter about your earache. That was the English."

In Moscow, one hour and forty minutes later, Alexei Rubinstein stopped with uplifted finger in the middle of dictating an interesting memorandum to his secretary, a sparse youth of Ukrainian extraction. " Stop ! " he said, and as he said this word his muscles galvanised suddenly, and the secretary observed his chief ducking suddenly, and while ducking disappear under the well of his own desk. A shrill wail passed over the Kremlin and subsided somewhere to the south. Alexei Rubinstein scrambled hurriedly from his recess. " Didn't you hear, you fool ? " he was shouting angrily. " That was a shell. A high-powered shell. They must be bombarding the Kremlin from the Sparrow Hills. Find out at once from the Commissariat of Defence."

Clutching a damp collar, the secretary hurried from the room. With shambling fingers Alexei Rubinstein turned the combination of the safe behind him. It clicked glibly and the door swung open. He extracted a small black bag, and, pressing a shaking thumb upon the spring-lock, gazed at its contents. They appeared to reassure him. There was the grey felt hat from Lincoln Bennett, the green covert coat from Burberry, the passport in the name of Arthur Robbins, the wisp of straw-coloured moustache, the bottle of hair-dye, the wad of German notes. As his secretary returned, Alexei Rubinstein placed the bag rapidly between his feet. "They think," stammered the secretary, "that it must be the English." "What English?" barked Rubinstein. "An English aeroplane, they think. One of the new sort."

The Commissar for Foreign Relations mopped his brow with a large green handkerchief. With a still trembling forefinger he dialled a number. "I want," he said, "the Embassy in London—no, you fool, I mean Berlin—yes, give me the Ambassador in Berlin—urgent."

He leant back in his chair and faced his secretary with a defiant smile. "We old campaigners . . ." he said. "Yes, it sounded just like a big shell."

"The horses," stuttered the secretary, "the horses of the Green Guard have stampeded. There have been many accidents already in the Red Square."

"Who cares about horses?" laughed Alexei Rubinstein, who at the moment was measuring distances from London to Moscow upon *The Times* Atlas. As the crow flies.

(3)

The fall of forty meteorites around him (for as such had Jules Boursicaut already formulated the passage of the rocket aeroplanes) was not the only shock to which, that June morning, the unhappy messenger of the Quai d'Orsay was exposed.

We left him leaning back in the seat of his aeroplane, clasping his portfolio tightly towards him, closing tight eyes, and praying ardently to God. He was praying for that blessed moment when five muffled bumps below him would indicate that Jules Boursicaut had once again been restored to the sacred soil of France. He would clamber busily from the aeroplane, laughing gaily at the pilot, extracting the cotton wool with which he had plugged his ears. And then rapidly, as befits a person carrying important despatches, he would walk across the trampled grass towards the official motor-car. There would be the faint smell of laburnum in the bois, the smell of watered asphalt in the Avenue Foch, the smell of beeswax as he stopped at the Ministry. And thereafter the smell of cabbage as he climbed his own staircase, the smell of coffee roasting as he opened the door of his own flat. And then Thérèse.

The picture of his wife, as viewed from the uneasy altitudes above Beauvais, did not come to Boursicaut with its usual association of anxiety and displeasure. She seemed so firm, so solid, so real. " Dear Thérèse," he murmured, his eyelids still closed tightly, the portfolio against his stomach relieving that queasy feel. " Dear Thérèse. How competent she is, how determined, how gifted ! "

At the thought of Thérèse's gifts the heart of Jules Boursicaut, for the second time in five minutes, stood stock still. It then began pounding rapidly. Boursicaut gasped.

" Great God ! " he gasped. " I have forgotten the article ! "

Unaccountably, irremediably (for was that not Beauvais swimming giddily below them ?), he had forgotten to deliver Thérèse's weekly fashion article to the *Sunday Mail*. The long envelope which contained it crackled ominously as he pressed his portfolio closer to a clammy breast. His ears, in anticipation, throbbed through the cotton wool with which he had stuffed them ; they throbbed to the anticipated screams and objurgations of Thérèse. She would strike him for this. She would take that large wooden spoon of hers and beat him with it about the head. Jules Boursicaut simply loathed being beaten by Thérèse. In the first place, it hurt. In the second place, it was unseemly, and, in a way, humiliating. The eyes of Jules Boursicaut, as he anticipated all these things, filled with tears of terror, self-pity, and remorse. It was all, he reflected, the fault of René Martin ; it was all the fault of this new pipe-smoking, grey-flannelled, slap-dash school of diplomacy. Had M. Martin, in his off-hand English way, not asked him that morning, yesterday morning, to share his breakfast : had he not forced him, with that ungainly lack of decorum, 'to take the chair opposite, then Jules 'Boursicaut would not have laid aside his portfolio upon the card-table which stood under the portrait of Maréchal Turenne. Had M. Martin been less disconcerting during the course of that now distant but highly distasteful breakfast, then Jules Boursicaut would not have omitted, when leaving, to advance in the direction of the portrait of Maréchal Turenne and to retrieve the portfolio from the card-table below it.

" You will return," the Ambassador had said as Boursicaut rose to leave, " at six this evening. I shall then be able to give you definite instructions. You must be prepared, however, to fly back to Paris at dawn to-morrow."

It was this word " dawn " which had upset M. Boursicaut, leading him to omit all recollection either of the portfolio or of Maréchal Turenne. He had had one dawn on Friday. It seemed monstrous that a second dawn, that of Saturday, should also be thrust upon him. As usual, he was being exploited, put upon, taken for granted, treated as of no account. Well—this time at least he would show them that the worm can turn : that a worm, when driven to combat in defence of human dignity, can become a python. Jules Boursicaut, descending the stair-case of the Embassy, tightened the muscles of his little back, feeling very like a python indeed.

" I'll show them . . ." he muttered fiercely as he emerged into a sun-splashed Knightsbridge.

He crossed to the Alexandra Hotel and engaged a bedroom. It was only when they murmured something about luggage that he remembered his portfolio. Yet even then he remembered it only as his luggage, as a fold of leather embarrassingly forgotten under the portrait of Maréchal Turenne. No—not again would he face the Embassy : not, at any rate, till six o'clock. He would shave: he would go to Hampton Court: he would return at five: and at six he would retrieve his portfolio, and make his stand about that dawn business. Jules Boursicaut, some two hours later, stalked amid the delphiniums rehearsing the firm, the virile words with which he would refuse to execute his instructions.

The hand of fate, that Friday evening, fixed its finger upon Jules Boursicaut, propelling him like some tiny pebble into the great wheels of history. It was in fact destined that Boursicaut should fail on Friday to deliver Thérèse's article to the *Sunday Mail*, in order that his attempt on Saturday to repair this omission might upset the calculations of three Cabinets. In saying this, we anticipate. It is necessary merely to record the fact that on his return from Hampton Court Jules Boursicaut retired to his bedroom and overslept: that it was not till 7.50 that he reached the Embassy, by which time the Ambassador had already gone out to dinner: and that it was not till 11.30 that night that Boursicaut, waiting uneasily in the hall of the Embassy, saw the great door flung open as His Excellency mounted the steps. Boursicaut rose sheepishly from his bench. An Attaché hurried up to the Ambassador with a message. "They have telephoned," he said, "from the Foreign Office. Mr. Bullinger wished you to be informed that the Cabinet have agreed upon their reply to the Note you delivered this afternoon. In the circumstances Mr. Bullinger feels that it would serve no useful purpose were Your Excellency, as suggested, to visit him at midnight. The Note will be delivered to you here in half an hour's time."

" No useful purpose . . ." murmured M. Martin. " That sounds categorical. I must telephone to Paris at once. And the British reply must be sent over to-morrow early. Ah! there you are, my dear Boursicaut. I fear that my letter and despatches will not be ready till after 1 a.m. It would be inconsiderate to keep you up as late as that and then to pack you off at dawn. No—if you leave Croydon at 7.30 and go straight to the Quai d'Orsay the despatches should be in the hands of M. Poncet by eleven at the latest. That will be time enough. Meanwhile, my poor Boursicaut, I fear you must wait. You will find a comfortable sofa in the outer chancery. I shall let you know when I am ready."

Boursicaut bowed. The Ambassador crossed the hall and entered his study. He sucked his under-lip pensively and then slowly lit a cigarette. He strolled to the telephone and called the long-distance exchange. In twelve minutes he was speaking to M. Massigli at his private house in Paris.

" Look here," he said, " I don't like the look of things over this side. I was to have seen Bullinger to-night after the Cabinet. I have just received a message telling me that he is sending the British reply round here by hand. That looks bad. I warn you that there must have been some new development, as otherwise Bullinger, who, when I saw him this afternoon, was clearly anxious, would not have cancelled our meeting. I shall send over the British reply and my own comments by air to-morrow early. They will reach you about eleven. Meanwhile, my dear Massigli, I beg you do all that is possible your end to prevent the Press from getting wind of Cocquebert's Note. He may regret tomorrow that he ever sent it : he may wish to retreat. It is absolutely essential that the terms of the communication should not be known in Paris."

"Absolutely essential," repeated M. Massigli. "I have been insisting on that for the last six hours. Yet I have failed. At this very moment, I am convinced, the admirable M. Cocquebert is telling the lobby correspondents the whole story."

"Hell!" said René Martin.

"Triple Hell!" repeated M. Massigli. "Good-night."

The British Note arrived at 11.50. M. Martin read it carefully. "There is no limit," he sighed, "to human stupidity." And then very carefully, very moderately, he wrote a long despatch explaining Bullinger and his answer away. He rang the bell. "Get this typed," he said, "for immediate signature."

It was past midnight when Jules Boursicaut was summoned to the Ambassador's study. "On arriving at Paris to-morrow," said M. Martin, "you will deliver this despatch and this letter personally to the Assistant Secretary-General, M. Massigli. I have just warned him by telephone to expect you about 11."

Jules Boursicaut bowed. "Certainly, Your Excellency." He bowed again when he reached the doorway.

"Hi! Boursicaut!" the Ambassador recalled

him. " Isn't this your portfolio ? I think you
must have have left it here this morning."

Boursicaut retrieved the portfolio and bowed
again. He was very sleepy. It was only next
morning, as we have seen, that he remembered what
the portfolio contained.

(4)

At the same moment as Jules Boursicaut (feeling
relieved at escaping from all those meteorites, feeling
anything but relieved at the prospect of an impending reunion with Thérèse) landed at Buc aerodrome,
Mr. Walter Bullinger pushed his cup of coffee
petulantly aside.

" My dear Edith," he said, " if I *wanted* a third
cup of coffee I should not hesitate to say so. You
always pester me to eat or drink things which I do
not happen to want."

" But, Walter dear, you're looking tired. Pater
is looking tired, isn't he, Jennifer ? I'm certain
these morning rides, and on an empty stomach, are
too much for you. I feel somehow that Dr.
Troutwell . . ."

Bullinger made a gesture of impatience. That
was so like Edith. She was always bothering him
to see some new doctor, and then nagging at the
treatment which the doctor prescribed. A few
months ago it had been : " What you want, pater,
is a good jogging before breakfast. You're getting
livery. One can see that with half an eye." And
now that he had obeyed her counsel the jog had
become for her a grievance, almost an enemy. She

would sit there presiding over his belated breakfast with an injured expression on her face. " Keeping pater company," she called it, and she brought her knitting-needles with her in order to jag his nerves. Why the hell should she keep him company when her own breakfast had not only been eaten but already cleared away ? And Jennifer, too, with her long straight neck and her hay-fever ? " Oh, curse ! " thought Bullinger, scraping greengage jam upon a triangular remnant of toast.

" Jennifer, dearest," said Mrs. Bullinger, " get pater another piece of toast."

" But I don't *want* another piece of toast."

" Now, Walter, don't get irritable. You always get so irritable after your morning ride. Why, you're quite flushed ! Remember you have got a Cabinet this morning at 11. Why on earth that man Furnivall should force you to attend a Cabinet on Saturday morning passes my comprehension. If you weren't all so terrified of that horrid clammy man you'd go on strike."

" There isn't a Cabinet this morning. We had it last night."

" Last night, Walter ? You never told Edith. No wonder you look tired. Jennifer ! Fetch pater another cup of coffee."

Bullinger, at that, started shouting. He yelled. And then he checked himself. A sudden, a glorious idea, had occurred to him.

" By the way," he said, " I must go down to Angley this morning."

" To *Angley* ? " Edith repeated with exaggerated astonishment. " But I thought there was some crisis on ? You told us that you would have to go to Chequers."

"The crisis is off," mumbled Bullinger. "It has been solved," he added pontifically. "It was solved last night." There was a note of defiance in his voice, since he was not himself convinced that what he said was true. Doubts had assailed him during his morning's ride. Doubts about the Shah, about Pantry, about Spencer Furnivall. Doubts, above all, regarding the wisdom of his own Note to the French Government. Assuredly he had snubbed M. Cocquebert: but was it ever a wise thing to snub a foreign politician ? Walter Bullinger confessed to himself that this snubbing business, however pleasant, might lead to reprisals. He felt, in fact, that he had done poorly at yesterday's Cabinet. He felt he needed a rest. And, after all, to-day was Saturday: to-morrow would be Sunday. Nothing much could happen over the week-end. And what he required more than anything was to be left undisturbed for a few hours: he required to *think things out*.

"Yes," he repeated, "I shall go to Angley this morning." And then with a further inspiration he added: " —and by air."

"By air ? " echoed Edith, mingling with her usual note of resigned astonishment that sharper note which meant that her astonishment was not resigned in the least.

"Yes," Bullinger answered, rising firmly from the breakfast-table, pushing back his chair with virile decision—" yes, I shall hire an air-taxi at Hanworth. I shall try to get that young pilot

Clitheroe, that nice boy who flew me to Aix that time that Furnivall got measles. I shall be at Angley before twelve. We can land in Long Meadow. Perhaps you and Jennifer could join me in the evening? You might take the 5.2 from Paddington, which will get you to Cheltenham by 7.31."

Edith gathered up her knitting with Christian resignation. "My dear Walter," she said, "one cannot really keep pace with all this continual chopping and changing. One day it's Chequers, and the next it's Aix or something. I suppose you expect me to telephone to Mrs. Bewley and tell her that you will be there for luncheon and Jennifer and I for dinner, and that everything must be in apple-pie order by the time you arrive? And only last Tuesday she wrote asking particularly that she should be given some warning if we were coming for the week-end. She meant to do the books. I told her she might."

"What books?" asked Bullinger.

"Really, Walter! The Library, of course—you know that vacuum cleaner and all those dust-sheets."

"I shan't want luncheon. I don't care a damn about the library. All I want is to get down there quickly and alone."

"Alone," he repeated with wounding emphasis. He did not slam the door. He merely shut it sharply: which, considering that his wife had neither need nor desire to remain with Jennifer in the dining-room, was an ill-mannered, unrestrained, unharrovian thing to do. Then he rang for Miss Ramsden. She was to telephone to Hanworth aerodrome and try to get hold of that young Clitheroe. In any case an air-taxi must be ready at once to land him on the Long Meadow at Angley Manor. And Jakes would be required to take him to Hanworth in five minutes.

Jubilant with liberation, he almost ran upstairs.

Dick Clitheroe, some forty minutes later, met Mr. Bullinger at the aerodrome. "Cheerio!" he said, having a liking for old Bullinger, and being by nature inclined to treat elderly gentlemen as if of his own age. "I say," he added, "that sounds a good show the Air Ministry have put up with their new rockets."

Bullinger paused. He stood still. "What show?" he blinked.

"Oh, it came through on the wireless, at 10. I thought you'd know about it, being in the Government, so to speak, and all that. Well, they made Paris in just under the half-hour, and forty minutes later they were over Berlin; they should be getting near Moscow at this minute—and back here by luncheon, mark you. Well, here's the old bus. Not much of a rocket, I fear, but I'll guarantee to get you to Angley before twelve."

Bullinger had turned pale. He stood stock still beside the aeroplane while the pilot fiddled inside with the contacts. "Paris?" he murmured, "Berlin? Moscow?" And then he smiled sarcastically. "Really," he murmured, "it was very considerate of Pantry to omit New York."

Dick Clitheroe climbed out of the aeroplane and stood beside him while the propeller raced. "And what's more," he shouted to Mr. Bullinger, adjusting his helmet, "three others have gone off to visit the Yanks. They should reach Lakehurst about two-thirty and be back in Kent by sunset."

"And New York?" muttered Mr. Bullinger to himself.

Yet none the less he followed Clitheroe as he climbed into the machine.

(5)

Jane Campbell, on that Saturday morning, woke with a sense of dissatisfaction. Her dinner with Shorland had been anything but a success. There was something wrong about that young man: even about his looks. There were moments, there were certain angles, at which, with his full lips and golden hair, he appeared to emerge integrate from a pan-athenaic festival. A sculptured effect. Yet there were other moments, other angles, at which he recalled, not the young men upon those attic friezes, but the horses with which those young men so muscularly coped. There was something about his nose, about the bone in his nose, about the set of his eye-sockets, about the splay of his nostrils, which suggested a horse.

John Shorland, when she came to think of it, was an ugly animal. And flabby.

Young men, thought Jane, who have a tendency to look like young horses should possess equine muscles. They should have short, lumpy bones. The bones of John Shorland looked long and fibrous: she feared that the calf of his leg, if viewed from behind, would wobble whitely as he walked.

These errors in drawing and construction did not count, of course, when he was a flustered, pathetic John, crumpling the *Economist* in twitching fingers. But when he became a competent, analytical John, toying with tissued toothpicks, turning them this way and that, one felt somehow that a horse should be less mental and more robust. There was about John a constant error of proportion: a lack of harmony between his loose white body and his tight red mind.

Yet, when she came to think of it, was his mind so very taut? Of course it wasn't. It was a lush mind: it ran to leaf: it was not a red mind at all, it was a green mind. It was a pompous, pontifical, sententious mind. It was a mind with great fat leaves like rhubarb, or rather gunnera. It was not a nimble mind: it was neither alert nor gay: it was a drab mind. John Shorland was drab.

"And to think," Jane snorted, "that only yesterday I imagined that I was in love with this unfortunate young man!"

Jane dabbed her nose angrily with a small powder-puff and walked briskly and emancipated into her sitting-room. She poured herself out a large cup of tea and opened the *Morning Express*. A black headline screamed at her across the central page. "France insults the British Empire." The leading article opposite was printed in heavy type with double spacing: it was headed "Hands Off!" Jane dropped the *Morning Express* hurriedly and picked up *The Times*. "M. Cocquebert's indiscretion," she read, and then more closely :—

" *Paris : midnight : by telephone.*

The President of the Council of Ministers on leaving the Chamber to-night divulged to the lobby correspondents that the French Ambassador in London has this afternoon delivered to the British Foreign Secretary a Note summoning Great Britain immediately to evacuate the island of Abu Saad and to restore it to Persia.

M. Cocquebert read to the assembled journalists a prepared statement in which he explained that France, as the second greatest Moslem Power, could not have remained indifferent to the appeal addressed to her by the Shah of Persia.

' It is time,' he said, ' that France should assume the responsibility involved upon her as the trustee of Western civilisation and as the guardian of the democratic tradition. It is not consonant with our destiny to stand aside with folded arms while yet another Islamic country falls a helpless victim to the imperialism, the cupidity, of Great Britain. Fully conscious of the grave responsibilities we are assuming, the Government over which I have the honour to preside have felt that the moment has arrived when it is incumbent upon us to call a halt. It is not an ultimatum which we have addressed to London : it is not even a menace : it is a firm and friendly warning. Nor do we stand alone. In making this gesture we are assured of the support of the Governments of Russia,

Germany and the United States as well as of the moral approval of all civilised peoples.

'Our task,' concluded M. Cocquebert, 'may be arduous and difficult: yet our duty is imperative: and our determination unflinching. At this moment there are no political parties in France: there are only Frenchmen."

Jane allowed *The Times* to drop limply from her fingers. She swallowed her tea. She drank a second cup. And then she picked up *The Times* again and turned to the leading article.

"The news," she read, "which reaches us from our Paris correspondent as we go to press. . . . It would be vain to deny. . . . Ill-timed as may seem M. Cocquebert's action, intemperate as is his language, yet full allowance should be made. . . . The British public will know, as in the past, how to temper justified indignation with needful equanimity, how to safeguard our national dignity while not . . . There are moments when it becomes necessary to face the naked facts and to state the issues bluntly, without fear or favour. Such a moment has now struck. At the risk of appearing brutal in our frankness, we feel bound to record the opinion that the situation created by the undiplomatic procedure of M. Cocquebert, although by no means critical, may yet, unless guided by moderation and firmness, lead to developments of the very gravest significance."

Jane glanced hurriedly at the clock. The hands stood at 9.50. She rang the bell. "Rose," she said, "I must get down to the office at once. Telephone for a taxi."

As she drove past Grosvenor Gardens she observed the Humber of Mr. Bullinger waiting outside No. 34. " Poor Walter ! " she thought, " this will be a blow to him. I suppose he's off to the Cabinet."

Yet in fact (as we know) the Secretary of State was not off to the Cabinet. He was off to Hanworth aerodrome. It was only when the machine was over Maidenhead that Walter Bullinger realised that he (being irritated at Edith calling him pater, saying he looked tired, pressing upon him a cup of coffee which he did not desire) had omitted to open his morning paper.

CHAPTER VIII

M. JULES BOURSICAUT reached the Quai d'Orsay
that morning at a quarter to eleven. He sprang
lightly from the car, flinging over his shoulder a
careless, and as it were accustomed order to the
chauffeur. "You will," he said, "await my
return," and having said it he bustled importantly
into the bureaux, bustling upstairs, bustling along
the corridor on the first floor. He told the huissier
at the end of the passage that he wished to see the
Assistant Secretary-General without one moment's
delay. The huissier, sitting there in his little
cubicle upon a kitchen chair, was not in the least
impressed by the bustling of Jules Boursicaut. "It
is very urgent," the latter panted, for there had
been many stairs. "I have this moment arrived
from London by air. M. Massigli will be
impatient to receive my despatches."

Slowly the huissier took off his pince-nez, placing
them in a soft leather case. Carefully he slid the
case into the top left-hand pocket of his waistcoat,
glancing downwards to make certain that it was
safe. With great deliberation he folded the *Petit
Parisien* and rising rheumatically laid it upon his
seat. And then with aching steps he slouched
along the corridor, entering the fourth door on the
right. In a few seconds he again emerged and

holding the door open behind him made with his chin an upward movement in the direction of Jules Boursicaut. Clasping his portfolio tightly, Boursicaut hurried in.

" Ah ! " exclaimed M. Massigli, leaning back at his writing-table. " There you are, my good Boursicaut ! I have been awaiting you anxiously. You have the despatches ? "

Jules Boursicaut opened his portfolio and extracted from it reverently a slim canvas bag attached to a large label and many scarlet seals. M. Massigli reached forward for a desk-knife and slit the strings around the neck of the bag, placing the released label carefully upon the pen-tray. He then pulled out the two envelopes and placed them side by side. " Your receipt-form, my good Boursicaut ? " And as he signed the receipt the Assistant Secretary-General stretched out his left hand for one of his many telephones. He asked to be placed in communication with M. de Margerie, the Chef de Cabinet. " Is that you, Roland ? " he said. " Massigli here. The London despatches have this moment arrived. You might come up for a few minutes. What ? Oh, I see ! Very well, I'll bring them downstairs at once."

M. Massigli gathered up the two envelopes and was about to hurry from the room when his kindly eye fell on the humble waiting figure of Jules Boursicaut. He paused for a moment, tapping his teeth with the desk-knife which he still held in his hand.

" My poor Boursicaut," he smiled, " I fear that I must ask you to wait for a few minutes. We are in full crisis. The Minister has just arrived, and wishes to see these despatches immediately. There may be further instructions. I very much fear, my poor Boursicaut, that you may have to fly back to London within the hour. I will leave word that your car and aeroplane must remain in readiness."

At that he indicated politely a hard Empire settee by the window. Clearly it was upon that settee that Jules Boursicaut was expected to wait. Breakfastless. Placing his bowler upon a file of the *Moniteur Officiel*, he sat down. He waited. The idea occurred to him that it might be tactful to employ these leisure moments in talking to Thérèse: she might be anxious: she would certainly be anxious about her manuscript for the *Sunday Mail*. Yet which of those four telephones communicated with the outside world? And was it in any case fitting that he, a mere courier, should use one of the telephones of the Assistant Secretary-General? Jules Boursicaut decided that it would be more fitting just to sit and wait. He sat. He waited. And then suddenly he had an idea. " If," he thought to himself, " they really send me back to London this morning I shall certainly be sick. Yet, on the other hand, I shall just have time to deliver Thérèse's article to the newspaper. If I get it to them by six this evening that will be time enough." Boursicaut, on achieving this calculation, felt relieved.

Meanwhile, in the high study of the Minister for Foreign Affairs, the Secretary-General, M. Léger the Directeur Politique, and M. de Margerie the Chef de Cabinet, had gathered to assist M. François

Poncet in grappling with what had by then become a highly intricate predicament. Lavish royalist tapestries, framed in the carved oak of the Third Republic, soared above them: the Savonnerie carpet was soft about their feet: the windows stood open to the garden terrace, and the faint splutter of a hose sprinkling the syringa mingled refreshingly with the silk and ormolu of the room.

M. François Poncet, the Foreign Secretary, was leaning back in his high chair as Massigli entered, and on his handsome face was an expression of righteous indignation. His advisers, deferential and troubled, clustered around him.

M. Massigli, as is the convention in the French foreign service, advanced towards his chief and shook him warmly by the hand.

" My dear Massigli," sighed M. François Poncet, " here's a nice kettle of fish! Let us at least be frank among ourselves. Let us admit from the outset that the intervention of the President of the Council in this unhappy affair has placed us all in an impossible position. Yes," he continued, leaning forward and rapping at his desk with a malachite letter-weight—" yes, that charming M. Cocquebert has, for you will excuse the word, bitched the whole business. Bitched it completely," repeated M. François Poncet, rapping sharply upon his table with the letter-weight.

M. Massigli, being a Normalien, had a weakness for categories. " Primo," he began, " Monsieur le Ministre . . ."

" In the first place," interrupted M. François Poncet with some asperity, " it was unwise of

M. Cocquebert to insist, against our expert advice, upon sending such a Note to London. In the second place, having sent such a Note, it was idiotic of him to have divulged the fact before the British Government had had time to reply. And in the third place, it was criminal,—yes, criminal—to have made this appalling indiscretion without troubling to read the urgent memorandum which I sent down to him at the Chamber. Had he read my memorandum, he would have learnt that the Russian Government had broken our united front and were about to invade Persia on their own. He would not then have talked so big about our responsibilities as a great Moslem Power, about our guardianship—great God!—of democratic tradition. . . . Excuse me, gentlemen, but there are some things which even a politician finds it difficult to endure. Yet I ask you—in the whole history of France can you recall a single instance of such reckless idiocy, such insane egoism?"

M. Poncet, at that, raised helpless hands towards the smiling figure of Henri Quatre, who, across the tapestry to his left, flaunted a gay, blue-scarved assurance in marked contrast to the black perplexity of M. François Poncet, to the drab silence of the officials by whom he was surrounded.

It was M. Massigli who broke the silence.

" Monsieur le Ministre," he said, " the messenger has just arrived from London bringing the text of the British reply. . . ."

" The British reply?" snorted M. Poncet. " We have all heard that reply this morning. The whole of Paris from Ménilmontant to Neuilly knows of that reply. The reply of the British Government to the idiotic gesture of M. Cocquebert was to send their rocket aeroplanes screaming above the chimney-tops of Paris. And mark you, gentlemen, the next time they come . . ."

M. Léger broke tactfully upon the Minister's monologue.

" Monsieur le Ministre," he said, " allow me to remind you that the Council of Ministers is to meet in twenty minutes. Will you allow me meanwhile to read to you a short summary which I have prepared of the messages received this morning ? "

M. François Poncet made a gesture indicating that he was prepared for anything.

" From Tehran," began M. Léger, reading in that aloof voice adopted by professional diplomatists who indulge in the craft of letters—" from Tehran we hear that the Minister of Court, on receiving the Russian ultimatum, was closeted for two hours with the Shah and then drove straight to the British Legation. It is surmised by our Minister that the Persian Government may already have concluded with Great Britain an agreement to settle the Abu Saad question, so to speak, out of court."

" Capital ! " snorted M. Poncet, with embittered irony. He had risen from the table and was pacing the room, still clutching a malachite paperweight in indignant hands.

" From Moscow," M. Léger continued pacifically, " we hear that three gunboats left Baku last night and should by now be off the Persian port of Pahlevi."

" Excellent ! "

" Our Embassy in London have telephoned to say that the English papers, of whatever shade of opinion, have reproduced M. Cocquebert's statement in a most sensational form. The editorial comments are, without exception, unfavourable, the general tenour being that French intervention is dictated solely by a desire to inflict humiliation on the British Empire."

" Superb ! "

" Our Embassy in Berlin has just telephoned to say that at 9.30 this morning a fleet of British rocket aeroplanes swept over the city from west to east. The German Cabinet has since then been in continuous session."

" Charming ! "

" The *Île de France*, now two days out from New York, has wirelessed that she encountered three or possibly four British rockets at dawn this morning obviously bound for Lakehurst."

" Splendid ! "

" A communication was received by post this morning from Geneva stating that the Secretary-General, at the urgent request of the Persian Government, had placed the Abu Saad question as the first item for consideration at the Council meeting on June 11."

" Ha ! ha ! Good ! Very good indeed that last bit. . . ."

The full irony of M. Poncet's laughter was curtailed by the hurried opening of the door opposite. M. Poncet paused. An attaché entered, bowed awkwardly to the Minister, and handed a strip of paper to M. Léger. The latter read it, and looked startled.

"A telephone message," he said, "at this moment received from London. It seems that Mr. Bullinger, the Foreign Secretary, has just left the capital by air for an unknown destination. . . ."

M. Poncet, at that, flung his letter-weight with a crash upon the table.

"Now that," he shouted, "is the last straw—positively the last. I am not responsible for this dreadful situation. The Note was despatched against my urgent advice. I shall no longer assist Cocquebert in disentangling this unhappy country from the morass into which he has led us. Gentlemen, I now leave you. I leave you for the purpose of once again handing to M. Hippolyte Cocquebert, President of the Council of Ministers, my resignation from a post which by his idiocy he has rendered untenable. There is a point, a limit beyond which . . ."

"Monsieur le Ministre . . ." they protested in chorus, knowing full well that it was far too late for M. Poncet to resign. Yet the Minister had already stalked indignant from the room.

M. Massigli picked up the two envelopes and handed them to M. Léger. "I suppose," he said, "that Boursicaut, the London messenger, had better wait."

"Certainly," Léger replied. "He will have to fly back to London within the next two hours."

(2)

Dick Clitheroe swung his aeroplane into a perfect landing upon Long Meadow. He turned round and laughed at Walter Bullinger as the propeller slowed to silence. He looked at his wrist-watch. It was eleven-forty.

"Pretty neat that," he laughed, "for a two-year-old! Or not?"

Mr. Bullinger, whose ears were still throbbing from the drone of the engine, caught little more than the purport of this remark. He smiled in response. Assuredly Dick Clitheroe was a charming young man.

They walked together across the meadow to where the neo-Elizabethan chimneys of Angley Manor showed straight and orange above the elms. They entered the shrubberies through the wicket gate, and emerged upon a sun-drenched lawn.

"I should like," said Bullinger, "to ask you to stay for luncheon. I should like that very much: my wife won't be here till eight. Yet, in the first place, there may be no luncheon. And, in the second place, I have got to work."

"That's all right," laughed Clitheroe. "I shall fly the old bus back to Hanworth. But I could do with a drink."

"You may have a drink," chuckled a truant and, as such, boyish Secretary of State—"you may, in fact, have several drinks."

They walked across the lawn, Clitheroe swinging his leather helmet by the chin-strap, Bullinger darting happy eyes to right and left. Yes, Pearl Queen was doing splendidly this year, and even Excelsior had consented to flower. The *Hyacinthus candicans* (how obstinate Edith had been about them—said she hated white) were showing clustered

206

lily-of-the-valley leaves. The agapanthus in the terrace tubs had already thrust thin flower-stalks above their floppy leaves, each stalk bearing a green ace of spades. That would mean blue splodges upon the terrace in July. Tapping with his truss of keys upon the French window of the morning-room, Walter Bullinger felt warm and comradely towards the agapanthus.

Lypiatt, sedate upon the parquet, appeared. A welcoming but not a very genial smile spread across his features. Evidently the household had been much disturbed. There was a moment of suspense while Lypiatt slid the little bolts which secured the French window.

" How are you, Lypiatt ? " asked Bullinger, anxious to appease.

" Very well, sir, thank you. There have been several 'phone messages during the last hour. The Prime Minister, sir, he telephoned himself, asking what time you were due to arrive. And would you ring him up ? Very anxious he seemed, sir, if I may say so. Then the Foreign Office have been on the 'phone almost continuous. And the news-papers. I took it on myself to inform the latter that your destination was unknown. They were most insistent."

" Splendid, Lypiatt, very good indeed. Now look here. Mr. Clitheroe, who has just flown me here from Hanworth, wants a drink. See to it that he has everything he requires. As for myself, I have some urgent work to do, and must be left completely undisturbed. I shall go down to the wood, probably, but in any case I shall not be available to anyone. If the Prime Minister telephones again tell him—yes, tell him that I have not yet arrived. Say the same to everyone. Let's see —it's now getting on for twelve. I shall be back here at one. I shall go down to the wood. Well, I shall say good-bye, Clitheroe, and many thanks for a superb flight. I am sure Lypiatt will give you all you need. Oh, yes, Lypiatt, I should like to take the morning papers down with me to the wood. I left in such a hurry this morning that I forgot . . ."

"Very sorry, sir, but there ain't no papers, not so to speak."

"What do you mean, Lypiatt—no papers?"

"Well, sir, Mrs. Bullinger gave instructions that when the family were in London . . . Of course there's cook, sir: she has her *Morning Mirror* regular . . ."

Bullinger made a gesture of impatience. "Doesn't matter," he added; "but send the hall boy down to the village to get a full batch of papers. I shall read them at luncheon."

With a friendly wave at Clitheroe, the Secretary of State retreated backwards across the lawn. He disappeared behind the rhododendrons. "How like Edith," he was thinking, "to stop the papers when we are away for a few weeks! A small mind, I fear, and economical. Edith has a penurious soul."

Bullinger had said to Lypiatt that he was going to the wood. That was a lie. He knew very well, even as he said it, that he had no intention of going to the wood. He was going to the island, that hidden sanctuary where he had sulked so often as a boy. Still holding in his hand the truss of keys with which he had tapped upon the French window, Bullinger strode happily down the nut-walk towards the lake. He allowed the truss to splay itself open on his palm, and then with the thumb and fore-finger of his left hand he pounced upon the key of the boathouse. A stubby little key, treasured always as perhaps the shyest of Bullinger's secret intimacies.

As he turned the corner by the silver birches the surface of the lower lake shone below him flattened by the saucer leaves of lilies. The sound of the sluice reached his ears. He started running: he panted slightly as he fitted the key into the padlock. The familiar smell of the boat-house creaked open as he swung the door: cool shades of brown and green. The punt, as he pushed hard with the paddle against the slats of the surround, shot gurg-ling into sunshine and water-lilies. Bullinger laid down the paddle and took off his coat. He flung the coat negligently towards the bow of the punt. He sat at the stern and began to paddle. Then he clambered forward again: holding the collar of his coat in his teeth, he fumbled, as if in someone else's pockets, for tobacco and a pipe. The punt, meanwhile, was swinging sideways towards a large yellow lily. Walter Bullinger regained the stern and with a touch of the paddle headed for the island. There, at the place he landed, was the old stump which, thirty-six years ago, he had hammered in with a croquet mallet. He remembered also (it must have been the next holidays) nailing on to that stump a little aluminium name-plate which he had stamped at a station automatic machine. "Walter Bullinger," he had stamped. Rather German it had looked at the time, the letters being all the same height and shape. He searched for it on the now-decaying stump. A small section only remained. "Walte . . ." he read. The rest had fallen off and been submerged. Submerged in public life.

In this truncated fashion did the Secretary of State re-establish contact with himself at seventeen.

He hid the punt among the flowering rush: the poplars rustled above him. He stepped on to the island. A moorhen cluttered off, trailing a straight, splashed line towards the further bank. A little grebe, delicate mother, fluttered around anxiously, diving and lapping round her tiny brood. "*Podicipes fluviatilis*," murmured Walter, having been a bird-snob as a boy. He scrunched on towards the centre of the island, where there was a clearing with two silver birches and a marooned clump of bracken. The bracken was fresh and sticky to the touch. He dropped his coat upon it and lay down: he joined his hands behind the nape of his neck: he looked up through poplars to the sky above. And what on earth had he done to himself in those all-but forty years?

How pleased father would have been! How wrong his father always was! Wrong about life, and what enjoyment was, and what was pleasure. "Walter," mother would say, "Walter, dearest, are you sure that you are not just pretending?"

"Are you quite, quite sure?"

That was the worst of it. He was never sure:
never quite, quite sure.

Was he sure, for instance, about the crisis?
Not think about the crisis. Was he sure, was he
quite, quite sure, about Edith? No, not think
about Edith. Was he sure of anything except that
he lay there, aged fifty-three, as he had lain, a limber
figure, at the age of seventeen? Giddily, with half-
closed eyes, he felt himself upon a pinnacle of time.
He looked behind him. The sharp smell of
bracken filled his nostrils with the smell of boy-
hood. How recent it all was! As if Monday or
Thursday last. Yet, in between, such a lot of
other things had happened. There had been
Edith. How peaked she looked the night that
Jennifer was born! The poplars rustled slumber-
ously. And that man at Havre during the war
who called him " Bullwinkle "—" Bullwinkle, my
dear sir, are you quite sure, my dear sir? " " Are
you quite sure, Bullwinkle, that you are not just
pretending? " Then the division bell echoed out
across the Terrace. " My dear lady, I fear I must
leave you for a moment.—Tony, help yourself to
strawberries. Yes, I'm coming, I'm coming."
Hurrying to early school: the dinner-bell; quick
or I shall be late for chapel. . . .

Bullinger woke with a start. It *was* a bell.
The Secretary of State roused himself stiffly and
creeping to the edge of the island peeped between
the willows. Lypiatt was hurrying like a black
retriever along the bank, ringing a large hand-bell.
" Sir! " he shouted at intervals. " Sir! sir! "

" What," thought Bullinger, " a silly sort of

shout!" And then he sighed. "That means I'm wanted. That means I've been caught."

Slowly he crunched back through the willow shoots and released the punt. He put on his coat again, tugging tidily. Slowly he pushed off from the island and paddled towards the bank.

So this was the end of his escape? How odd, always, was this mystery of displacement. He had been in London, in the dining-room: he was now at Angley, on the lake. Two completely different places. Yet he had brought himself with him. The same self. The same walls and furniture and ceiling. The same unhappiness. The same incessant worry.

How unaccountable, for instance, was the fact that he had flown to Angley! Edith had pressed upon him a third cup of coffee, and a hurricane had risen, whirling him like a feather towards the island. Furnivall would not understand that sort of thing. Even Jane, who sympathised, would find it difficult to explain. There was, in fact, nothing about it which was even vaguely explicable. He would not endeavour to explain. A sad silence, lit by a smile of inner justification—that would be the attitude to adopt. It was not an easy attitude, but he would adopt it.

Lypiatt observed his master when the latter was half-way across the lake. Still ringing the hand-bell, he hurried towards the boathouse.

"Oh, sir!" he panted, "there's an aeroplane arrived, and one of those Foreign Office gentlemen, and three motor-cars, sir, with Press reporters; and the 'phone, sir, has been something chronic."

"Very well," said Bullinger, "I can come now."

He felt different. He felt younger. Whatever happened now, he would no longer pretend.

(3)

On reaching the Foreign Office, Jane Campbell, without taking off her hat, walked straight to the Private Secretaries' room. What did it matter now? John Shorland was now no more to her than a young man with a face like a horse. She was glad in a way—no, she was glad in *every* way—that the Private Secretaries' room had become for her of no more importance than any other room in the office. Just a room it was : a room containing two civil servants, Peabody and Shorland : a room where one obtained necessary information.

"Good-morning, Mr. Peabody!"—she entered briskly, swinging her hips a little with what Shorland had once called her girl-guide gait—"Good-morning, John. Is the Secretary of State coming straight here, or has he gone to No. 10? I passed his car in Grosvenor Gardens."

Peabody advanced towards her with his wonted alacrity.

"Good-morning, Miss Campbell; we're early to-day. Have you ever seen anything so absurd as this morning's papers? One would imagine that we were on the brink of war. Though I must say that *The Times* . . ."

"But we *are* on the brink of war, Mr. Peabody, that's the whole point."

" My dear Miss Campbell, really . . ."

Shorland was telephoning to Paris. He held up a pencil as a warning that they should cease their chatter. He was holding the receiver in his left hand, and scribbling notes on the blotting-paper. " Yes," he was saying, " yes, got that : yes. For God's sake man, hurry up ! don't be so slow about it."

He put down the receiver and looked at Jane.

" Those damned rockets," he said, " seem to have frightened the Parisians out of their wits."

" What rockets ? " said Jane : she was thinking that his eyes were very straight eyes : blue lances : not equine at all.

" Why, Pantry's rockets, of course. Is it conceivable that in this year 1939 an old crook like that can still bluff and . . ."

The telephone shrilled again.

" Yes, yes ! " Shorland answered impatiently. His indignation with the Air Minister transferred itself to the young lady at the exchange. " Yes, I'll hold on . . ."

He raised the receiver at them. " Berlin," he said. He transferred the receiver to his left hand and picked up his pencil.

" Yes, yes. Shorland here. Yes, Patrick, of course I can hear you. What's it all about ? No, he's not here yet. Expect him any moment. How's that ? Oh, yes, the rockets. How many ? You couldn't see. Exact time ? 10.15 or 20, Berlin time. That makes 9.15 here. Yes, there seems to have been some sort of panic in Paris also. Yes, of course I'll tell him. But he's not here yet. Not *here*, h-e-r-e. Got that? Right! I may ring you up later."

Shorland slammed the receiver back upon its ebony stand.

"This telephone business," he said, "is becoming a curse. Instead of sending telegrams or even messages to the Communications Department in the ordinary way, these lousy Embassies have developed a habit of telephoning to you or me. It gives them a sense of personal contact with the Secretary of State. By the way, where is our beloved Bullinger this morning? I should have imagined that with all this splash in the papers he would have hurried here by half-past nine. Talking of splash, incidentally the Pantry rockets have reached Berlin. They'll be in Moscow before the morning's out. Now how on earth a Cabinet composed of people who, though not very bright in the head, are at least educated, can at least read and write—how they could have allowed that old crook . . ."

The telephone rang again.

"Yes, yes," said Shorland. "Private Secretary F.O. here. No, he hasn't come yet. We expect him at any moment. No, I shouldn't do that. He's probably left already——" He glanced at Jane, who nodded confirmatively—"Yes, he must have left Grosvenor Gardens some five—ten minutes ago. Yes, I'll tell him to ring up the Prime Minister the moment he gets in. Right!"

"You know, Jane," Shorland resumed, "I believe that old pig Pantry has played the dirty on them. I can't conceive that a man like Bullinger, who, with all his flabbiness, is a decent old codger . . ."

Again the bell shrilled.

"Yes," said Shorland, "Private Secretary F.O. speaking. Oh, it's for you, Peabody. Why can't the exchange put your calls through to your own telephone? It's for you—German Embassy."

He rose, leaving the receiver lying on its side. He walked to where Jane was standing by the window.

"Yes," Peabody was saying, "I should love to. Where did you say? Right! St. James's at 1.30. Thank you, my dear Kleinroth."

Shorland was disagreeing with Jane's suggestion that he should at once telephone to Grosvenor Gardens to find out about Bullinger. He disliked warm telephone receivers. "Give him five more minutes," he said.

"But he *ought* to be here," Jane insisted, tapping with an impatient toe. "It looks so odd."

John Shorland strolled slowly to his desk. He picked up the receiver. "Get me," he said, "the Secretary of State's private house."

"Of course," he said, turning to Jane, "he may have dropped in at the French Embassy on his way here. You know how pally he is with René Martin." The bell rang.

"Is that Grosvenor Gardens? Private Secretary Foreign Office here. Has Mr. Bullinger left yet? Oh, he has? About twenty minutes ago? Was he coming straight here or to Downing Street? What? Say that again. Hanwell? The asylum?

Hanworth? Oh, yes, of course. To Angley, did you say? But it isn't possible. Here, hold on a second! Oh, damn! they've rung off."

"Jane," he said, "the Secretary of State has bolted. He's bolted by aeroplane to that ghastly house of his at Cheltenham. Now what on earth possessed him to do that?"

Jane's nose twitched violently. She walked rapidly to the telephone. "Exchange," she said, "Miss Campbell here. I want to talk to Mrs. Bullinger at the Secretary of State's private house. I want to speak to her personally."

"He must have gone off his chump," said Shorland, "complete nervous collapse."

"Not in the least," snapped Peabody. "I fully see his point. It's you people who are creating the artificial atmosphere of panic and sensation."

"Halloa!" said Jane, who had again grasped the telephone. "Halloa! Oh, is that you, Edith? Jane Campbell here. Look here, it isn't really a fact that Walter has flown down to Angley? . . . But what on earth possessed him? He must be got back at once. Why *shouldn't* he? But, my dear Edith, haven't you seen the papers? This French Note. No, Edith, not boat—Note. It's been published. . . . He said it was solved, did he? But that's impossible; he can't have thought that when he read the papers this morning. . . . You mean he didn't? Are you sure of that? But how unlike him! He's all right, isn't he? I mean he's perfectly well . . . ?"

Jane's voice trailed off into conventional civilities. She banged down the receiver.

"Look here," she said, "you two. This is awful. The Secretary of State at breakfast this morning conceived the sudden whim to fly down to Angley. He drove to Hanworth. But the point is that before leaving he never read the papers. He thinks, or pretends to think, that the whole show was over the moment the Shah offered us a direct settlement. He doesn't know about Cocquebert's statement to the journalists. He doesn't know about the rockets. Look here, John, we must catch him at once at Angley and bring him back. Get hold of a machine—the Air Ministry will give you one—and fly at once to Angley. You can land on that large meadow to the north of the house. Meanwhile you and I, Mr. Peabody, have got to hold the fort. No, this is anything but a joke. Walter's whole position is at stake. And far more than that. Good God! Mr. Peabody, don't look like that; surely you realise now that every second counts?"

Shorland was already at the telephone. "I want the Air Ministry, urgent," he said. Jane was at the other desk and had taken Peabody's receiver off its stand. "I want the Prime Minister," she said. "Miss Campbell speaking."

"Air Ministry?" said Shorland. "Private Secretary F.O. speaking. Give me Commodore Christie. Well, I'm afraid you must cut in—this is very urgent. That you, Christie? Shorland here. Sorry to cut in. Look here, our Secretary of State has flown to Cheltenham. I've got to get him back here before two. Can I have a service machine? I shall have to fly the old man back, you understand. That all right? Splendid! Yes, I shall be there in twenty minutes."

"Oh, Mr. Furnivall," said Jane, in her brightest, happiest voice, "Walter asked me to get into touch with you the first thing this morning, but I have been so terribly rushed. I am so sorry. We all thought last night that it would be a good thing if at this moment he pretended to leave London. It will reassure opinion here if they know that he has left for his usual week-end. People abroad will not believe this, and will be puzzled by his disappearance. It will be a good thing to give them something to puzzle over during the next few hours. Far-fetched, you think? Oh, surely not, Mr. Furnivall—yes, I know we should have consulted you, but there was so little time. In any case he will be back here by two or so. Yes, of course you can telephone. He should reach Angley in about half an hour from now. Cheltenham 58, the number is. Oh, not at all, Mr. Furnivall—I am only sorry that I did not explain earlier; you must have been at a complete loss to understand. Oh, not at all. . . ."

Jane sighed deeply. "God!" she said to Shorland, "what lies one has to tell!"

Shorland seized his hat, a red box, a file of telegrams, and a notebook containing material for an article he was writing on the geography of Pytheas. Peabody, feeling ignored yet olympian, passed into the stenographer's room holding some letters in his hand. John hesitated at the doorway. Jane was standing by the window. He walked quickly across the room and seized her by the shoulders. His fingers gripped her as if ten points of steel: he shook her. "Jane," he said, "you are magnificent!" And then he kissed her very hard. The door slammed behind him.

Jane returned to the telephone. "News Department," she said. It was absurd, he wasn't flabby in the least. She could still feel ten fingers upon her shoulders: there would be a bruise. "Oh, is that you, Mr. Crossland? Jane Campbell speaking. Look here, the Secretary of State has staged a diplomatic absence. You'd better put out two messages ten minutes between each. First let the foreign correspondents know that the Secretary of State left Hanworth by air this morning, but that you have as yet no conception where he has gone. Then wait ten minutes—no, better wait twenty minutes—and put out another message, this time for our own Press. Say that the Secretary of State left Hanworth this morning for his usual week-end at Angley Manor near Cheltenham. Neither must be official statements, of course—just indications. Yes—of course I will. I'll shoulder any responsibility that may arise."

And how fantastic to have thought him like a horse!

"Exchange, Miss Campbell speaking. I want you to put through a call every ten minutes to Angley Manor, where the Secretary of State should shortly be arriving. Cheltenham 58, the number is. I must talk to Mr. Bullinger the very moment he arrives."

(4)

A little lever among the great greased cogs of Big Ben clicked suddenly, and dropped. A wheel to the left spun glistening into hurried motion. The four heavy clappers jerked outwards, a jerk a second, till they reached their fullest span. Then one after the other they swooped upon the wincing bronze, pounding sixteen times. A bruised silence followed, pierced by the scream of gulls. And through the drifting echoes of that prelude thundered the twelve deep notes of noon.

"Pass along, please! Pass along there, *if* you please!" The patient voices of policemen rose above the heavy shuffle of the crowds. Restless and slow-moving, a double tide lapped along White-hall, checking at the iron gates which barred the entrance to Downing Street, checking again by the garden railings in front of the Air Ministry, sending out a sparse runnel through King Street and under the Horse Guards Arch, massing in a black pool against the courtyard of St. Stephen's. Silent was the crowd, impelled by dumb curiosity, moving to the slow impulse of a general surmise. Against this shambling monotone, isolated noises detached themselves in sharp precision. A man leaning against the wall of the Home Office coughed rasp-ingly. The cry of a child. The laughter of a group of students darting in and out of the slow mass like gnats above an evening pool. The cry of a hawker selling paper flags: "Union Jacks a penny! Union Jacks a penny!" The noise of gears grating as the three-decked buses lumbered from the pavement. "Pass along, please! Pass along there, *if* you please!"

The yellow vans of the Federation of London Newspapers flashed and swung in and out of the slower traffic. Impatiently they would pause by the curb, and a bundle of papers would be flung to the expectant street-seller, wrapped in their own poster. Never, since the days of the Egyptian crisis, had the Federation of London Newspapers had such a bumper morning. The great engines of the F.L.N. (inappropriate in their steel dignity to the hourly foam which they produced) rose and fell, rose and fell. Edition after edition slid down the steel shoots to the waiting vans. With thick black pencils the sub-editors, sipping whisky, heightened the tone of their posters as the temperature rose. "R.A.F. Sensation" had been succeeded at 10.5 by "Pantry answers the French." At 10.15 had come "Panic over Paris," and at 10.30 "Rockets reach Berlin." "The Now to Moscow" of 10.40 was succeeded by the "New York Next" of 10.45. At 10.50 a more raucous note crept into their exclamations. "What about Europe Now?" flamed across London, to be supplanted by 11.10 by "Europe Trembles." At 11.20 the vans had run out, and forty lorries from Carter Paterson were urgently engaged. The sub-editors, in a fever of patriotic effort, slashed and scribbled. The accountants' department rushed from their desks and guided by the Assistant Circulation Manager manned the lorries. A touch of realism, of British common sense, was struck at 11.40 by "Rockets Latest" followed by "And

Still We Go On." Feverishly the latter were scrapped at 12.5 by " Foreign Secretary. Sensation," and by the more explicit poster of 12.40 " Bullinger Disappears." The crowd, being accustomed to the hysterics of the F.L.N., received these exhortations calmly. Silently they slouched along Whitehall.

Mr. Bullinger, at the time, was passing, captured, over Wallingford. The Thames below him shone like an eel. He was reading the messages which Shorland had brought him. He felt suspended, cool, detached. That to the left, there, must be Chequers : yes, there was the rose-garden. Bullinger smiled grimly. No, whatever Furnivall might indicate, he would refuse to resign. He was flying to London to prevent a war. That drone around him was an insistent reminder that it rested with him to prevent the atomic bomb. Bullinger felt uplifted, confident, secure. He placed his hand upon Shorland's knee : he wished to assure that troubled young man that his chief possessed a sense of mastery. Shorland looked embarrassed. " Quite certainly," he thought, " the old man is off his chump." Bullinger smiled : shyly.

Herr von Dieckhoff emerged into the Wilhelmstrasse with an anxious expression on his face. It had not been a satisfactory Council, it had been indeterminate and vague. The Minister of Defence had obviously not wished to disclose to his civilian colleagues the full measure of his own knowledge. He had suggested that a Committee of Three should be appointed to consider the situation.

" There are certain facts," he said, " which to so large an assembly I am unable to disclose." That had sounded not rude merely, but ominous. Herr von Dieckhoff decided that he would lunch at Pelzer before returning to the Ministry. The Chancellor, the Foreign Secretary and the Minister of Defence had remained behind in the Reichskanzler-palais. " This," thought Herr von Dieckhoff, " is the sort of thing which happened in July 1914."

Alexei Rubinstein was again attempting to tele-phone to Baku. It was very difficult. He had said that in no circumstances must the gunboats open fire upon the port of Pahlevi without provoca-tion. The commandant at Baku had been slow at the uptake. " Openly ? " he had said. " No," Rubinstein had shouted, " open fire." " At once ? " the Commandant had enquired. " No," yelled Rubinstein, " *not* open fire." " Then open what ? " the Commandant had bleated on. The conversa-tion ended without mutual esteem or understanding having been established.

M. Hippolyte Cocquebert, for his part, was striding up and down the room, emitting the words " Sacred Blue ! " Never had he attended so venom-ous a meeting of the Council of Ministers. M. Poncet had been worse than patronising : he had been rude : he had actually offered to resign : it had taken the united efforts of M. Cocquebert and the Minister of Ways and Communications to in-duce him to withdraw that decision. M. Cocque-bert felt personally injured. It had all been most unfair. How could he explain to the Cabinet what Raoul Thierry had threatened, what he in his turn

had said to Raoul Thierry? How could he explain
to them that M. Paul Sebire had confessed to Madame
de Juvenel that if he succeeded in ousting Cocquebert he would " settle the Tunis question once and
for all " ? How could he divulge that, on Thursday
last, when the Note to London had been at last
accepted, he had overheard Poncet say to Leger,
" Well, after all, it doesn't matter much, we can
always get Martin to explain that it isn't serious,
that it's merely a sudden whim of our dear friend
Cocquebert " ? How could he convince them that
his indiscretion to the journalists had for this reason
been the most calculated indiscretion which he had
ever made ? How could he assure those glum faces
that he, Hippolyte Cocquebert, simply loathed
foreign affairs and had wanted only to keep Sebire
out, and to prevent a war with two, if not three of
the Italian Republics ? It was unfair. It was
worse than unfair : it was dangerous. Yet—and
that was something—M. Thierry could scarcely put
his question now.

At Tehran, that afternoon, the thermometer,
though it was 5.30 p.m., stood at 104° in the shade.
The sky spread white and merciless above that tawny
upland : even the shadows—and there were few of
them—assumed the colour of dust. The lizards
up at Shimran flickered dustily across the parched
stones of the river-beds : and in the town itself the
large leaves of the plane-trees dropped one by one,
now upon a burning roof of corrugated iron, now
upon some petroleum tins abandoned beside an
arid well.

The gardeners up at Dilkusha passed and repassed, splashing water upon the parched alleys. The Shah, with unbuttoned collar, sat in a garden tent which faced the north. He was thinking heavily. From time to time a deep pectoral regurgitation indicated the profundity of his thoughts. In the shadow of the tent the Minister of Court remained standing with his hands crossed reverentially below his chest.

The Shah spat suddenly upon the carpet. " Yes," he said, " tell the Russians that I shall withdraw the Bill from the Majlis and tell the British that their terms are unacceptable. It was a false move, that, about the concessions. You gave me wrong advice. We must now return to our original standpoint. Russia is too close to us: too strong. I am prepared even to grant the Abu Saad concession to the four Powers. You may tell the Russians at once."

The Minister of Court bowed deeply, stepping backwards towards the curtain of the tent. At that moment a shrill scream descended from the upper air upon them. The Minister of the Court dropped rapidly upon all fours: the Shah with a flash of the hand drew his revolver and began firing among the already fleeing gardeners. Three mules came crashing through the flower-beds, their eyes strained in terror. The Shah stood at the entrance to the tent, his revolver still smoking in his hand. A clamour arose from the adjoining villa. A gardener, who had been wounded in the thigh, lay whimpering among the salvias. The Captain of the Escort came running across the terrace towards them.

" Your Majesty is unhurt ? " he panted.

" It was a shell," said the Shah, his little blood-shot eyes squinting to left and right like those of a buffalo.

" Undoubtedly, Your Majesty," assented the Captain of the Guard.

The Minister of Court, being a man of the world, had regained his composure, his upright position, and his advantage.

" Or perhaps," he suggested, " it may be the new English aeroplanes which travel at a thousand miles an hour."

The Shah glowered in front of him in silence. Slowly he slid his revolver back into the loose pocket of his tunic.

" Attend to that man," he said, indicating the gardener. The Captain of the Escort retired. A hint of evening breeze sighed through the parched oleanders.

" And now," said His Majesty, turning almost genially to the Minister of the Court, " we must consider what reply to return to this Russian outrage. A thousand miles an hour—it is incredible ! You have already sent a telegram to Geneva ? We must discover at once how far, and for what price, the English . . ."

And thereupon His Imperial Majesty, in a small, gentle voice, outlined a further change of policy : unaware that the situation had reached a stage at which the actions of the Persian Government had become wholly immaterial : unaware that, even as he spoke, that scarlet smudge in a crisp morning sky had descended shrieking upon New York.

CHAPTER IX

(1)

IT was 1.10 p.m. The crowd upon the hot pavements of Whitehall had thinned since noon: only loungers remained, apathetic and listless, waiting for they knew not what. In the great public offices the typewriters ticked ceaselessly, and ceaselessly the telephone bells shrilled. A string of motor lorries lumbered out from the courtyard of the War Office: four armoured cars, emphatic with searchlights, stood outside the Air Ministry: the high iron gateway which in 1933 had been erected at the entrance to Downing Street remained permanently closed: a squad of mounted police patrolled through Great George Street and Parliament Square. The great red buses, indifferent to these symbols of uneasiness, swayed up and down.

Arthur Peabody, washed and cool, emerged from the side door of the Foreign Office and out on to the glitter of the Horse Guards Parade. Entering the Park, he strode diagonally, preoccupied and purposeful, in the direction of the St. James's Club.

Peabody, once again, was feeling displeased. There was, he confessed to himself, no possible doubt about it: he had made a grave miscalculation regarding that Abu Saad question. He should have realised from the first that this was something more than a commercial matter : that it was something more than a shady concession obtained by an ex-Major in Skinner's Horse : there was more in it, even, than the usual delays and inconsistencies of a disagreement with the Persian Government. It had grown into an Anglo-French issue : it had, since Cocquebert's amazing statement to the lobby journalists, since our own equally turgid demonstration over Paris and Berlin, become more than an Anglo-French issue : it had become a *crisis*. There was no use denying it : one must always face the facts : this Morris concession had swollen unaccountably into the " *Crisis of June* 1939." And he, Arthur Peabody, owing to a sudden whim of disinclination (was he becoming impulsive by any chance ?), had chosen for himself a back, an awkward, an ungainly, seat in this historic drama. Yes, he, Arthur Peabody, had a seat in the third—nay, the fourth—row of the dress-circle ; if not in the pit. Clearly, he must at once resume his rightful place in the counsels of Europe : clearly, he must at once descend from his inglorious eminence and take his seat in the stalls. It should have been Arthur Peabody and not John Shorland who flew to Angley. At the realisation of this fact he made the motion of striking off the head of an iris with his umbrella : the iris, although Peabody knew it not, was called " Ambassador " : the fact that he did not strike the iris was due, not to his knowledge of its title, but to his knowledge that it was the property of His Majesty's Office of Works. He swung his umbrella viciously above the proud head of " Ambassador " :

he passed onwards : he crossed the Mall with almost surreptitious caution ; and then manfully he cut across the Green Park towards Piccadilly.

Peabody, though now determined at once to resume his full functions as Principal Private Secretary to the Secretary of State, had not, as yet, acquired that expert grasp of the more detailed aspects of the crisis which so central a position would now, not necessitate merely, but entail. True it was that he decided there and then, with a decisive swing of his umbrella, to devote the whole afternoon to mastering the bewildering intricacies of the problem. Nothing, by 4.45 p.m., would catch him unprepared. Yet history did not consent, on that Saturday, June 4, to wait till tea-time : history decided (a little meanly) to catch Arthur Peabody at luncheon. And she caught him out.

It may be of solace, none the less, to those who are pained by the intervention of the Furies in important human affairs, to be assured that, even had Peabody possessed that meticulous knowledge of the Abu Saad problem which had, during the last thirty-six hours, been acquired by John Shorland : even had he been gifted, as he was not gifted, with the antennæ of Jane Campbell : he might still, all careless, have been guilty, when lunching with Dr. Kleinroth, of that pregnant inadvertence which gave to the immediate development of the crisis so unexpected a twist.

Shorland, in Peabody's place, might, it is true, have known better where the ice was thin. Peabody, as will be seen, deliberately selected as the area of his gyrations the very spot which Shorland would have avoided. Yet even Shorland did not know, as we now know, that the German Government were hesitating to come to a decision until they could obtain reliable answers to two vital questions. The first of these questions was: "Do the British possess in England sufficient stocks of the Livingstone alloy to enable them within a few weeks to manufacture further rockets?" The second question was: "Has Mr. Walter Bullinger flown to Stockholm?" To each of these two questions Arthur Peabody, as we shall shortly see, furnished Dr. Kleinroth with authoritative, but wholly inaccurate, replies.

It is possible for us to-day, informed as we are by the publication of most of the official correspondence, enlightened as we are by those two remarkable books, the *Enthüllungen* of Dr. Breitscheid and the *Anklage* of Dr. Jakob Altmaier—it is possible for us to determine exactly what stage the fears and expectations of the several Governments had actually reached by 1.30 p.m. on that Saturday, June 4. In order that the significance of Arthur Peabody's indiscretion (a significance which Lord Limpsfield in Volume III of his Memoirs appreciates but, as usual, misinterprets) may be fully weighed, it is necessary, at this point, to anticipate our narrative to the extent of disclosing knowledge which, at that time, was the property of only three or four men.

It has been indicated that by the early afternoon of that day, four out of the six protagonists were already lost in the false entrenchments which they had unwisely occupied, and had thereby long since surrendered the power of initiative or control.

231

Monsieur Cocquebert had, it is true, succeeded in staving off the interpellation of M. Raoul Thierry, but in order to do so he had landed himself in a salient from which it was dangerous either to retreat or to advance. He was at that moment already ascending the red carpet of the Elysée for the purpose of handing to the President of the Republic the resignation of his Government. Alexei Rubinstein had, it is true, done something to demonstrate to the Central Asian Republics that the hand of Moscow still held the knout, but in so doing he had not only broken faith with his confederates, but had exposed himself to the embarrassment—nay, the bad example —of giving to a small Oriental Government an excuse to appeal, and perhaps successfully, to Geneva. The Shah, by trying to get the best of both worlds, had incurred the simultaneous hostility of Great Britain and Russia ;—a thing which no right-thinking Persian likes to do. And Walter Bullinger, having shirked both Pantry and Furnivall, had sidled into a belligerent position towards France, whereas he would have much preferred a benevolent position—vague, non-committal, ex-ally, and righteous.

Two men alone still retained any liberty of action. The one was Mr. Hans P. Scholle, President of the United States. The other was Herr Treviranus, Chancellor of the German Reich.

Mr. Scholle at that moment (it was 8.25 a.m. at Bar Harbour) had just been riven from the first scoop at his grape-fruit by an urgent call from New York. He rejoined his family around the breakfast-table wearing an expression of pain and indignation upon his frank though pimpled face. Silently he continued to gouge his fruit: to the bright, the fervently matutinal, questions of Mrs. Scholle, he answered only in monosyllables: " Well, Mr. President . . ." had ventured Admiral Purves, ingratiatingly adjutant—the Admiral had been snubbed. " Those Britishers," mumbled the President eventually, having taken a large gulp of iced water, " are getting fresh." Yet for the present we are not concerned with the distress of Hans P. Scholle. We are concerned with what was happening at that moment in Berlin.

The situation disclosed by the Minister of Defence in secret conclave with Herr Treviranus, the Chancellor, and Herr von Hoesch, the Minister for Foreign Affairs, was both intricate and precise. General Lynau had begun by giving his two colleagues an instructive survey of the origins and development of the rocket and the stratosphere planes. He had taken them right back to 1929 and had quoted largely from the *Wege zur Raumschiffahrt*, which had in that year been published by Professor Hermann Oberth of Mediasch. He had then passed lightly onwards to Professor Goddard and M. Esnault-Pelterie; and had thereafter given them a detailed account of the stratosphere experiments of 1932 to 1935. It was nearly two o'clock before General Lynau reached the point of his discourse; but the point, when it came, was significant enough.

The introductory passages of General Lynau's statement, although instructive, had not been irrelevant: he had shown that hitherto the use of rocket or stratosphere planes for purposes of war had been hampered by the difficulty of finding a material capable of withstanding the initial strain. It was not merely that a combustion chamber was required strong enough to compress solid explosives in place of oxygen, and withal light enough to enable the machine to ascend rapidly from the atmo- to the strato-sphere : it was also that the terrific frictional heat engendered necessitated qualities of resistance which no metal yet discovered could supply. Essentially this same problem applied alike to the rocket and the stratosphere plane. The latter, rising to a height of 50,000 feet, its engine power maintained by super-charges, could travel, once that refined altitude had been reached, once the right metal had been discovered, at some 800 miles an hour, and would be both invisible and inaudible from the earth. The rocket, on the other hand, could, even with the Livingstone alloy, scarcely average more than 600 miles an hour, and possessed the additional disadvantage of being audible (at this General Lynau smiled grimly), and even visible, from the ground. Conversely, the rocket had the advantage which the stratosphere planes lacked, of being able to fly very low indeed and to select its objectives.

The aeronautical research department of the Reichswehr-ministerium had for years been experimenting with different types of alloy. They had now discovered a deposit which, although it produced a new metal suited to stratosphere planes, could not compete (and they must face the fact) with the Livingstone alloy for atmospheric machines.

This element had been discovered at Helström, in the Hernösand district of Sweden. A private German Company had been formed, under the name of the Hamburger Schmirgel A.-G., and had obtained in February last a concession from the Swedish Government covering the mining rights at Helström. Two stratosphere planes had already been constructed for experimental purposes and at their recent trials had averaged 900 miles an hour. Within ten weeks it would be possible to construct some eighty more, which, with the aid of the Althausen bomb, could certainly do grave damage to any very large town or congested district. So far, so good. There remained, however, two elements of uncertainty. Although the British possessed no bomb of the capacity of the Althausen, yet the fact that their rockets enjoyed immunity from attack by any other atmospheric machine, plus their greater carrying capacity and visibility, would, were they able to manufacture a sufficient quantity, give them a great initial advantage. In the second place, the Swedish Government were unaware of the true nature and purposes of the Hamburger Schmirgel A.-G., and would, if informed, certainly cancel the concession.

For these reasons the decision appeared to depend upon two, at present unknown, considerations. First: " Can the English manufacture immediately a large number of rockets ?" Second: " Will the Swedish Government remain unaware of the true nature of the Helström deposits, at least until such time as the Hamburger Schmirgel A.-G. have extracted all the material required ?"

The Chancellor—thus concluded General Lynau at the end of what had surely been a very long disquisition—would now recognise that he, as Minister of Defence, had been right in withholding these particulars from the full Cabinet. They were known in their entirety to only two men in Germany, to himself and to Major Kleinroth, his chief of staff. In so saying General Lynau told the truth : for he was unaware that Major Kleinroth had informed his brother in London of the opportunities and uncertainties involved in the Helström deposits.

Having concluded his exposition, the General leant back in his chair, eyeing the shocked perplexity of his civilian colleagues with saddened contempt. There was a silence in the room.

" If I may venture," continued the General, " to depart for an instant from my purely technical province, I should suggest that this is the moment for which Germany has been waiting for over twenty-two years. Our hands are free. I repeat it, our hands are free. We are not, as we were in 1914, hampered by any alliance. We can act realistically. If we are *absolutely* certain that the answers to the above two questions are favourable—if we are quite certain, that is, that England can produce no more rockets—if we are certain that our Swedish deposits will enable us uninterruptedly to construct as many stratospheres as we need : then we can, of course on our own terms, join with France against England. If, on the other hand, the answers are unfavourable, or ambiguous, then with equal advantage we can join with England against France. The one fatal mistake would be to oppose England before we are certain that the mastery of the air lies with us. Consider, for instance . . ."

The telephone upon the Chancellor's writing-table had for some time been shrilling insistently. Herr Treviranus rose to answer it. A look of incredulous astonishment spread across his handsome sailor face.

" Gentlemen," he said, " this is most perplexing. That was our Ambassador in London. It seems that the British Foreign Secretary has left suddenly by air for an unknown destination."

The fist of General Lynau crashed upon the table. " That British Secret Service," he shouted, " they are the devil! Do you know where the British Foreign Minister has flown to? I can tell you. He has flown to Stockholm. He has flown to tell the Swedes."

Herr von Hoesch, rising in his chair, smiled at the General with exhausted indulgence. " My dear General," he said, " even supposing that the English have found out about your Helström deposits, Mr. Bullinger would not fly himself to Stockholm. At least, I scarcely think so. At least,—but then where else can he have gone?" None of the three German Ministers could find an answer to that question.

(2)

Ignorant of this interesting conference, Arthur Peabody walked nimbly across the Green Park swinging his umbrella. A cloudless sky opened above the wide expanse of grass: the proletariat, with opened shirts, lay basking in the sunshine, prone and scattered as on a battlefield. Cautiously did Arthur Peabody cross Piccadilly, glancing appraisingly from left to right. It was with a professional smile already glinting between his lips that he climbed the steps of the St. James's.

Dr. Kleinroth, in the leathered lounge, was sitting alone in front of two glasses of sherry. He rose as Peabody entered, and enquired whether he would like a wash. Peabody replied that he had washed already, but that it would be convenient for him to dispose of his hat and umbrella : amicably they walked together towards the hat-room : rocking slightly, the bowler of Peabody was abandoned upon its peg : they returned to the lounge. Dr. Kleinroth motioned Peabody towards the sherry. "Thank you," said Peabody, "I should much like a glass of sherry. Such a *clean* wine, I always say." And that was how Dr. Kleinroth's luncheon began.

It was only later, in the dining-room, at the moment when Peabody had surrendered to the solicitations of his host and agreed to strawberries ; at the moment when it was evident to both of them that purely social conversation could no longer be prolonged ; that the finger of history, questing, intervened.

"Cream ? " asked Dr. Kleinroth.

"Please," said Peabody. "Extraordinarily early strawberries are this year."

"They come from France," Dr. Kleinroth answered.

"Ah yes ! how stupid of me ! By air.

"Talking of air," Peabody continued, since he was feeling uplifted by the Liebfraumilch, " talking

238

of air—what, my dear Kleinroth, do you feel will be the effect abroad of this aerial demonstration which our Air Ministry have staged? I don't mind telling you between ourselves that I do not like it. I consider it, as a gesture, both unfortunate and ill-timed. People abroad will regard it as a deliberate act of provocation, if not as an overt threat. I must say that I don't blame them. I don't mind confessing, my dear Kleinroth, that the first I heard of the whole business was when I read it on the tape this morning."

"Yes," said Dr. Kleinroth, " I can myself well believe it. It has always struck me, during the many years I have served in this country, as quite extraordinary how you people in the Foreign Office are over-ridden by the other Ministries. One day it is the Treasury: the next day it is the Board of Trade: the Foreign Office are always the last to be consulted and the last to know. I understand all that, since I have now been eleven years in London. But I find it difficult to convince my people at the Wilhelmstrasse. In this very case, for instance, nobody in Berlin would seriously believe that the Foreign Secretary could have concealed so important a matter from his own *chef de cabinet*."

"But, my dear Kleinroth," interrupted Peabody, flushing quickly, " you have got it all wrong. I flatter myself that Mr. Bullinger has only once concealed anything from me. And that was when, in December last, he was so good as to recommend me for a K.C.M.G. in the new year's honours. He confessed it to me afterwards when this particular K.C.M.G. had been filched from me by Macready, the Prime Minister's secretary. ' This,' said the Secretary of State, ' is the only thing since we have worked together which I have ever hid from you.' Rather charming . . . what ? "

Dr. Kleinroth was a persistent man. He was not to be diverted from his purpose by the red-herring of Bullinger's charm.

" Do you," he said, " seriously mean to imply that the Cabinet, that your chief in particular, were not aware of this intended flight ? "

" Oh, well . . ." said Peabody, gazing hurriedly at the Angelica Kaufmanns in the ceiling—" well, you see, they knew about the rockets, of course, and about the trials and all that. But they did not know where those trials were to take place or when. Had they done so, I should naturally have advised Mr. Bullinger to insist upon a postponement."

" You will have some port, yes ? " asked Kleinroth politely.

" Thank you—yes, I should like a glass of port-wine. Such a *clean* beverage, I always say."

" Yet all the same," continued Dr. Kleinroth, " it does strike me as odd how little you people at the F.O. are admitted into the *insides* of things. It is so different at the Wilhelmstrasse and at the Quai d'Orsay. You know, it is a commonplace with us down at the Embassy that the foreign correspondents always know what your Cabinet have decided twenty-four hours before that knowledge has percolated through to you Civil Servants."

Peabody much disliked being called a Civil Servant. He swallowed his port hastily to cover his irritation.

" Will you have kümmel, or benedictine, or perhaps some brandy ? "

" Thank you,—yes. I should like a glass of brandy. I always prefer it, even at luncheon, to those sugary liqueurs. Such a clean wine . . ."

" For instance," interrupted Dr. Kleinroth, " you know Elbogen, I think, the correspondent of our *Tageblatt ?* Such a clever man ; and a gentleman too, which makes a difference. Well, Elbogen telephoned to me just before I came out to luncheon and told me that there were only six rockets, and not ten, as your Air Ministry gave out."

If there was one thing that Peabody disliked it was foreigners suggesting that any British Department of State could be untruthful. It was with dignity that he answered :—

" He was wrong in that. There are ten. There are in fact eleven, if you add in the one which went a fortnight ago to New York."

" Yes, I know," said Kleinroth—" I know that that is the correct official answer. Yet I prefer in all such matters to take my information from Elbogen, who possesses sources of information which are closed to you and me. Have another brandy ? Waiter—another two brandies. For instance, he has discovered that you have no stocks whatsoever in this country of the Livingstone deposit—or whatever it is that makes the metal for the rocket aeroplanes. None whatever. Beyond the six machines you have already, you have nothing at all. Now I truly believe that you, my dear Peabody, in spite of your position, had no conception of that ? "

R   241

Peabody loathed Elbogen with a devouring passion. It seemed to Peabody that the worst horrors of the Press were concentrated in the person of that fraudulent, unctuous, elephantine and ubiquitous crypto-Jew. At the thought of Elbogen the blood flamed furious to his head.

"I fear," he said in icy tones, "that in this matter the omniscient Elbogen has gone pretty thoroughly off the rails. As a matter of fact, if you want to know, we have accumulated stocks of the deposit for the last six months. We have enough now, in this country, to last us for eight years."

That was Peabody's first inadvertence, well meant, but untrue.

"Yes, yes," replied Kleinroth, retaining, though with a colour heightened by the chase, his bantering manner—"yes, I know that is what you have been told to say. But there again I prefer the information of our friend Elbogen. Though I will confess to you that in one point this morning Elbogen was, as you say, completely off the rails. It will amuse you. He told me that he knew for a fact that Mr. Bullinger had flown to Paris. Now you and I, my dear Peabody, know at least that his destination was somewhere very different . . . ?"

Dr. Kleinroth paused, smiling. Peabody's mind worked hurriedly. What was it that Miss Campbell had been telling the News Department that morning when he had re-entered the room after dictating? Something about it being a good thing to keep the foreigners in a state of ignorance. Yes—that was it: keep them puzzled.

"You will say," Dr. Kleinroth was continuing—

" you will say, I know, that the Secretary of State
has left for a week-end in the country. While I
was waiting for you downstairs I read on the tape
an Exchange message (obviously inspired) to that
effect. But do you seriously imagine that this will
be believed upon the continent ? You English are
so childish—so clumsy, if I may say so—about this
sort of thing. You see, I know as well as you, my
dear Peabody, that Mr. Bullinger left Hanworth
aerodrome to-day, not at 10.20 as you said
but at dawn ; and that he was bound for Stockholm."

Peabody winced. He winced visibly. He also
coloured scarlet. He had really winced from
startled surprise at so fantastic a statement. He
had coloured at realising that Dr. Kleinroth was
trying to inveigle him towards an indiscretion.
And why on earth Stockholm ? It had nothing
whatsoever to do with the business. Well, if it
pleased, if it puzzled Kleinroth, let him believe that
the Secretary of State had flown to Stockholm.
Dr. Kleinroth, watching Peabody closely, derived
the conviction that he had winced, had coloured, in
distress at the accuracy of his, clever Kleinroth's
information. Peabody by then was gazing at the
Kaufmanns in the lozenges. Yes, Miss Campbell,
who knew all the details, had certainly told the News
Department to keep the continentals in a state of
suspense. He turned upon Dr. Kleinroth a discreet but winsome face.

" My dear Kleinroth," he said, " you people at
the German Embassy know far too much."

" Now, this statement," began Dr. Kleinroth,

veering rapidly away from acquired thin ice, " this **statement** of M. Cocquebert . . ."

Peabody followed his discourse with affable attention. He glanced at his watch. " I am afraid . . ." he said. Dr. Kleinroth rose with unexpected alacrity. " Yes," he answered quickly, " I also must hurry back."

" Let us walk together," said Peabody, " as far as the Duke of York's steps."

" No," said Dr. Kleinroth, with unwonted briskness. " I must get along to my Embassy at once." And so saying he hailed a passing cab.

Peabody, swinging his umbrella manfully, thinking how much he disliked that fellow Elbogen, strode across the Green Park. By the time he reached the Foreign Office, Dr. Kleinroth, from Carlton House Terrace, was already connected with the Reichswehr-ministerium in Berlin. He was talking to his brother.

" Yes," he was saying, " I think I have got the information you require. Our friends have been accumulating the stocks for the last six months and have ample material. And you were right about Stockholm. He left at dawn this morning. Certain ? Yes, I think you can be certain—my information comes from an absolutely reliable source. Not very intelligent—but truthful and well-informed. Yes, Max, I think you can count on it."

Dr. Kleinroth replaced the receiver feeling that he had done the State some service.

But he was wrong.

(3)

M. Hippolyte Cocquebert, at the very moment when Arthur Peabody at the St. James's Club was draining his third glass of Liebfraumilch, descended the steps of the Elysée.   He was no longer President of the French Council of Ministers : he was merely M. Hippolyte Cocquebert, deputy for Vézelay. The journalists in the courtyard thronged around him : he faced their cameras with an expression of injured rectitude : he explained.

" Yes, gentlemen," he explained, " it is true that I have this moment handed to the President of the Republic my own resignation and that of my colleagues. You ask me my reasons ? I am now, as a private citizen, at liberty to give them. It had been my earnest endeavour, in the strained situation which has so regrettably arisen between ourselves and Great Britain, to maintain, and at any cost, the honour and the dignity of our beloved country. There were those, however, among my opponents— there were those even among my own colleagues— who preferred that France should remain for ever subservient to our friends across the Channel. Internationalism, gentlemen, whether of high finance or of low politics, is an insidious enemy.   Until the last moment I fought undaunted and alone against external intrigues, and internal treachery. I have been beaten, gentlemen.   Yet there are worse things than defeat : I have now taken the only course open to a man of honour, to a veteran of 1914.   I have surrendered the sacred task entrusted to me :

I have disengaged my responsibility : France shall be my judge."

" Judge," scribbled the journalists, and gazed at M. Cocquebert, expecting more. He stood there, meditating some phrase about France having lost a statesman and gained a poilu. He thought better of it : such phrases required to be extremely polished and impulsive. With defiant dignity, M. Cocquebert raised his hat to the expectant journalists and entered his car. The wheels crunched and crackled on the gravel of the court-yard : and as they did so, two other cars entered from the Rue du Faubourg St. Honoré. M. Cocquebert recognised the first of these two cars as being the white Renault of M. Paul Sebire.

By 2.30 that afternoon it was known in Paris that M. Sebire had formed a coalition government of the Right–Centre : that M. Raoul Thierry had accepted the Ministry of War : and that Mr. François Poncet had consented to retain in the new ministry his former office of Foreign Secretary. At 2.45 the members of the newly constituted Cabinet met at the Presidency of the Council. M. Sebire invited M. Poncet to inform them of the international position.

The statement of M. Poncet was short and to the point. He explained that the crisis had already passed through two phases, and was now entering upon the third. The first phase, the Abu Saad phase, had ceased to have any central reality from the moment that the Shah's action had disunited the four Powers, from the moment that the British Government had settled the dispute by a direct deal with Tehran. The second phase—the Anglo-French phase—had been introduced by M. Cocquebert's unfortunate Note, by his still more regrettable indiscretion to the lobby journalists, and by the curt and almost insulting reply from London. That phase, with the fall of the Cocquebert Cabinet, had also passed. M. Cocquebert had become the scapegoat of his own delinquencies : his resignation would go far towards appeasing the excitement in London and the anxiety abroad.

An expression of beatific relief spread from face to face. M. Poncet stilled it with uplifted forefinger :—

"We are now," he said, "entering upon the third phase—a phase which is rendered difficult, and I might add dangerous, by two new factors. The first factor is this morning's brutal demonstration on the part of the British rocket planes. It would, but for this factor, have been easy to arrange a settlement with the London Cabinet by expressing some form of regret for M. Cocquebert's Note and indiscretion. As it is, such an apology would be regarded as having been wrung from us by the menace of the British rockets. Our friend Cocquebert attributes his sudden fall to the panic created by this morning's raid. He is right in so doing. Had it not been for the rockets it would have taken us at least two days to force Cocquebert to resign. Yet if we now apologise to England he will use his influence with the Press and in the Chamber to attack us for having capitulated to an insulting threat. That, gentlemen, is the first factor which renders the present phase of the crisis so difficult.

I now come to the second factor—the factor which, in my opinion, renders it not difficult only, but acutely dangerous."

M. Poncet paused, gazing at the troubled faces of his novice colleagues.

"This second new factor," he continued, "is the disappearance of the British Foreign Secretary. I confess that his sudden and wholly unaccountable departure has caused me grave anxiety. The authorities in London, with engaging simplicity—or rather with that arrogant insouciance which is so irritating a feature of British diplomacy—have given out that Mr. Bullinger merely flew to his house in the country; this confirms my perplexity and my disquiet. An hour ago, when I last communicated with our Embassy, Mr. Bullinger had not yet returned to London. Assuming, as we must assume, that he started at dawn, he has already been absent for more than ten hours. Where has Mr. Bullinger flown to? And why? I do not wish to appear alarmist, yet we must envisage every probability. We must, gentlemen, envisage the probability that Mr. Bullinger has flown to Berlin!"

The sound of that dread word sent a tremor through the Cabinet. The blue line of the Vosges flickered like lightning before their eyes. The hereditary menace made them feel hereditary. There was an anxious pause. It was M. Thierry who first found his voice.

"Tell us," he said, "what do you propose?"

"Obviously," answered M. Poncet, toying slowly with his pencil, "there is no time to lose. Obviously, also, we must to some extent throw ourselves upon

the mercy of the British Government. And equally
obviously we must not, if we can possibly avoid it,
afford to M. Cocquebert and the Press an opportunity of rousing against us a patriotic agitation.
My proposal is determined by each of these three
considerations. It is this. That I should within
the next half-hour send back the air messenger to
London with instructions calculated to meet all our
difficulties. In the first place, I shall send an
official Note couched in the strongest language, pro-
testing against the flight of the rockets over Paris.
I shall point out that the flight was not merely
discourteous and provocative, but that it constituted
an express violation of Article XVII of the Air
Convention of April 1937. I should then insist
upon a formal apology from the British Government
and reparation for the physical and moral damage
which has been caused. That would be our official
Note. I should accompany this Note with a private
and secret letter to our Ambassador. In that letter
I should explain all our difficulties. I should make
it clear to M. Martin that his action must be guided
entirely by the consideration whether or not the
British have come to any understanding with Berlin.
If they have,—then, gentlemen, I fear that complete
and immediate capitulation on our part is the only
course. The Note of Protest must not be delivered
and a full apology must be given for M. Cocquebert's action. If, on the other hand, M. Martin
can satisfy himself that Mr. Bullinger did not in fact
fly to Berlin, then we can deliver the Note of Protest,
and if need be, show the Note to our critics in the
Chamber and the Press. In no circumstances,

however, should the text of the Note be published. It would create an outburst in England. I should thus authorise M. Martin to take the British Government into our confidence: to explain to them our difficulties and our regrets: to beg them neither to publish the Note nor to take it too seriously. This, gentlemen, is my proposal. I do not in general believe in such equivocal and ambiguous gestures of diplomacy. In this case, however, it is essential. I ask that my policy be approved."

M. Sebire, blinking round the table, signified that the proposal of M. Poncet had been endorsed by the Cabinet. The Foreign Secretary rapidly returned to the Quai d'Orsay, and within a few minutes the instructions had been drafted and signed. At 3.20 p.m. M. Massigli handed to Jules Boursicaut two long envelopes. The one contained the official Note, the other the private instructions.

"My poor Boursicaut," he said, "you must hurry back to London. There is not one moment to lose. The Ministry of Aviation have been instructed to provide for you the fastest machine which they possess. You should be at Croydon by 5. Remember, my poor Boursicaut—every second counts."

Jules Boursicaut retrieved his bowler from the side table. He had not breakfasted, he had not lunched. He stopped the swaying motor at St. Cloud and purchased some chocolate, a loaf of bread, and a half-bottle of cognac.

The latter was a most unfortunate purchase.

(4)

Sir Charles Pantry, seated at his desk in White-hall Gardens, replaced the receiver with a smile of satisfaction. The smile of Sir Charles Pantry was not a pleasant spectacle, nor, had he known it, was his satisfaction wholly justified by facts. He had, it is true, just heard from Marden that the machines engaged upon the European flight had all returned to safety. He had, it is also true, been reading with appreciation the pæans of patriotism, the eulogies of himself, with which the F.L.N. had plastered the pages of their afternoon editions. Yet had Sir Charles Pantry possessed either the tem-perament or the knowledge to take a more balanced view of the situation, his pleasure, at that moment, would have been soured by the acids of anger and doubt. " Yes," he murmured to himself, pushing the telephone away, resuming his pleased perusal of the *Evening Express*—" yes, I must say I have taught that old pansy Bullinger how to handle a crisis. And what's more, the country knows it." Yet even as he said so, a firm, a recaptured Bullinger was closeted with the Prime Minister across the way. And Mr. Furnivall, startled by Bullinger's per-sistence, had just agreed that Sir Charles must be called upon to resign.

" You see . . ." Bullinger was saying.

Spencer Furnivall had often wished that Bullinger would not begin each sentence with those irritating words, " You see." It was worse than the " I mean " of Petticue. Really, his colleagues had the most annoying tricks. Furnivall made a gesture of impatience. Bullinger ignored it.

" You see, it is not that I object to your having, during my absence this morning, given to the Press the text of my reply to Cocquebert. I think it was a mistake to do so, and had you only delayed a few hours you would have heard that Cocquebert was no more. He is sure to make capital out of this publication, if only to weaken the position of his successors. And our one hope of reaching a peaceful solution is to come to some immediate arrangement with the Sebire Cabinet, who are men of honesty and sense. Yet I quite see, my dear P.M., that some public gesture had to be made in view of the hysteria roused over here by Cocquebert's Note and his statement last night. I am not surprised that people here interpreted both of them as a deliberate challenge. I quite see that in the circumstances you could scarcely have deferred all action pending my return. But none the less, now that both Notes have been published, some striking gesture of appeasement is necessary. The French have made this gesture by dismissing Cocquebert. We must reply to it by dismissing Pantry. Either I, my dear P.M., or Pantry must go—and you will be the first to see that great anxiety would be caused were I myself to resign."

Mr. Furnivall tapped slim fingers silently. He had never seen Walter Bullinger in so personal, so aggressive, so arrogant a mood. Bullinger, from the moment he had entered the room, had been different somehow. He *looked* different. He had refused to give any explanation of his extraordinary flight to Angley. "I had my reasons," he had said, "and to my mind they were good reasons. Time alone will show whether I was right. For the moment, we have no time. We must at once concentrate upon what is to be done here and now. We can't look back, or waste valuable minutes in explanation, we must deal with the situation as it stands this afternoon. And the first thing is this. Pantry and all his doings must, whatever the consequences, be at once repudiated."

Yes, Bullinger was different somehow. The Prime Minister leant back in his chair seeking for some phrase which should neatly define this exact shade of difference. He found it. Hitherto, Bullinger had been like a posthumous portrait; very resembling and all that, but lacking that individual look about the eyes. Bullinger had suddenly ceased to be like a posthumous portrait. The Prime Minister was so pleased with this intricate discovery, that he found himself actually agreeing, more or less, with what Bullinger had said.

"Yes," said Spencer Furnivall, his beard upwards, "I really think that on this occasion our dear friend Pantry has gone rather far. We must at once repair the damage. You may tell the French Ambassador if you like that the rocket flight was an error on the part of the Air Minister which the Cabinet as a Cabinet (Furnivall at that laughed his silent laugh) are not prepared to overlook. Then to-morrow morning we must all meet at Chequers. You can repeat to Pantry, in Cabinet, what you said to the French Ambassador. I shall support you, and add that your statement was made with my full authority. He will then resign. It will be an amusing scene. But at the same moment we must issue a State of Emergency Decree under the Defence of the Realm Act. I will ask Belisha to have everything in readiness. That will muzzle the Press. After their experiences with Dora at the time of the Egyptian Crisis the F.L.N. will scarcely dare to print what Pantry will then tell them. Yes, it will be a delightful little drama. And without the F.L.N., Pantry, I rejoice to think, is powerless. Yes, I shall ask Bob Boothby to take the Air Ministry. He is so reliable and popular. Yes, that will be the best solution, and meanwhile . . ."

" Meanwhile," said Bullinger, " we must square the Yanks. I must telephone to Washington immediately."

Twenty minutes later the Secretary of State was speaking on the long-distance telephone.

" Is that you, Reith ? " he said. " Thank God ! I was afraid you might have gone off somewhere for the week-end. Pretty hot your end, I expect. This end's as hot as hell. In fact, we're in the very devil of a mess. Can you get the President by telephone ? Better not ? Well, anyhow, go down to the State Department at once and lay all your cards straight on the table. Apologise, before they say anything, about the rocket planes. Hint that Pantry has muddled the whole thing and may have to resign. Tell them that we have come to a direct settlement with the Persians about Abu Saad, and indicate that we should be happy to hand over the concession to a group on which American interests would be fully represented. Tell them that their friends the Russians are at this moment bombarding the Caspian ports.   Make it quite clear to them that we rely on Washington to help us in preventing a war over this side of the Atlantic.   You can say we shall go to any lengths to meet them.   Have you got all that, Reith ?   I shall send you formal instructions by telegraph.   Meanwhile don't put anything in writing, but get in a verbal representation just as quick as you can.   Oh, yes—and you can put most of the blame for the whole thing upon that bloody ass Cocquebert.   Have you got all that ? "

Sir John Reith blushed hotly at the epithets applied by Mr. Bullinger to M. Cocquebert.

" I understand perfectly," he said, mingling with an accustomed tone of efficiency, a note of christian reproof.   " I shall attend to it immediately.   I trust that your official instructions, when they reach me, will be equally explicit, and perhaps a shade less . . ."

" A shade *what* ? " shouted Bullinger, who still believed it necessary to raise the voice when speaking to America.

" Well," hesitated Sir John, " less violent, perhaps. . . ."   He hoped that Mr. Bullinger had seen the point.   The Secretary of State had not. He had already replaced the receiver and asked to be put into immediate communication with Sir Neville Henderson, the Ambassador in Berlin.

CHAPTER X

(1)

JANE CAMPBELL, that afternoon, was feeling out of it. She was feeling more than out of it: she was feeling flat. She was feeling more than flat; she was feeling uneasy.

For one crowded hour had she quaffed the nectar of autocracy. For one hour that morning had she controlled the whirlwind: she had taken risks, she had assumed responsibilities, which no permanent official would have contemplated for one instant: she had shown the civil servants that when it came to a crisis it was the front bench figure who took control. Even Sir Reginald Talbot—not a very subservient man—had accepted her instructions: aged gentlemen had scurried along corridors in execution of her behests: the ten taut fingers of John Shorland had gripped in admiration: through the trim vulcanite of her telephone she had given orders which would effect the destinies of millions: her hand, for some eighty minutes, had rested upon the levers of the world: she had been brave and calm: she had been virile, resourceful and decisive: she had with untrembling fingers made gestures of courage, vision and intelligence: and then, at 2.40 p.m., Walter Bullinger had returned.

He had said: " Well, Jane, I gather from Shorland that you have done your best to cover my retreat."

She said: " Yes, Walter; it was difficult to know what to say. I hope you approve of our explanations ? "

Bullinger hesitated. " I think," he smiled, " that they were very ingenious. Your loyalty, my dear Jane, has really touched me. Only wasn't it all rather far-fetched, rather—if I may say so without appearing to criticise—rather unnecessary ? "

Jane's face fell suddenly. She looked mortified. Bullinger walked to the window and looked down upon the lake.

" Of course," he said, " I ought not to have left London this morning. It was a mere chance, really, that I forgot to look at the papers. It was a combination of chances which impelled me to fly to Angley. One can never explain those sort of chances. It is always better to leave such impulses unexplained."

" But at least," Jane interposed, feeling disconcerted, " no harm can have been done ? "

" I hope not," Bullinger answered, without smiling. " You see, I am always a little afraid of the ingenious. It is so terribly unprofessional, and in this job the amateurish always leads to trouble. Besides, Jane, it wasn't true what you told the P.M. And lies are an unending bore. Nor did I like that bit about the ' unknown destination.' My butler at Angley said the same thing. But it ought not to have been said up here. You see, it will make the foreigners imagine all sorts of nonsense. And even in this country it gives to my movements a news-value which is highly inconvenient."

" News-value ? " Jane repeated the words unhappily. Bullinger left the window and crossed the room towards his desk. There was something different about Bullinger. Jane noticed it from the way he walked. He had lost his jaunty gait, his gay anglican manner : he moved slowly : he seemed depressed but confident : there was about him a saddened confidence more convincing than the chest-patting bluster of his former manner. He had gained in reality.

" You see," Bullinger continued, and this time he smiled a trifle wearily, " to the Yellow Press, information, however serious and important, possesses no news-value whatsoever. The withholding of information, even on the most trivial matters, *does* possess it. If you tell every paper everything, you can be certain that no paper will publish anything. Information, I repeat, is never news provided it be full, accurate and not exclusive. On the other hand, to withhold information produces the emotional effect of the mystery or puzzle. That, to the Yellow Press, is always honey, especially if it is a personal mystery."

" I see," said Jane, lamely.

" Of course," Bullinger continued, " I grant you, Jane, that in any case no one abroad would have believed that I chose this morning to fly to Angley. Yes, I grant you that. It was foolish, it was perhaps insane, of me to go. Yet I can't tell you, Jane, how glad I am that I went."

Jane smiled. " Yes," she said, " you look a

different man." Yet undubitably she was crest-fallen. Bullinger laid a gentle hand upon her shoulder.

" Don't worry," he said. " I expect it is all right. I must now dash across to No. 10. We shall have to get rid of Pantry at any cost. I shall be back about four. Have you lunched, Jane? Better go out and get some luncheon—it's striking three already."

Jane passed into the Private Secretaries' room.

" Well," Shorland grinned, " I fear that the Secretary of State was not wholly pleased by our stratagem ? "

" No," said Jane, " he wasn't. He said," she added, " that it would give him news-value. He said it would confuse people abroad."

Peabody came across to Shorland's table. " Yes," he said, " the foreigners can't make it out at all. I have just been lunching with Kleinroth. He had got it firmly into his head that the Secretary of State had flown to Stockholm."

" Stockholm ? " echoed Shorland. " Now what made him think of that ? There must have been some reason for it. And what on earth did you say ? "

Peabody laughed knowingly. " Oh, I allowed him to remain under that misapprehension."

" Did you ? " said Jane.

" Then he was very inquisitive about our stocks of this Abu Saad deposit. I thought it best to let him know the truth. It was rather an awkward moment, but my experience tells me that no harm is ever done by confessions of power. So I told him that we had been accumulating supplies since March."

" But we haven't," said Jane.

" Surely," Peabody answered, " surely, Miss Campbell. I remember reading it in the Cabinet minutes. It struck me forcibly at the time. Pantry definitely confessed to the Cabinet that he had been accumulating these stocks for the last three months."

" No," said Jane firmly, " no, not at all. You have got it all wrong, Mr. Peabody. What happened in March is that we sent a few coolies and some A.P.O.C. tankers to Abu Saad. That was to mine the stuff. But we haven't got it yet. It won't be here for at least another two months."

" Lud ! " said Shorland.

Peabody looked confused. " Oh dear ! " he said, " Oh dear me ! "

An awkward silence followed. Jane was about to tell Peabody that he must at once inform the Secretary of State of this unfortunate error. But she checked herself. She had had enough, for one day, of telling other people to do things. She was not, at the moment, feeling instructive.

" Well . . ." she said vaguely, and left them. She returned to her room. She went to the window and stood there gazing across at the Admiralty. The flowers on the table below her claimed her attention. How badly irises did in water ! These had been fresh on Thursday, and now by Saturday afternoon they were already wrinkling stickily. She crossed to the table and fetched a pair of scissors. As she snipped the dead buds she felt uneasy ; out of it ; flat.

(2)

At 4.0 p.m. Herr von Schubert, German Ambassador in London, descended the Duke of York's steps and walked unwillingly in the direction of the Foreign Office. He was sunk in thought. He was thinking that the telephone conversation which, only half an hour previously, he had held with Berlin, was the most futile conversation which he had ever conducted. He was feeling troubled and uncertain. In the first place, he did not relish receiving instructions of such vital importance on the telephone: it was a bad modern practice, which led all too frequently to misunderstandings, if not to repudiation. Being of the older school of diplomacy, Herr von Schubert preferred the written to the spoken word. In the second place, he did not care for the instructions themselves: they struck him as sensational and based on insufficient evidence. They were worse than that: they were provocative and mischievous: they were the sort of instructions which led to enmities and even war. Herr von Schubert glanced at the bronze figures on the plinth of the Guards' Memorial: four firm young chins under four firm steel helmets: he sighed heavily: he was that rare type of elderly man who much dislikes the thought of young men being killed. There were few things which filled him with such acute distaste as belligerent instructions. He wished now that he had told the Wilhelmstrasse that he must refuse to obey such orders. Yet how, in the heat of an engagement, could a General in the field defy headquarters? At least he had told them that he doubted the correctness of their premises and loathed their conclusions. He would send a despatch that very evening in which the whole conversation should be recorded in writing. History, at least, should mark and learn.

The Wilhelmstrasse themselves had clearly disliked their own message. They had underlined the fact that it arose from a decision of the whole Cabinet. "The Reichskanzler," they had said, "felt it necessary to put to the vote the proposal of the Minister of Defence." That was a discreet way of implying that neither Treviranus nor von Hoesch had approved the decision. Of course they hadn't approved. Yet the decision, the instructions, remained. And as a result he must obey the behests of General Lynau. Herr von Schubert ground his teeth in rage. With dragging footsteps he walked up the steps into Downing Street: he entered the courtyard of the Foreign Office: slowly he ascended the staircase: an office-keeper seized his hat and stick: with a reserved expression Herr von Schubert entered the room of Walter Bullinger.

The Secretary of State appeared less genial than was his wont: he was clearly preoccupied: dispensing with the usual affabilities of small-talk, he went straight to the point.

"My dear Ambassador," he said, "I am glad to see you. I wish to apologise to your people for this morning's incident. I can assure you that the despatch of the rocket planes over Berlin was a measure conceived without the knowledge or approval of the Cabinet. It is a measure which we regret. I may add that I am seeing the French

Ambassador at five, and that I shall make a similar apology to him. The whole incident, which was most unfortunate, was due to an error of judgment on the part of my colleague of the Air Ministry."

Herr von Schubert had not expected this apology. It rendered his own instructions even more inappropriate and silly. He bowed with dignity, accepting Bullinger's excuses with generous lack of comment. A silence ensued.

The Ambassador was wondering if he should ask Bullinger outright whether in fact he had flown to Stockholm, whether in fact the British had accumulated huge stocks of this Livingstone deposit. Such were the two premises upon which the German Cabinet had based their conclusions. He himself had considered them absurd. " Oh, but no ! " the voice had answered from Berlin, " we know it for a fact. Our information was absolutely authoritative." Being an old diplomatist, Herr von Schubert did not like asking questions which might have to be answered by a direct untruth. It was irksome for him, liking Bullinger as he did, to watch that harmless little liberal telling lies. He therefore refrained from mentioning the premises on which his Government had based their conclusions : he passed at once to these conclusions themselves.

" Mr. Bullinger," he said, " I have been instructed by my Government to make to you a communication of the utmost secrecy and importance. This Abu Saad question, as you will agree, has, owing to the action of the French Government (an action, I need scarcely assure you, undertaken without consultation with their associates), ceased to be a mere matter of a British monopoly in the Persian Gulf. It has become a direct and vital issue between France and England. . . ."

" Oh," interrupted Walter Bullinger, " but that's all right."

". . . and England," continued Herr von Schubert. " My Government fully understand that the challenge publicly addressed to you by France. . . ."

" Oh," interrupted Walter Bullinger, "but it wasn't France. It was just that ass Cocquebert. And he's gone."

". . . will not, and indeed cannot, be ignored by an Empire such as yours. . . ."

" But it *can*," protested Bullinger, " and what's more, if I have anything to do with the business, it most assuredly will."

The German Ambassador mopped his brow. Really Mr. Bullinger and his interjections were making it all very difficult.

" In the conflict," he began again, " which is now bound to arise between London and Paris, my Government are ready, nay anxious to accord, you every support. . . ."

" Well, really," exclaimed Bullinger, " that's very civil of them. Very civil indeed! Yet I don't quite see . . ."

" My Government," resumed the Ambassador, " cannot but feel that this conflict. . . ."

" But there isn't a conflict! " protested Bullinger.

". . . this conflict which has deliberately, and wholly gratuitously, been provoked by France . . ."

" Oh, come, my dear Ambassador, I mean, really . . ."

". . . by France, furnishes her two neighbours with an occasion to put an end, once and for all, to this neurotic instability of Paris, which for twenty years or more has been as a malignant growth in the body politic of Europe. The moment, they feel, has now arrived when joint and above all powerful intervention on the part of the British Empire and Germany would not only remove this constant source of disquiet, but would place the continent once again upon a just equilibrium, upon that balance of order, justice and authority which constitutes the only firm guarantee of future peace."

The Ambassador paused, conscious that in his endeavour to render his communication less foolish he had succeeded only in becoming cumbrous.

"Oh, my word!" said Walter Bullinger. And a silence ensured.

The Secretary of State rose from the sofa and took his usual walk to the window. Two of the pelicans were evidently asleep. The third was probing a dry bill among the wet feathers at the base of his spine. Bullinger watched them for a few moments and then returned slowly across the room.

"I'll tell you what," he said. "Your people over there are exaggerating. I admit that things looked pretty nasty last night, and that the publication of the two Notes has scarcely eased relations between London and Paris. But I am confident that with Sebire and Poncet in power we shall come to some reasonable understanding. After all, they are both men of sense : they have no desire to precipitate a quarrel : you won't find a man like Sebire addressing an insulting Note to London and then publishing it before we have had time to reply. A gesture of conciliation on either side will calm the public excitement. I have this moment heard from Washington that the Americans are in no sense anxious for trouble. The Russians are out of it, ·having embarked upon a little adventure on their own. With the Persians we have already come to a direct agreement. It is with all the more pleasure, therefore, that I learn from you, my dear Schubert, that your Government also will assist us in finding a sensible exit to this unhappy muddle. Believe me, my dear Ambassador, I am very grateful to you and to your Government."

Herr von Schubert hesitated : he looked at Bullinger : had the Secretary of State deliberately misunderstood the purpose of his communication ? Or had he merely evaded it ? There was upon the face of Bullinger a sympathetic, yet a shrewd, smile. A strange thought darted across the mind of Herr von Schubert. Supposing that, after all, Walter Bullinger were not a very stupid man ? He dismissed this hypothesis. He took his leave.

Walking back across the park he reflected how very difficult it would be to explain all this to the Wilhelmstrasse. Mr. Bullinger, whether by skill or from stupidity, had evaded giving any direct answer about joint intervention. It was distressing to reflect how vague, how unwelcome, how damnably difficult would be the report of the interview which Herr von Schubert must now telegraph to Berlin.

The Ambassador sighed heavily as he climbed the Duke of York's steps.

(3)

M. Jules Boursicaut, that afternoon, started to feel sick even as he climbed into the aeroplane. The air above Buc was pocketed and bumpy : Boursicaut vomited exiguously above the Bassin d'Apollon at Versailles. By the time they reached Beauvais he was feeling very ill indeed : the spires of Amiens received what remained of his loaf of bread : upon the pine trees of Le Touquet did he lavish the remains of his chocolate : cognac alone remained to him as they lurched above the terraced gardens, the attic propylæa, of Lympne. It was a confused, a drunken Boursicaut, who in record time landed at Croydon.

One thought (a persistent centre around which his impressions whirled as in a toy snowstorm) was the thought of Thérèse's article. If he could reach the offices of the *Sunday Mail* before 5.30, then all would be well. It was seven minutes past five when he landed at Croydon. He swayed fussily towards a taxi. His courier's passport, as also his lack of personal luggage, dispensed him from all Customs formalities. It was only 5.32 when the taxi, hooting vociferously, lurched along Tudor Street and swung to rest in Salisbury Square. Plunging a shaking hand into his portfolio, M. Boursicaut grabbed Thérèse's envelope. He dashed up the steps of the *Sunday Mail* and informed the porter that he must see Miss Geraldine Smithers at once. He had been there before. He knew the way. There was a door there to the right with a

fanlight of frosted glass, and across it the words
" Home Page " in black letters.

Boursicaut pushed the door. He knocked. He
entered. Miss Smithers at the moment was engaged
at the telephone. Boursicaut slammed down the
envelope upon her desk.   " The article," he panted,
" of Mélisande. It is not too late ? " Miss Smithers
placed her hand over the mouth-piece. " Pardon ? "
she said.   " This is the article," panted Boursicaut,
" on the Paris fashions. The Mélisande article for
to-morrow. I have brought it from Paris by air.
In record time. I am not too late ? " Miss Smithers
nodded. " That will be all right," she said. And
then she continued her conversation on the telephone.
" Home Page Editor, *Sunday Mail*, speaking. Is
that Simpsons ? Oh, is that you, Mr. Fryer ?
Geraldine Smithers here. About those blocks of
the frigidaires. They won't do at all. They will
have to be undercut again. I thought I had made
it quite clear yesterday . . ."

Jules Boursicaut hesitated. They were so strange,
these Ladies of the Press. He bowed awkwardly,
gobbling above his bowler. Miss Smithers nodded
briskly back at him : a dismissive, rather virginal,
nod. Boursicaut clattered down the staircase and
lurched back into the taxi.

" Embassy," he panted—" the French Embassy
in Albert Gate, and as quick as you can." He opened
both the side windows. The breeze of evening,
that clear draught along the Mall, eased his throbbing
temples. Was he in a fit state to appear before the
Ambassador ? Probably not. He felt cold in the
wrong places, and in the wrong places he felt hot.

Better just dash in hurriedly (for had he not flown in record time from Paris ?), hand the two envelopes to an attaché, and then be off again. If he did this very quickly people might not notice. It was always best to hurry when drunk. Scarcely had he come to this decision when he was faced simultaneously with the Embassy door and the approach of hiccoughs.

He bustled up the steps and rang the bell. " I want M. Lebrun," he said angrily to the responsive footman. M. Lebrun, a trifle puzzled, appeared from the Chancery. M. Boursicaut thrust the two envelopes into his startled hands.

" For His Excellency," he mumbled. " Very urgent. Record time from Paris. Feeling very ill. Yes, I have no time for the receipt. To-morrow morning."

So saying M. Boursicaut bundled back into the cab. "Alexandra Hotel," he shouted and as he did so he descried upon the lips of the driver the elements of a sardonic smile. The cab was already edging its nose into the Knightsbridge traffic. M. Boursicaut would demonstrate that he was a man of substance, of official weight. He leant his head out of the window. " No," he said, " not the Alexandra. Drive me to the Savoy Hotel." On reaching that discreet but impressive frontage, M. Boursicaut was impressed. He climbed from the cab grasping a now empty portfolio. He scrutinised the taximeter carefully ; and, after much fumbling, pressed thirteen shillings into the driver's hand. The cab backed for a moment, and then crackled out into the Strand. M. Boursicaut hesitated : the soft radiance of the Savoy, the glint through the windows of the reception desk, destroyed his courage. Grasping his portfolio, still swaying a little, he crossed the street and booked a room at the Strand Palace Hotel. And it was in this way that when, an hour later, M. Boursicaut was most urgently wanted, he could not be found.

(4)

Miss Geraldine Smithers, having concluded her conversation with Mr. Fryer of Simpsons, leant back in her chair. She sighed. That Mélisande woman was really intolerable. Again and again had she been asked to send over her articles by Friday evening ; again and again had these articles only reached Salisbury Square by the afternoon of Saturday. She must be a slipshod woman, that Mélisande ; a careless woman : a bad journalist in any case. And inconsiderate. Miss Smithers sighed irritably as she reflected how inconsiderate that Mélisande woman really was.

To-night, for instance. The article would first have to be translated into English, and by Geraldine herself. There was no other member of the staff who was familiar with the French language. As always, the article would be either too short or too long. Mélisande never seemed to realise the difference between 1250 and 1320 words. Then the blocks wouldn't fit. That would entail snipping and measuring. Miss Smithers loathed that side of her functions. It would mean that she would have to stay on at the office until after seven. And she had arranged that evening to dine with Lucy Bentheim and to go on to a Chatham House lecture. With loathing in her heart, Miss Smithers stretched forward and took the envelope which Jules Boursicaut, but five minutes ago, had flung so oddly upon her desk.

She slit the envelope with her paper-opener, and extracted its contents. Her first impression was that Mélisande had abandoned her usual flimsies in favour of a stiff and superfine quality of paper. Her second impression—and it was one of relief—was that Mélisande had substituted for her usual violet scribble the firm legibility of an expensive typewriter. Her third impression was one of blank astonishment. She read as follows :—

> " *M. François Poncet. Ministre des Affaires Etrangères à M. René Martin, Ambassadeur de France à Londres.*
>
>

Paris.

ce samedi 4 juin 1939.

>
> *Monsieur l'Ambassadeur,*
> *Le raid inautorisé qu'ont opéré ce matin les aeronefs britanniques oblige le gouvernement français d'insister à ce que. . . ."*

Miss Smithers gasped. She laid the document down upon her blotter and retrieved from the wastepaper basket the envelope in which it had been contained. She had been far too angry, while slitting open that envelope, to observe either the address, or the heavy seal by which it was closed. Yes, there could be no possible doubt. Into the hands of Geraldine Smithers had fallen a secret despatch addressed by the French Government to their Ambassador in London. "Geraldine," she said to herself, "pull yourself together. The scoop, at long last, has arrived. Keep your head, Geraldine, and acquire merit."

She reached for the telephone and spoke to the sub-editor's room. "That Mélisande article," she said, "has not turned up. It will have to drop out. You must put in its place that tosh which Lady Betchingham has written about the Ethel Smyth symphony."

Having given these instructions, she returned to her scoop. She smoothed the stiff paper under a dry palm. She read the despatch from end to end. "Gosh!" exclaimed Miss Smithers. "Well, I'm damned!"

Having uttered this exclamation she seized her scoop and walked briskly upstairs to the editor's room.

Mr. Stanley Primmett, editor of the *Sunday Mail*, was a man of great experience and slight education. The former quality gave him a certain unstable assurance : the latter defect rendered him suspicious. Mr. Primmett was invariably hostile to all forms of knowledge which he did not himself possess. The scope of Mr. Primmett's hostility was therefore wide: the area of his assurance, on the other hand, was much restricted. Few men in England possessed a quicker grasp, a more vivid memory, of the by-elections of the last twenty years. He could tell you, without a moment's hesitation, the exact total of votes polled by Mr. Petherick—unsuccessful

Labour candidate for the Langport division in 1928. He could recall, as if it were but yesterday, exactly what Mr. Osiah Bundle had said at Dorking in 1926. Nor was this, his knowledge of our legislators, confined only to statistical or public data. He possessed inside knowledge also. He knew—and was happy to share that knowledge with the readers of the *Sunday Mail*—which of our front-bench figures preferred tea for breakfast, which of them had an antipathy for cats. Yet to the wider and more durable aspects of public life the temperament of Mr. Primmett was not attuned.

Miss Smithers was thus aware, as she climbed the staircase, that Mr. Primmett would have to be handled with tact. He would not, she knew, take very readily or immediately to her scoop. In the first place, it was her scoop, and not his. In the second place, it was couched in the French language—always a source of animosity to Mr. Primmett. And in the third place, it dealt with foreign politics—a subject which, as the editor frequently repeated, possessed no news-value whatsoever.

It was thus with no exuberance of expected triumph that she entered the editor's room ; the key of her approach was modesty, diffidence, a puzzled and solicitous appeal for guidance.

" Mr. Primmett," she said, " I'm sorry to bother you, but I have come up against a snag. I want your advice. An odd thing has happened. By some chance I have received, instead of the usual weekly article on Paris fashions, the original of a secret despatch from the French Foreign Minister to the Ambassador in London."

" Which Ambassador ? " said Mr. Primmett.
" The British Ambassador ? "

" No," answered Miss Smithers, " not exactly,
Mr. Primmett. We haven't got an Ambassador
in London at the moment. It is addressed to the
French Ambassador. It's written in French, and
as far as I can make it out is of some importance.
It deals with those rocket planes which are still
excellent news-value. It instructs the French
Ambassador to demand an apology and compensation for the moral and physical damage caused to
the Parisians. I think, if you agree, that it is almost
front-page news. We could put it in in facsimile,
and add a translation in the front column. It
might even serve for a leader. I know that Mr.
Douglas is short of a subject this week."

Mr. Primmett, as was his wont when faced with
problems outside the orbit of his own knowledge,
adopted a coy tone of banter.

" I see," he smirked. " You have been pur-
loining official documents. You remember what
Mr. Bucktrout said at Malvern after the Borthwick
case. . . ."

" But, Mr. Primmett," interposed Miss Smithers,
" I'm afraid that it's all rather urgent. You know
how pleased The Chief always is when we get something really exclusive. No other Sunday paper can
possibly have got hold of this document. I daresay that it's not really very important, but it's
certainly authentic, and above all it is undoubtedly
exclusive. I can't help feeling that The Chief
might like to have it splashed. You know how he
hates the League of Nations. And if he does decide

to use it, the whole layout will have to be scrapped. There's little time to lose. Shall I knock off a rough translation which you could telephone down to the Chief ? "

Mr. Primmett smirked, wishing thereby to convey that his assent was due to kindly indulgence rather than to any form of agreement. " Very well," he smirked. " There's no harm in asking him—so long as you are certain it's exclusive. After all, we can always make it *look* like news."

Four hours later the great engines in the basement were rotating wildly. The Chief had pronounced it to be not merely news, but front-page news. And there must be a strong leader by Douglas, in a patriotic vein. Upon the front page, dominated by stream headlines, appeared a facsimile of M. Poncet's despatch.

M. Lebrun, on receiving the two envelopes from the pale but apoplectic Boursicaut, had walked rapidly towards the Ambassador's study. " Monsieur l'Ambassadeur," he said, " the despatches have this moment arrived."

M. René Martin stretched out an impatient hand. " Thank you," he said. " You have already telephoned to explain to Mr. Bullinger that I could not keep my appointment for five ? Let me see, it is now nearly six. Telephone to the Foreign Office and ask whether I can see the Minister at six-thirty ? "

M. Martin returned to his desk and opened the first of the two envelopes. It contained a long private letter from M. François Poncet himself.

He was instructed to visit the British Foreign
Secretary immediately and to lay all his cards upon
the table. He was to explain that the new French
Government desired nothing better than to resume
normal relations of good-neighbourship with Great
Britain. They regretted the terms of M. Cocquebert's Note, and they regretted even more the discourtesy shown by that gentleman in giving the
substance of that Note to the Press correspondents.
To that extent the situation had been eased by M.
Cocquebert's resignation. On the other hand,
public opinion in Paris was much excited, especially
by the demonstration of the British rocket planes.
M. Cocquebert was evidently determined, now
that he found himself in opposition, to render impossible the task of his successors. Some gesture,
therefore, was essential, if only to take the wind out
of M. Cocquebert's sails. The French Government therefore felt themselves obliged to address
a Note of protest against the flight of the rocket
planes, which was demonstrably a violation of the
Air Convention, and to demand an apology and
compensation. The text of this Note would reach
the Ambassador under separate cover. They
trusted that the British Government, realising their
internal difficulties, would agree to facilitate their
task. The Note would not of course be published,
nor would its terms be make known either to the
Chamber or to the Press. The most that M.
Poncet would say, if interpellated, was that negotiations were in progress with the London Cabinet.
He begged the latter, in the interests of a reasonable
settlement, to accord him satisfaction.

M. Poncet's letter, which had clearly been composed under the pressure of time, went on to say that these instructions applied only if M. Martin, from his own information, was quite certain that Mr. Bullinger's mysterious flight of that morning had not been undertaken for the purpose of getting into touch with any representatives of the German Government. Were any understanding to exist between the British and the German Governments, then the position of the French Government would be far more serious, and there must be no question of antagonising the British Government by raising the question of the rocket flight.

Having read these instructions, M. Martin glanced at the clock. It was time to go. He could read the Note itself on his way to Downing Street. It was so like Paris to imagine that Mr. Bullinger had flown to Berlin. M. Martin knew and understood Mr. Bullinger. He was perfectly certain that that sentimentalist had in fact, as had been officially stated, flown to Angley. He was certain also that, so long as nothing were published, Mr. Bullinger would be quite prepared to help M. Poncet by accepting the Note and returning some form of apology. "In fact," chuckled Martin to himself, "the old man will be delighted to have this against Sir Pantry."

Chuckling in this way, he entered his Renault. He pulled the second envelope from his pocket and started to read. He read as follows :—

"Avec les beaux jours l'on voit apparaître les chapeaux à bords moyens et les grandes capelines, soit en crin uni, ou à dessins de fantaisie genre dentelle, soit en pailles d'Italie vieilles ou teintes de tous les tons pastels, très élégants. Ces capelines se garnissent de guirlandes de fleurs aux tons diaprés : quelques petits chapeaux de feutre de couleurs claires sont assez prisés pour la demi-saison.

"Dans sa nouvelle collection très complète, d'une homogénéité parfaite, Chanel montre des robes du jour de ligne droite à peine evasée : taille basse, encore abaissée par derrière : robes avec boléro qui s'arrête à demi-taille, manteau long, droit, avec martingale. . . ."

M. Martin, for one moment, imagined that this was some sort of code newly devised by the Quai d'Orsay. He retrieved the envelope. He read the superscription. "Article," he read, "for Sunday, June 5."

"But what on earth . . ." murmured the French Ambassador. And then he laughed. "Well, anyhow," he chuckled, "that rules out any possibility of presenting a Note."

The car had by then reached Downing Street. M. Martin's interview with Mr. Bullinger was in every way successful. It was only when he returned to the Embassy, when he enquired further of M. Lebrun, that it dawned upon them that Boursicaut might have blundered. Many hours were wasted in trying to locate that gentleman. The Alexandra Hotel knew nothing of him. The Savoy—for the footman had heard him shout such an address— bore no name resembling Boursicaut upon their list. Yet Paris, when consulted in the matter replied that not only had Boursicaut been given that Note, but that it was absolutely essential that it should at once be retrieved.

It was not retrieved.

(5)

"So you see," said Walter Bullinger, "everything has fitted in nicely."

"I'm sure I hope so," Jane answered.

"But surely, my dear Jane, surely we are now almost out of the wood? The Cabinet meet at Chequers to-morrow morning early. Most of us are going down there to-night. I shall explain how I have had to apologise for that rocket idiocy both to the French, the Germans and the Americans. Why, even Rex Leeper has been told to mumble some form of excuse to Rubinstein. And, what's more, we've got in our apology before any of them asked for it. That makes a difference. It will be quite easy on Monday to explain to the House how, so soon as we realised that we had unwittingly violated the Air Convention, we at once offered reparation. The House of Commons never object to apologies so long as they are unsolicited. They find them gentleman-like. What they hate are apologies which are not wholly spontaneous : they find this variety an act of cowardice. That's why it makes such a difference having got in our apology first."

"Yes," said Jane, "it does make a difference. But it won't make any difference to Pantry."

Bullinger walked to the window.

"Pantry," he murmured, gazing down upon the lake, "will have to go. I'm not sorry myself. He was always a confounded nuisance in Cabinet."

"But," said Jane, "he will be even more of a nuisance outside."

Bullinger re-crossed the room slowly. Taking wide steps along the pattern of the carpet: his head lowered: watching his toes.

"I know, Jane. That will be awkward. So awkward, in fact, that the P.M. is going to muzzle him for twelve hours: he is going to proclaim the State of Emergency under Dora. I know that sounds drastic—but it doesn't matter so very much on a Sunday. The Exchange will be closed, and if there seems any danger of panic we can proclaim a Bank Holiday on Monday. After all, the State of Emergency under the new Dora isn't so very excessive. It's far the mildest of the four stages. If I remember rightly, it only affects the newspapers and certain banks. By Monday afternoon I shall have made my statement. On Tuesday we can return to the normal. Pantry's bubble by then will have been neatly pricked."

"Well," said Jane, prodding with her nose, "I don't like it. The whole scheme seems artificial to me, and dangerous."

"The whole crisis," Bullinger answered, "has been artificial. I felt from the very first that it was all so damned unnecessary. Yet once people begin to think in terms of crisis they end by behaving critically. Take the Germans, for instance. Do you know, Jane (and you must keep this strictly to yourself), von Schubert this afternoon practically offered me a defensive and offensive alliance against France ? "

" Von Schubert ? But why, in heaven's name ? And on what conditions ? And what on earth, my poor Walter, did you say ? "

" Well, I pretended, of course, that I hadn't understood. He hinted vaguely that we should join to upset the Versailles settlement and the two League decisions about Danzig. He talked of ' continental equilibrium.' When a German says that, I always know he means the Corridor. Yet I confess that I was taken aback."

" Did he ask you about Stockholm ? "

" Stockholm, Jane ? What on earth do you mean ? "

" Well, the Germans have got it into their heads that you flew this morning to Stockholm. For some reason which I can't fathom they seem to regard this as most important. They are also under the impression that we have huge stocks of the Livingstone deposit. That also strikes them as a vital point. You know how impulsive they are."

" Stockholm ? Deposit ? My dear Jane, I really don't follow."

" If you think it important, you had better ask Mr. Peabody. He will tell you the whole story."

Bullinger crossed to his writing-table and pressed the buzzer. The green baize door swung open, disclosing the alertly subservient features of Arthur Peabody.

" Look here," said the Secretary of State, " what's this fantastic story about my having flown to Stockholm ? Miss Campbell says you know something about it."

Peabody blushed. Really, this was most embarrassing. He shot a glance of irritation at Jane Campbell. Of course she was a mongoose : no, a ferret, burrowing, nosing, sneaking out.

" It was like this, sir . . ."

Haltingly, but with marked frankness, Peabody told his foolish little tale. Mr. Bullinger, for once, displayed annoyance.

" You should have told me at once," he said ; " it is all most unfortunate, most indiscreet."

Peabody winced as if he had been struck in the face. The Secretary of State had already grasped the telephone. " German Embassy," he said, " I want to speak to Herr von Schubert, personally."

Arthur Peabody hesitated for an instant, and then disappeared behind the green door. Indiscreet indeed ! He, Arthur Peabody, with twenty years' experience, dubbed indiscreet ! And in front of that Miss Campbell ! How he loathed all politicians ! He barked sharply at John Shorland, who asked him what was wrong.

" Is that you, Schubert ? " Mr. Bullinger was saying, standing beside his desk, leaning downwards towards the receiver. " Bullinger here. I say, I have just heard that my Private Secretary inadvertently gave your Counsellor to-day some wrong information. He told him that we had large stocks of the Livingstone deposit. We haven't. We *shall* have in three months, but we haven't got it now. He also allowed him to suppose that I had flown to Stockholm. Now that is fantastic. I flew down to my own little place in the country on private business. I was only there an hour. Less than that.

For goodness' sake, my dear Schubert, don't allow your people at Berlin to get wrong ideas into their heads. There are muddles enough in this business as it is. No, not at all—on the contrary, I should have let you know before, but I only heard of it this moment myself. No—not in the least. Of course not."

"Well," said Walter Bullinger, "I've nailed one lie to the counter anyhow."

He hadn't.

There is a type of German mind which prefers the improbable to the obvious. General Lynau, Minister of Defence, possessed that type of mind. When told that evening of the explanations furnished by the British Foreign Secretary to Herr von Schubert, he snorted aloud.

"Sly dogs!" he snorted. "How like their cant and bluff! Obviously they think they hold all the cards and can keep us dangling. The negotiations with London must be pursued without relaxation: if need be, the crisis must be precipitated."

It was, to do him justice, not only his passion for the improbable which convinced General Lynau that Peabody's indiscretion had been accurate, that Bullinger's subsequent disclaimer was a trick. Since that very evening he had heard that the Swedish courts had found a flaw in the terms of the concession of the Hamburger Schmirgel A.-G., and that the Swedish Government had incontinently transferred the Helström concession to the Gruvak-tiebolaget Hernösand, Smergel.

An occurrence for which Walter Bullinger was in no way responsible.

CHAPTER XI

(1)

EARLY on Sunday morning Sir Charles Pantry drove down to Chequers. He was in the worst of tempers. Upon the seat beside him bounced Mr. Petticue, President of the Board of Agriculture and Fisheries. Mr. Petticue, when at Cambridge, had won the quarter mile. The eager, the attentive, look inspired and, indeed, necessitated by that event, had remained with him in after life. Mr. Petticue believed in keeping fit : this belief had given him a delicate digestion, thin dry hands, much insomnia, and (about the eyes) a pink and questing look. Mr. Petticue did not care for Sir Charles Pantry : he found him bloated and humiliating. Sir Charles Pantry, for his part, despised Mr. Petticue : he considered him sycophantic, weedy, and half-baked. Yet on that Sunday morning of June 5, 1939, these two were linked together by a common grievance. They each felt that the Prime Minister, by not inviting them to sleep the night at Chequers, had been guilty of a studied insult. Other Ministers had slept and breakfasted in the luxury of that feudal mansion. Pantry and Petticue had been asked to leave London at 8.30 a.m. For the Cabinet meeting had been fixed for 10. A most invidious and significant distinction.

They were silent, nursing their grievance, until they reached Chalfont. Then Petticue spoke.

" By the way," he said, " did you see the papers before starting ? "

" Only the *Observer*," growled Sir Charles Pantry. " That fellow Garvin makes me sick. He's getting pink. He's as bad as that League of Nations fellow in the *Sunday Times*. ' Hectic adventurism,' indeed ! That's how he describes my rockets. I tell you, Petticue, that fellow ought to be taken out and shot."

" But haven't you," fluted Petticue, fiddling at his tie with fingers as thin as a withered chestnut leaf—" haven't you seen the *Sunday Mail* ? They've got hold of the text of the new French Note."

" Note ? " gobbled Sir Charles, and at that he began to probe with a hairy hand among the cushions behind him. He extracted a thick wedge of newspapers and pulled from among them the *Sunday Mail*. He opened that weekly with a wide and furious gesture. Petticue ducked.

" It's on the front page," he fluted.

Sir Charles Pantry turned back to the front page. The headlines streamed and screamed. " Another insult," they shouted, " from France." " *Sunday Mail*," they yelled, " obtains exclusive text of French challenge to Great Britain." " The British Empire," they hooted, " is summoned to apologise." " What," they screamed, " will Pantry do ? "

The Secretary of State for Air read onwards. He choked. He gobbled. The wedge of neck above his collar turned purple and then blue. The thoughts of Petticue scurried frantically among the corridors of his brain searching for some formula which might tell him how to deal with apoplectics in a car. The large frame beside him began to heave and shake. Mr. Petticue peered at his neighbour in acute alarm. Sir Charles Pantry was laughing: there could be no doubt that those jerks, those gulpings, indicated laughter. The seizure of Sir Charles Pantry was not one of illness, it was one of restored vitality. He had a stroke of exuberance. "Ha! ha!" he shouted, "I have got the ——s now!"

He had used a word which Petticue, ever since his Cambridge days, had much disliked. A coarse word. A word which to Petticue suggested the most shaming associations. The springs of the upholstery twanged to the heavings of Sir Charles Pantry's laughter.

"That," thundered the Air Minister, "will dish their pretty little game. They can't sack me now."

"I'm afraid," suggested Petticue, "that I don't quite follow."

"You're *afraid!*" echoed Sir Charles Pantry, throwing into the words that ocean of contempt which he entertained, not for Petticue particularly, but for all civilians.

They drove on in silence. From time to time Mr. Petticue peeped upwards at his formidable neighbour. From time to time Sir Charles Pantry set the springs twanging by another deep rumble of delight. They were approaching Amersham.

"Stop the car," exclaimed Sir Charles Pantry, "I must telephone at once!"

Obediently Mr. Petticue leant forward and tapped the window. The chauffeur turned his head. Mr. Petticue held up an arid finger indicating " Stop ! " The car came to a standstill in front of the " Penn's Arms." Rumbling purple, Sir Charles Pantry descended and entered the inn.

" You won't be long ? " piped Mr. Petticue ; " we haven't got much time."

The wide back of the Air Minister was his sole response.

Sir Charles Pantry, having been escorted into the bar-parlour, closed and locked the door. He then went to the telephone and put through two calls.

The first was to the Air Ministry. The Resident Clerk at Whitehall Gardens was just finishing his Sunday breakfast. He had at that very moment absorbed a large mouthful of marmalade and toast. On hearing the thunderous voice of Sir Charles Pantry he gulped hurriedly.

" Yes, sir," he spluttered, " I can hear you perfectly."

" Well, look here," began Pantry, " you've got to get hold of the Under-Secretary immediately. I told him not to leave London this morning. He must go round to the Admiralty at once and get them to wireless to the *Albatross*—no, not Albert Ross, you fool—the *Albatross*—*tross*, you idiot—the ship which has taken Rocket I.A. upon the bomb experiment—got that ?—anyhow, Sullivan will know. Well, look here, it's now 9.35, he should be round there soon after 10—suppose the message gets off at 10.30—*what* message ?—why, you fool, the instructions to go ahead at once—Sullivan will

287

understand, he was with me yesterday when I sent
orders that they were for the moment to suspend
operations. Tell him that this French Note, the
one in the *Sunday Mail*, alters all that—we can now
afford to go ahead—ahead, you fool—bang the
bomb—no *bang*, I said—got that? Well, if he
can get that off by 10.30 it will reach them soon
after 5 a.m.—their time, of course—just before
dawn—they mustn't lose a moment—we must get
the news back here before to-night—time for full
splash in to-morrow's papers—got that clear? My
God! young man, if you make a mess of this I
shall have you flayed alive—the name?—what name?
—but I told you, you fool—*Albatross*—the aeroplane
carrier. Spell it?—I'll see you damned first—your
business is to obey orders and no questions—got
that? Right!"

Sir Charles Pantry's swivel eye glared at the
ceiling with the cold blue of a periwinkle.

His second call was to Lord Dorking, Chairman
of the Board of Directors of the Federation of
London Newspapers.

"That you, Dorking?"—Sir Charles Pantry
collected himself. He readjusted the tone of his
voice, which still retained its ministerial ring—"Is
that you, Lord Dorking? Charles Pantry here.
How are you, my dear fellow? Splendid, thanks.
Look here, I suppose you've seen the *Sunday Mail*?
What did you say? Oh! *scoop*. I thought you
said 'scoot.' Ha! ha! . . ."

The laughter of Sir Charles Pantry echoed
horribly against the deal boarding of the bar-
parlour.

"Ha! ha! Very good indeed. Well, in any case my resignation is off. Can't do it, you know. Can't run away in the face of such a challenge. I'll stick to the guns, and you people keep the powder dry. Yes, I'm just on my way there now, merely stopped here at Amersham to give you a ring. Yes, of course I will, I'll let you know the moment the meeting is over. Or, better still, I'll drop in for luncheon on my way back to town. I've got another bit of news for you. Pretty fruity, I can tell you. It will give you a fine splash for to-morrow. Yes, I will certainly. About one or so. I've got the car. Till then, old man. . . ."

Sir Charles Pantry unlocked the door and thrust half a crown into the palm of the barman. He then rejoined an impatient Mr. Petticue.

"Sorry," he mumbled, "absolutely essential."

The car turned to the left before they reached Great Missenden. Twenty minutes later its wheels crunched on the gravel forecourt of the Prime Minister's country residence.

(2)

They learnt from the parlour-maid (she was one of Furnivall's affectations) that the meeting of the Cabinet had been put off till 11. The Home Secretary had telephoned that it would not be possible for him to reach Chequers before that hour. Sir Charles Pantry made no visible effort to conceal his indignation. He stamped his heavy foot upon the stone floor of the outer hall. He

said " Damn ! " three times. Even Mr. Petticue
was cross. " A little inconsiderate," he twittered.
" They really might have warned us before we left
London ! They must have known."

The indignation of Sir Charles Pantry would
have been even more fervent had he known the true
cause of the Home Secretary's delay. Mr. Hore
Belisha was, in fact, putting the finishing touches
to a draft Order in Council enforcing the Defence
of the Realm Act (State of Emergency) Regulations
Schedule A. And, as we know, the whole purpose
of that Order was to prevent Sir Charles Pantry,
after his impending dismissal, from starting an
agitation in the F.L.N.

Even as it was, Sir Charles was angry enough.
He stalked into the inner hall, his great black boots
tocking loudly upon the polished boards. " And
where," he shouted, " is the Prime Minister ? "

" I think, Sir Charles, that he is taking a little
walk with Mr. Bullinger upon the down."

Pantry snorted in disgust. He lowered his huge
frame into a chintz arm-chair. He stretched his
two feet in front of him.

" Perhaps, Sir Charles, you would wish to see
the Sunday papers ? "

" No," snorted Pantry, " I should *not*."

The parlour-maid withdrew.

Mr. Petticue meanwhile had wandered off towards
the rose-garden.

Walter Bullinger meanwhile was walking with
the Prime Minister upon the down.

" It is a pity," Furnivall was saying, " it is a
thousand pities. Never again shall we be granted

such a heaven-sent opportunity to rid ourselves of Pantry. Yet seriously, after that publication in the *Sunday Mail*, the thing can't be done. It would be thought that we were dismissing a British Cabinet Minister under orders from the Quai O'Orsay. No, it simply can't be done. Pantry will have to stay. Whatever possessed Poncet I cannot imagine, nor can I conceive how the *Sunday Mail* got hold of the document. But one thing is certain—that beastly Note is certainly authentic."

" But it wasn't *delivered*," protested Bullinger. " Surely that makes a difference ? After all, I saw René Martin yesterday evening. Nothing could have been more friendly, more helpful, than his attitude. He never mentioned any Note. He said that he would at once convey to his people my apology about the air-raid. I told him that if it would strengthen Sebire's hand, I had no objection to the latter publishing the fact that we had formally apologised for our violation of the Air Convention. After all, I shall tell the whole story myself in the House to-morrow. We shall survive till then at least. But really, my dear P.M., there was not one word said about the Note. I believe it to be a forgery."

" No," sighed Furnivall, " it's authentic enough —one can tell that from the facsimile."

They were retracing their footsteps down the hill towards the house. It lay below them, mellow and somnolent in the early sun. Behind and above stretched a wide sweep of down-land turf.

" I tell you what," said Bullinger. " May I telephone before Cabinet to René Martin himself ?

It can do no harm. I know that he will tell me the truth."

The Prime Minister paused, jabbing with his shooting-stick into the turf so that it showed a round of chalk.

" Yes," he said, " do that. It's worth doing."

" Right ! " said Bullinger. " I'll hurry at once."

He almost ran down the path between the stunted shrubberies towards the house.

He was thinking : " How this place has been let down since Ramsay MacDonald's day ! Ramsay understood it : he felt at home here : he fitted in. The others simply have not known how to behave. No dignity. No harmony. No sense of history. Vulgar they are. Even Furnivall looks out of place : those grey flannel bags, that Norfolk jacket : looks like a teacher of geology at some girls' school : digging at fossils for young ladies upon the Folkestone cliffs. Whereas Ramsay . . ."

But by that time he had reached the house. The voice of Pantry aroused the high echoes of the hall. Bullinger slipped in by the garden door and dodged behind a high Chinese screen. He passed on unperceived to the Prime Minister's study. He shut the door. He bolted it. And then he telephoned to the French Ambassador.

" Is that you, Martin ? Walter Bullinger here. I am speaking from Chequers. We have got a Cabinet in twenty minutes. Look here, what am I to say about that publication in the *Sunday Mail* ? Is the thing authentic, or not ? "

" Yes," the Ambassador answered. " Yes and no. It is certainly a correct facsimile of a Note

sent to me yesterday by the Quai d'Orsay. I
know, moreover, how the *Sunday Mail* got hold of
it. I shall tell you one day. It will make you
laugh. But the point is that I was given full discretion regarding the use I should make of that
document. The fact that you began our interview
by tendering so generous an apology for the air-
raid would in any case have made me decide in no
circumstances to deliver a Note of that nature. I
am perfectly prepared to tell the Press on my own
responsibility that no such Note was ever addressed
to the British Government by this Embassy. You,
for your part, can affirm that no such Note was ever
received. If pressed upon the point of authenticity,
let us both be most undiplomatic. Let us tell the
truth. After all, it's a very reasonable truth."

"Yes," said Bullinger, "I'll try. I mean I'll
try it on the Cabinet. I'm not sure that it will
work. You see, there is more behind it all than
you realise. Anyhow, thank you, Martin. Now
I know where I stand."

Bullinger replaced the receiver thoughtfully. He
had not liked the sound of Pantry's voice behind
the Chinese screen. Furnivall, that morning, had
been a different Furnivall. He had looked ridiculous, of course : he had looked like a geologist : but
he hadn't sneered. Yet Pantry wasn't different.
He was the same sort of Pantry as he had been on
Friday. Walter Bullinger began to feel that he
also was the same Bullinger as on Friday. The
effect of the island was wearing off. For a few
hours his focus had been sharp : for a few hours his
centre, for once, had remained in the middle. As

he rose to unbolt the door Bullinger had a sense of that familiar slipping feel inside. He sighed. Patting his breast pockets cheerfully, he advanced with jaunty anglican footsteps into the inner hall.

" Dear me ! " thought Furnivall, " our friend Bullinger has recovered that posthumous look."

They walked together in the rose-garden.

(3)

The Cabinet, at 10.55, assembled in the dining-room. The Prime Minister, in accordance with the Downing Street ritual, sat in the middle. Mr. Petticue, somewhat to his embarrassment, found himself at the head of the table, ensconced like a praying mantis in a Cromwellian arm-chair. Mr. Furnivall glanced silkily around and then began :—

" I am sorry," he began, " to have dragged you all down here on Sunday. Yet a meeting in Downing Street would have entailed even greater publicity. We must be careful to avoid anything like a public sensation. There is nothing which alarms the British public so much as the thought that their Government is functioning on a Sunday. Partly sporting their feeling is, partly sabbatarian."

The Cabinet smiled politely. They were accustomed to such introductory flippancy. They did not like it, but they had come to expect it. Pantry, alone among them, drummed hirsute fingers upon the shining oak.

" We are here," continued the Prime Minister, " to discuss what I observe is described in the newspapers as ' the crisis.' I am unaware myself that any crisis exists. I can myself see nothing more in the present entanglement than a series of fortuitous misunderstandings, which can easily be dissipated by a little tact, a little firmness. Our friend Bullinger will be able to tell us that the resources of diplomacy are not yet exhausted."

Bullinger did not care for that last sentence. Furnivall had sneered: there was no doubt about it: the Prime Minister had again started sneering. The pulses of Walter Bullinger fluttered like young rooks. He glanced at Pantry. Rapidly, almost furtively, he deflected his glance.

"You see . . ." he began. The slim white fingers of Spencer Furnivall had begun to tap already.

"Well, it's like this," continued Bullinger. "You see, these air-raids over Paris, Berlin and Washington—I mean New York . . ."

"*Air-raids?*" thundered Sir Charles Pantry. "Not in the least. What are you talking about? Trial flights, they were, and nothing more."

"Well, these flights, or whatever we choose to call them, were not in accordance with the Air Convention, an international instrument which we ourselves sponsored and which we signed. No, Sir Charles, I beg you not to interrupt. Technically we should have given twelve hours' notice, and in any case we should not have flown low over any town of more than twenty thousand inhabitants. The inhabitants of Paris, Berlin and New York exceed that number. Considerable material damage has been occasioned. The horses at the Halles— the Covent Garden of Paris—and also in Berlin . . ."

" *Horses !* " snarled the Air Minister, his eyes goggling, one towards the carpet, the other upwards at the Tudor ceiling.

" Anyhow, we were, technically and morally, in the wrong. Foreseeing the protests, the unanswerable protests, which would be received, I decided to forestall this difficulty. To each of the three, no, four, Powers concerned, I have addressed an ample and as it were spontaneous apology . . ."

Sir Charles Pantry, at this, rose purple from his seat. He pointed at Bullinger a large and furious finger. He gobbled around his collar, and then the word came :—

" *Apology* . . . ? " he yelled.

" A spontaneous apology, wholly unsolicited. . . ." The voice of Bullinger was even, but his fingers toyed unevenly with the papers before him, " . . . and I added that we should be willing to pay compensation for any damage done."

Sir Charles Pantry, at that, sat down as abruptly as he had risen. His fist descended slowly but very violently upon the table. A lupin in the centre vase started at the impact and fell sideways across the shining wood.

" My dear Pantry," said the Prime Minister, " please control yourself. Personally I consider that our friend Bullinger acted with commendable promptitude. I am sure that the majority of my colleagues are of the same opinion."

A faint rustle of acquiescence passed round the table.

" He had no right," stuttered Pantry, " to apologise to foreigners without the approval of the

Cabinet as a whole. A thing like that, involving the prestige of the Empire, is a Cabinet matter. The Foreign Secretary had no right . . ."

" Pardon me ! "—the voice of Furnivall was as silk—" pardon me, my dear Pantry, but surely your air-raid should also have been submitted, before you took independent action, to the approval of the Cabinet as a whole ? "

Pantry, blue as a raw steak, blinked heavily. He leant back in his chair, drumming with ten fingers upon the table. His eye detached itself as a plumbago blossom from a sheet of indigo. He half rose, and then again he seated himself. He lifted his right hand and wagged a finger across at the Prime Minister : it was an unconvincing wag : as that of a coquettish prize-fighter.

" No ! no ! " he gobbled, " that won't do, Furnivall. Not after that French Note in the *Sunday Mail*. It simply won't work. Not after that Note it won't. You wouldn't survive an hour, and you know it. You know very well, Furnivall, that you could not face the House, still less the country, were I, at this moment, to resign. No ! no ! Mr. Furnivall, I've got you *here*."

And at that Sir Charles Pantry made a plebeian gesture with his thumb ; a gesture as if crushing some bug or flea against the table. A painful silence ensued.

" The Note to which you refer "—the voice of Furnivall was no longer silken, it was a voice of ice—" the Note with which, it seems, you desire to blackmail myself and my colleagues, is of no importance whatsoever. No such Note was ever

addressed to us : no such Note was ever received.
We ignore the publication. And I take it therefore that by the *majority* of my colleagues the
Foreign Secretary's action in repudiating these air-
raids is entirely approved ? "

A ripple of anonymous assent passed over the
Cabinet. Again the fist of Pantry descended upon
the table. A second lupin, from sheer nervousness, swung sideways on to the oak. The gasps of
Sir Charles Pantry were the only other sounds
which filled the room. Suddenly he pushed back
his chair and rose. His voice was no longer
thunderous : it was not even raucous : he wheezed.

" Right ! " he wheezed, " then I resign. But,
my God ! the whole gang of you will be ousted by
Thursday. Every man jack of you—got that ?
And I don't mind telling you where I am going at
this moment. I am going to Dorking, to Lord
Dorking. Put that in your pipes, you snivelling
lot of . . ."

The slamming of the door interrupted the last
words which Sir Charles Pantry addressed to the
Furnivall, or indeed to any, Cabinet. There was a
general feeling that his final sentence, had it not
been muffled by the slamming of the door, would
have been a wounding sentence. A strained, an
almost penitential, silence followed.

" And now," resumed the Prime Minister, " my
dear Belisha, have you your draft Order in Council ?
I should explain that we have found it necessary to
impose, as from 2 p.m. this afternoon, Schedule A
of the State of Emergency Regulations. The Home
Secretary, in a few minutes, will drive to Windsor.

The order will be posted immediately. And by the way, my dear Belisha, it might be a good thing if your Department were to indicate to the F.L.N. that any disclosure of proceedings in Cabinet will most certainly entail a prosecution under the powers thereafter devolving upon us. It would be as well to make that quite clear in advance. And now, my dear Bullinger, perhaps you can sketch to us the general outline of the statement which you propose to make to the House to-morrow afternoon ? "

"You see . . ." Bullinger began. The fingers of Furnivall joined and separated, joined and separated : slim and dry.

We are not, however, in the least concerned with Bullinger's statement. For even as he opened his discourse, looking blandly round at his colleagues in the dining-room of Chequers, a scarlet aeroplane slid away from the greased platform of the *Albatross*, and screamed across the western Atlantic. A glistening cylinder sprang into the air, and with decreasing speed, circled down towards the indigo waters. Rocket I.A. screamed onwards. The cylinder splashed and sank.

It was the immediate effects of this experiment which rendered nugatory the speech which Walter Bullinger had prepared for Monday.

(4)

The exact range of the explosion remains to this day a matter of some controversy. The records at the Air Ministry are, in so far as they go, precise enough. It is clear that it had at first been decided to release the atomic bomb at a point in the western Atlantic which is known to oceanographers as Nares Deep. It was felt, however, that this particular depression of the ocean-bed was too contiguous to Porto Rico, and a more distant pocket, situated near the intersection of Long. 72 with Lat. 34, was (unfortunately) selected instead. The bomb itself was timed to explode some five minutes after its release from the rocket plane. It had been assumed, and incorrectly, that the circumference of explosion would not be wider than thirty miles. The pilot and observer of Rocket I.A. were instructed to fly due west on leaving the *Albatross* and to allow a period of six minutes by the chronometer to elapse : the bomb was then to be released : it was estimated that at the moment of explosion the rocket plane would already have reached a point some fifty miles distant. These calculations, in several important particulars, were at fault.

The most striking of these particulars was the destruction of the United States Scout Cruiser *Omaha*. The loss of Rocket I.A., the foundering of the *Albatross* herself, were purely national disasters, and as such manageable. The disappearance of the ss. *Calamares* of the United Fruit Company might, in its turn, have been attributed to the perils of the deep. And the tidal wave which overwhelmed the cities of Charleston, Myrtle Beach and Mount Pleasant, involving a loss of eighty thousand lives, could readily, but for the *Omaha*, have been ascribed to some submarine eruption, and, as such, to the act of God. But the unfortunate thing about the *Omaha* was that she knew; and told.

At 1.30 a.m. on that Sunday morning the *Omaha* had addressed to H.M.S. *Albatross* a wireless message enquiring her identity and her business in such unusual waters. The latter, with some ostentation, had replied that she was an aeroplane-carrier of His Majesty's Navy. She added that she was engaged in experimenting with depth charges of a highly dangerous nature, and she strongly advised the *Omaha* to keep at a distance of not less than forty miles. Captain Meerschaum of the *Omaha*—better known by his posthumous appellation of "dare-devil Otto"—was struck by the discourtesy of this communication. Not only did he regard it as fresh in tone, but he regarded it as anti-American in substance. The more he thought of it, the more did Captain Meerschaum become convinced that the presence, the impertinence, and the intended action of the *Albatross* were aimed, not merely against the Monroe Doctrine, but against the freedom of the seas. At 2 a.m. he repeated to Washington the substance of these two messages and asked for instructions. A reply reached him at 4.40. He was instructed to keep the *Albatross* under observation and, while not running any unnecessary risks, to investigate the nature of her experiments. Captain Meerschaum at once released one of his two aeroplanes with orders to locate the *Albatross* and to keep her in sight. The aeroplane rose rapidly in the crisp air of dawn and climbed to a height of three thousand feet. The *Omaha*, who at the time of receiving instructions was some thirty miles east of the *Albatross*, steamed westward. It may be supposed that at the moment of the explosion the two ships were little more than eight miles apart.

The orders which, as we have seen, Sir Charles Pantry telephoned from the " Penn's Arms " at Amersham reached the Admiralty at 10 a.m. and the *Albatross* at 5.15 a.m. by Jamaica time. The bomb must have exploded at 5.30 a.m., and it was 8.50 a.m. when the aeroplane which had been detached from the *Omaha* crashed in a field near Carthage in North Carolina. The pilot was dead. But the observer (and this was the regrettable part) lived long enough to tell his story.

He explained how, shortly after five, they had reached an altitude from which both the *Albatross* and the *Omaha* were clearly distinguishable. Visibility had been excellent and, while still keeping the *Omaha* in sight, they had circled high above the *Albatross*. At about 5.20 they had seen an aeroplane, a red aeroplane, being released from the platform. Some six minutes later they had observed towards the west what they at first took to be a waterspout, but which in a few seconds assumed the form of a white bank of fog. At the same moment they observed both the *Albatross* and the *Omaha* heel over on their sides and sink within thirty-five seconds. Almost simultaneously the white bank of fog, which was travelling with extreme velocity, obscured the scene of the disaster. The pilot had dived towards the fog below them, and in a second they had been wrapped in a sheet of scalding steam. The pilot, who was wearing shorts and a thin vest, must have been killed almost immediately. The observer, who had put on a leather coat above his pyjamas, and who wore gauntlets, was scalded only upon the face. The aeroplane meanwhile had shot above the fog and was travelling westwards. He had managed to climb into the pilot's seat and gain control. The sea below was hidden by the steam, which changed gradually to a thick black cloud whirling westwards with the speed of a hurricane. It was only when he saw the Alleghanies rising ahead of him that he had thought it safe to descend.

(5)

President Hans P. Scholle was aroused early that morning by a telephone message from Washington. A terrible disaster had occurred upon the coast of Carolina. A tidal wave had overwhelmed the city of Charleston and the townships of Myrtle Beach and Mount Pleasant. Relief ships were already proceeding to the spot, but it was feared that very heavy loss of life had been occasioned. The President, still in his dressing-gown, sat down at his desk and addressed to the mayor of Charleston a telegram of condolence. It was a well-worded telegram, and having written it the President returned to his bathroom in a mood of pleasurable achievement. He hummed gaily to himself above the shaving-soap. It was a lovely morning up there at Bar Harbour. President Scholle, for once, was feeling eupeptic.

From that moment, however, things began to go wrong. The little green packet which contained his razor-blades was empty. He rang for his negro valet. The man, not expecting the President to rise so early, was feeding the ducks. Some twenty minutes elapsed before he could be retrieved. The President, during those twenty minutes, had remained encased in soap. He was no longer feeling eupeptic. He dressed sulkily and went down to the verandah. They were already laying breakfast upon the wide round table. The sight of the fourteen plates, the clatter of forks and spoons, roused him to fury. Day after day, it was always the same. Never alone. Always the bright solicitude of Mrs. Scholle, always the flat, flattering faces of his staff. Never alone, never unengaged, never unsurrounded. " Good-morning, Mr. President, I hope you slept well." " Good-morning, good-morning ! " Those flat smiles. Those unctuous voices. Mr. Scholle seized the *Philadelphia Ledger* angrily and stalked off towards the laurel bushes. He was not even allowed to see or to open his own letters. At this very moment that toady Daventer was slitting open envelopes, deciding which of the letters Mr. President might have. He was nursed, cozened, cossetted. He wasn't himself any more, he was a prize bull. The khaki figure of a detective slipped tactfully between the bushes in front of him. Mr. Scholle sank upon a garden bench with rage in his heart. He opened the *Philadelphia Ledger*. He read a spirited leading article in which his birth and origin were flung into his face. " America," he read, " tottering to decay under the guidance of a Jewish immigrant from Bremerhaven." It wasn't true. He had been born at St. Louis. And it was Hamburg that his father came from. And, damn it all, he loved America with the jealous passion of his race. Mr. Scholle tore the *Philadelphia Ledger* into small pieces. It was while he was still holding these pieces—an embarrassing handful—that Mr. Daventer came running through the shrubberies. "Mr. President!" he panted, "you are wanted urgently. A call from Washington. The British have sunk the *Omaha*." Still holding the remains of the *Philadelphia Ledger*, the President hurried towards his study.

"No, Daventer," he said ten minutes later, "no —these things must be done at once. Within half an hour the whole country will hear this news from Carthage. It is fitting, at such a moment, that their President should be the first to speak. Leave me, Daventer. I shall write that message myself."

It was for reasons such as these that the statement issued from Bar Harbour did not bear that stamp of culture and control which we are apt to associate with presidential pronouncements. Mr. Hans P. Scholle had been deeply moved. He showed it. True it is that he had good cause for indignation, both personal and righteous. True it is that he was justified in voicing the horror with which this outrage was regarded by his countrymen. True it is that history would have sympathised had he expressed to the full the anger and the sorrow of his people, had he demanded the most complete reparation for the wrong which had been done. Unfortunately, however, the President, being angry and pressed for time, was tempted into an undue exuberance of thought and language. It was unfortunate, for instance, that he should have gone so far out of his way as to drag in that passage about the *Maine*—an allusion which escaped the majority of his readers and listeners, but which was painfully startling to those who knew. Yet even to the unhistorical the purport of the presidential statement was clear enough. It was to the effect that Great Britain, having wantonly destroyed a unit of the United States Navy, having butchered in cold blood some eighty thousand American adults and children, was " attainted " of murder. And that the United States, conscious of her leadership of the civilised world, would see to it that this crime should not escape " unpunished."

This petulant statement was issued from Bar Harbour at 9.31 a.m. New York time. It reached Paris at 2.4 and Berlin shortly after 3.0. Its effect on Europe was immediate. M. Paul Sebire, at 4.30, handed in the resignation of his Government, and M. Cocquebert, with triumphant footsteps, again climbed the steps of the Elysée. By 6 p.m. on that Sunday evening M. Cocquebert was in telephonic communication with Herr Treviranus at Berlin. By 6.50 p.m. he had conducted a rapid, but extremely pregnant, conversation with Alexei Rubinstein. By 7 p.m. that evening Mr. Hans P. Scholle was assured from Washington that France, Germany and Russia were fully prepared to support the United States in any measures she might take to exact reparation from Great Britain.

Mr. Spencer Furnivall, meanwhile, had returned very hurriedly to London. He gazed round upon his miserable colleagues with a silky but uncertain smile.

"Well, my dear Bullinger . . .?"

"You see . . ." began the Secretary of State. His voice trembled.

CHAPTER XII

(1)

JANE CAMPBELL that Sunday morning woke with a renewed feeling that she was unwanted. Her conversation with Bullinger on the previous afternoon had been important enough so far as it went. But it had not gone very far. And now, away from her influence, the Secretary of State had disappeared to Chequers. This thought did not fill Jane with either confidence or pleasure. Spencer Furnivall, she felt, did not understand Walter Bullinger: and, what was more, he exercised upon him a disconcerting effect. The Secretary of State was apt to become so affable, so muddle-headed, in face of the disconcerting. Jane wished that she were there. She *ought* to be there: so ought Sir Reginald Talbot: the issue, primarily, was a Foreign Office issue: both the Permanent and the Parliamentary Under-Secretaries should certainly have been invited to attend. Furnivall possessed a slack, untidy mind. Jane straightened the fork to the left of her plate, pondering over the slipshod mentality of the Prime Minister. Walter Bullinger, if it came to that, also possessed an untidy mind. Jane straightened the spoon to the right of her plate and went on with her breakfast. Sir Reginald, on the other hand, possessed the tidiest mind she knew. It was a lovely mind. Jane finished her porridge, reflecting how much, now she came to think of it, she respected Sir Reginald Talbot.

Then she remembered that she must telephone to the office. She was connected to the Resident Clerk. No, nothing very important had come in over-night. In fact, they were a dull lot of telegrams. Should he ring her up if anything interesting happened later?

"Yes," said Jane, " that would be good of you, Mr. Crichton Stuart. I shall be in all morning. No. Hi! stop—I shan't. I forgot. I am lunching in the country. You can get me at Tunbridge Wells 186. Yes, better write it down. I shall be there till five."

She laid the receiver back upon its little rack. She was feeling better. After all, she was still a person of consequence. And it had been a good idea that about lunching with her mother. Jane always had good ideas once she started telephoning. It was a brisk, a gay Jane who rang up the garage and asked them to bring round the little Austin at eleven. " Rikki come too," she said. Then she remembered that John had begged her not to " talk baby " to her dog. " Rikki," she repeated, " you may come with me." That sounded cold. Heavens, how pompous, how insufferable, John could be! She dialled furiously for the Toll exchange.

" Mummy," she said, " I simply can't bear London any longer. May I motor down to luncheon?"

" To-day, dear?" Lady Campbell's voice was surprised and disapproving.

" Yes, Mummy, I hope you don't mind ? I'll bring something with me—a tongue or something. No, you don't like tongue. Anyhow, I'll bring something. Don't get in anything extra. Oh, I forgot it's Sunday."

" Very well, dear. At one-thirty, sharp."

" But, Mummy, if it's a bore I can easily lunch on the way down. If I get to you by two . . ."

There was no reply. Lady Campbell, as was her habit, had cut off in the middle of the conversation.

Jane was usually amused by this timid idiosyncrasy on the part of her mother. It arose, so Jane said, mainly from a physical fear of modern inventions, but to some extent also from a persistent belief that telephone conversations, on the analogy of telegrams, were charged for at so much a word. That morning, however, she was not amused : she felt mortified and snubbed. " Really," she thought, " Mummy might at least have *sounded* pleased."

Thus thinking, she observed that a strip of marquetry upon her writing-desk had become unstuck. A shaft of pleasure pierced her gloom. There were few things in life which occasioned greater joy to Jane than the sight of small objects requiring Durofix. For the next ten minutes she was neatly, happily, employed. It was with recovered equanimity (for she was not a subscriber to the *Sunday Mail*) that Jane Campbell, half an hour later, sped along the Kent arterial.

Her mother, at Rusthall Lodge, was welcoming, delighted, almost disarmed. She took her out to see the azaleas. She showed her how, this year, she had defied the slugs by sprinkling orange peel among the stocks. They sat down upon the white bench under the catalpa. " Now," said Lady Campbell, " tell me all your news."

" Mummy," Jane began, " you know John Shorland ? I mean I've told you about him, haven't I ? "

" A young man, isn't he, at the Foreign Office ? Yes, what about him ? "

" He wants me to marry him."

" But, my dear Jane, how old is he ? "

" Twenty-four, Mummy, I'm afraid."

" Well, that," said Lady Campbell, " doesn't make much difference. I always say that people should marry other people who are much younger than themselves. Your dear father . . ."

" Yes, Mummy ; but in your case it was the other way about."

" That makes no difference at all, Jane, no difference whatsoever."

" He's very young," said Jane—" I mean he's young in mind too."

" Well, dear, you can develop him, I'm sure. You're so clever, Jane. Besides, he comes of a good stock. And he's the heir, isn't he ? "

" Yes, Mummy. I think he is. But then I'm not sure that I like him very, very much. At least, I like him terribly in some ways and in other ways I . . ."

" Do you respect him, Jane ? That is the only thing that lasts in marriage, or that matters."

" *Respect* him, Mummy ? What an odd Victorian question ! I never thought about it."

" Well, Jane, think about it now."

" But, Mummy darling, we never respect people nowadays. It isn't done. I mean, it doesn't enter our heads exactly, we haven't got that sort of . . ."

" I daresay not," said Lady Campbell; " but I'm right all the same. Think it over, Jane. Try to clear your mind of everything else, and then ask yourself that question. It's the vital point. And now, darling, we must go into luncheon, or Margaret will begin to fuss. And don't talk about this thing in front of Margaret."

They chatted during luncheon of indifferent matters. Margaret brought the coffee and left them.

" Well, Mummy . . ." Jane began. But at that moment Margaret reappeared hurriedly.

" You're wanted on the telephone, Miss. A call from London."

Jane went into the little drawing-room and took up the receiver.

" That you, Miss Campbell ? Resident Clerk here. We've just had a telegram from Washington. There has been some sort of disaster in Carolina, a tidal wave or something, eighty thousand dead, and an American cruiser has been sunk. It seems that one of our new rocket planes was experimenting with a depth charge. The President appears to have gone clean off his head. He has issued a message saying that we have committed murder and must be ' punished.' I never read such a thing. Yes, of course—I got on to Chequers at once. They will be up here within the hour. I think you had better come too. Sir Reginald is here already. And by the way, Miss Campbell, a State of Emergency Order has just been issued. So far

as I know it only affects the Press and the Exchange,
but you had better bring your official pass with you.
They may hold up traffic for a bit on the Kent
arterial. Yes—Mr. Bullinger comes here direct.
They are meeting at Downing Street at 4."

Jane was still looking startled when she returned
to the dining-room.

"Mummy," she said, "something ghastly has
happened. They have been experimenting with
that atomic bomb. It seems that it has done fearful
damage in Carolina and one of the American cruisers
has been sunk. I must get back to London this
very minute."

"Who's they?" said Lady Campbell.

"Well, we, I suppose—I mean the Air Ministry—
that dreadful man Sir Charles Pantry. And I
begged Walter to make quite certain about that
atomic bomb. And now we may be let in for a
war."

"War?" said Lady Campbell, having resumed
her knitting, "War with whom?"

"War with everybody," said Jane, swallowing her
coffee in desperation.

"But surely, my dear Jane, how ridiculous you
are! If the bomb is as bad as all that, and if we
have several of them, no one will dare to go to war.
Not if we have enough of those bombs. Besides,
in any case, darling, you can't dash off like this
directly after luncheon. You know how easily . . ."

Jane kissed her mother hurriedly and ran to her
little car. The sky above the expanse of the Kent
arterial was soft and wide. Two phrases were
circling in Jane's mind. The first was "Do you

respect him, darling ? " The second was " If we really have enough of those bombs ? "

Did she ?

Had they ?

(2)

The Secretary of State returned from the Cabinet shortly after five. Jane peeped round the corner of the baize door. He was standing by the side table gulping tea. He looked boyish and forlorn. A tin tray stood upon the table, and on the tray were arranged a brown teapot, a milk and water jug, a white cup and saucer, a dish of hot toast, a pot of raspberry jam. The Secretary of State always insisted upon raspberry jam. Jane's heart went out to him.

" Walter," she said, " are you terribly busy ? May I come in ? "

He straightened himself immediately, throwing back hearty episcopal shoulders.

" Ah ! " he exclaimed, " my dear Jane ! Come in at once. You are more than welcome."

" Go on with your tea," she said, and walked towards the sofa. She lit a cigarette slowly, fitting it gradually into one of those long cardboard holders which so irritated John. " Well," she said, " and what did you decide ? "

Bullinger remained standing above her, munching toast. He spread some jam upon the toast and munched. " Pantry," he mumbled, " has resigned. As a matter of fact he resigned this morning. Dear me ! How long ago that seems ! "

" But about America and the rest ? "

314

"You have seen Scholle's statement. An extraordinary business. So undignified in a way. So childish, didn't you think, Jane? I thought it childish."

The Secretary of State beamed boyishly at her over his toast. Clearly he was feeling the strain.

"But what," Jane repeated, "have the Cabinet decided to do?"

"You have seen," said Bullinger, "our State of Emergency Order? As a matter of fact, we had decided upon that order even before the American incident arose. But it comes in useful, don't you think, Jane? I think it comes in useful."

"Yes," said Jane, and waited silently.

Bullinger, she was glad to see, was lighting his pipe. That was a good sign. He always became less anglican once he had lit his pipe. It interrupted the more jaunty variety of his talk.

"You see . . ." he began, and the match above the pipe blazed and sank to his inhalations. He lit a second match. It was more successful. He gave four rapid puffs to assure himself that the pipe was fully kindled. And then he sank wearily beside Jane upon the sofa.

"You see . . . I mean what a mess! Nothing like it ever. You know, Jane, motoring up from Chequers this afternoon I kept on asking myself at what point I had made mistakes. There is something very odd about this crisis. It opens and shuts continually like a grey door in a nightmare. At one moment it seems closed, and then one finds that it's been open all the time. You know what I mean?"

He lit another match. "You know the feeling?"

he asked, puffing till the inside of his fingers glowed pink around the bowl.

"You see, Jane, it changes so. It began in Persia. We thought in terms of Abu Saad, of the Muscat leases. I remember I was worried about them. I remember standing by the window over there, feeling that it was all very complicated, unnecessary and unfair. Unfair on me, I don't know why exactly, but I felt aggrieved. Yes, Jane, I felt aggrieved. Yet what a little thing that was! How long ago!"

"Yes," Jane answered, "it all seemed so manageable so long as it remained intricate. It is this appalling simplification of the issues which is now so terrifying. In gathering cohesion the whole business has gathered force. How distant the Abu Saad phase feels at this moment! And then there came the second phase—the Cocquebert phase. That also seemed tremendously important at the time."

"Yes, Jane, and I remember that on that Thursday evening—no, it must have been on the Friday—I was so pleased in Cabinet. Yencken's telegram arrived, the one about the Shah's offer, just as I was about to make my statement. It seemed so opportune at the time. Such a score. I suppose it was a score at the time. But only a tiny score. I blame myself for having been so anxious to take the trick."

"Then there came the third phase"—Jane's nose prodded as she made her points—"the third phase, Walter, when von Schubert made that odd suggestion, and the Sebire Government came into power. By the way, Walter, Sebire has resigned

—have you seen it on the tape? We shall have our Cocquebert back. And then there was that bit about your going to Angley. Really, Walter, I have never understood that bit in the least."

" And they thought I had gone to Stockholm, and the French, it seems, imagined I had gone to Berlin. Do you realise, Jane, that all this happened yesterday? And then came the fourth phase. Actually this morning. We got rid of Pantry. The crisis seemed over. That was this morning, Jane, at about half-past eleven. . . ."

" And now, my poor Walter, we have reached the fifth phase."

" Yes," said the Secretary of State, staring abstractedly at the paper frill in the fireplace, " we have now the fifth."

There was a silence between them.

" And do you know," Jane began again brightly, " I worked for hours at that first phase? The Abu Saad phase. I wrote a memorandum about it . . ."

"So did I," said Bullinger, "I sent a memorandum to the Prime Minister. And I mentioned the bomb —I did really, Jane. It is in writing. We were right at the time. It *was* important. One always gets the proportions wrong when one looks backwards. You were right to fuss about the early stage. Only I don't think we saw the point. I mean we bothered about Persia and the Muscat leases. We did not have the courage to admit that the essential point, as in March of last year, was Pantry and his rockets and his bomb."

" Yes," said Jane, " the Muscat leases were so much more manageable. They looked better on paper. The other was not a paper question. It was a personal question, a question of character . . ."

" I know," said Bullinger. " That's where I went wrong. I tried to avoid things. I tried to avoid awkwardness, scenes in Cabinet, even over-work. At the back of my mind, from the very start, I knew that these rockets were dangerous and that the bomb might be fatal. Yet I was too *shy*, Jane. That's what comes of being a gentleman. One always becomes shy about important things."

" And optimistic," Jane added.

" And optimistic," Bullinger confessed.

A pause followed.

" And now," said Jane, " France and Germany will join the Yanks."

" Of course," said Bullinger.

" And what shall we do ? "

" I haven't the least idea," replied the Secretary of State.

" So you decided nothing ? "

" We decided to wait until to-morrow."

" Was that a good thing to decide ? "

" Perhaps not. But something else might have been worse."

" Well," said Jane, " if the worst comes to the worst, there is always the League of Nations. We had forgotten about them."

" Yes," said Bullinger.

" And then, Walter, after all, there *is* the atomic bomb."

" No," said Bullinger.

" But there must be, Walter, if you can make one, you can make a thousand."

"My dear Jane, the point to realise is that Scholle was right. That bomb means murder. We have already murdered some ninety thousand people. Let us stick at that."

"But you're being sentimental, Walter. They don't *know* it was a bomb. They don't realise that what happened to Charleston may happen to New York. They think it was some sort of depth-charge. Surely it would do good to tell them it was a bomb?"

"The only thing," said the Secretary of State, "that the Cabinet *did* decide this afternoon was to stick to this depth-charge theory."

"But you can't, Walter. There is the opposition."

"But, my dear Jane—conceive of the alternative. There is public opinion. Would they for one second allow us to grovel to the United States if they knew about this atomic bomb? And grovel is what we shall have to do."

Jane's nose pointed fiercely in the air. It was a banner of freedom.

"Never," she exclaimed, "Never! never! never! Anything but that!"

"Well, anyhow," sighed Bullinger, "that is what we shall decide in Cabinet. Apart from my own views, there are several other Ministers who would certainly resign were there any further question of the bomb. That would mean a Government either of extreme left or the extreme right. It would mean the end of Liberalism in England. It would entail disasters far more terrible than any that we can suffer at the hands of the four Powers. No, Jane, surrender—complete and utter—is our only course."

319

Jane rose quietly. " I must go," she said, " I must leave you."

Her hand rested for a moment upon Bullinger's bowed shoulder.

She walked quickly from the room.

(3)

" Jane," said John Shorland that evening, " are you dining anywhere ? Let's dine together and talk it over."

" Talk what over ? "

" Not ourselves, Jane. We can't talk about that at present. Talk the crisis over."

" Very well, John—if you like."

" Let's get to the Jardin, Jane. I'll be there at eight."

Jane winced. " No," she said hurriedly, " not the Jardin—anywhere but that."

He looked surprised at her vehemence. She felt saddened by his insensibility. Yet it was an impersonal sadness : she felt free now that she had ceased to respect him. She had never respected him.

" Very well," he said, " we can go to the Café Royal."

" No," Jane answered, " I'll give you dinner at my house. We shall be quiet there. I'll go back at once and warn Rose. She is really quite good-tempered about that sort of thing."

A few minutes later she was driving past the unsolaced frontages of Pimlico. " One ought to be able to do something, there must be something that one ought to do." These words drummed in Jane's ears the whole length of Ebury Street. They still circled in her mind as she climbed the neat staircase of No. 34 St. Leonard's Terrace. They wheeled back at her when, in her almost clinical bathroom, she looked at her face in the glass. It was a pale face, but defiant. Jane smiled sadly at it. " A Charlotte Corday," she murmured, " without a Marat."

She was silent during dinner, allowing John to talk.

" The Secretary of State," he was saying, " has, I fear, had a complete relapse. He was more solid yesterday afternoon than I have ever seen him. Yet to-day he has gone to pieces again. He bounced like a celluloid ball. You know, Jane, those little balls which dance in a stream of heated air. Pitiable it was, positively pitiable. After you left the office the telegrams began to pour in by the hundred. Each telegram, each telephone call, was worse than the last. The block, the old Abu Saad block, has been reconstituted with a vengeance. The Germans have issued their beastly Vorbereitung decree, which, as you know, is pretty close to mobilisation. The French are concentrating all their submarines at Brest, even the Mediterranean ones, which looks as if they were certain about the Italian republics. They have also wirelessed to their merchant ships to make for the nearest French, or, if more than two hundred miles distant, neutral, port. We intercepted that. And the Russians have landed two brigades upon the Persian coast, and have established a regular bridgehead at Pahlevi. It seems also that they are concentrating all the Caspian shipping at

Baku. But the worst news comes from Angora and Kabul. It really looks as if Rubinstein had brought off some concentration of Eastern Powers against Persia or rather India. And as for the United States, the whole country seems to have gone up in flames. The Washington Embassy, as well as our Consulate at St. Louis, have been attacked and looted. We can't make out what has happened to Reith. And meanwhile all that the Cabinet have done is to recall the fleet to Rosyth, and to issue their Emergency Regulations, Schedule B. Of course it's lucky that it's Sunday. The public do not yet seem to have caught on to the danger. There was a small crowd in Downing Street, but nothing like the crowd we had after the Cocquebert Note. Meanwhile the Home Office have muzzled the B.B.C. Nothing except Government communiqués are to be allowed in to-morrow's Press. Bullinger was trying to dictate the main communiqué just before I left. It was pitiable, Jane, I can't tell you. Peabody and I took turns to interrupt him with some fresh piece of ghastly news. He was bouncing up and down the room, slapping his breast pockets—you know that trick—and at each message that we brought him he became more jaunty, more exuberant, more gay. Hopeless he was ; I ceased even to be sorry for him. When I brought the Kabul telegram he had reached the end of his communiqué. " A full statement of the position will be made in the House of Commons to-morrow by His Majesty's Principal Secretary of State for Foreign Affairs." He intoned that sentence, Jane—it was a sort of magnificat."

Jane interrupted at this stage. " Exactly at

what time," she said, " will he make his statement ? "

" Oh, after questions—about 3.40, I suppose."

" Yes, after questions," Jane repeated the words slowly, pointing with her nose. " Go on, John," she smiled wearily, " continue your catalogue of woe."

" Of course," John continued, " the Service Departments are doing something. They have got to carry out the items in Schedule B. All telephone communication, except of official calls, has been severed with the continent. The Channel steamers are being diverted from Folkestone and Dover to Newhaven and Havre. Can't think why. And by the way, Jane, it's to be a bank holiday to-morrow. The Stock Exchange won't open till Tuesday. . . ."

Jane was not listening in the least. She was thinking with her chin upon her palm.

" Let's go into the other room," she said. " You will have to get back to the office in a few minutes. Yes, bring your brandy with you."

For a further twenty minutes John Shorland poured out his catalogue of happenings. And then he checked himself.

" Jane," he said, " I don't believe you have heard a single syllable. You haven't been paying the slightest attention."

" No," said Jane, " I haven't. But I'll tell you what I *have* done. I have made up my mind. I have decided what to do."

" Do ? " echoed John, gazing up at her. For she had risen and was standing beside the fireplace.

" Yes, I have made up my mind. I have come to a decision. It will seem to you a rather sensational decision, but there it is. It's no good your trying to dissuade me. I am quite firm about it. And of course, if I tell you, you must keep it to yourself."

She sat down again, leaning forward in her chair.

"This explosion, this American disaster, has inevitably destroyed the thinking capacity of half the world. It will be some time before people recover their reason, and then it will be too late. This bomb of Pantry's has released emotions which no wisdom, no cleverness, no surrender even, on our part can possibly tame. Above all, it has released hatred. Now there is only one human emotion stronger than mass-hatred, and that is mass-fear. We must summon fear to our assistance. That, John, is the only possible thing which we can do."

Shorland remained silent. He made no comment as she continued.

"The Secretary of State is to make his speech after questions to-morrow. I propose to forestall that speech. The Cabinet have decided that, whatever happens, the legend of the depth-charge is to be maintained. I propose, before Bullinger makes his statement, to tell the whole truth."

Jane rose from her chair and paced slowly up and down the little carpet. She poked, she burrowed, with her nose.

"Yes, it is really easier than you think. I can get a friend on the other side—I could get Oliver Baldwin—to put a Private Notice Question on the subject of the *Albatross*. As the Secretary of State is making his big speech later, I shall in any case be taking Foreign Office questions. I shall say that the *Albatross* was experimenting, not with depth-charges, but with an atomic bomb. I shall say that the range of destruction of these atomic bombs, for the manufacture of which we alone possess the required alloy, was wrongly estimated at thirty miles. I shall say that, as a result of this deplorable accident, we must now assume that a single atomic bomb is capable of destroying all matter within a circumference of seventy to eighty miles from the point of explosion. That, I think, is all that it will be necessary to say."

Shorland remained silent.

" Of course," he said at last, " you would give that answer entirely on your own. I mean you would, in actual fact, be acting treacherously towards the Cabinet in general and to Bullinger personally. Apart from other considerations, such action would ruin your career. It would mean that from that moment you would have to retire from public life. And there would be no return."

" Yes, John, I know that. I don't pretend to like it. I hate it. But we must see the thing in proportion. Once I am convinced that this is the only possible hope . . ."

John Shorland rose.

" Yes," he said, " I think you are right. I *know* that you are right. Bless you, Jane. I must be getting back now. I promised Peabottle I should be back soon after nine."

He left her hurriedly.

(4)

John Shorland was much relieved, on reaching the Foreign Office, to find that Peabody had not returned. He skimmed his hat in the direction of the peg and hurried across to his own table. "Exchange," he said, "can you get me Reuter's immediately? I want to talk to the Chairman himself." Having set this call in motion, he crossed to Peabody's table and picked up the second telephone. He asked for the News Department. "Private Secretary speaking. Is that the News Department? That you, Miles? John here. I say, look here, have you sent out that Government communiqué yet? Half an hour ago. Right you are. I say, you might send me down the final text as issued. Send it down at once. I'm rather rushed at the moment. Yes, I'm in my room." The bell on his own table had by that time started to ring. He dashed across and lifted the receiver.

"Private Secretary Foreign Office speaking. That Reuter's? Can you put me on to the Chairman personally? Oh, he's away, is he? Down at Rottingdean? Where did you say? Well, can you give me the number? I don't care a hell what instructions he left. This is most urgent and important. I am speaking on behalf of the Foreign Secretary, and I must talk to Lord Rottingdean himself and no one else. You have simply got to give me that number. All right. Sorry I was cross. Yes, I'll write it down."

Shorland scribbled a number on his blotting-pad and told the exchange to put through a trunk call urgent and priority. A minute later he was speaking to Lord Rottingdean in Yorkshire.

"Is that you, Lord Rottingdean? This is John Shorland speaking. I'm speaking from the Foreign

Office. Your people did not want to give me your
number, but I insisted. Yes, I'm very well, thank
you; rather rushed at the moment. Look here,
I've got to put out to-night a communiqué which is
very urgent and complicated. I want to make
quite certain of two things. First, that it does *not*
appear in the morning editions of any British newspaper. Second, that it *does* appear in every foreign
newspaper from Vladivostock to Los Angeles. I
shall have the text ready in about half an hour from
now. I shall then take it round by hand to your
office. It is too important to trust to ordinary
channels. What I want you to do is to ring up your
man in charge at the office and warn him that I shall
shortly arrive with a Government communiqué
which has got to be issued immediately. What's
his name? Hemming? Oh yes, I know, young
Fleming. Yes, I know him personally—that makes
it easier. Well, I should be much obliged if you
could ring him up and tell him to do exactly what I
ask. Impress upon him that the thing is vastly
confidential and all that. Thank you so much,
Lord Rottingdean. I'm sorry to have bothered you.
Only we can't afford to take risks of muddling this
message. Good-night—many thanks."

Shorland replaced the receiver with a gesture of
finality. That was that. He had burnt his boats.
It made him feel very clear about the head. He
opened the box which had just come down from the
News Department. He spread the Government
communiqué upon his blotting-pad and read it carefully. It was headed: " *Statement approved by
the Prime Minister and Cabinet, June 5. To be*

released for publication in first morning editions of June 6.

The text was as follows :—

" His Majesty's Government regret to announce that a very serious accident, involving the loss of many lives, occurred at dawn on Sunday at a point in the Western Atlantic some three hundred miles east of the coast of Carolina, U.S.A.

It is feared that H.M.S. *Albatross* has been lost with all hands. Rocket Aeroplane I.A. has not returned.

The United States Scout Cruiser *Omaha*, which happened to be in the vicinity of the accident, is reported to have foundered, and the s.s. *Calamares* of the United Fruit Company is also missing.

Shortly after the accident a tidal wave overwhelmed the city of Charleston, South Carolina, and the neighbouring townships of Mount Pleasant and Myrtle Beach, involving very considerable loss of life.

The United States Government, relying upon evidence furnished by the *Omaha* previous to the event, attribute this unfortunate disaster to certain experiments in a new type of depth-charge which, it is alleged, were being conducted at the time by H.M.S. *Albatross* with the assistance of Rocket Aeroplane I.A.

Pending full enquiry, His Majesty's Government do not desire to commit themselves to any opinion regarding the accuracy or the reverse of the American contention. Nor would any useful purpose be at present served by disclosing the text of the communications which have been received from Washington.

His Majesty's Government feel it necessary none the less to announce here and now that they are willing that these incidents should be submitted to full and impartial investigation. And they pledge themselves, should it be proved that the experiments which were being conducted by H.M.S. *Albatross* were in any way responsible for the accident, to offer all reparation within their power.

In view, meanwhile, of the strained situation which has inevitably arisen as a result of this disaster, His Majesty's Government have decided to put into force the provisions of the Defence of the Realm (State of Emergency) Act Schedules A and B.

It has also been decided that to-day, Monday, June 6, shall be regarded within the United Kingdom and in Northern Ireland as a Bank Holiday.

A full statement of the position will be made in the House of Commons this afternoon by His Majesty's Principal Secretary of State for Foreign Affairs. Arrangements are being made with the B.B.C. whereby this statement shall be relayed from the House to all stations."

" Ugh ! " said John Shorland.
Having uttered this expletive he pulled his Remington Portable towards him. He selected

from the rack in front of him the most embossed
of all his varieties of official notepaper. He took
three very clean carbons from the drawer. He
began to type.

John Shorland was as proud of his gifts as a
typist as he was proud of his facility for drafting
official documents without a single erasure. At the
end of twenty minutes his own communiqué was
finished. He slid it out of the Remington and laid
the carbon copies neatly to one side. He re-read
what he had written with an awful horror and a glow
of delight. It ran as follows :—

*Statement for foreign press approved by Prime
Minister and Cabinet. To be sent out through
Reuters at midnight on June 5. Not to be
released to any newspaper in the United Kingdom
or Northern Ireland.*

In connection with the disaster which has
occurred in the Western Atlantic the British
Government make the following announce-
ment :—

(1) The wreck of the United States Scout
Cruiser *Omaha*, as also the sinking of H.M.S.
Albatross and the s.s. *Calamares*, and the
tidal wave which broke upon the coast of South
Carolina, were not, as contended by the United
States Government, caused by experiments in
any form of depth-charge.

These accidents were caused by the experimental release from Rocket Aeroplane I.A. of
an atomic bomb.

(2) The British Government admit that the destructive range of this bomb had been seriously under-estimated. It had been assumed that the atomic bomb would possess a range of destruction not wider than thirty miles in circumference. It is now clear that the range of destruction for each bomb is between seventy and eighty miles.

(3) On learning of the disaster the British Government at once issued orders that no rocket or other aeroplane shall, in time of peace, carry any atomic bombs: all existing stocks have been isolated in such a manner as to render impossible the recurrence of any further accidents.

(4) The British Government recognise, none the less, that full reparation is due to the United States for the damage which has regrettably been caused. They are prepared to submit the incident to any impartial tribunal and to abide by any reasonable award which such a tribunal may pronounce.

(5) The British Government, moreover, recognising that these new and potent engines of destruction are inimical to existing civilisation, are prepared (subject to the condition outlined below) to pledge themselves to destroy within a period of six months their existing stocks of atomic bombs and to manufacture no further bombs in future.

They suggest for this purpose that the matter be referred to the twelfth Preparatory Disarmament Conference which is to meet at

Geneva on July 1 next. As a condition of their renouncement the British Government would, however, insist that all other Powers pledge themselves unreservedly to abandon all forms of aerial and submarine warfare, and to suppress their existing fleets of aeroplanes and submarines.

(6) Unless the Powers signatory of the Protocol of the Eleventh Preparatory Disarmament Conference signify their acceptance of this proposal not later than the 28th of the present month, the British Government will reluctantly be obliged to resort to progressive means of compulsion."

Having read through this composition with great care, John Shorland rang the bell. " Well," he exclaimed grimly, " I may, or may not, have saved the twentieth century. But I have certainly saved Jane Campbell."

" I shall want a taxi," he said aloud, " in five minutes in the courtyard."

He then took a large envelope, inserted his communiqué, and sealed it with three red seals. The wax was scarcely dry when Peabody, in full evening dress, appeared upon the threshold.

" Anything happened ? " he enquired.

" No," said Shorland, " nothing has happened for the moment. I must dash out and get a drink."

He drove straight to Reuter's.

(5)

It was not till eleven the next morning that Walter Bullinger arrived at the Foreign Office. The meeting of the Cabinet had been fixed for twelve. He emerged exuberantly from the lift and handed his grey top-hat, his lavender gloves, to the expectant office-keeper. "Good-morning, Sinclair," he said, and having said it he adjusted the carnation in his button-hole. "A lovely morning," he added, prancing, through a widely opened portal, into his room.

John Shorland entered immediately by the green baize door. He had been listening anxiously for the high hum of the Secretary of State's lift. He had been waiting to confess.

"Ah! good-morning, my dear Shorland! What a superb morning! I can assure you that the Park this morning, one can say what one likes . . ."

"I am afraid, sir, that I have something very unpleasant to tell you. It is essential that you should know about it before you see anyone else this morning. I am afraid, sir, that you will be deeply shocked. But I quite see that I have got to tell you before you speak to anyone else, before you see anyone else . . ."

The Secretary of State was standing beside his desk. He picked up a file of typewritten telegram sheets which had arrived since the morning's distribution. He hummed to himself cheerfully as he turned the sheets.

"Yes, my dear Shorland. Well, what is it?"

"Last night, sir, I gave to Reuter's a communiqué

which they sent out at midnight. It will have been published in the press of the whole world."

"Ah! Reuter's, of course!"—the Secretary of State was still humming snatches from 'Rigoletto'—"Ah yes, we forgot about Reuter's. That was thoughtful of you, Shorland. I am much obliged."

"But my communiqué, sir, was very different from yours. I think you had better read it at once. I have a copy here . . ."

Bullinger continued to turn over his telegram sheets humming gaily.

"But of course, my dear Shorland, naturally the Reuter message would have to be cast in a slightly different form. I have absolute reliance in your judgment. Not a Fellow of All Souls for nothing. There's no need to get agitated about it. I see that you are agitated, my dear Shorland. You are quite pale. Now that won't do at all. Not at all. At moments such as this, my dear Shorland, we must all keep our nerves rigidly under control."

John Shorland set his teeth in rage.

"You've simply got to read this, sir, before you read anything else. You can't get away from it. Whatever you may think about it, the fact remains that this Reuter communiqué is from now on the centre of the whole problem. I am afraid, sir, that you have got to read it, and at once."

He thrust the paper into Bullinger's unwilling hands. The Secretary of State read it slowly. On reaching the end of the first paragraph he sat down abruptly and began to read again from the beginning. "Great God!" he muttered. "My God!"

Then he looked up at Shorland. " I don't quite understand . . ." he said. It was not an angry look : it was not either frightened or puzzled : it was just a shy look. The Secretary of State was feeling overwhelmingly embarrassed. This, ineluctably, was about to be a most shaming scene.

He reached for the telephone. " This is the Secretary of State speaking. Please ask Miss Campbell to come to my room immediately."

" So you handed this to Reuter's last night ? Without any authority ? Now look here, Shorland, do you mean me to seriously believe, I mean seriously to believe, do you believe me to mean . . ."

His voice trailed off helplessly. He sank back into his chair. He seemed to have shrunk to half his size. He sat there huddled, fiddling with errant fingers round the edge of his blotting-pad. Tearing triangles. Jane Campbell entered. He roused himself.

" Jane," he said, " read this."

" Yes, sir," John Shorland answered—it was better to get it off while Jane was reading—" yes, sir, I do not try to excuse my action. I know that there is no excuse. I know the penalties for what I have done. But there is an explanation. I saw quite clearly that such a statement, such a menace, if you like, was the only hope. I knew that neither you nor the Cabinet would ever authorise it. I therefore took it upon myself."

Jane had finished reading the communiqué. She said nothing. She came and stood by the Secretary of State's chair. Bullinger again looked at Shorland. A crushed, a purple Bullinger. Yet, for an instant, from his colourless eyes there flashed something that was difficult to define. It wasn't anger. It was not even astonishment. It was certainly not admiration. It was something sharp and thin and almost hostile. Shorland never forgot that flash in the eyes of Walter Bullinger. It was not till long afterwards that he realised that it had been a flash of envy.

Bullinger turned to Jane. "Well," he said, "you gather what has happened! This young man has used his official position to issue a statement which is not only unauthorised, but a deliberate forgery. A statement which may well . . ."

The telephone bell rang before Jane could frame a reply.

"Yes," said the Secretary of State, "yes, Bullinger himself speaking. Oh, good-morning, my dear Ambassador! *What* did you say? I am sorry, Martin, but I can't quite catch. *Congratulate me?* But what on earth about? The Reuter message? Oh yes, I see, of course. Of course, Martin. Worked already? What on earth do you mean? No, that's impossible! You mean to tell me that your Government have agreed already? But surely that's very quick. Of course our friend Cocquebert *is* very quick, isn't he? Ha! ha! Oh, the Reuter communiqué? A masterpiece? Come, come, my dear Martin, you know, really! You are bringing a Note? Satisfactory, is it? Well, come along at once. We have a Cabinet at twelve. A thousand thanks, my dear Martin. No, nonsense, nonsense! —not in the least. You flatter me. One merely tries to do one's best."

He laid down the receiver and stared fixedly in front of him at the blotting-pad. " Extraordinary ! " he muttered, " quite extraordinary."

He turned to Jane.

" That was René Martin. He says that his Government agree with the conditions contained in our Reuter communiqué. Most extraordinary. No, don't go, Shorland. Wait here. There may be something in all this. We must work it out. It's very risky, of course, but, after all, forlorn hopes, you know, at such a moment. But what the Cabinet will say, I mean, really . . ."

Again the telephone rang. He answered it.

" Yes, yes. Walter Bullinger here. Oh yes, my dear Schubert. Good-morning. What do you say ? Good news ? Well, that's always welcome. Which communiqué ? Oh yes, of course, the Reuter communiqué. Well, I confess that I found it a bit menacing when I first read it. Yes, it's clear enough. Yes, I agree. It has cleared the air. *Enormous* good ? Surely, my dear Schubert, you exaggerate. Yes, of course I can see you. We have a Cabinet at twelve. I should like something definite before then. In writing if possible. So your people also accept our renouncement condition ? Excellent ! But bring a Note with you, there's a good fellow. I must have something final and definite to show the Cabinet."

Bullinger turned to Shorland.

" My God ! young man—you've done the trick ! That was Schubert that time. The Germans agree. This is really amazing—think of it, Jane—out of all this may come disarmament, real disarmament . . ."

The green baize door clicked suddenly. Arthur Peabody entered.

" Excuse me, sir," said Peabody, " but the American Ambassador has just telephoned. Your own line was engaged. He says he has received urgent instructions to open negotiations on the basis of the Reuter communiqué. I ventured to tell him that there must be some misunderstanding. To my certain knowledge no communiqué had been issued through Reuter's. He read me the text upon the telephone. I assured him at once that no statement of such a nature could possibly have issued from official sources. I begged him not to attach the slightest credence to anything so fantastic. It's extraordinary, these Americans, their childishness . . ."

" Oh, shut up !" Bullinger shouted, and he reached quickly for the telephone. " Get me," he said, " the American Ambassador—very urgent indeed."

He drummed impatiently upon the blotter till the call came through.

Jane came up to John Shorland. " You did that for my sake, John ? "

" Not in the least, Jane, I merely cribbed your idea."

" Oh, John, all the same. . . . Dear me, how I respect you ! I find it far nicer to respect people than to be in love with them. Don't you, John ? "

Shorland grinned. " I suppose so, Jane." The Secretary of State held up a finger, suppressive of all whisperings.

" Is that you, my dear Ambassador ? Walter

Bullinger here. I am afraid my secretary misled you about that Reuter communiqué. *Of course* it's authentic. I drafted it myself. Yes, that's what I thought. It simply had to be precise. Yes, I agree. But it does offer a solution, don't you think? Yes, I should love to see you, but the Cabinet meets in forty minutes, and I have the Frenchman and the German coming, also bringing Notes. I could squeeze you in at 11.50. And for God's sake man bring something in writing. The Cabinet always like to see these things in written form. But not at all, my dear Ambassador. One does one's best. No, really, you flatter me. One only tries to do one's best."

EPILOGUE

Extract from The Times, *June* 12, 1939 :—

" *Geneva, June* 11. The Council at this afternoon's session considered the appeal addressed to them by the Persian Government in connection with the landing of Russian troops on Persian territory. The Secretary-General announced that he had this morning received from the Russian Government a telegram stating that, in view of the withdrawal from the Majlis of the Bill cancelling all foreign concessions in Persia, orders had already been issued that the Russian troops and gunboats should return to Baku. The Council took note of this assurance."

Extract from The Times, *June* 27, 1939 :—

" His Majesty's Minister at Tehran to-day signed with the Persian Foreign Minister an agreement whereby Great Britain, on behalf of the Sultan of Muscat, renounced all territorial claims to the island of Abu Saad. An Anglo-Persian consortium is being constituted for the exploitation of all mineral deposits in the island."

Extract from The Times, *July* 15, 1939 :—

" Mr. Walter Bullinger, the Foreign Secretary, reached Victoria Station yesterday evening on his return from the Disarmament Conference at Geneva. He was met on arrival by the Prime Minister and Members of the Cabinet, as well as by the French, German, United States and Russian Ambassadors. The Persian Minister also was present. A large crowd had collected round the approaches to the station and was with difficulty controlled by the police. Mr. Bullinger, who was looking in the best of health, gaily acknowledged . . ."

Extract from The Times, *August* 1, 1939 :—

"Mr. Arthur Sidney Peabody, C.M.G., C.B.E., to be His Majesty's Minister at Berne in succession to Sir Ronald Pittledoe."

Extract from the Leeds Mercury, *September* 10, 1939 :—

"The chair of Greek History at our University, recently rendered vacant by the untimely death of Professor Moriarty, has been offered to the Honourable John Shorland, M.A., a Fellow of All Souls College, Oxford. It is understood that Mr. Shorland, who until recently was attached to the Foreign Office, has signified his willingness to accept this appointment. Mr. Shorland, though still a very young man, has many academic laurels to his credit. At Eton he won the Newfoundland, and obtained a first class in Responsions. His career at Balliol was no less distinguished. He is one of the few Oxonians who secured both the Newdigate and a Senior Wranglership. He may be certain that at Leeds . . ."

Extract from the Morning Post, *November* 5, 1939 :—

" A marriage is announced, and will shortly take place, between Jane, only child of the late Professor Sir Andrew Campbell, F.R.S., F.R.G.S., and Lady Campbell, of Rusthall Lodge, Tunbridge Wells, Parliamentary Under-Secretary of State for Foreign Affairs, and Sir Reginald Talbot, G.C.M.G., K.B.E., C.I.E., Permanent Under-Secretary of State for Foreign Affairs."

Extract from the World's Press News, *December* 6, 1939 :—

" We understand that Mrs. Gerald Snelgrove, formerly Madame Jules Boursicaut, but better known in ' The Street ' as ' Mélisande ' of the *Sunday Mail*, has accepted an appointment as Fashion Editor in the Vogue-Femina-Vie Heureuse-Good Housekeeping amalgamation."

Extract from " *The Londoner's Diary*," Evening Standard, *December* 20, 1939 :—

" The retiring Foreign Secretary, Mr. Walter Bullinger, is in many ways a remarkable man. Not only is he the only front-bench figure who, after the age of fifty, has managed to reduce his handicap from 9 to 7, but he has for long shared with Mr. Buchan Hepburn the honour of being one of the last of our public figures to wear a grey top hat in the House of Commons.

" The last time I lunched with Mr. Bullinger was shortly after his triumphant return from the final Disarmament Conference at Geneva. He told me . . ."

Extract from the Morning Post, *April* 6, 1940 :—

" The Earl and Countess of Cheltenham, accompanied by Lady Jennifer Bullinger, have left 34 Grosvenor Gardens for Angley Manor, Cheltenham."

Extract from Country Life, *July* 1942 :—

" Some of our leading horticulturists prefer to make the best of this climatic alteration. Lord Cheltenham, for instance, the President of the Royal Horticultural Society, has definitely come down on the side of those who believe that the Gulf Stream has been permanently diverted. He has transformed three of his orchards at Angley Manor into vineyards, and looks forward to producing wine, at first upon a domestic, but eventually upon a commercial scale. His Lordship is also experimenting both with Richmond and with Cavalla tobacco plants. We may look forward to the day when the ' Clos Angley 1945 ' or the ' Flor d'Angley ' becomes the ambition of our oino—or our kapnophils."

Extract from a wireless talk by Mr. Gerald Heard, September 1943 :—

" Then there is another extraordinarily interesting thing about this change in climatic conditions. Eels, as you know, are very odd creatures. Yet why have they suddenly disappeared from our ponds and rivers ? There are many ichthyographers who maintain that the eel has formed a distaste for our present hot summers and dry winters, and undoubtedly many of his old haunts are now covered with the wild rosemary and cistus. Yet, after all, there are eels in Provence, aren't there?, and our average drought has not yet reached the Provençal level. No—I fear that the climatic argument won't do with our eels. I incline rather to credit those daring investigators who contend that it is all the fault of the atomic bomb explosion in June of 1939. Such people point to the fact that the breeding-grounds of our British eel were situated in the Gulf of Mexico, after all not so very far from the point where the atomic bomb exploded. Now it is very extraordinary when you come to think of it that . . ."

Extract from the Financial Times, *October* 1943 :—

" We are informed that Sir Charles Pantry, at one time Air Minister in the Furnivall Cabinet, has accepted a directorship of the Bolivian Platinum Exploration and Investment Company. The other two directors are Mr. Roy Gomez and Howard Stanley-Lewis, Esquire."

APPENDIX I

[*How history is written*]

WE reproduce below the introduction written to the 1978 edition of this novel.

Joon 13, 1978.

Relistening resently Vol. III Lord Limpsfield's "*Forty Years in Downing Street*"—(publishd, Rae & Kristian, Gloster, 1949 : blattnerphond, Ekersly Rewīnd Serees, 1968-) rekognīsed passej on paj 328 deeling with krīsis of Joon 1939.

Rekalled how mī grandfather :—

[Harold Nikolson, d. 1958 : diplomatist, rīter, renter, passifist : tippikal erly-Georgian : sentimental, emoshonal, optimistik, induldjent, superfishal, unedukated, feebly hellenistik : hemd in bī relidjus, klas, " good-taste," publikskool, Oxfo'd, patriotik, nashonalist, borjoy, blokages : bad pituitary, worse adrenals : no sĕns of sinthesis : no kommuniti-feel : plump, roomatik, rosi, def, kurli, verri foolish]

—had kontended this passej " travesty of the facts," & insisted rīting what he klamed troo reko'd of those events.

Having diskuverd kopi of this his reko'd have desīded republish it in its original fo'm. Bekos provides admirabl instans muddelheadedness of last

tô kapitalist dekkads. Wil make no apologi for
retaning old-fashionabl stīl and spelling. Nor kan
be held responsibl long-windedness grandfather, his
fawls valyoos, his kompleet lak of enni narrativ gifts.

Meenwhīl prodyuse belô passej in Lord Limpsfield's memwīres wich drove mī grandfather kompôs
this windi wo'k.

EXTRACT FROM LORD LIMPSFIELD'S
*"Forty Years in Downing Street," Rae and
Christian, Gloucester, 1949, Vol. III, pp. 328 ff.*

" *But of all the many crises, national and international, which it has been my privilege to witness,
none was so sudden, so complicated, so protean, so
fraught with world-shattering possibilities, as that which
has been miscalled the Anglo-French crisis of June 2 to
6, 1939.*

" *I shall, I trust, be revealing no damaging secret if
I disclose that for several hours during the course of
those four or five days the fate of Western Civilisation
seemed to all of us to hang, as it were, by a thread.
The public, misled by the F.L.N. (that syndicate of
popular newspapers the suppression of which was one
of the many valuable achievements of the Mosley
Cabinet of 1942)—derived the impression that the
crisis was due solely to the ambition and to the
machinations of M. Cocquebert, the Prime Minister of
France. It was represented to them that M. Cocquebert had taken advantage of some trivial dispute in the
Persian Gulf to fasten upon the British Empire a
quarrel of the most envenomed nature. And they were
also taught to believe that, had it not been for the courage*

and enterprise of Sir Charles Pantry, Air Minister in the Furnivall Government, we should in all certainty have been exposed either to a humiliating surrender or to a disastrous war against the combined forces of France, Germany, Russia and the United States. It was the general opinion at the time (an opinion which I much regret to observe is echoed in Professor Scarrett's otherwise admirable monograph "Capitalist Diplomacy: Last Phase") that the civilian members of Mr. Furnivall's Cabinet, and the Foreign Secretary in particular, displayed throughout the crisis a lack of perspicacity, a lack of decision, a lack of virile courage, from which they were rescued solely by the forceful realism of Sir Charles Pantry.

" That impression—and I write as one who witnessed every stage of this sensational drama—was, and is, a false impression.

" Sir Charles Pantry, let me be the first to admit, was a great Air Minister : yet in Cabinet he exercised, and desired to exercise, no influence whatsoever. He was content to leave the broad lines of policy to be decided by the Prime Minister and the Foreign Secretary : his sole preoccupation was loyally and efficiently to execute the decisions which they reached. Nor must it be forgotten that at the supreme moment of the crisis, (at the moment when war between Great Britain and the United States appeared wholly unavoidable) Sir Charles Pantry had already resigned.

" The control of policy rested, during those anxious days, entirely in the hands of Walter Bullinger (subsequently Lord Cheltenham), His Majesty's then Secretary of State for Foreign Affairs. Even the Prime Minister confined his intervention to encouraging and

stimulating his more brilliant, and (if one may say so without offence to the memory of Mr. Furnivall) more active, colleague.

"*The name of Lord Cheltenham is a household word to horticulturists throughout the country : he is gratefully remembered as the man who financed and organised the Bullinger Expedition to Mazanderan in 1942, and it is to him we owe the discovery, cultivation, and popularisation of the* Meconopsis Angleyi *or green poppy.*

"*His merits as a statesman and as a diplomatist have been less widely recognised. The astounding lucidity with which, when others wavered, he grasped the essentials of the problem ; the dexterity and courage which he displayed in coping with the ever-shifting menace of that four-day crisis ; above all, his genius for calculated inaction interspersed with calculated indiscretion ; all these should have sufficed, were the true story known, to place his name upon the golden roll of great Foreign Secretaries ; to immortalise him as the equal of a Canning or a Salisbury, of a MacDonald or a Brendan Bracken.*

"*No, Walter Bullinger has been a prophet of too little honour in his own country. Upon the Continent, and in the United States, he is still regarded as a second Talleyrand, as a master of diplomatic finesse. His rapid negotiation, when the crisis first developed, of a separate agreement with Persia upon the ostensible* fons et origo *of the whole controversy ; his daring decision to permit the rocket aeroplanes (at that date an alarming novelty) to exercise their trial flights by flying low over Paris, Moscow, Berlin and New York ; the consummate mastery with which he staged a sensational dis-*

appearance on the very morning when the crisis cul-
minated : his perfectly timed ' indiscretion ' (conveyed
to the German Embassy through his private Secretary,
Sir Arthur Peabody) regarding our stocks of Livingstone
Deposit A : above all, perhaps, his communiqué to
Reuter's disclosing our possession of the atomic bomb :
and his final triumphant appeal to Geneva—all these
daring and deliberate actions have been recognised
abroad as proving him a man of consummate intelligence,
unflinching courage, and almost superhuman lucidity of
vision.

*" Yes, '—*Unus homo nobis . . . *' : and that man*
was Walter Bullinger.

" I remember, as it were but yesterday, his handling
of the Cabinet on the night of Friday, June 3. I may
perhaps be allowed, at this distance of time, to disclose
that there were moments when the more anxious among
his colleagues felt that Walter Bullinger lacked the
initiative, the grip, perhaps even the vision, to steer
the ship of state through the rapids and the reefs which
were then in front of us. How quickly, on that evening,
did he dispel their illusions ! How dramatically, the
next morning, did he prove their doubts to have been
unworthy ! Almost as a matter of course did he disclose
to them the firm, the dignified, language in which he
intended, that very evening, to reply to the French
Government. Almost incidentally did he communicate
to them his great coup in the shape of a direct arrange-
ment with Persia. And from then onwards, hammer
stroke after hammer stroke, he pounded with his strong
arm ; and brought his country peace with honour.

" The climax of his activity was, of course, his
amazing courage (at a moment when the sinking of the

349

U.S. cruiser ' Omaha' seemed to render war inevitable) in issuing on his own responsibility a statement of which, had they been consulted, the Cabinet would never have approved.   Walter Bullinger staked everything upon a single card.   It turned up (if I may use a homely expression) trumps.   The twentieth century was saved from disaster unparalleled.   And having accomplished this great deed, Mr. Bullinger, like Cincinnatus, retired to his farm.

" I recollect, for instance, a conversation, which I held after the crisis was over, with Jane Campbell, at that time Parliamentary Under-Secretary at the Foreign Office.   She confessed that she herself . . ."

In this manna Lord Limpsfield kontinyoos his diskors. Hav kwôtd enuff however indikat mī reeders general līns his interpretashon this obskyure krīsis. To Limpsfield's emoshonal individualism mī grandfather opposes mental individualism. Interesting see how both ekwalli silli, ekwalli fawls.

LEONID NIKOLSON,

Kent Kommuniti Fa'am No. 468.
Sissingherst, Joon 13, 1978.

APPENDIX II

[Not printed]

PORTWAY REPRINTS

Non-fiction

Braddock, Joseph	HAUNTED HOUSES
Cardus, Neville	DAYS IN THE SUN
Cobbett, William	COTTAGE ECONOMY
Day, J. Wentworth	GHOSTS AND WITCHES
Edmonds, Charles	A SUBALTERN'S WAR
Gandy, Ida	A WILTSHIRE CHILDHOOD
Gibbons, Floyd	RED KNIGHT OF GERMANY
Gibbs, P.	FROM BAPAUME TO PASSEHENDAELE
Grant, I. F.	ECONOMIC HISTORY OF SCOTLAND
Harris, John	RECOLLECTIONS OF RIFLEMAN HARRIS
Hitchcock, F. C.	STAND TO: A Diary of the Trenches
Jones, Jack	GIVE ME BACK MY HEART
Jones, Jack	UNFINISHED JOURNEY
Jones, Jack	ME AND MINE
Lowe, George	BECAUSE IT IS THERE
O'Mara, Pat	AUTOBIOGRAPHY OF A LIVERPOOL IRISH SLUMMY
D'Oyley, Elizabeth	JAMES, DUKE OF MONMOUTH
Price, Harry	THE MOST HAUNTED HOUSE IN ENGLAND
Price, Harry	THE END OF BORLEY RECTORY
Stamper, Joseph	LESS THAN THE DUST
Stoker, Bram	FAMOUS IMPOSTERS
Tangye, Derek	TIME WAS MINE
Tangye, Derek	WENT THE DAY WELL
Thompson, P. A.	LIONS LED BY DONKEYS
Vigilant	RICHTOFEN—Red Knight of the Air
Villiers, Alan	SONS OF SINDBAD
Von Richtofen	THE RED AIR FIGHTER

Fiction

Ainsworth, W. Harrison	GUY FAWKES
Anthony, Evelyn	CURSE NOT THE KING
Anthony, Evelyn	IMPERIAL HIGHNESS
Ashton, Helen	FOOTMAN IN POWDER
Barke, James	THE END OF HIGH BRIDGE
Barke, James	THE SONG IN THE GREEN THORN TREE
Barke, James	THE WELL OF THE SILENT HARP
Barke, James	THE WONDER OF ALL THE GAY WORLD
Barke, James	THE CREST OF THE BROKEN WAVE
Barke, James	THE WIND THAT SHAKES THE BARLEY
Benson, R. H.	LORD OF THE WORLD
Benson, R. H.	COME RACK, COME ROPE
Besant, Walter	DOROTHY FORSTER
Blain, William	WITCH'S BLOOD

Jones, Jack	LILY OF THE VALLEY
Jones, Jack	THE MAN DAVID
Jones, Jack	COME NIGHT: END DAY
Jones, Jack	TIME AND THE BUSINESS
Jones, Jack	CHORAL SYMPHONY
Kersh, Gerald	NINE LIVES OF BILL NELSON
Kersh, Gerald	THEY DIE WITH THEIR BOOTS CLEAN
Keyes, Frances Parkinson	VAIL D'ALVERY
Keyes, Frances Parkinson	IF EVER I CEASE TO LOVE
Keyes, Frances Parkinson	FIELDING'S FOLLY
Keyes, Frances Parkinson	LARRY VINCENT
Keyes, Frances Parkinson	THE AMBASSADRESS
Keyes, Frances Parkinson	HONOR BRIGHT
Keyes, Frances Parkinson	LADY BLANCHE FARM
Kirkham, Nellie	UNREST OF THEIR TIME
Knight, L. A.	CONQUEROR'S ROAD
Knight, L. A.	DEADMAN'S BAY
Knight, L. A.	JUDGEMENT ROCK
Kyle, Elizabeth	THE PLEASURE DOME
Lawrence, Margery	MADONNA OF THE SEVEN MOONS
Lawrence, Margery	NUMBER 7 QUEER STREET
Lewis, Hilda	PENNY LACE
Lewis, Hilda	THE DAY IS OURS
Lewis, Hilda	BECAUSE I MUST
Lewis, Hilda	STRANGE STORY
Lindsay, Philip	THE LITTLE WENCH
Lindsay, Philip	PUDDING LANE
Lindsay, Philip	THEY HAVE THEIR DREAMS
Lindsay, Philip	LOVE RIDES TO BUTTERMERE
Lofts, Norah	REQUIEM FOR IDOLS
Lofts, Norah	WHITE HELL OF PITY
MacDonell, A. G.	HOW LIKE AN ANGEL
MacGill, Patrick	CHILDREN OF THE DEAD END
Mackenzie, Compton	POOR RELATIONS
Mackenzie, Compton	THE PASSIONATE ELOPEMENT
Mackenzie, Compton	EXTRAORDINARY WOMEN
Macpherson, I.	SHEPHERD'S CALENDAR
Macpherson, I.	LAND OF OUR FATHERS
Macpherson, I.	PRIDE IN THE VALLEY
Macpherson, I.	HAPPY HAWKERS
Macpherson, I.	WILD HARBOUR
Masefield, Muriel	SEVEN AGAINST EDINBURGH
Maturin, Henri	MELMOTH THE WANDERER— 3 volumes
Morrison, Arthur	A CHILD OF THE JAGO
Morrison, Arthur	TALES OF MEAN STREETS
Mundy, Talbot	TROS OF SAMOTHRACE
Myers, Elizabeth	A WELL FULL OF LEAVES
Neill, Robert	MIST OVER PENDLE
D'Oyley, Elizabeth	LORD ROBERT'S WIFE
D'Oyley, Elizabeth	YOUNG JEMMY
D'Oyley, Elizabeth	THE ENGLISH MARCH
D'Oyley, Elizabeth	EVEN AS THE SUN
D'Oyley, Elizabeth	PLAY ME FAIR
D'Oyley, Elizabeth	THE MIRED HORSE
Oliver & Stafford	BUSINESS AS USUAL
Oliver, Jane	THE LION AND THE ROSE
Oliver, Jane	NOT PEACE BUT A SWORD